Any

'Immensely readab̲   ̲ ̲g̲.̲ ̲ ̲ut-loud moments), irreverence, and inventiveness, yet unexpectedly moving. Never mind the length, feel the quality.'

Ellin Stein, Arts Journalist. Author.

'Screenwriters often make the best novelists, and Mendelson is no exception. He grabs you from the start and tells his stories with economy and stealthy humor. You'll be chuckling all along the way.'

Courtney Daniels, Filmmaker. *What other couples do.*

'Imaginative, funny and poignant.'

David Lister, *The Independent.*

'Paul A Mendelson is a master of the art of storytelling. Once again, he has created believable characters whose adventures are narrated in his usual, witty and very readable prose.'

Barry Kester, author of *Round in Circles,*
the story of Rodgers and Hammerstein's Carousel

'A short story, a novella and a novel! The choicest of spoils. I laughed and I cried.'

Paul Harrison. BAFTA-winning director.
Ballykissangel, Touch of Frost

'Sitting down with Paul A Mendelson's book feels like spending time with your articulate, storytelling best friend. Searingly human, keenly observed and nuanced. A great read.'

Micky Levy, filmmaker and screenwriter (USA)

'In a time when laughter is in short supply, this funny book leads the way. From the misfit romcom to the brilliantly noted murder mystery, it deftly switches from touching and insightful to hilarious in a heartbeat.'

Andy de Emmony, BAFTA-winning TV and film director.
Father Ted. Four Kids and It.

'A triumphant quartet of differing literary styles, bound together with sharply drawn characters, joyous wit and deft plotting. Einstein; I Can't Be Ill, I'm a Hypochondriac and Lost Souls are collectively genius, feelgood and redeeming, while A Perfect Murder Story is precisely that. Go to any lengths please to read this book!'

Colin Edmonds, scriptwriter and novelist

'Witty, perceptive and so cleverly written. Mendelson has the knack of creating quirky characters and then gently revealing flaws we all recognise in ourselves. A joy to read.'

Steve Levinson, broadcaster and journalist,
From Fleet Street to Tweet Street

'Paul A Mendelson has a rare skill, conflating different literary styles with ease. His character descriptions are extraordinary!'
Olga Swan, author of best-selling novel *The Mandarin Seeds.*

'Any Lengths to Please is predictably funny but you also run the gamut of emotions. Entertaining, highly readable and just full of good things!

James Scott, Executive Producer at Circus Studios.
Fisherman's Friends.

'Insanity rules. I laughed out loud!'
Barry Mendelson (No relation, honestly!)
Entertainment Mogul USA

ANY LENGTHS TO PLEASE

A short story, A novella, A novel
And a brief confection

Paul A. Mendelson

The Book Guild Ltd

First published in Great Britain in 2024 by
The Book Guild Ltd
Unit E2 Airfield Business Park,
Harrison Road, Market Harborough,
Leicestershire. LE16 7UL
Tel: 0116 2792299
www.bookguild.co.uk
Email: info@bookguild.co.uk
Twitter: @bookguild

Typeset in 11pt Minion Pro

Printed and bound by CPI Group (UK) Ltd, Croydon, CR0 4YY

ISBN 978 1916668 119

British Library Cataloguing in Publication Data.
A catalogue record for this book is available from the British Library.

To M.
Words count.
Yet words can't even begin...

Short story – *a piece of prose fiction that can typically be read in a single sitting and focuses on a self-contained incident or series of linked incidents. Word count is typically anywhere from 1000 to 4000, however, some have up to 15,000 words.*

Novella – *narrative prose fiction whose length is shorter than most novels, but longer than most short stories, with a distinction based on word count. A range between 17,500 and 40,000 words is commonly used for the novella category.*

Novel – *a relatively long work of narrative fiction, usually between 50,000 and 110,000 words.*

A Literary Confection – *a frivolous, amusing or contrived play, book, or other artistic or literary work. Of any length that pleases.*

THE STORIES

EINSTEIN

If you knew Cassie Nordstrom as I do, it wouldn't at all surprise you what she did on that plane coming back from LA to JFK. Although the upshot of this particular intervention might leave you reeling. It sure did a number on me.

As it was a pretty full aircraft, Cassie apparently found herself sitting between a dapper man in his mid-sixties and an equally (to her) elderly and rather elegant lady of a similar age. So naturally – well, at least natural for Cassie – they all got to talking. In fact, they chatted pretty well non-stop throughout the flight, meals included. Cassie isn't one to let a lightly curried chicken or the odd bout of turbulence stem her flow.

She soon discovered, not through prying but more out of her genuine interest in people – all people, folks who wouldn't interest you or me, waifs and strays included – that both her companions were sadly widowed and lived in different parts of New York State. The gentleman on her left had been to LA to visit a long-standing and now quite unwell client, whilst the window-seated passenger had made the long trip to ensure that she didn't lose touch with her recently 'emigrated' grandkids.

They in turn learned that Cassie was in her mid-thirties, single – though not for the want of trying – and an accomplished artist, teaching at a major NYC art school, who had travelled right across the country to catch a show by one of her favourite ex-students. Not even a solo show, just one in a pretty large group.

Nothing unusual in all of this, you might say. Just a pleasant, relatively brief encounter, three people flying solo, as they each mostly do, passing the time and chewing the fat (and the pretzels) on an ordinary cross-country journey.

But wait, the journey isn't over yet.

As the plane was coming into land and the erstwhile threesome were making their separate preparations for onward travel, Cassie turned to each of them and smiled that lovely open smile of hers, as she opened her pocketbook.

"Hey, guys," she said. "I've enjoyed this plane ride and our conversations just so much. Know what, I'd like to give each of you my card. That's me right there, see? Cassie Nordstrom. Good Swedish stock. And I'd sure appreciate it if you each gave me one of yours."

Surprised but far from unenchanted, the older man and woman willingly accepted an unsurprisingly arty business card from Cassie, then each of them fished out a more functional one of their own to add to her collection.

Now comes the good bit.

Cassie immediately took the man's card and handed it to the woman. Then she repeated the gesture but in the other direction. And here's what she said:

"I think you guys should hang onto these. After what I've seen going on these past few hours, I'd never forgive myself if I let the two of you leave this plane without them."

The elderly couple were married in the fall. They invited Cassie to the wedding. She came willingly, but on her own.

*

Okay, so I've known Cassie since we were kids in grade school, and now she's a devoted and dutiful godmother to both of mine, God save her. When she told me over too quick a lunch near her school about the wedding she had recently attended upstate

4

and the momentous plane ride that had preceded it, well, I just shook my head.

"What?" she said, with that sweet, confused smile of hers, running her hand through her hair, the way she does when something ruffles her. I'd kill for that hair – rich, natural blonde. Who has natural blonde hair these days? Only Swedes, and she hasn't been one of those for generations!

"You," I said.

"I know," she said, with a weary sigh. "I see two people who just ought to be together and I have to fix it. I'm in the wrong line of work, aren't I?"

"Sure are," I agreed.

As indeed I had to, seeing as how six years ago she got me and John Feltman, her downstairs neighbor, together over dinner at her apartment. My oldest friend does a good dinner. (Six years, one mixed set of twins later…!)

"And while we're on the subject…?"

I hate – well, sort of hate – to quiz Cassie about her love life, because it's rarely good news, even though she never loses hope. But what are friends for? And there's really no point my telling her that she has everything a man could wish for, because a guy would have to be blind not to pick that up from her dating profile alone. Looks, personality, intelligence, GSOH, breeding, bizarre fashion sense – they all shine through. She's even got childbearing hips, for crissakes.

"Well," she says, with a coy smile. "I have met someone. Okay, not actually met, as in—"

"Met?"

"Sure, but oh Laura, this guy…"

"You could have written his profile yourself."

"Exactly, but I couldn't have got it so right. Peas in a pod. He loves art, the more contemporary the better. The man's even an accomplished painter himself."

"He could do your apartment. The walls are peeling."

"You noticed. I must get that fixed, but it'd mean taking all the pictures down. Oh, and he loves literature, the theatre, travel, animals, kids—"

"To molest, murder?"

"He didn't specify. I know you think all the guys who register on these sites are serial killers or sex offenders, but most of them are just ordinary decent people looking for—"

"Not you, obviously. But I imagine this one's different."

"Ignoring your cynicism, yes, he is. Checks every box and then some. We could be soulmates. And we're meeting on Thursday to see the Nicholas Party exhibition in the city."

"The what?"

"Swiss, lives in NYC and he's brilliant. Gwilym – that's my guy's name – loves him and so do I. Isn't that fate?"

"Gwilym? What is he – a hobbit?"

"His father's Welsh. From Wales."

"Playing the Welsh card. Sly bastard. Well, Ms Nordstrom, box twenty-nine C4 whatever, make sure you tell me how it goes. Every last detail. I'm not so interested in what kind of coffee you invite him up for, in case you need to abridge it."

"I've got a feeling about this one, Laura. He's a seismologist! And no snide remarks about the earth moving."

"Would I? Well, just remember – seis isn't everything."

"I have no idea what you mean."

*

And know what – maybe she really didn't. I sometimes think it's the blank spots that make me love her so much.

I did not grill Cassie for information. At least not straightaway. In fact, I was pretty good and gave her a wide berth for the best part of four weeks. That's almost a whole month. Not that Cassie called me once in that time, which made me think – made me hope – that things were going well.

When she did call me, it was on a different matter entirely.

"Laura, you remember that dear couple I met on the plane?"

"The time Cupid was flying Delta."

"Exactly!" she said and had the grace to laugh. "So, they're in town over the weekend, taking in some shows, and I'd love you and John to come over for supper to meet them."

"And you'll be…?"

"Cooking. Well, yes."

"I'll give you one extra word but after that no more clues. And you'll be 'with'? And I don't mean 'child', although mind you—"

"Oh, you mean Gwilym. Well, actually—"

"Don't tell me he welshed."

"Oh, ha ha. No. He was very nice. Really. Sweet. We just didn't have anything in common."

"*You had everything in friggin' common!* He was practically your clone. Not that your other disasters haven't 'checked all the boxes.'"

"I know." She sighed. "Maybe it's me. Maybe some people are just, I dunno, hardwired to be single. I meet these perfectly nice, decent guys, guys who seem just the job, y'know, on paper, and it simply doesn't happen. And trust me, it's not for the want of trying."

"How about the sex?" I asked. Did I mention we've been pals since grade school? These are the sort of questions you can ask.

"I knew you'd ask, Laura. I'm surprised you don't want to see the videos."

"*You took videos?*" Now even I am shocked.

"Of course we didn't! But if we did, at least I'd know how to get the lighting right. I minored in film."

I didn't say anything. The best things come to those who wait.

"It was fine. It was perfectly adequate."

"What every guy wants to hear. Bet that's already on his Tinder profile."

I could hear the sadness in the silence, sense the sighing in her breath. And I knew when to back off.

"Oh, Cassie," I said. I didn't need to say more, did I?

"I know," she said, which was all she needed to say. "So, will you and John join us? On Saturday."

"Sure. I'll tell my mom if she doesn't come babysit, she'll never see her grandkids again. Usually works."

*

It actually didn't. Mom had a bridge tournament but fortunately our elderly neighbors upstairs stepped in, so they're the twins' grandparents now. It's called tough love.

We had a great evening. I always love going to Cassie's apartment anyway, regardless of the guest list. It's like stepping into an art gallery, only a whole lot warmer and less clinical. And with better food.

You can hardly move for artwork – some of it her own, naturally, but so many pieces created by current or former students, many of which are gifts of gratitude. Not that my friend isn't only too willing to spend more than she earns to give some of these talented if deluded youngsters the sort of kickstart they need.

I have no idea whether the apartment walls are expanding, but each time I visit there's more stuff on them (maybe she's a hoarder – I watched a TV show on that and then plowed through my own apartment with trash bags).

I'll be honest, I'm not crazy about every individual item yet somehow when they're all together – and we are talking sculptures here, too, and photos and what I think they call installations – they form this amazing cocoon of color and light that seems to embrace you and takes you over in waves of warm creativity the moment you step through the door (which itself is also festooned with tiny paintings and drawings – go figure).

Needless to say, Adam and Eleanor, the older but newer couple, were delightful and, of course, absolutely made for each other. Sickeningly so. Even my John thought they were perfect together and he gives misanthropy a bad name. In fact, he kept calling them Adam and Evelyn most of the evening, so something must have gotten through to him. Either that or it's early-onset dementia.

Unlike so many of the dinner parties we go to these days, where conversation seems to begin and end with Trump and the narcissist boys' club, this one was refreshingly free ranging: the current parlous state of the art and theatre worlds, the scary prospects for our kids in this unpredictable age but wasn't it always thus, climate protection and energy conservation without tears or inconvenience. And, of course, the customary passing around of photos of our kids and grandkids with John saying that, as the other couple had eight between them and we only had two very little ones, we were entitled to boast four times as long on each. Or, in his words, 'kvell', as he's an occasional Jew.

Perhaps we were being insensitive, or maybe the dessert simply needed a lot of preparation, but it was during this mutual admiration fest – "Oh, isn't he gorgeous! – She? Oh, isn't she darling?" – that Cassie rose from the table a tad abruptly and excused herself into the kitchen, where she remained for some time.

The sheepish silence she left in her wake endured only until we were certain that the kitchen door was firmly closed and the banging and clattering of utensils were at their height. Then it was time to discuss the topic that was foremost on our minds and probably had been even before the evening started.

Cassie Nordstrom.

And men.

Surely there was someone out there who was just right for our wonderfully kind and gentle, sweet and talented friend?

Some wonderful soul who really checked all the boxes, even ones that hadn't been invented yet.

All we had to do was put our impeccably coiffured (except for John's) heads together.

And think.

*

As luck would have it, this past December was my sister's turn to host our mom for Christmas (our father having moved on to sunnier climes and spouses many years earlier). Since my sister and I were long estranged – in fact, Cassie was more of a sister to me than my elder sibling ever was – and seeing as how John's family don't go much for Christmas but peak bigtime on Thanksgiving, we found ourselves either resigning to a quiet family holiday at home or foolishly hoping some generous soul might whisk us all away.

The whisking came quite out of the blue, courtesy of the delightful Adam and Eleanor, with whom we had, as they say, 'clicked' and who so graciously invited us to spend Christmas with them in their splendid and happily capacious home in upstate New York (without even a preview of our twins!). Their own families were fortuitously with 'the other sides' this festive season, our kind hosts, like John's folks, having been on Thanksgiving detail.

And, of course, our Cassie, matchmaker supreme, would be the guest of honor.

I should explain that Cassie's parents are both flourishing and somewhat obsessed academics, who spend every holiday that God and their faculties give them exploring different countries and putting it down on their tax returns as research. They have implied – well, more than implied – that they are pretty certain Cassie wouldn't wish to be lumbered with two boring oldies in the holidays, not when she has such a vibrant social life of her own, but they know for sure that they'll all be together either when she's finally a mom or at that inevitable time when they can't even remember what they had for breakfast (this Christmas it would probably be La Paz's finest *empanadas fritas*, and they'd have the photos and receipts to prove it).

How Cassie came to be such a nice and caring individual is beyond me. Unless she simply took the road less travelled.

So anyway, on Christmas Eve off we all drove to the wilds of upstate New York, which, if you don't know it, is so unlike New York City as to be in a different, distant state, if not planet. The folks are WASP without being waspish, and brashness can't get through the Catskills or over the Susquehanna.

Cassie doesn't have a car, in fact, she doesn't even drive, so we sat her in the back with the twins, which seemed fun for her and acted as a useful buffer to stop my guys from actually killing each other (our daughter, Lottie, has a left hook LaMotta would have given his right arm for).

We had no real idea who or what awaited us. And neither, even more so, did Cassie.

*

It must have been around 7pm on Christmas Eve when Irwin Rance turned up.

We had all settled into Adam and Eleanor's gorgeous colonial home at the ass end of nowhere earlier that afternoon. Oh, my God, the space! Three acres of land you could happily lose yourself or your children in. Set well back from the road and a little way from the nearest small town.

As we had driven up, we could see that the front was beautifully landscaped, with a sculpted lawn like something out of a movie or *Better Homes and Gardens*. I know I sound like a realtor, but you had to enjoy what was going on here. So much lawn! So many shrubs. The traditional entrance, the cathedral ceiling, the gleaming white columns, the whole place reeking of class and tradition, even though it was probably only built within the last twenty years.

Don't get me started on the kitchen. Country style with thick granite countertops, a breakfast island the size of Sardinia and all open to the huge but still surprisingly cozy family room, with its welcoming wood-burning fireplace and sumptuously festooned Christmas tree. Can you hire professional Yule festooners? I just bet you can.

And when Eleanor had said to me, "Laura, you and John and the wee ones can take the Blue Room, Cassie dearest, yours is the Green" (who has rooms named after colors?), I should have held out for the Green, because that's how I was feeling right then. Is that terrible of me? At least it's honest.

I could sense Cassie nudging me, if only with her mind, as she gushingly admired the décor, which I have to say was pretty damn classy. I've been in plenty of big homes where it was taste-no-object, but these guys knew what they were buying and decorating. And Cassie sure recognized, or at least could appreciate, the artwork that nonchalantly speckled rather than simply dominated the rooms. "You've got a Yankeleyevich!" she'd shriek. I made that name up, but you get the picture, even if there's no way most of us could get that picture!

Lottie and Benjy had just enjoyed the biggest and possibly the longest bath of their short twin lives. Nicely overfed and snuggled into their best going-to-ritzy-house pyjamas, they were making reluctant goodnights when the doorbell rang.

"That'll be the cops," said Adam somewhat enigmatically, as he stood up. Eleanor just smiled.

And a few minutes later, after some unintelligible doorstep mutterings, Officer Irwin Rance walked into the living room. I say walked, but invaded might be more accurate. The guy was big. And not just vertically. Don't get me wrong, he wasn't obese, he was more sort of oval. His head was the smallest thing about him, even though it was probably much the same size as that of his fellow males in the room. A room which suddenly appeared a whole lot smaller. I could tell that the kids were fascinated yet maybe a tad scared. But that could have been the uniform and all the fun things attached. Benjy began to nuzzle into me, but I don't think either of the twins blinked once.

Cassie, of course, smiled amiably and guessed, as we did, that this must be the local officer of the law, if not the entire neighborhood force. And unless there was a prowler on the loose and the sheer thought of it was making him smile, he had probably just rocked up to dispense or even enjoy some Christmas cheer.

"Everyone," said Adam cordially, "this is Officer Rance, and he's come to arrest you all for being city folk." With this he tried and failed to put his arm round his guest and settled for a manly pat on the back.

"Good evening, folks," said the uniformed visitor, "and a merry Christmas."

"I told Irwin to call in after he'd finished his rounds, so I could give him his festive bribe." With this he handed the man a package which I guessed was pretty fine bourbon or scotch. A litre of it, at least. "Season's greetings, Irwin."

"So, Irwin," asked a smiling Eleanor, as the man practically grabbed the bottle and began to rip off the delicate packaging. "Are you spending the evening with your mom?"

"My mom's in a home now, Mrs Bryant."

"Oh, of course Irwin, forgive me," she berated herself. "Well then, you must have supper with us."

I can't say that we reacted to this suggestion with total equanimity, but we gave it a good try. Maybe it was the fact that he was a stranger, and we weren't expecting to have to get to know someone new just yet. Perhaps it was that he was a policeman, and I don't care what anyone says, they're different and we feel different around them. Not proud of it, but I can see why cops usually prefer the company of other cops. But in this town, I was guessing that whatever other cops there were had drawn the short straw this year, the red and gold one with *Christmas shifts* written all over it.

Or maybe it was because it was Irwin.

"Yeah?" mulled Irwin, looking a gift horse straight in the mouth. "What you cookin'?"

"Will pot roast do?" asked Eleanor, with a warm smile.

We could see that Irwin was giving this some thought. "If you got a Bud to go with it," he suggested.

"Michelob okay?" ventured Adam.

"Guess it'll have to be."

I sneaked a look at Cassie, who was staring at the man in fascination. I have no idea whether she thought he'd be great to sculpt, a challenge to pair off with a large friend, or simply a species of humanity she had never before encountered.

Interestingly, Irwin wasn't paying particular attention to either myself or Cassie. As neither of us are totally grotesque, and Cassie herself is not far short of beautiful, I found this, to say the least, interesting. But it could have been because Officer Rance's attention was pretty much fully taken up with the huge bowl of pecans and almonds that Eleanor had honey-roasted earlier in the day and which was now sitting on the small occasional table near the fire. I could tell that Eleanor was on the point of telling Irwin to go on and help himself when Irwin went on and did exactly that. With a hand like one of those grabbers in the glass cases in Coney Island.

"Mm, these are good, Mrs Bryant," praised the man.

"Thank you, Irwin. I'm glad you like them."

Irwin was proceeding to show everyone just how much he liked them when John and I decided almost simultaneously that it was time that our sleepy, yet strangely wide-eyed, offspring needed the day's final visit to the Blue Room.

I could sense Cassie looking at us a bit forlornly as we each picked up a mesmerized twin and made for the stairs. Especially when Eleanor went to check out if she had made sufficient food for an extra guest – or maybe three or four. Adam rose courteously to help her.

"See you at supper," said Cassie, which came off less as a casual throwaway and more of a plea.

As we left, I could hear her say, "So, Irwin, what do you do for a living? Is – what I'd usually say – ha! But not to someone with a gun and a badge. Or even with just a gun!"

I realized this was gonna have to be a very quick bedtime story for my guys.

*

Dinner – or supper as Eleanor liked to call it, in order to stress the casual and really-no-bother nature of what turned out to be a veritable feast – was what you might term tricky.

Not that our Irwin, bless him, didn't have conversation. He did – and fulsome it was, too – but hardly of the type we were used to. It was composed mainly of small-town gossip and local petty crime; youngsters gone off the rails and older residents gone off the roads. In both cases, drink tended to be heavily involved. As indeed was supper. The narrative was also delivered with a full mouth and a rapidly filling belly. Irwin clearly enjoyed his food.

"And old Mrs Schwarzkopf, she went and tied her big ole dog Billy to one of that long line of shoppin' carts outside of the ShopRite Supermarket over on Main Street, thinkin' it was a friggin' metal hitchin' post or somethin'. Next thing you know, Billy spies Karen Cooper's little schnauzer on the other side of the road and decides it's high time he did a bit of butt-sniffin'. So, what does the old critter do? He goes and hightails it across that busy thoroughfare, draggin' a line of – oh, about twenty – big empty shoppin' carts with him! Jeez, the noise. Cars hootin', smackin' into each other, shoppin' carts clatterin' into people, traffic, shop winders. Folk screamin' all down Main Street. Like

Armageddon it was, only worse. Ha! Never seen anythin' so funny in my whole life."

"Weren't people hurt?" asked Cassie, full of genuine concern.

"Oh, sure," chuckled Irwin. "Hospital was kept real busy for days. No fatalities or deaths or anythin'. Just a few broken arms 'n' legs."

"And how was old Billy?" persisted Cassie.

"Oh, I had to shoot him. Boy was he mad." Irwin must have seen our open mouths and eyes filled with horror. "Joking, ma'am. Billy's fine. Only thing we shoot in this town is the breeze, ain't that so, Mr Bryant?"

"You said it, Irwin," agreed Adam, with a smile.

And so the conversation went on, local tale after colorful local tale. Until Irwin suddenly stopped, and a look very much resembling contrition appeared on his face.

"Oh shoot, here's me rattlin' on about myself and I ain't even asked you people what you do to earn your bucks." He smiled up at Cassie. "You first, ma'am."

"Well, Irwin, I'm an artist."

"Yeah, well that's great, but what you do for a livin'?"

"That's what I do. I make art – and I teach others. To make art."

"Oh Jesus H. Christ!" said Irwin Rance and grabbed himself another bread roll.

*

It was between the main dish and dessert that I managed to slip out and join Eleanor in the kitchen.

"Well, what do you think of our local cop?" said Eleanor, as she swiftly garnished the next course.

"Different," I replied, diplomatically. "Refreshing," I hazarded. "But hey, Eleanor, remember what we discussed at Cassie's – y'know, when she was out of the room?"

"I do indeed."

"So, when's this guy of yours coming? The one who's gonna change things for our little pal."

Eleanor turned to me and smiled. "Laura, you just met him. He's here."

Before we went back into the living room, me with my head still reeling and my arms laden with the most delicious and elaborate 'just-rustled-up' desserts, Eleanor whispered one single word. Well, not so much a word as a name. Not just a name but an icon.

"Einstein."

I had no idea what the hell she was talking about. And no time to ask. Especially as we returned smack into the middle of a riveting conversation.

"The head was on one side of the freeway and the body on the other. Never seen that before, Carrie, and I seen a good few traffic incidents."

"It's Cassie. And goodness, how awful, Irving."

"It's okay. You can call me Irving."

Cassie looked mortified, as if she had deliberately got the cop's name wrong as some sort of revenge for his error, which I know for sure the girl wouldn't do. But Irwin appeared surprisingly gracious.

"Oh, Irwin – it is definitely Irwin, isn't it? – I am so so sorry. I really didn't mean to… I must have been a bit discombobulated, y'know, by your fascinating multiple pile-up story. Well, anthology of stories."

"Not too gruesome for you?" enquired Irwin, concernedly. "I know arty ladies from the city can get the vapours at stuff like this."

"The vapours?"

"You know, you can watch all sorts of things like this at the movies and on TV and in the theater…"

He pronounced it the disdainful way, 'the – ater', an arena I had much frequented in the pre-twin and pre-COVID eras, but have shamefully to confess that the decapitation and severance-themed plays and musicals had totally passed me by.

"But when it comes to real life…"

"Don't you like the theater then, Irwin?" asked Cassie, tempting fate.

A scoff consisting in equal parts contempt, Michelob and homemade bread roll was the only response. But Cassie, a now somewhat outraged Cassie, was on a roll of her own.

"We get real life in Manhattan, y'know. I have two very close friends who got mugged only last year." It sounded almost as if she was bragging. "I may work in an art school but some of my students – especially the ones from overseas – can verge on the suicidal."

"I ain't surprised," commented Irwin, "having to look at Picasshole all day. They should go to a ballgame."

Now it was Cassie's turn to snort.

"What you got against sports, lady? Fresh air, good company, hot dogs. No suicides there."

"You should be a therapist," said Cassie.

"I know," agreed Irwin.

And so the evening progressed. In its own way John and I found it all quite fascinating. Well, when I wasn't ransacking my meagre mental attic for what all I knew about Einstein.

Cassie and I weren't able to connect until well into the night, when we met entirely by chance. We might have been able to pass legitimately on the way to the bathroom, but of course the Blue and Green rooms had their own ensuite. So, it took synchronized bouts of insomnia to bring us together in the darkened kitchen.

"*What the -?*" was all she said.

"I know!" I said. I certainly wasn't going to tell her about Eleanor's plan because I had not the faintest idea in hell what it was, but then I'm surely no Einstein.

"Did you *hear* the guy?"

"Cass, I was sitting next to you. And by the way, neither

John nor I, nor even our wonderful hosts, could get a word in edgewise."

My dear friend looked at me with a genuine astonishment only enhanced by the unpolluted, or at least less polluted, moonlight. "What do you mean?" she said.

"Well, you and Irving—"

"Irwin," she corrected. "His name's Irwin."

"Well, you and Officer Irwin were discussing art, theater, sport, food all evening."

"No, we weren't!" she protested. "Well, okay, I suppose we were, but only because he was dumping on everything I love."

"And vice versa."

"Shooting innocent animals on weekends, getting wrecked watching the Super Bowl, taking bets on America's Got Talent! Eating garbage? Oh, please."

"Well, I've got some bad news for you," I said.

"What?"

"Adam told John over their pre-retiring cigar, Irwin has nowhere to go tomorrow. So, he's coming here for Christmas lunch."

"You are kidding me!"

"Nope. Do you know anything about Einstein?"

"Relatively little."

So at least the poor girl could still smile.

*

It wasn't a different Irwin Rance – or 'rancid', as Cassie had referred to him uncharitably at breakfast then instantly regretted it – who turned up at around 11.30 Christmas morning, after we had all exchanged extravagantly-wrapped gifts by the tree and the kids had expressed almost hysterical relief that Santa had found his way here without the Empire State to guide him. But it was a slightly mellower one. This was notwithstanding the huge musical

Santa Claus hat he turned up wearing, whose pointed red peak bobbed and whirled dervishly to the rhythm of a pre-recorded chip singing a raucous and bluesy 'Merry Christmas' over and over, and did I say 'over', again.

The twins, who had only just calmed down from the gift-giving and had to be physically extracted from all the candies Eleanor and Adam had showered on them, went crazy once more. And the town's only off-duty policeman lapped it up.

Within seconds Irwin was on all fours, right at their level, so they could both of them tap his still frenzied hat and giggle manically until their noses ran. Five minutes later they were inside the police car that was parked right outside the house.

For the next half hour at least, it was all flashing lights and sirens and loudhailers. 'Come on out of there mister, with your hands up, or we're coming in' sounds pretty weird from the amplified mouth of an over-excited four-year-old, and I even doubt that the words were ever uttered on duty by the man himself. I found myself on the cusp of wishing that he had brought his taser with him, when he returned to the house, carrying a relentlessly gleeful kid in each arm.

"Sorry," said Irwin. "I hope we didn't hold you guys up."

We all shook our heads, which still had cop sounds ringing in them. It was then that Irwin appeared to notice Cassie.

"Hey, Cassie! Cool dress. Didn't realise last night with all that woolly stuff on you that you had a pretty decent figure under it. I certainly enjoyed arguin' with you n'all over supper. Hope I didn't come on too strong. I'm sure your art and theater and stuff ain't all bullshit."

It was then that I saw from Cassie the first smile towards this man that wasn't composed entirely of disbelief and bewilderment.

"Well, to be honest, Irwin," she confessed, "some of it really is. And before you think I'm just a snooty, highbrow Manhattanite, I actually hail from small town Pennsylvania and have been known to wolf down more than one hot dog at a ballgame. With relish."

"See, Mr and Mrs Bryant, I knew the girl didn't really have a broom up her ass," said Irwin, which I suppose my friend had to take as some sort of compliment.

"No, Irwin, the girl really hasn't," said Eleanor. "Shall we go into the living room? I thought maybe we'd have some of that fruit punch I've got nicely warming up, then take a little walk before our meal. We'll probably all be far too sated and sleepy afterwards." She took Cassie's arm. "Cassie, I'm sure Irwin might like to see some of your students' work – y'know, those pieces on your phone you showed me back in New York."

"Oh, I'm pretty certain Irwin wouldn't, Eleanor," laughed Cassie.

"Hey," protested Irwin, "I'm pretty sure I would. If some suicidal kids have taken all that trouble to draw somethin' weird, least I can do is take a look. Might give me some clues, y'know. And hey, I'm not a complete Phyllis Stein, whoever the hell she was."

I caught Eleanor watching this exchange and could stand it no longer. I practically dragged her into the kitchen, saying, "Let me just help you with that punch, dear."

As soon as we were out of earshot and Irwin was back on all fours showing the twins how traffic casualties shouldn't try to move a muscle or they could die, I cornered Eleanor by the huge cut glass punchbowl.

"Excuse me saying this, Eleanor, but when Cassie saw the way you two guys were connecting on the plane, she could tell straightaway you were meant for each other. Are you honestly telling me…?"

"I'm not telling you anything, Laura," she said, a tad enigmatically.

"Einstein," I sort of half-grunted, as if it was the worst cuss word I could find.

*

The walk in the nearby woods was brisk, convivial and pretty uneventful. At least, up until the time Benjy secretly stuffed his face with some of the candies he wasn't supposed to enjoy until after lunch and which we had foolishly thought we had confiscated in their sticky entirety. We normally police this sort of thing really well – and I don't mean in an Irwin Rance 'put those Skittles down and come out with your mouth open' kind of way. But John and I must have each of us taken our eye off the ball and hadn't noticed that a few had gone into his tiny pocket and then into his not-so-tiny face.

We took more notice however – and it still makes me want to heave whenever I think of it – around about the time poor little Benjy began to choke. After what must have been barely two seconds of watching our tiny guy in total blind panic, both his and ours, we ran to him from different angles and even fought with each other to do the Heimlich, something we had never done before and to our shame weren't exactly sure how it went (hey, come on, they say even Heimlich only got to do it that one time).

Meantime, above the terrified choking and Lottie's equally terrified but infinitely healthier screaming, we could hear Cassie and Eleanor muttering some sort of useless encouragement from the sidelines: "Hit his back – hold his tongue." I could sense that Adam was on his cell to someone, but God knows who, and I was beginning to fear, as my heart and breath simply stopped, that it was in God's hands anyway.

Then a calm and increasingly familiar voice cut through the babbling.

"Step aside, folks, could you please?"

I felt a huge and very strong hand practically pushing me out of the way, as did John, so Irwin clearly wasn't going to wait for an answer.

After that it all happened so swiftly. The big guy Heimliched the hell out of our little man, expelling the toxic bon-bon along with most of his tasty and oversized Christmas breakfast. Lottie couldn't have been more fascinated if an alien had burst out of her brother's stomach.

John and I were almost too busy comforting Benjy and each other to thank the big man for undoubtedly saving our son's life. But Cassie had no such hesitation.

"Wow!" she said. "Just wow!" she elaborated. "Guess you must have done a lot of these."

"Just two," he admitted. "But this is the first one that worked."

And as if there weren't enough people crying at this point, Irwin Rance's open face suddenly became streaked with tears. Cassie Nordstrom tapped his arm so very gently, offered him a handkerchief then buried her face in Eleanor Bryant's beautiful winter coat.

Christmas improved considerably after that.

*

"Please tell me you didn't organise the whole choking thing," I said to Eleanor, in a moment when Cassie wasn't helping to me to clear up the debris from lunch.

Actually, to be honest, Cassie was being pretty useless at this point. Could have been the alcohol – our girl is not the greatest drinker. But she had certainly been making pretty good headway with the vintage Cabernet Sauvignon over our very fine meal, at the same time as she was trying far too hard to make it up to Irwin for all the unkind things she had said (not that many) and all the ungracious thoughts she had allowed in (quite a few, which, of course, Irwin didn't have any idea of until she tipsily blurted out her regrets at even entertaining them).

"Don't be ridiculous," said Eleanor, looking quite stern.

Yet right then her eyes began to sparkle, and I could tell it wasn't from tears left over after the horrors and what-coulda-beens of this morning. Believe me, I was still having plenty of them and even the finest wines from Chile wouldn't be taking the edge off those guys for some good while.

"But did you see how she looked at him, after he had saved your son?" said the old lady.

"Well, we all did," I countered. "John woulda given the man a blowjob if he'd asked him." (Maybe the drink was having more of an effect on me than I had thought.)

"Be that as it may," said Eleanor gently, "but I do believe, albeit rather too dramatically, that a point may have been made."

"*What friggin' point?*" I responded, perhaps just a tad too loud. "And if you carry on about Einstein just once more, I can't be responsible for what I'll do with a stray sprig of holly."

Eleanor stroked me gently on the cheek and instantly reminded me of my mom.

"Do you know what Einstein said, Laura?"

"Sure. E = mc squared. Pretty damn obvious, if you ask me. But what the hell?"

"Do you know what else he said?"

"Not offhand," I admitted, feeling pretty bad I wasn't better informed of the wild genius's other bon mots.

"About insanity."

Now she was giving me fucking clues. I was just starting to hate her.

"No, Eleanor, but you're rapidly driving me to it." I began to nibble at stuff in a leftover dish. I do that sometimes. Now and then. Too often.

So finally, she told me, but I still didn't get it. Well, at least not straightaway.

"Insanity, Laura," explained Eleanor, "is apparently doing the same thing over and over again and expecting different results. Of course, I imagine the great man was talking about scientific experiments."

"Of course he was," said I. Like I knew. "But what's that got to do with Cassie and – *ah*!" So then I got it. Sort of. "You mean like…?" I left Eleanor to complete the thought she clearly and misguidedly believed I'd fully formed.

"*Exactly!*" complimented our host. "It's what poor Cassie has been doing for far too long. Scouring those awful websites for people exactly the same as her."

"Guys who check all the boxes."

"Do I check all the boxes with Adam? Of course I don't. Do you and John?"

"No way!" I said. "If we'd put our profiles out there online, we'd never ever have hooked up! Not in a million. One example: I can hardly work a cellphone. He's so into gizmos and technology, I tell folk there are three people in our marriage – John, me and Alexa. The only thing we two have in common—"

"Is that you warm to each other's differences and love each other to pieces. I could see that straightaway."

"And now we can moan about our kids together!" I added. "That's bonding."

But then the most awful thought struck me, as I looked back into the living-room and watched Cassie and Irwin playing a game with the twins on the floor.

"Eleanor, you're not saying, Cassie and Irwin…?"

"Don't be so friggin' stupid, Laura," said the woman with a smile. "Cassie Nordstrom and Irwin Rance? Now, that *would* be insanity."

There was still some of that wine left in a bottle. But not for long.

*

Naturally, we ran a post-mortem of the entire visit in the car driving home. And it was all pretty positive, except of course for the horrific near-death choking incident. We took care not to bring that up – no pun intended – but turned out, Benjy couldn't stop talking about it. Not just talking – full re-enactment, sound effects included.

"I coulda died," he kept saying. "I coulda choked myself to dead!"

"I wish you had," said Lottie finally, when she could stand the lack of attention no longer. Which did at least serve to shut the little guy up for a while. That and the extra cuddles from Cassie, who I could see through the vanity mirror seemed really deep in thought.

It was John who finally introduced the elephant into the room – and I mean no disrespect to Officer Rance with that remark.

"Well, Irwin sure wasn't the sort of guy I was expecting to meet," he laughed. "But you know something? I'm kinda really glad I did."

There was a silence and then from the back we heard a very quiet Cassie.

"So am I," she said, thoughtfully.

John and I just glanced at each other. The glance might have gone on a fraction longer, had Benjy not decided to 'choke' all over again.

*

The next time Eleanor and Adam came into town for a theater-fest, we met them at their hotel for an early drink. They were able to tell us with some delight that our friend and saviour Irwin had recently become engaged to a sweet young woman he had known since high school. A dental hygienist.

We were, naturally, delighted, as was Cassie, even though she hadn't herself 'arranged' this particular match.

Perhaps she had been too busy arranging one of her own.

Dale was sitting beside us, in the elegant lobby of the Algonquin. A sweet guy, an air-conditioning contractor in Brooklyn, with precious few of the same interests as Cassie but an enduring interest in and concern for Cassie herself that melted even this old cynic's heart.

They couldn't keep their eyes off each other. Or their hands. I felt Eleanor's eyes darting between them and me and I knew there was only one thing to do.

Raising my glass, I said, "I'd like to make a toast."

They all looked at me.

"*Einstein!*" I said, rather too loudly.

"*Einstein!*" said the others, raising their own glasses in turn, although only two of us remained un-mystified.

I gather that this has now become a well-recognized and oft-employed toast in the watering holes of Manhattan, although as yet nobody has been able to explain its provenance.

Kind of insane, isn't it?

I CAN'T BE ILL, I'M A HYPOCHONDRIAC

A woman's hands are pulling a dish from an oven. As we move out, we see a lively family in a typically 'messy' suburban kitchen.

The father and the cute 8-year-old boy are at the table, while Mum potters at the cooker. The boy is diligently setting out the cutlery, his dad is tossing the salad.

Meantime a teenage girl of around fifteen has her back to them all and is chatting on her phone, totally oblivious to, or at least disinterested in, what's going on around her.

"So, where did he take her?" asks the girl. "What – for *Valentine's!"*

"Sophie, love," intrudes a masculine voice. "We're having supper now."

"He is so mean!" continues the girl. "I'm telling you, she could do so much better. He did the same with Abigail."

Now an older, female voice dares to interrupt. "I've made that Fisherman's Pie you like."

Now the girl on the phone is laughing. "Yeah right…"

"Made with real fishermen," jokes the dad, for his son's benefit and perhaps his own.

Mum moves across and playfully wafts the steaming dish in front of the girl. Very gradually she turns round. "Made with smoked cod," announces Mum, "prawns and scallops in a cheese and…"

"Switch this fucking thing off," says a voice we haven't heard before.

"It hasn't finished yet, Leo!" protests the large, bearded man still hovering beside a massive TV monitor. He looks disgruntled but also a tiny bit fearful, as he tries not to meet the gaze of the person who had patently seen quite enough.

"Doubt that it was going to surprise me, Phil," responds the unimpressed creative director, whose expansive office this is. "And it's all so... *white*. Even the sodding fish. Not exactly ticking the diversity box."

Suddenly Phil Morrison feels very old. He is only in his early forties – well, forty-five – and still has most of his once red, now rusty brown hair, yet he just has to glance through the clear glass walls of his considerably younger boss's vast office, into the aquarium in which his ad agency colleagues busily swim, to feel like something out of *Jurassic World*, but without the rejuvenating special effects.

Leo is just twenty-nine, barely a year older than Phil's partner-in-creative-crime way back down the corridor in their own far cosier office, the young art director who is almost equally responsible (or culpable) for the commercial that has just apparently met its fishy end.

Because he is patently wealthier and more successful than his underlings, Leo is more scruffily dressed. His hand is forever shooting forcefully through his luxuriant, almost aggressive mass of blond hair, especially in moments of intense irritation or thought, as though trying to outwit a fly on the back of his neck. Phil is often surprised that this involuntary action doesn't cause the man to keel right over.

He is, in fact, doing the hand business right now, but as Phil finds it disconcerting and just a wee bit unhygienic, he decides to take a swift look around the office. This doesn't exactly cheer him. Aside from its size – large enough to accommodate Phil's current living room and probably his first marital flat – the place is festooned with framed press ads and mini posters the great man himself has conceived, stills from lauded commercials he

32

has created over his stellar career and gleaming awards from advertising festivals around the world, of which there are many, some in cities Phil is not fully convinced actually exist.

For some reason there is also a hefty remote-controlled model aeroplane on a table, which Phil and his art director have presumed is visible evidence of a rich and disarmingly humanising outside-life, a much-loved and rather unexpected hobby or simply the latest costly acquisition of a seriously overpaid arsehole.

As Leo talks, mostly about how shamefully antediluvian and uninclusive Phil's latest commercial is and indeed the entire, seemingly interminable 'Fish Family' campaign – a campaign designed to promote the British fish industry, which to Leo's chagrin, it has done pretty effectively over the years – the copywriter's eyes fall on Camille, the personal assistant Leo imported from his last advertising agency as soon as he could find a place to offload the extremely efficient older lady whom he inherited.

Camille, who does tick the diversity box, is the only sure evidence to which Phil can turn in order to convince himself that Leo may have some redeeming features, as she has never been anything other than friendly and accommodating to him.

"And I didn't see any steam," concludes Leo, because he could tell that Phil's attention had wandered, which he charitably puts down to age.

"There *was* steam, Leo!" protests Phil. "We had a guy on set blowing out steam the whole time. Do you want to see it again?"

"Christ, no!" says the young creative director, as if the older man has just flashed him. "Anyway, who cares, it's the last one." He fondles the aircraft, either not noticing or simply ignoring the shock on Phil's face. "Maiden flight, Sunday."

"The campaign's been a success, Leo," protests Phil. "The ads work."

"A white van 'works', Phil. Don't make it a Lamborghini."

Phil notices as ever the cod Cockney accent, as if dropping the odd 'aitch' and employing bad English is suddenly the great leveller.

"We're going to wake this bloody agency up, eh Camille? Well, I am. *And* the new talent I'm bringing in. That's what they've hired me for."

"Uh huh," says Camille. "Would you like a coffee, Phil?"

"Er, yeah. Decaff, please. No milk – unless there's some soya. Or almond. One sweetener. Thanks, Camille."

"He's not staying," corrects Leo. "At least, not long enough for you to sort *that* bollocks out. Need to talk, matey." He picks up some papers from his desk and strides off.

Phil offers Camille a smile and a shrug, which is sweetly reciprocated, and follows his new boss like a prisoner going to the gallows.

He knows that he really has to clarify before they reach his office whether he is still on the account in question and, indeed, the worst fear of every adman, if he is on any account whatsoever. Phil has seen too many of those movies where a guy leaves his office for the last time, as colleagues watch or try not to, bearing one solitary brown box with all his life inside. He also ponders that the box is always exactly the same type and thinks that the box company must be making a fortune.

As they walk towards Phil's desk, a trek which in itself is a rare show of democracy and team spirit on Leo's part, the great man nods to his creative staff, most of whom are relatively new to him and some of whom, like Phil, are fearing that this could be at best a passing acquaintance.

There are, of course, those who have encountered Leo before, in other lives and agencies, and are either praying that he recalls their talent favourably or that he has forgotten any unintended slights on his meteoric journey upwards. He himself knows that his reputation has gone before him, albeit only a few miles up the road from Knightsbridge to Paddington, and he revels in his feline status amongst the fairly mixed loft of pigeons.

The creatives he passes are unnecessarily young and in copywriter/art director teams although, as Phil himself would attest, the demarcation between the two disciplines has become considerably more blurred over the twenty-plus years he has been in the industry. Yet he would readily admit that his gift for rather elegant copy is significantly more worthy of praise than his ability to render a rough idea or layout, imaginative as it may be, using stickmen and a bit of collage.

Leo taps a young man on the shoulder. "New plane's in my office," he tells him warmly. "Stroke it and weep. Liked the ad." As the guy beams and moves on, Leo tells Phil, "Nineteen. Work placement, straight out of college. Can't hardly read or write – but they don't give awards for reading and writing."

A junior art director, jet black hair tucked under a bright red beret, sits at her drawing board as they approach. Phil notices with some disapproval that the creative director's demeanour has subtly changed to exude boyish charm and most probably excess testosterone. His judgment is tempered only by the realisation that he is most probably doing the exact same, only to infinitely less effect. This reminds him once again, like a familiar dig in the ribs from the person in question, that he has a wife of long standing with a serious birthday coming up.

"Delkron Tools," says Leo, suddenly.

"Oh, yeah," responds Phil, although he has no idea to what the man is referring and wonders if, yet again, his own mind has been wandering.

"They want us to pitch," explains Leo, as if to an idiot.

"Fuck me!" says Phil, who rarely swears but feels that perhaps he should be doing more of it in present company. "That's a big one. Fuck."

"Five mill. More and more punters are having to DIY it themselves. Times are hard, Phil," he says empathically, then just as suddenly laughs. "Especially for the guys who make the crap they're running now!"

Phil winces. Grace of God and all that. They pass a woman about Leo's age carrying some artwork.

"I can't let that ad go out, heart."

The art director looks understandably upset.

"We'll talk. It's fixable." They move on. "Bet she's pouting. Is she? We... you know. Not here. At her last place."

Phil looks shocked.

"You were young once, Morrison. Or so I imagine. So – Delkron meeting, 4:30, my gaff."

Phil pauses as it sinks in. He's excited yet nonplussed. And a little bit nauseous.

"Sorry – you're asking *me* to do it? The Delkron pitch!"

"I know. Baffling, eh? You wouldn't be my first choice – or my eighth – but their new marketing chief knows you, he mentioned you by name. Derek Curtis?"

Derek...? thinks Phil, trying desperately to remember. Or, failing this, to make out that he does.

"Oh, yeah. Derek. Shit! He was a client of mine, before he went to – Lord, it must be a while ago. Good old Derek, eh," he adds, for luck.

"Well, good for you, matey. Bizarrely, they like The Fish Family. They're a conservative lot. Head office in Ohio, you know. Homespun... ageing. Just don't give me *'The Delkron Family'*."

"I have done other stuff, Leo," protests Phil. "Before – before you arrived. *And* since," he adds, hastily.

Leo raises a sceptical eyebrow, a gesture Phil hates at the same time as wishing he could do it.

"But I'm told you ain't won us any new business in eighteen months."

Phil wishes again that people wouldn't say 'ain't' when they're clearly not born to it. He also wishes he didn't get distracted by things like this.

"I've held on to the stuff I've got!"

"Not what it's about, heart, is it?"

Phil stares at the younger yet senior man. The implications are clear. But Leo has already turned down another corridor, on his way either to the boardroom or the unisex toilets, leaving just a few encouraging words in his wake.

"I want to see the steam!"

*

Deciding that a trip to the gents, much as he himself needs one right now, could look weird, Phil Morrison decides to return to his office.

The room is smaller and a good deal messier than the one he just left. It also boasts far fewer awards and one less model aircraft. What's more, instead of an incredibly efficient and personable Camille seated opposite him, Phil Morrison has Keval, who is fast asleep with his head on his open but untouched and still gleaming layout pad.

The older man tiptoes into the glassy room then plonks himself down at his desk, on the adjustable chair with his personal back-friend attached and begins to tap loudly on the keyboard of his company laptop.

Keval starts to stir.

"Oh, *sorry*, Kev. Did I wake you? We're pitching for Delkron."

The reaction from his young and, at least in Phil's eyes, multitalented art director to the prospect of a full-scale creative pitch, part of the warp and weave of any major advertising agency – the lobbied for, sought after, love-hated adrenaline charge – is not one of excitement or even understandable trepidation. It is a long, drawn-out groan.

"Another sleepless night?" asks Phil, a touch more empathically. "How's the wee one?"

Keval stares blearily at Phil, his usually sparky, dark brown eyes now reduced to narrow slits, and spreads his hands about twelve inches apart. "How can something this big cause so much trouble?"

"I ask myself that every day," sighs Phil. To which Keval has at least the grace to smile. Then a less whimsical thought strikes the already harassed senior copywriter. "*Shit* – I'd better phone Nancy. She is going to kill me."

"Oh, come on, Phil. She's got to be used to late ones by now."

"No... no," explains the older team member, already seeming quite upset. "It's her birthday coming up again. But a major one this year. Big Four O. And every time I'm working. *Every bloody time!* We were going to Paris for a long weekend. Went there on our honeymoon. *Shit!*" He begins to speed-dial on his phone.

Keval shuffles over to the coffee maker as if he's approaching Lourdes. "Do what I did for Jyoti's twenty-fifth."

"Give her a baby? Been there."

"*Surprise party!* Tons of brownie points."

Phil waves the ringing phone. "I'll suggest it now."

It takes just a second and a stare from the coffee maker.

"Oh. Right."

For some reason Phil chooses to adjust his groin. Keval notices and throws him a look.

"Can you get a hernia just from stress?" wonders Phil out loud. Keval, who knows that such questions, offered up with some regularity, are simply rhetorical and that he isn't Google, just continues to make the coffee.

*

In the lobby of his building, at the base of a stylish, plant-filled atrium, Phil once again wishes that he had the glass contract or even the cleaning concession for this cool, modern and necessarily trendy address. As most of the people milling around him on his departure from work this early summer evening appear equally cool and trendy, and indeed some of them almost see-through themselves, Phil has discovered a reassuring affinity with Arthur, the dour security man of a certain age now standing beside the desk.

"Arthur. Hi."

Arthur immediately disappears behind the glass-canopied desk and emerges with a jar of pills bearing a Japanese label.

"Got those things you asked for, Phil. The son-in-law brought them in from Tokyo last night."

"Brilliant," says Phil, immediately stuffing the jar into one of his pockets, as if it contains one of the most illegal and dangerous substances known to man rather than a natural energy-booster that he read about in one of the newspapers scattered around the agency. He really wishes he could stop buying arcane remedies and medicaments for diseases and conditions he doesn't yet have but might wish to head off at the pass. It's like a drug.

"How's he doing over there?"

"Coining it," says Arthur, proudly. "What's in 'em?"

"Fish innards. For energy. Apparently, the Japanese swear by 'em. Although, interestingly, I've a feeling they're the one people who don't actually swear. Fuck knows how they manage. Ha! What do I owe you?"

"Tenner'll do."

Again, as he swiftly pays the man, Phil feels like he is connecting with his dealer. *I'm in a business where cocaine is as available as CoffeeMate*, he tells himself, *and I'm anxious about buying fish oil!*

"You watch, Arthur. I'll be a new man."

As Phil walks away, gently massaging his groin, Arthur remains unconvinced.

*

"Delkron Tools... Licensed to Drill. Delkron. DelkrON – DelkrOFF – DelkrON... DelkrOFF..."

Phil opens the door to his cosy, heavily mortgaged Edwardian semi, still busily sloganising, and is immediately assailed by his fifteen-year-old daughter. Somehow, it always feels with this young person as if he has suddenly found himself in the centre of a heated conversation, with absolutely no memory of the original point of entry.

"She like really pissed me off at school today. Okay, so she's planning this big thing at the pub on Saturday, right? And she *knows* that's the day I work for Susie's mum, yeah? Bloody Abigail – like she is *so* out of order."

"Pub?" says Phil, when his daughter is obliged to pause for breath and it's the only word that has failed to evaporate in the deluge. "You're barely fifteen!"

"Thanks for missing the point."

Phil realises that it is probably inappropriate – in fact, no probably about it, at least where Nancy is concerned – but he finds himself smiling at the young girl, who is managing to appear both womanly and childlike at the same disconcerting time. He knows only too well that she is – well, was – the inspiration for 'Fish Family Girl'. The trouble is he sometimes feels that Erica knows it too and is just feeding him lines. Well, too late kiddo, that fishing boat has sailed.

"Other than that, how was your day?" he asks, dumping his bag on the Victorian settle in the hallway and slinging his lightweight jacket on a clothes hook beside it, in full and troubled knowledge that he should be hanging it up properly upstairs, so that it doesn't crease or get brushed to the ground by children rushing headlong up and down the narrow staircase. Sometimes he wonders why he finds life so complicated. He has been told several times that he lives in his head, but he knows that nowhere else would have him even as a lodger.

Erica answers his question with a shrug then does her duty by responding in kind.

"How was yours?"

"We are *pitching* for Delkron Tools!" he announces momentously.

"Uh huh," says Erica.

"Where's Mum?" asks Phil, hoping the second-house audience will be more responsive than the first.

When Erica points upstairs, Phil taps his daughter's arm lightly and lowers his voice. "Listen darling – I want to do her a surprise party."

"Uh? Who?"

"Mum! For her big birthday. You know. But it'll have to be after the pitch."

Erica just stares at her father. "She would so hate it."

"No, she wouldn't!"

"Oh, like you're a woman."

"Come on Ric, love," says Phil, changing tack. "You will help?"

Rather than colluding in her father's insane clandestine plan, Erica instantly becomes louder and crosser.

"*Dad, I've got revision*! As you keep sodding telling me."

Inevitably, Nancy now appears on the stairs and just as predictably Erica swishes past her and upwards, most probably to avoid being reprimanded for shouting, swearing or just being Erica.

"Bonding?" asks Nancy.

"*As if!*" responds Phil, in his awkward but well-honed parody of a teenager, then reverts instantly to husband-overwhelmed-with-contrition. "Hey, sorry about—"

"Sorry about – Paris? Being late? Paris?" She laughs wryly, which Phil knows from experience means that she is *so* not amused.

"What?"

"*Delkron Tools!* Phil, you can't even knock a bloody nail in."

"I can, too!" protests Phil, because he actually can but not that straight and he'd need to be reminded exactly where they keep the hammer. He can tell that Nancy is on a roll, so he won't mention in his defence his earlier campaigns for sanitary towels.

"I've got a whole list of un-begun jobs." She gets her counting fingers out, which is always a worry. "For starters, there's the sink—"

"Nance, I can't lose this one. Leo wants me out."

She stops listing and listens.

"I'm not joking, love."

"Phil, he can't." She has no idea whether this is true, so they both know that hers is an expression of righteous outrage rather than chapter and verse of employment law.

"He's smart," explains Phil. "The big boys trust him; they brought him in – and he's made it pretty clear what he thinks of me. He's already sent the Fish Family to a watery grave."

Sometimes Phil surprises himself with his ability to find the most felicitous expression, even in moments of anger, distress or panic. Yet he also deems it oddly pathetic rather than some extraordinary linguistic gift.

Before Nancy can respond, a little dynamo in Spider-Man pyjamas suddenly hurls himself at Phil, causing him to reel backwards into the hallway radiator.

"Hi, Dad. Can I have a biscuit?"

Phil brightens and swings his eight-year-old around enthusiastically.

"Course you can, mate," says the besotted dad.

"You've had three already," amends Nancy. "And Daddy, you'll put his shoulder out again, like you did on Southend Pier. Back to bed, Toddy. Scoot." She glares at Phil. "'*Course you can*'?"

Todd scoots back upstairs, biscuitless. As he watches the vivid pyjamas recede, Phil feels a sudden twinge down below. He shifts uneasily.

"Oooh!" He winces. "Nance, can you pull something – down there?"

"Not right now I can't, you smooth-talkin'—"

"No." He almost laughs but doesn't. "I mean… can one… you know?"

"Eh? Oh, I don't know, Phil. You could. You could pull a nostril."

As she walks off into the kitchen, Phil can almost watch her body sag. He feels contrite that yet again he has bothered her, almost immediately after trudging in, with the latest tiny ache of the day. 'The lunatic twinge', as she once called it, quite wittily in his professional opinion. He decides not to mention Arthur the security man's new fish tablets.

"Hard day?" he asks solicitously.

"Remember my car thief?" she says, without turning round.

"Which? The one who only does Jags? Didn't he keep his appointment?"

"Oh yes," nods Nancy despairingly. "Parked his latest Jag right there in the Probation Office car park. He must think we're all such idiots."

Phil hugs her comfortingly from behind, then gently cups her breasts, which he enjoys and she doesn't appear to find hugely inappropriate, even in the midst of professional discussions of a criminal nature. But tonight, for different reasons, she tries extra hard not to succumb.

"I'm still cross, Phil," she says, quietly. "Every time we make a plan. *Every* bloody—"

"I know. I do, Nance. I'll make it up to you. Promise. You'll see. I'll fix the sink."

She has to smile at this.

"I've still got to read a load of stuff, y'know, for tomorrow."

"And tomorrow and tomorrow. Have your supper first."

The phone in the kitchen rings and Phil immediately stiffens. For some reason he always associates the landline with bad news.

Of course, he has occasionally been correct – there was that time when his mum passed away, and six weeks later Nancy's dad – but these calamities, or at least sadnesses, were naturally far less frequent than those occasions when a call has been purely social or someone with nothing to sell trying to sell him something.

Erica is down the stairs and on the case.

"It's for me," she announces, grabbing it. "Hi!... oh. Hi, Grandpa." She can see Phil waving wildly and shaking his head like he's at some sort of southern revival meeting. "I'm fine... and Todd's fine, Mum's fine, Dad's fine... they're not called O-levels anymore. Yes, he's here."

Phil, looking instantly drained and that he'd like to strangle his treacherous daughter, takes the phone.

"Hi, Dad... I'm fine... uh huh... listen, Dad, can you tell me about it tomorrow? I'm only just in from – no, I've not been working all this time, I'm having an affair. ... Just some girl from the office." He swiftly shakes his head to Nancy, somewhat unnecessarily. "Tomorrow, promise."

No sooner does he down the phone than Erica grabs it and walks off.

"Erica, where's your mobile?"

"Recharging."

Phil sometimes wonders if his life is on some sort of time loop and he's just living the same day over and over again but without becoming any wiser.

In just under three hours' time, he will stop wondering this. Perhaps forever.

*

Nancy and Phil lie side-by-side in bed reading work documents on their iPads, as they are too often obliged to do by the demands of children and household duties. And life. They would prefer a decent book or even, at times, an indecent one.

As with so many long-standing pairs there is a ritual, a mating dance, which in this case commences not with the clicking of legs or the fanning of feathers but with the deft removal of reading glasses. This night it is Nancy's turn to whip them off.

"Got a lot more to read?" she begins, casually.

"A bit," replies Phil, still struggling to get his head around the vast – and to him, totally unnecessary – range of Delkron tools and appliances. "Not a lot." He turns towards her, looking under his spectacles. "You?" He notices her temptingly naked eyes.

"I could finish the court reports in the morning," she breathes, huskily.

"I can do my notes on the tube," he responds, with a come-hither glance, coolly divesting himself of his own eyewear. "If I get a seat, of course. Sometimes at the very last minute they go and just cancel—"

"Enough."

He feels the warmth of Nancy's lower thigh against his freshly washed bedtime jockey shorts and puts his arm round her. "Are the kids asleep?" he murmurs smoothly.

"Bloody better be. You're not too tired?"

"Admen do it in thirty seconds," he purrs, which makes Nancy giggle.

It isn't until they have finished making love and are easing gently towards a hopefully profound and relatively untroubled sleep that Phil decides to make conversation.

"Sorry about Paris."

"You're forgiven. This time," she replies sleepily, assuming that this is the last time they'll speak until the cruel morning alarm.

In this she is deeply mistaken.

"Nance… Nancy…? Are you asleep?" says Phil, just over an hour later.

"Mmhmm… huh? What is it?" asks the now just slightly less asleep person next to him.

"I've got something," explains Phil. "Down here."

Whilst admiring his constitution, Nancy finds herself less enamoured with the timing.

"Oh, Phil, love... please."

"No, no," he protests. "I didn't mean – I think I've found something."

"What... in the bed?" She is still very much asleep, or at least wishing herself so.

"No. Me. Here – feel."

"*Philip!*"

His voice becomes far softer yet infinitely more compelling. "Please, Nance. I think I've got a lump."

"What sort of a lump?"

"I dunno. A lump lump. It's down there. You know. The one on your side."

Nancy, who is now quite a lot more awake, realises that she has to go exploring. Very gently she burrows an arm under the covers. "Where? There?" She tries.

"Uh uh. Give me your hand. No. Bit further down. It's just—"

"Hang on," says Nancy, moving closer and turning onto her side. She shuffles up against him and realises that her nighty has rolled right up, but this is hardly going to be of any moment right now. "Can you shove up the bed a wee bit?"

Phil does so and at the same time switches on his bedside light. Nancy gets an immediate shock and flinches.

"*Aaah!*" She continues her quest. "No... I can't feel any... Phil, there's nothing there or I'm sure I would have, y'know, when we... oh!"

"What? What 'oh'? What, Nancy?"

"Well, there might be something. A little – well, something, I dunno. Is it sore?"

"Not really. Maybe a little. Not 'sore' sore. Is that good or bad?"

"Well, I like things not to be sore, as a general rule."

"What do you think it is?"

Nancy has no idea. "You know you... it's probably always been there."

"No," corrects Phil. "It hasn't. I'm down there a lot."

"Well, if you're worried, love, see the doctor in the morning."

"Yeah, good luck with that. And I'm not getting my bits out on Zoom – you never know who's looking in. Or recording. Oh, I can't anyway tomorrow. We're off to Nottingham first thing."

"Oh Phil, come on. Leo will understand."

"Have you *met* him? Leo wouldn't understand if my leg was hanging off. We're seeing the Delkron clients up there. I already know one of them. That's the only reason I'm... if I hit it off with them, it could really swing things for the pitch. And right now—"

"Okay. See the doctor the day after. It'll probably be easier anyway with some notice."

"Mm... could you maybe ring them and make an appointment? Tell them it's me."

"Er... yes. Okay," says Nancy, who can't quite see why she should be the one doing it, whilst at the same time feeling churlish for even hesitating. "You'll have to leave me the number of your loyalty card," she says, aiming for a lightness of tone.

"Ha ha. Thanks, love."

Satisfied, up to a point, Phil switches off his light. The silence lasts around ten seconds.

"Nance, you don't think...?"

"No, Phil. I don't. Look, there's really no point in worrying about things until they happen."

Phil sighs at this arrant nonsense.

"Just try and sleep, love," she adds.

"Yes. Okay. Love you."

"Love you."

For the rest of the night Phil Morrison lies awake in his bed, terrified. He has no idea, nor will he for some time, that just inches away from him, in the same recently and rather pleasantly rumpled bed, his wife is doing much the same.

*

"Well, maybe that's 'cos nobody's ever bloody *asked* Tarantino to do a cider commercial!"

Leo is talking loudly on his mobile, running his hand through his hair as he leans casually on a standard, creative-director issue, top of the range Tesla. He is munching a 'designer' bacon sandwich.

Standing beside him, respectfully awaiting permission to enter the almost pristine machine, are Phil, Keval and Amara, an enviably bright and extremely personable planner/researcher in her early thirties.

Amara is also very tall, so Phil finds himself puzzling over whether to suggest that she might be more comfortable sitting in the front next to Leo. Would this be an act of simple courtesy or an insensitive reference to her unusual height? And, as she is most probably of African heritage, would there also be an unconscious slur of some unspecific genre thrown in there for good measure? He wonders if everyone finds modern life such a minefield. Watching the team dextrously arranging their bags and laptops in order to accommodate coffees and breakfast, a routine he still finds a challenge, he somehow doubts it.

But then again, none of them have just discovered overnight that one of their appendages has a small but solid-feeling lump on it. So perhaps he shouldn't beat himself up – especially not this morning, when they're all off to meet his professional destiny and, albeit to a lesser extent, their own, on an industrial estate just this side of Nottingham.

He suddenly realises that Leo is talking but this time not on the phone.

"…And this is how I see it, Amara. Right?"

She nods, as if she should be impressed that the man has remembered her odd-sounding name amongst so many.

"You've got your Mr..." At this he puts on a voice like nobody Phil has ever met or heard but is clearly meant to be the man on the street. "'Oh yes, I converted my entire loft over a wet Whit weekend – two beds and a bath' and you've got your man who has to fix a shelf 'cos both his books have fallen down and... you've got Phil."

"Mm? Sorry?" Phil realises he has gone miles away again and that it hasn't passed unnoticed.

Amara slips nimbly into the silence. "You're what we've recently substratified, using all the available research data, as a GALMI."

"GALMI?" says Phil. "General... Attitudinal...?"

"'Get A Little Man In!' – Joke? Ha ha. Oh, come on, Morrison. Chill!" laughs Amara.

Usually, Phil would be right in there with Amara, laughing readily. He likes and admires her, enjoys her company. She was the one who told him once that her entire department was suffering from Researcher's Disease: 'Broken down by age and sex.' He has used that a lot, sometimes without attribution. But this time he is in job-saving mode.

"At least I'm not yawning," he says, nodding towards Keval.

"Oh. Sorry," shrugs the younger man.

"Ah, bless," coos Amara. "C'mon, Daddy, photos!"

"I'm eating!" groans Leo, opening the car and graciously beckoning them in. "The suits will meet us up there. You got kids, Phil?"

Phil slides into the rear with Keval and starts tapping his phone. "Still the two I told you about, Leo. Just gotta make a quick call."

He burrows into the ridiculously comfortable seat and hopes that the sounds of the car will drown out his side of the conversation. Unfortunately, being a Tesla, there is precious little sound other than Leo's ultra-cool and utterly unidentifiable music that immediately wafts through the hidden speakers, so he has to whisper.

"Oh hello. Can I speak to Mrs Morrison please? It's her husband."

After what seems an indeterminable wait but really only takes until the car reaches the end of the busy road on which their agency sits, Nancy picks up her phone (Phil knows that she has her mobile off when she's with her clients and prefers that he goes through whoever is triaging the landline).

"Hi, love... is everything—"

She doesn't have a chance to finish.

"No, not yet... you know you can never get through first thing... Phil, why would I book the lady doctor? Hang on a second."

While Nancy is clearly talking to a colleague, Phil takes the opportunity to examine his crotch through his trousers. Unfortunately, Amara chooses this moment to turn round in her seat and hand back Keval's phone with his baby photos on display. She decides to ignore Phil's 'exploratory', regarding it as something men just do, for reasons best known to themselves, and simply compliments Keval on his new son.

"Don't worry," comes Nancy's rushed voice, "I'm on the case. Have a good meeting."

As Phil returns the phone to his pocket, he keeps replaying Nancy's words in his head. She sounded normal, didn't she? Not frantic or even particularly concerned. Preoccupied. Possibly even a little insensitive?

Doesn't she care at all?

Had Phil quizzed Nancy's PA at the Probation Office, a young man who is currently staring at his boss with mild curiosity and the first tingles of concern, he might be feeling less uncertain. As it is, he realises that yet again he has missed a pivotal tranche of the Thoughts of Director Leo and would be wise to focus just that bit harder.

*

When Phil had called Nancy again that day, this time from the Delkron executive bathroom mid-briefing, and reported that happily the lump hadn't grown (but neither had it diminished), she was able to respond that an appointment had been made in his GP's actual surgery the following morning. So, there would be no exposing himself on Zoom or anywhere else, other than exactly where he is now, on the efficient young medic's couch.

"Mmhmm. Does that hurt, Mr Morrison?" asks the doctor, squeezing firmly.

"Er... not unduly," admits Phil, although surely no man could go through having his testicle squeezed by another without feeling at least some moderate discomfort.

"This?" suggests the younger man, somewhat over-enthusiastically.

"Well... mm, maybe... no... no, I don't think so. I'd ask you to try again, y'know, for luck, but I don't think I will."

"Fine," says the unsmiling doctor. "You can get dressed now."

Phil pulls his pants up, wondering how many more times he will have to drop everything before – well, who knows before what? The GP is busily tapping his computer.

"So... what do you think it is?"

The doctor continues to tap. For some reason Phil immediately equates a lot of typing with something serious – 'nothing to report' wouldn't take this long. He tries to take a peak.

"Probably nothing," continues the GP, still rooted to the screen. "I suspect that it's just a hydrocele. That's a collection of fluid in the scrotum."

"Oh, fine," says Phil, with a huge but not unpleasant sigh. "Ha... you know, for a moment—"

"But I'm going to send you to someone. Just to make sure."

"Make sure of what?"

"That it is what I think it is."

Phil tries to will the man to make full eye-contact but for whatever reason the young and highly efficient doctor appears glued to his machine.

"What if it's not... you know? What you're pretty sure it is. Can I have your second opinion now?"

"They're a good team at the hospital. One of the best. You shouldn't worry."

"It's what I do," explained Phil, nodding towards the computer. "I'm half your hard drive."

The doctor finally rises to see his patient out. Otherwise, he fears the man might never go. "Better that than someone who leaves things till it's too late. You'll get a letter soon, about the appointment."

"Great. Thanks. What do you mean 'too late'?"

For the first time the GP appears a bit nonplussed. "Just an expression," he sighs, and goes back to the safety of his computer.

*

When Camille walks into Phil's office the next morning with yet another Delkron document and glimpses the detailed anatomical diagram of male genitalia filling Phil's entire laptop screen, the young woman simply assumes that it is in connection with some client account, probably of a medical nature, of which she and possibly even her boss have not yet been made aware. Even allowing for Phil's age she can't believe that this could have any other contraindications, despite the almost rapt attention it is receiving from its concerned onlooker. Noticing Camille's entrance, he immediately clicks off.

"Bit of freelance," he murmurs, in a slightly pleading way. "Needs must."

Camille just smiles, throwing a sympathetic look across to a bemused Keval, and backs away, almost bumping into Leo on his troop visit. The office is already like a mini Delkron showroom, with pristine tools and sample packaging everywhere.

"Okay. *Quorum!*" announces Leo, for some reason pulling Keval half off his chair and into a vice-like grip, which both members of the creative team assume is meant to signify camaraderie rather than slow death by strangulation. "Just had a chat with upstairs. I want to use fucking great posters."

"Doesn't that depend on what we want to say?" says Phil, instinctively.

"Yes, Phil. We want to say we're an agency that does fucking great posters." He picks up a huge drill and handles it like a Colt 45, doing some quick-draw stuff which, for one brief, unkind moment, Phil wishes would conclude in the puncturing of a minor artery.

"Listen, guys, I know you're both pro's and you're going to give us all a good, solid campaign – and I guess it'll sell a lot of drills and stuff – but for once let's have something just a bit more out there, a bit more in your face. One for the company showreel, eh? For when the BMWs and Guinnesses of this world come calling."

The 'guys' stare at the man, just a tad offended by the assumption that their ideas will be resolutely and unsexily workmanlike. Leo picks up Phil's solitary award from a shelf.

"We need first scribbles by Thursday, for the suits. And not just the posters – I want telly too, duh obviously."

"*Thursday?*"

"Problem, Phil?" asks Leo.

"We can do it in our sleep!" promises Keval, swiftly. When Leo looks at him, the young man just shrugs.

"Half the world's after this bugger," says Leo. "We have so got to get it. No – too English." He starts to send himself up, as if channelling *Mad Men*. "We are going to fucking nail this baby, guys. Bigtime. Group hug!"

They recoil as he approaches them, which just makes him laugh. The man glides out, but not before throwing Phil a look.

"Thursday," he repeats.

"It's his mum I feel sorry for," grumbles Keval, as the creative director moves on. "You okay, Phil?"

"Yeah. Fine. I'm fine. Er, Kev...?"

Keval looks at his older and now clearly perturbed partner, but Phil just shakes his head.

"No, nothing. It's okay. Got any ideas – other than homicide?"

Keval picks up his trusty red magic marker and bares his perfect teeth.

*

"*Delkron Industrial Strength Vacuum Cleaners*," mutters Phil, as he enters his local NHS hospital. "*I've seen the future, and it sucks.*"

To his surprise but also concern, Phil hasn't had to wait too long for his appointment. He either has a very grave disease or a very good GP. Or possibly both.

Hospitals make Phil feel ill. He suspects that, even allowing for his own make-up, he is hardly unique in this. However brightened, tarted up or even clinically exclusive these institutions may be, they are rarely Disneyland for most people, unless these perhaps are people making their final farewells to a dying relative they despise but from whom they are more than anxious to inherit.

He's going off on one again. *Think Delkron not death*, he tells himself. Yet it isn't that easy when he sees blue signs all around him, directing him to the venue's multifarious attractions – *Accident and Emergency* – *Radiotherapy* – *Imaging* (whatever the hell that is) – *Morgue*. He thinks he may have made that last one up.

It is some while until his name is called. Meantime, he spends a fruitless forty-five minutes trying to guess what each of his fellow patients are in for and what power tools they might have in their sheds. He has just decided on 'Mr Sander', a bulky man in his mid-fifties who is reading the Daily Mail back pages first, when his own name is called out loud. "Mr Morrison. Lump on right testicle." (He probably imagined that last bit too.)

The consultant is a kindly Scot in his early sixties, who introduces himself as Mr Pringle. His professional warmth and distance from a computer screen curiously only heighten the fear.

As expected, he invites Phil to lie on the couch with his pants around his ankles, so that the man can have a good old rummage, which he certainly does. Instinctively, as the man squeezes and explores, Phil reckons that this person knows exactly what he is doing, although he has no idea what it might feel like to have a person down there who doesn't know what he is doing. He hopes he never shall.

"You can put your kecks back on now, Mr Morrison," the older man says finally, with a gentle smile.

Mr Pringle then proceeds to write his notes, with an expensive fountain pen, in total silence. Phil eventually wonders, from the length of time it is all taking, whether the man is in fact outlining a game-changing article for the British Medical Journal, one that will turn the world of testicular lumps on its head.

Eventually the amiable Scotsman turns back to his patient. "Well, I reckon the best thing we can do for you is take a wee look, eh?"

"You just have, Mr Pringle."

The doctor smiles. Phil notices that he has slightly yellowing teeth and wonders if he's a smoker. He also wonders what this says about him and decides that it says he's a smoker.

"A *proper* look," explains the man. "Under general anaesthetic."

Phil, who has been standing throughout this conversation, sinks onto the couch once again. The fear, which curiously had diminished as fascination with the process and the expert conducting it took over, now floods relentlessly back in.

"So, what do you think?" he manages to say. He is not convinced that he really wants to know.

Mr Pringle leans forward over the desk, although Phil can hear him just fine. "I'll go through the options, shall I? It could well be nothing, it very often is, perhaps just an excess of fluid. But if when we investigate further, we do find there's a wee tumour in there, then we would need to remove the testicle."

He waits for a moment, as if he is already anticipating Phil's next question.

"What – the whole thing? Why?"

"So we can examine it and find out exactly what sort of laddie we're dealing with."

"Uh huh. Tumour? That's – that is cancer, isn't it?"

"Aye, well it can be, Mr Morrison. But—"

"And forgive me, this is still all a bit – you'd definitely have to remove the whole…?"

Mr Pringle nods regretfully. "After that we'd send you for a scan, just to check if there's been any spread – and then we'd probably give you a dash of radiotherapy."

The specialist is never certain whether patients take in everything he says. He knows for sure that he appears to scare men shitless, young and old, on an hourly basis.

"O-kay," says Phil, shaking his head almost involuntarily, as if to suggest otherwise. "This has come at a rotten time."

Mr Pringle smiles a touch ruefully. "One day I'd love someone to tell me a really good time for having your scrotum investigated. – So, you're in advertising. What's the day's big project? You guys always have a *'big project'.*"

"Oh, er… Delkron Tools. We don't have it – we're pitching."

Mr Pringle beams enthusiastically. "Ah. Well, I hope you get it, Mr Morrison. I'm a great fan of Delkron Tools. I use them all the time."

An image of a man in scrubs bearing down on his lower portions with a whirring circular saw flashes through Phil's mind.

"I hope they're not what you're going to use on me," he says, with what he hopes resembles a smile.

This cracks Mr Pringle up. "Och, it's great that you can still laugh!" he chuckles.

"Why?" asks Phil Morrison.

*

In the evening, after another long, head-banging day, preambled by vague excuses as to his early absence from work, Phil makes himself even more miserable by watching the BBC News Channel.

"Nance, what if it is... you know... cancer?" he says, still looking at the TV but taking nothing in other than the universal pall of gloom. "Ha – I can't be ill, I'm a bloody hypochondriac!"

"Oh, Phil," says Nancy, because it sounds like something to say, even when she has absolutely no idea what to say. All she knows is that whatever she says that isn't utterly bland or deliberately non-committal could be dangerous and wrong.

"*They can't just chop one off!* Like a branch or something. Or a coconut."

She turns to him.

"Okay, maybe not quite a coconut. But I'll be... lopsided! And what if they don't catch it all – what if I spotted it that bit too late? It could have been down there just growing and growing. The silent killer."

"Phil love, you'd have noticed. You said so yourself. And nobody's found anything yet. Maybe – maybe you should just try to, y'know, take things one little step at a time."

Phil switches his eyes from the television to glare at his wife in fury. Nancy feels herself recoiling. She has no idea what has sparked this sudden rush of anger.

"*I'm not one of your fucking clients, Nancy!*"

Instantly she feels tears come to her eyes but just as swiftly tries to blink them back. She can't let him see her weepy. Not now. Not today. She didn't mean to get him so worked up and still has no idea what she has said, as it's not even one of the phrases she recalls ever using with her clients. But perhaps she does regularly employ it, which was why she could call it up so effortlessly. She looks across to Phil, wanting at least to shrug an apology, but he has already sunk back into the sofa and closed his eyes.

Nancy realises with a jolt that whilst she might think she knows how her husband's mind works, after all these many years, right now she has absolutely no idea.

*

A woman's hand goes into a hefty toolbox. From it she removes a well-used Delkron DEL46HD electric drill, plugs it in and switches it on. The whirr is powerful and reassuring.

The woman is not the only occupant of this smart but still not completely finished new kitchen. Nor is she the only one deftly handling a Delkron power tool.

Erica (15) and Todd (8) are happily improving their home alongside her. Erica is nimbly cutting a fresh piece of wood with her DEL53J Jigsaw, while Todd happily sands away at the floor with the very latest, state-of-the-art DEL72S electric sander.

They all turn in delight as the father of the house strolls in and admires their handiwork. He looks like he hasn't a care in the world. The kids immediately switch off their tools and run over to him. Nancy smiles at him 'bravely', clearly concerned and emotional.

"Oh, hi, darling," she says. "How did it go?"

Phil is the picture of insouciance. "Well, the old doc says it could be a malignant tumour on my right testicle."

Now it is Erica's turn to look worried. "Oh no, you poor thing. Are you very scared, Daddy?"

Phil just laughs. "Scared – me? Nah. Worrying's your mother's job, eh love? Well, that and using her new Delkron DEL46HD Hammer Drill."

A teary Nancy moves towards Phil, overflowing with love and compassion. She forgets that she is still brandishing the huge, throbbing drill.

"Whoa," says Phil, recoiling with a chortle, "let's not jump the gun here, eh sweetheart?"

They all laugh together as a family, as Nancy switches off her DEL46HD.

A masculine voiceover cuts in. "Delkron. For men who value their tools."

Logo and out.

*

Phil sits staring at his bowl of cholesterol-friendly oats, berries and nuts, all currently fighting for their lives under a deluge of calcium-enriched almond milk. Erica is making her lunch out of whatever she fancies in the fridge. The sensor that tells her the fridge door needs to close again in order to keep its cool might as well be beeping to its bloody self.

Nancy moves across the kitchen with a sigh and flips the door shut, in an exaggerated gesture that is totally meaningless, except of course to the chilling food.

"What sort of operation?" says Erica, finding the perfect balance between showing she's interested and signalling not that much.

"It's called an exploratory. They just open me up—"

"With a knife?" asks Todd, who has heard fragments of this from the hallway and is deliciously intrigued.

Phil looks up at his young son from his barely touched bowl

and is struck once again by the innocence in those enormous blue eyes and half open mouth.

"Sort of," he explains, "but they put me to sleep first, Toddy. Well, I hope they do. Sometimes they don't give you quite enough anaesthetic and you're still—"

"Phil," warns Nancy.

"No, it'll be fine, Toddy."

"There is *no* hazelnut yoghurt!" moans Erica, opening the fridge again.

"Take one of the others."

"I don't *like* one of the others!"

Phil looks at her then at Nancy, as if a bit of concern from their daughter might be nice.

"What do they do after they've knifed you?" asks Todd, still fascinated.

"Well, they just have a little rummage, Toddy. Like putting their hand into a bag of sweets. And if they find anything they really don't like—"

"They sort it out straightaway," says Nancy, swiftly.

Phil glares at her, like an actor who has just had his best line trampled. "It doesn't need bloody two of us, Nancy!"

"*Forest fruits!*" gripes Erica, in disgust. "Is it sore at the moment? You don't look sore."

"How does sore look?" asks Phil, grumpily. "No, it's not sore, Erica. Well, maybe the odd twinge. Especially when—"

"Okay. Bye." She grabs her yogurt-less bag and goes off to school.

"Well, that was heartwarming," says Phil, when his daughter has gone.

"She did ask if it was sore," defends Nancy, looking back at the closing door.

"Amit Patel's only got one ball," announces Todd, suddenly.

"Has he, love? That's interesting," says Nancy, who really is curious. Amit's mum has never mentioned it to her. She knows from old what Phil might have said, or even sung, in jollier times. Something about Hitler. She smiles reassuringly to her son, who does look a tad more concerned about his father than his sister appeared to be. But then again, so does the fridge.

"Well, don't you worry, darling, Dad's going to be just fine."

"Not after I've told Leo," points out Phil, opening up a whole new arena of potential catastrophe.

*

"*Oh shit, Phil!*"

As Phil and Leo are walking together along the corridor, deep in conversation, which always reminds Phil of a scene straight out of The West Wing, Leo has suddenly stopped.

"Fuck me!"

Leo walks on, shaking his head at how the world constantly conspires against him, and almost bumps into a young art director emerging from an office.

"Saw the shots, love," says Leo, in a tone the younger man takes as enthusiastic. "Don't crop in too tight. The client paid an arm and a leg for that beach." He turns back to Phil as they reach the lift, by which time the first shock wave has begun to subside. "Listen mate, your health comes first. Has to, obviously. Can't you put if off for a few weeks?"

Phil talks faster than he thinks he ever has in his life, as if that life is already running away with him. "I'll give you a cracking campaign, Leo. I've got to have a quick ultrasound and some blood tests, takes no time at all, then wait a week or so before the op and – and I'll be in and out of hospital. They don't keep you around too long on the national health, provided you've got a home to go back to. Which I still have, thankfully. So, Delkron…?"

Leo is starting to pace outside the lifts. "Well, that's okay. No, that's cool. I mean, what can I say?"

Phil can see that the man is royally pissed-off and taking the sudden outcropping on Phil Morrison's right testicle as a personal affront.

"Leo…"

"The clients *know* you now. They bought into you! You were doing that 'interested' thing they like."

"I *was* interested, Leo. And there's absolutely no need to farm it out to other teams. We're going to win this one. Trust me."

The lift opens and Amara emerges, almost obscured by a thick pile of charts and documents. Leo barges into the lift and turns back to Phil, as the doors close.

"Get well soon, Philip." He makes it sound more like an order than the front of a greetings card.

Amara looks at Phil, who immediately helps her with the files then worries again that this might have come off as a bit sexist. It did, but Amara can clearly see that the man is shaken, so she just lets him get on with it.

"Are you okay, Phil?" she asks, in genuine concern.

"Never better, Amara," he says, with a bravado that is only slightly diminished by his adding, "except I've got what looks like a malignant tumour on my right testicle. Well, left testicle, if you're looking at it. Not that you…"

Amara retrieves her files and gently walks him back to his office. He tells her about the hospital on their way.

*

Nancy is folding up Phil's clothes as he shuffles back in from the bathroom in his hospital gown. She has never seen him looking more vulnerable and finds herself, even after some two decades of marriage, not knowing what to say. Or perhaps she does know what to say but is far less certain as to how whatever she says will be taken. Sometimes she feels that she should say nothing at all, but she knows that she is not great with silence and, in any case, that's one thing that could definitely be taken the wrong way.

"Phwoar!" is what she hears herself saying, which fortunately appears to be just fine.

"We try," says Phil, doing an awkward twirl. "Listen, Nance – '*Delkron Tools – they'll do you a power of good.*'"

"I like it. 'Power of Good'. It's... nice."

"It's crap, Nancy! You see, the problem is they're really quite superb tools – apparently, what the hell do I know? – but they are pretty expensive. Compared to – well, to all the others."

He gets onto the bed and into himself. Nancy can recognise it – dear Lord, hasn't she seen it often enough? At school shows, church services, family gatherings, even occasionally at the theatre, but this, of course, is a first. She decides just to tidy quietly around him, until eventually the silence becomes too oppressive to bear.

"Erica and Abigail aren't speaking. It's official."

"What, over the pub thing?"

Nancy knew that her wandering husband would slip back into reality with the promise of a story. "Turns out there's a lad they both fancy. Jamie Woolcot. You remember – used to be at East Lodge with her. Anyway, Abigail made it Saturday on purpose, so Erica couldn't come."

"God, I'm glad I'm not a woman," says Phil, then looks down along his body. "Mind you..." He suddenly pauses and holds out his hand. "I'm trembling, Nancy – is that normal?"

Nancy just nods because she imagines that it must be and she's hardly going to say 'no, it's just you, you wuss'. But he's already moved on to a new panic.

"Oh, listen – if my dad calls, just don't tell him, okay? About any of it. *Please.* I really don't need..."

Nancy just shakes her head, but he has no idea whether this is in disagreement or just despair.

"So, what am I supposed to say, Phil – 'Oh, he's fine Desmond... no, I tell a lie'?"

Phil is grateful not to have to respond, as his eyes and bowels are already registering the entrance of a smiling nurse. She is with a porter, who begins to unlock the bed, prior to transportation.

"Hello, Mr Morrison. Are you ready?" she says, which is a bit of a stupid question in Phil's opinion.

He gazes upwards at Nancy, clearly terrified. And, she thinks, pathetic, in its least pejorative sense.

As he slowly arranges himself on the bed, preserving his modesty, for what it's worth, she grips his hand tightly and feels his far clammier one gripping shakily back.

"I'll see you later, darling," she says. "It'll be fine. I'll be here, my love."

She gives him her warmest, bravest, most resolutely loving smile, which lasts until the back wheels of her husband's latest conveyance have completely disappeared.

*

"Hello… Erica?… Todd? Anyone there?… I left a couple of messages on your mobile. Thought you might be home by – well, Daddy's out of his operation. Still fast asleep. So… don't worry, okay? Er… right, no other news. I'll see you later. Oh Erica, you did remember to pick Toddy up from school? – Okay, love you."

If Nancy were able to see her children, she would be reassured that they were indeed both safe and well.

Not exactly safe and well at home. Todd is well into the big bag of chips provided by his sister, while Erica chats and smokes happily in the street with her pals. Even his sister's friend Abigail gives him a nice smile as she passes by the little group, which is actually more than she gives his big sister.

Erica has no idea how long she needs to babysit her little brother and, right now, neither does her mum, but it could be a while. Nancy is currently sitting at her husband's bedside, the curtains drawn, as he lies there groggily surfacing. Very gently she takes his hand, which feels unfamiliarly cold.

"N… Nancy?"

"I'm here, love."

"Did they…?"

She waits but she knows what's coming.

"Did they cut it off…?"

"Yes, love. Yes, they did."

Phil Morrison just nods, as if he thought as much, and goes back to sleep. Nancy leaves him for a few minutes in order that she can vomit privately in the nearest ladies' toilet, then returns to be at his side.

*

When she spots her children walking up the path, as she turns to park in the drive, Nancy Morrison feels all her anger about absolutely everything boiling up at the same speed as her car window slides down.

"*Where the hell have you been? Where the hell—*"

"Yeah… okay!" says Erica quietly, looking around for any neighbours who might be settling down for the show. "Calm down. Toddy was really worried, yeah, so I got him some chips and we went for a nice walk to help him chill. Then to Sarah's for tea. Took his mind right off it. How's Dad? Same as you said on the phone?"

Nancy switches off the engine, gets out of her car and slams the door, only noticing that her window is still open after she has fully locked up. So now she has to go through the whole rigmarole of unlocking, switching on and closing again which annoyingly dilutes a totally justifiable rage, just when she had wanted it to flare up with renewed vigour.

"He's okay. He's fine, love. The operation went really well."

"See, Toddy? Told you."

Nancy opens the door and almost shoves her children inside. "You smell all smokey."

Erica shoots her brother a warning look, but his mind is elsewhere.

"Did they open Daddy up with the knife?" he asks.

"Just a little, pet. And they took a tiny piece away. So they could examine it. I think I've got some of that fig cake left in the fridge."

"What piece?" asks Erica, removing her smokey blazer and launching it briskly up the stairs.

Nancy goes into the kitchen. She sorely needs to sit down but knows that she might not get up again, possibly ever, and she still has plenty to do this evening.

"The testicle."

Erica just stares at her, as if this has come from left field. For a moment, Nancy wonders if she herself has been playing it too calmly, but there seem to be no rules or strategies for this sort of thing.

"*What – the whole bollock?*"

"Thank you, Erica. Anyway, he'll be fine. You can manage with one. You can even have kids with one testicle."

"Like Amit Patel," says Todd.

"No, I meant…"

Erica grabs her mobile from her pocket. "I need to call—"

"Won't you just sit with us, Erica?" says Nancy, gently. "Please. While we're having our cake. You *still* smell smokey."

"Dad *is* going to be okay?" says Erica. "You said."

"Oh yes, love. Don't worry." Nancy starts handing out the cake. She notices that her hand is shaking. "It'll take time, but he'll be – he'll be fine."

She tries to look more reassuring than she feels, but Nancy can already tell that her teenage daughter, who suddenly seems so small and young, is just confused.

"Do they let Daddy keep his tentacle?" asks Todd. "In a box."

*

There are cards and flowers next to Phil Morrison's bed. These are mostly from friends and family, although there are some from work colleagues, including Keval and Amara. Leo's has yet to arrive.

Whilst still in some pain, kept at bay with a self-administering but regulated morphine drip, Phil is managing to scribble with reasonable legibility – at least to his own eyes – on a lined yellow A4 notepad. His medium of choice.

"Not drawing me, are you?"

The man in the opposite bed, a cheerful, balding Londoner who is probably just a few years older than Phil, is watching him with fascination.

"Not unless you're an electric drill," says Phil, not really wanting to engage in conversation.

"That your job – drill-drawing? Name's Dave, by the way," says the man, who is clearly up for a chat.

"Advertising. I write… ads."

"Yeah? Written anything I've seen? Name's Dave."

"You said. Oh. Mine's Phil. Er… the Fish Family?"

"*You wrote those!*" exclaims Dave, in wonder. Phil, somewhat uplifted and slightly chastened by his earlier standoffishness, just nods. "I thought they was rubbish," says his new friend in the opposite bed. "No offence."

"None fucking taken," mutters Phil to himself, treating his body to a tiny morphine shot.

He has just returned to his rubbish-in-progress when Nancy arrives with more cards and flowers. She notices that Phil is working and is surprised, although she knows that she shouldn't be. *Perhaps it's a good sign*, she muses, although really she has no idea and is just going by instinct and hope. She has a feeling that he'll be spouting slogans in his coffin.

"Hi, love, how are you?" she says, with a cheeriness she is not totally feeling. "Good to see you're working – but you mustn't, y'know, overdo it."

"*He wrote that Fish Family!*" comes a chirpy voice from across the way.

"I know. I'm the fishwife," she says, turning to acknowledge the man. She points to the screens. "Do you mind if I…?"

"I'll whistle if a nurse comes," chuckles Dave, as his view is swiftly blocked.

Phil rolls his eyes as Nancy smiles.

"Has Mr Pringle been round yet?" she asks.

"Not yet, no. Even total strangers are telling me my work's shit now! I'm amazed they don't just get up a petition."

"Oh, don't listen, love. And whatever he says, we'll… deal with it. Mr Pringle, I mean. Not—"

"Nance, I showed you what it said on the internet. The cancer can spread to the lymph nodes and then, well… " He just shrugs, as if to suggest all bets are off.

They are interrupted once again.

"Here he comes!" announces Dave. "'*Great British Fish. Great Thinking.*'"

"See. You bloody remembered it!"

The screen is pulled back. Mr Pringle enters – with another taller, balding man in his late forties. Mr Pringle wears his usual warm smile, but his companion appears quite dour and serious. Even his suit seems morose.

"Hope we're not interrupting something?" greets Mr Pringle cheerily, nodding to Nancy. "Such as the new sparkling Delkron Tools campaign."

"Not a thing. Morning er… Mr Pringle," says Phil, his eyes on the other man.

Nancy starts to rise. "Would you like me to… ?"

"Och, not at all. You stay, Mrs Morrison. We won't be long. This is my colleague, Dr Hirst. He's an oncologist. A cancer specialist. He'll be looking after you from now on."

Dr Hirst nods sombrely, as if there's no more to be said. Had he been introduced as a mortician, Phil wouldn't have been completely surprised.

"So, how are you feeling today?"

"A bit sore. Down there." Phil offers up a sample wince, in case his surgeon doesn't quite know the term.

"Aye, it will be for a while," reassures Mr Pringle. "You just take it easy okay. No DIY! You know the drill – ha! And we've had the results now."

Phil feels the familiar chill that ripples through him whenever news of any sort is coming. He can sense the bile prepping for a return visit. "Oh. Right."

"The tumour was what we call a seminoma."

This is a term Phil knows. You don't become a black belt in Googling medical websites and men's cancer chat-lines without recognising a seminoma when you hear it. And he is also aware that the operation he just had was a 'partial orchidectomy', which he thought sounded like something you should hear about on Gardeners' Question Time.

"It's the sort of tumour we'd expect in a man of your age."

Mr Pringle now turns to his colleague with a well-practised over-to-you nod.

When Dr Hirst begins to talk, his face appears to light up with an almost boyish enthusiasm, which Phil finds infinitely more sinister than his earlier lugubrious silence.

"Indeed," says the man. "So, next step – we'll make you an appointment for that scan, as I believe was mentioned, so we can check if the tumour was contained in the testicle or if the cancer has spread at all."

"What happens if it's spread?" asks Phil.

"Then we'll give you a course of radiotherapy."

Phil appears quietly hopeful. "Right. So, if it hasn't spread, that's job done."

The two doctors exchange a swift look. "Well, no, we'll give you the radiotherapy anyway. Protocol. Just in case. Belt and braces stuff.

"Okay – but then I'll be fine, yes?"

"We… jolly well hope so," enthuses Dr Hirst with a hopefulness that isn't wholly infectious. "But I'm afraid we won't know for absolute certain straightaway. Which is why you'll come and see us for tests at regular intervals. Blood, chest X-rays, that sort of thing."

"How long for?" says Nancy, even before Phil can ask, which irks him a little. Whose seminoma is this anyway?

"About the next five years or so."

Phil's hand goes out to grab Nancy's.

"Hope it's fish for lunch!" pipes a voice from beyond the screens.

*

Nancy sometimes wonders if her clients reckon she leads a charmed life.

She was a Samaritan for several years and the standing, somewhat dark joke at the centre where she volunteered was that they would one day respond to a caller with, 'You think *you've* got problems!' Fortunately, Nancy's troubles had never been anywhere near as grave or desperate as some of those she heard on each shift and with which she hopefully empathised. Today, however, she is finding it unusually hard to offer her usual one hundred and ten percent to the person on the other side of her overloaded desk.

The person, a good-looking and dangerously charming man in his early thirties, with a broken nose but sparkling teeth, doesn't appear to be over-bothered.

"The way I see it, Nancy," he explains cockily, "it's like coming off the drink. It's not that you can't… it's more that when everyone else you know's still doing it, you ain't got that much incentive."

"You could stop hanging around with criminals," suggests Nancy.

"Nancy, they're the only game in town."

Nancy sighs, despairingly, although she does appreciate the dilemma. "Mr Grainger, this isn't Las Vegas. And I'm Mrs Morrison."

"You see how hard it is for me to make straight friends?"

She has to smile at this. She often wonders whether she should like some of these clients as much as she does, but she tells herself they're not bad people, they've just been doing some bad things. He checks out the smile and returns it, as he takes a pack of cigarettes from his denim shirt pocket.

"You don't mind if I…?"

Nancy points to the big *No smoking* sign that he must have seen. Mr Grainger just shrugs. Worth a try.

The door opens and Andrew, her PA, comes in. He is wearing his concerned look. "Sorry to interrupt, Nancy. Phone."

Nancy gets up, perturbed yet also displeased, then turns back to apologise to her client and confiscate his cigarettes. "Will you excuse me, Mr Grainger?"

"It's your Phil," whispers Andrew, on their way out, "otherwise I wouldn't have—"

"Andy, I'm with a client!" She sighs as she takes the office phone. "Hi, love. Is everything alright?" she says, swiftly. "… Sorry Phil, I can't chat now. When I'm through here I'll just make a quick supper for the kids then I'll be right over. See you then. Promise."

Ignoring Andrew's worried glance – and, indeed, those of everyone else in the office; the sort of looks Nancy has been observing recently, where the head tilts to one side in sympathy and the 'aahs' hang unspoken in the air – she goes back towards the interview room.

To her surprise, Mr Grainger is standing at the door, simply watching her. As if he can sense that something isn't right.

"Sorry about that, Mr Pearson," she apologises and then wonders why he's staring.

"Grainger," he corrects kindly, without seeming to have taken offence. "Hey, Nancy, I can't expect to have you all to myself."

"Yes, you can, Mr Grainger," she says, firmly. "This is *your* time."

The 'You think you've got problems?' remains unspoken.

*

"A lot of celebs do DIY, Leo. Harrison Ford was a carpenter – 'Whether repairing the lost ark, or putting up a bathroom cabinet, Harrison Ford turns to Delkron for star power'. And, of course, there's Jesus. – No, that was an attempt at frivolity, Leo. – Yeah, I know."

Phil sits in the chair beside his hospital bed, talking on his phone. He still looks frail and pained.

"Okay, no worries, I've got loads of other ideas. I'll bike some over this afternoon. – Eh? – *Soon* Leo, I'll be back in the office real soon. *Really* – yeah, bye."

"Who's Leo?" asks Dave.

"Just someone I work with."

"Did you do that Guinness ad – y'know the one with the—"

"Yep, that'd be one of mine, Dave."

"Yeah?" says Dave, clearly impressed. "What about that one with, who was it – Elton John?"

"Uh huh. Well, I was part of a team. Good old Elton."

Before Phil can admit to the creation of anything else that springs into Dave's gogglebox mind, Erica walks in, still in her school uniform but smelling less smokey. She appears quite ill at ease.

"Hello. School's out," says Dave, predictably.

"Oh, hi, love," says Phil, surprised but clearly delighted. "Close the curtains, would you?"

Erica pulls the curtains round, as Phil shuffles awkwardly back onto his bed so that she can sit down.

"Bye," says Dave.

"Is that the one who's getting on your—"

"*Ssshh!*" warns Phil. "Dave's my number one fan – now that he thinks I wrote all his favourite ads."

Phil can sense that Erica clearly has no idea what to say to him, but he feels too weary, especially after his regular tricky conversation with Leo, to help her out or make much conversation.

"Is it hurting?" she asks eventually, which feels like safe albeit uncomfortable ground.

"A bit. From the op, not from the er you know. But they've done their little tests and they... know what to do about it now. Two or three weeks of radiotherapy..."

"Uh huh," mulls Erica. "That's good, isn't it?"

Phil waits, in case his daughter wants to elaborate, but she clearly doesn't. He wonders to himself why she isn't more interested. As soon as the silence becomes too much to bear, he decides to change the subject.

"So – have you thought about Mum's surprise party?"

Erica looks either amazed or appalled. "*Is that still on?*"

"Why not?" challenges Phil.

"Well... we could do it next year. Or not at all."

"I might not... I might not have time next year. And her big birthday will have been and gone. You will help, won't you love? *Erica?*"

Erica is clearly not thrilled. "Yeah. Okay."

Phil decides to read into this curt response a subtext of barely suppressed enthusiasm.

"Great. Good! Well, for starters we'll be needing invitations. Nice fancy ones – you know, with some lovely graphics. You're terrific at art."

"Dad, you work with artists all day." She watches his face, as it registers disappointment. "It's just, like… I've got a lot on my mind… things are a bit crap at school. Abigail's—"

"Erica, you do know I've got cancer?"

She looks shocked and perhaps offended. "*Course I know! Dad?* But you're going to get better, aren't you? Mum said."

Phil thinks that he should agree with this upbeat assessment from his wife, but he's finding it depressingly difficult. He knows that the vast majority of people – well, men – with his condition do make it through, albeit lopsidedly, but finds himself inevitably identifying with that tiny but desperately unlucky minority who don't.

"Mum'll need a bit of help when I get back," is all he can manage.

"She told me," Erica sighs. "Like about a million times."

In the silence they stare at each other. Phil tries to smile at her, and she tries to smile back. Finally, she picks up her schoolbag and rises from the chair.

"I'd best… you know, before it gets dark."

Phil nods, although he hasn't previously noticed that darkness was a particular impediment for his daughter.

"Yeah. You stay safe. Thanks for coming, love."

"That's okay. Oh, the girls at school wish you better."

"Eh? *Erica* – you never told them!"

"It's not like you caught something. Y'know, down there."

"No," agreed Phil. "I'm blessed. Do I get a kiss?"

Erica bends stiffly towards him. They peck at each other's cheek with some difficulty. As soon as she goes, Phil returns to his pad and his project. He doesn't notice Erica turning slightly, as she pulls back the curtains, to glance at him before she leaves.

"Walkers Crisps?" comes the inevitable challenge.

"Uh huh," says Phil, already back to power tools.

*

74

A couple of days later, at the same time as her recovering husband is preparing to pack up his stuff to come home, Nancy resolves to corral her daughter into helping prepare this same home as somewhere he might feel comfortable. Or at least not too uncomfortable.

The little TV from the kitchen is now on a pine chest of drawers opposite their bed, freshly picked flowers sitting in a small vase beside it. Nancy knows that Phil will barely notice the flowers, unless they are planted right in front of the TV screen, but she thinks that he might just sense their absence after the hospital. And anything that brightens the room has to be worthwhile, hasn't it?

"*Are all my tights in the wash?*" asks Erica, steaming in.

Nancy wonders why every single question this teenage girl chooses to ask expresses itself as either a challenge or a criticism. The only other teenage girls she has 'on file' with which to compare are herself when she was young (a joy and a treasure) and those currently belonging to her friends (just as bad, if not worse). Everyone tells her that it will pass, which for any parent has to be a relief yet, somewhere, also a sadness.

"Have you checked your floor?" mutters Nancy. "Hey, while you're here, help me with the bed. I want it all to look nice for Dad. And I've got to go pick him up in a few minutes."

Erica lifts up a huge pair of loose tracksuit bottoms from a chair and eyes them with distaste. "These are really cool."

"*Erica!* They're to make it less sore for poor Dad. Y'know, down there. They are a bit gross, aren't they?"

If Phil could witness his girls laughing together, sharing a moment, even at his expense, he might feel more heartwarmed than ridiculed, but it's a tough call and the 'girls' (although he knows from Erica's glares that he must not ever call them this, especially not Mum's 'grown-up' friends) are sufficiently sensitive to share these things strictly in private.

Meantime, the patient is indeed diligently completing his own preparations.

"What's the next thing I'll be seeing on the telly then, Phil?" asks Dave.

At least this will be the final question, thinks Phil, as he sits patiently beside his packed suitcase, in uncomfortable but just about bearable pain.

"Oh, this and that – you know. Well, you never really know. I suppose that's part of the excitement. And the angst."

"Yeah. Gotcha. – Hey, Phil, do you want to, you know, keep in touch? Like a support group."

Er, no.

"Er... yeah. Be... great, Dave."

"Wouldn't be for long."

Phil looks at the man as this registers, but Dave has already turned towards to the door.

"*And here comes the fishwife!*" he announces breezily.

"Hi, Dave," greets Nancy, as she strolls in. She notices Phil's face, which even for him looks glum. "You okay, love?"

*

Phil's study is small and almost overwhelmingly cluttered.

In the past he would have said that it was the place in the house where he felt most at home, his haven and refuge, surrounded by his books, his music, his computer, his mess and an impressive array of gadgets designed to relax a person. These range from Newton's Balls (and Phil hasn't refrained from telling him, 'you're lucky to have them, mate') to any number of objects of various levels of squidginess that will instantly remove tension from a person the moment that he/she (but mostly he) grips them in an angry vice.

Today, however, as he hunches baggy and unshaven over his keyboard, writing a commercial out loud, with Def Leppard playing from the tiny speakers on his desk, he is feeling anything but comfortable.

"*'Open on two brawny guys holding rival power drills, like they're Colt 45s in a shoot-out'.*"

Phil doesn't notice Nancy in the doorway, still in her coat, carrying a pharmacy bag. So he can't be aware of how appalled she is. At least, not until she switches the music off and he turns painfully around.

"I don't know how you expect that wound to heal!" she says, plonking his assorted medicaments, some hospital-prescribed and others personally requested, down right in front of him.

"Nance, the world doesn't stop just 'cos I've been in hospital."

"No, but it can turn bloody well without you!"

Phil resumes his typing. "That's rather the problem, isn't it?"

"Oh, please!" says Nancy, feeling the anger and despair shaking up like some noxious cocktail.

"You do know there's only one in five people in advertising over forty? One in five!"

"You told me. Every week since you were thirty-five. For God's sake, Phil! If you're not fit and well, they won't give you your radiotherapy."

"Well, *there's* an incentive! I only hope those hot little radiotherapists can control themselves when they see what I've got to offer."

Nancy feels wrong-footed, the conversation straying inevitably into areas she wants desperately to avoid, at least for now. Yet, she is determined to be cheery.

"You're still man enough for me, kiddo," she says.

He gets up, ignoring the sharp catch in his groin, and moves round his chair to cuddle her. For reasons even she might find hard fully to explain, Nancy feels quite uneasy. When he kisses her on the lips, she simply accepts it without reciprocation. She feels ashamed by her reticence and can only source some justification in her not wishing to cause him even more discomfort or to make him feel that he can run before he can hardly walk. Yet she is not totally certain that she believes it.

Phil appears to have less of a problem interpreting her stance. "Yeah. Anyway, mustn't stop." He switches the music back to even louder than before and taps some random keys on his keyboard. "And I'm going back to work tomorrow," he says quietly.

Now Nancy is in no doubt where she stands. "*No*, I'm sorry. *You are not!* You are bloody not, Phil! For pity's sake, you've only been home what a couple of days! You're still healing. You've got the phone… you've got email… that new scanner you went out and—"

"Nancy… they think I'm dying."

She says nothing because there's nothing to say, or at least nothing that won't inflame him more.

"And if I don't win this pitch, I might as well be."

"Jesus, Phil!" she finally manages to say.

"*This is my cancer – okay?*"

He carries on typing, this time for real.

Nancy knows that she is spoiling for a fight yet is only too aware that she can't get into one. Not now. Not yet. Perhaps not ever. So, after a moment of intense centring and equally fervid simmering, she simply leaves the room. Hiding the tears that are there.

When she emerges from the once again raucous study into the relative quiet of the landing, she sees Todd watching her. Immediately her face brightens and her eyes twinkle, which annoyingly just causes the tears to squeeze out even more.

"Daddy's going back to work tomorrow, Toddy. Isn't *that* good news?"

*

When Phil enters the lushly carpeted office, Leo, Keval and Amara are poring over an array of scribbled roughs on the floor.

"Knock knock!" chirps Phil, with Oscar-winning cheeriness. Amara and Keval turn immediately and hurl gratifying beams of love at him, as does Camille from her desk. Leo forces out a more restrained smile.

"Hey, it's the man himself!" says Leo, as Amara rises to offer Phil a welcoming kiss. Keval gives off signals that he too would kiss his creative partner if he did that sort of thing.

"Camille, see who's here! Coffee… coffee! Make it strong. You look… you look terrific, matey. How you feeling?"

"I'm getting there, Leo." Phil thinks he looks as far from terrific as Aleppo is but appreciates that the situation isn't easy for anyone. "Hi, guys."

"It is *so* good to see you," says Amara, her head instantly cocked to one side. "Are you sure you're ready, Phil? These things take—"

"Course he's ready!" insists Leo, the urologist. "Amara? That Lance Armstrong had one of his lopped off and he won the Tour de France seven times!"

"Couldn't he have just shaved his legs?" says Phil. No one laughs but he can see the two women exchanging sad looks. "That was meant to be a joke."

Through the ripples of kindly mirth, Phil can watch Leo trying to satisfy his curiosity, whilst tamping down his squeamishness.

"So, do they really…?" He makes a scissors gesture as Keval joins him for a quick wince.

"Actually, they make an incision in the groin, then they—"

"I don't wanna know!" shrieks Leo. "I don't want to know. Shit, I hope it doesn't happen to me when I'm your age."

"Can happen at any age, Leo," says Phil, helpfully.

"Statistically," adds Amara, "it's mostly younger men who get it."

Phil is finding this conversation almost as painful as just standing here, with his dressing still on and the wound inexorably stretching and healing. He decides to point to one of the rough ads. "That one works," he says. "I wasn't sure."

"Yeah," says Leo, thrilling to the sound of a subject changing. "I had young Kev here work up those ideas you sent over. Hey, I've seen far worse from blokes with two bollocks."

"*Leo!*" chides Amara. "So that's it then, is it Phil? I mean, with…"

"Yeah that's it, Amara. Aside from the scan."

"Scan?" asks Keval.

"It's just like this metal doughnut thing – checks they've got it all. Which they probably have. And then a swift dash of radiotherapy."

Amara tuts in sympathy.

"Only Monday to Friday." He doesn't dare look at Leo. "For a week. Or three."

A groan from Leo, which sounds very like a long drawn-out 'fuuuuckk'.

"And I'll come straight on to work afterwards each day. Won't take long. You're in and out of there, apparently. Zap zap zap! It'll be fine."

"Right. Yeah. Whatever," says Leo. "Hey, you just get better, Phil… all that matters. Yeah."

Phil, who knows what matters most in this room, squats uneasily down to look at the roughs splayed out on the floor, wondering if he'll actually be able to rise up again unaided, and in relative silence, when the time comes.

"We have so fucking got to win this one," mutters Leo.

*

"*Spread!*"

The Morrisons sit in the oncologist's office, looking shell-shocked.

Phil recalls his recent helpless terror, going through that

horribly brilliant machine. Or rather the machine going over him. The operators graciously permitted his ordeal to be accompanied by music of his choice, whilst ordering him to keep entirely still throughout. This had forced him to select something that wouldn't automatically set his feet tapping and his head bopping. He had only realised when the contraption began to whir that he didn't really like Coldplay that much and that it didn't pacify him in the slightest.

"Spread?" he asked the oncologist again, who wasn't looking any cheerier than on that first ominous bedside visit. "How far has it spread?"

"To the lymph glands at the back of your abdomen. Have you been getting backaches at all, Mr Morrison?"

"Phil. You can call me Phil. Most people who fiddle with me down there do. – Er, yeah. A bit. Lower back. And shoulders. And neck, actually. And I think a bit of jaw. And head. I thought it was just stress. Not good, is it?"

"It most probably *was* just stress. Phil," reassures the man. "Our backs do tend to bear the brunt of what the mind and our emotions throw at us. But all that this means is the radiotherapy will have to work just a tiny bit harder. I honestly wouldn't let it faze you too much."

A mobile starts to ring. Nancy rummages in her bag, looks at her phone and swiftly turns it off. "Work – sorry."

When they are walking out of the hospital, Nancy turns to Phil. "Did you have to say that thing about 'fiddling?'"

"Is that your main concern?"

"No. Of course not. He said it shouldn't faze you."

"Do I look fazed?"

"I can't tell anymore," admits Nancy, grasping his hand. "We'll get through this, love."

"'We'?" says Phil.

*

The Delkron kids are happily doing their DIY in the kitchen. Todd is up a ladder with a drill, fixing a shelf. Erica is planing some wood.

Phil and Nancy stroll in cheerily from outside, still in their coats, hand and hand.

"Hey, Dad, how did it go?" says their concerned teenage daughter, her face riven with apprehension.

"Total breeze," grins Phil. "Looks like it's the old radiotherapy Monday to Friday for me, kids. Zap zap zap!"

The children look delighted, as if their dad is off to Club Med.

"But before it starts," announces Dad, turning towards his wife. He suddenly whips open his overcoat, revealing an elaborate Workman's Belt, bristling with power tools, etc., of every shape and size. Nancy is clearly impressed, even as she shakes her head at him. What a card.

"The Delkron X918 Masterbuilder Tool Belt," he explains. "I'm going to do all those odd jobs round the house. Starting with that sink."

Nancy turns to her offspring. "I just don't know where he gets the energy from."

"Plenty left over where that came from, eh Mum?" says Phil cheekily, striding across to the sink in question.

Nancy blushes slightly, as Erica and Todd share a 'parents!' look.

The voice-over declaims: "Delkron – for men who are always on the job!"

*

Nancy is reading her daily reports in bed, with an unfamiliar lack of focus that quite upsets her. Phil's planning brief sits open on his iPad, yet his hand is barely moving, and the eyes are fixed somewhere between the curtains and infinity.

Glancing across, Nancy speaks softly, as if not wishing to

unsettle him. "Phil, you know the balance is due on Erica's school trip?"

"Mm? Oh, God, does she have to go?"

"She wants to go. Her pals are going. I know it isn't cheap—"

"Okay – but let's just, y'know, take it easy."

"I know, don't worry."

She gives him a little kiss, then pulls away. He gently yet firmly eases her round to him once more.

"Do you really want to?" she says, equally gently. And firmly.

"I'd like to know if I still can, Nancy."

"Of course, you can. Mr Pringle said."

"It's not Mr Pringle who's had his three-piece suite re-upholstered."

Whilst not their most romantic of foreplays, Nancy is sufficiently wise to see how important this is right now for the man lying next to her, the person looking everywhere but in her direction. For some reason, a song lyric rushes into her head – something about when people touch and too much honesty, and she wonders why the mind tends to wander at just those times when it should be most focused. She'd be rubbish in the SAS.

As he lies on his back, Nancy cuddles up to him, kissing him first on the cheek, then softly on the lips. For the first time in ages, she notices a kind of contentment come upon him, an aura of something vaguely resembling peace. And now she senses his whole body gearing up to a response, new energy hotly coursing, as he turns towards her with an urgent, still impressive vigour. The pain immediately shoots through him, so searing and acute it causes Phil to yelp and instantly pull away.

"Is it the wound?" asks Nancy, although she knows there's little else it could be.

"*Of course, it's the fucking wound!* Wait a minute."

He tries desperately to find a different position, one that might cause him at least a fraction less pain. He has ruled out total painlessness as an achievable goal. At least for now. Nancy knows that she should also twist her weary body to accommodate him, but she is at a loss as to exactly how or where. Or in which direction.

"Meet me halfway, Nancy!"

"Sorry. Sorry, darling. What should I do?"

"Well, turn on your side so I don't have to twist so far! *For Christ's sake, Nance!*"

"How? Which side? I don't know what to do, love... please, tell me what to do."

"Never mind." Using his elbows to take the weight off his lower body, Phil finally manages to hoist himself on top of her. "That's it," he says, looking down at her. Waiting. Breathless.

Then, before she even has time to understand what he wants or for what exactly he is waiting, he simply shakes his head and moves off her with a sigh.

"We should probably just give it time, love," she soothes. "It'll happen, you'll see. There's absolutely no reason why..." She can hear herself rambling on but finds it almost impossible to stop, even when he slowly starts to get up and stumble away "Phil, my sweet..."

She lies alone in the bed, just staring at the open doorway.

In the bathroom, Phil is staring too. First at his pallid, despondent face in the mirror then, as he pulls out the elasticated band of his unfetching pyjama bottoms, down at his diminished self. He thinks Nancy might just be able to hear his small, desperate sobs, but he really doesn't care.

*

The big room looks seriously intimidating. Cold. Clinical. Which is hardly surprising, thinks Phil Morrison, as this is exactly what it is.

When he enters, lost and scared, in yet another hospital gown, he feels dwarfed by the large, cheery Trinidadian radiotherapist and her young assistant. They watch him as he takes in the apparatus, the control room, the warning signs on the walls.

The table.

"Do you expect me to talk?" he quotes to himself.

"Hi, Mr Morrison, I'm Paula," says the senior radiotherapist. "Now, don't you go worrying – we're a lot less scary once you get to know us. Aren't we, Karen?"

The sympathetic young assistant nods, her head already cocked to one side as she observes her patient.

"Does it, you know, hurt, Paula?" asks Phil.

"You won't feel a thing. Now just slip your gown off."

He does so – a tad shyly.

"That's it. After a few days you could start to get a bit tired. On you go, sir. Onto the table." He tries to mount the beast without losing his dignity or his modesty.

"How tired?" he asks. "And please, call me Phil."

"Pretty tired, Phil," admits Paula. "And your skin might feel a little tender. But we'll give you some cream."

"Nausea?" added Phil. "I read on the internet it can make you nauseous."

Paula starts to arrange the equipment in order to hone in on him. "Could be. But you don't want to read too much on the internet, or you'll think if we press the wrong button you'll turn into Spider-Man. Now, you have to lie really still while we line you up. You don't want any of this going where it's not supposed."

"I heard about one guy in my position who was offered an artificial testicle, y'know, to replace the... anyway, when they were doing the procedure, they couldn't find the new prosthetic ball anywhere, so the doctor said, 'oh, just pop in a nice, big pickled onion, he won't know the difference'. Couple of weeks later the guy comes back to the doc, who of course asks him how he's doing. The bloke says, 'absolutely fine, doc, but funny thing – every time I see a cheese sandwich, I get this massive erection.'"

Paula and Karen laugh themselves silly.

"Heard it before, haven't you?"

"Yes," admits Paula, "but not this week. There we are. All set."

Then they go out of the room.

"Where are you going?" calls the abandoned patient.

"Don't worry – we'll be back in a few minutes."

Phil lies there on his own, just staring at the machinery. Through the intercom he hears Paula's voice. "You just try and relax, Mr Morrison. But see that you don't move while you're doing it."

He has never felt less relaxed in his life. So, he thinks about the upcoming Delkron pitch. Which fortuitously scares him rigid.

*

A week later Phil is sitting on the dusty floor of his agency office, poring uncomfortably over roughs and storyboards with Keval, who for some reason keeps staring at him. Phil hopes that this has purely to do with professional approval for a piece of creative work but fears that it is more likely to be sympathy for someone who's currently looking like warmed-up shit.

A large, hand-drawn rough reads *Advanced DelkrONics* below the huge *ON* button of a serious power tool (both *ON*s are in red). Phil slaps it enthusiastically.

"That one works you know, Kev. As a smart sign-off. You can animate it *and* it's branded. Sometimes I think guys like Leo get so wrapped up in the 'big gobsmacking idea', they forget we're all about selling a bloody product."

"How'd it go this morning?" asks Keval, as he has done most mornings.

Phil just shrugs, not exactly sure how it went. He's well into his radiotherapy now and weary both of it and from it. The chest feels raw, the head foggy as hell and for some reason he reckons that he could eat for Britain. Perhaps this latter is to replace the energy in his body that the process itself depletes, but he truly expected to be losing weight right now not putting it on. Isn't that what cancer is all about? He is wondering idly how much a single excised testicle might weigh, when he notices a very young man and an equally youthful woman glancing through the glass wall at them. Keval picks up on Phil's look and turns.

"Who are they?" he asks.

Phil nods warmly at them. "Couple of kids Leo's got on the cheap. Work experience. They even make you look old."

Suddenly Leo appears, waving warmly at the kids, as he steams into the cluttered office.

"Okay, guys," he announces, without preamble or a hug, "here's the plan. I want you to do me a half-dozen fuckity-fuck dazzling OMG campaigns that we are *not* going to sell 'em on the day."

Phil and Keval just stare at the man.

"No, sorry Leo – lost me already," says Phil, shaking his foggy head.

Leo looks at Phil like he's inherited an idiot then squats down to grab a rough from the floor.

"O-kay, guys," he says slowly, in case estuary English isn't their first language. "You show 'em a great idea, yeah? Make 'em cream all over it, yeah? I mean, *really* cream. And then…" He crumples the first rough savagely into a tiny ball and throws it casually over his left shoulder. They watch as it hits the glass door then disappears behind a large plans chest. Before they can enquire if the man is having a rather violent stroke, Leo simply says, "Sorry, gents."

"Er, that's alright, Leo…?" says Phil, understandably. But Leo is on a roll.

"I was saying 'sorry' to Delkron. '*Sorry, gents*'? So then you show 'em another cracking campaign," he continues, at an even louder and more excited pitch. "Same strategy, the one we've all nailed down with the suits, but a totally different execution. And holy cow – *this idea is even better!* So, what do we do?" He picks up another rough and repeats the same destructive process, only with greater force and velocity. Phil tries to save the idea, but Leo simply smacks his hand away and carries on crumpling. "... Ap... pap... pap!" he chides. "Now same again, chaps. Sorry, *encore une fois*, Delkron!"

Keval deftly glides the remaining ideas away from the madman as Phil just stares.

"Notice a pattern emerging?" says Leo, rhetorically, pulling any vulnerable roughs back into range. "We do this, say, five, six, maybe even seven times. All blinding ideas. All pushing the envelope. All kaput. By the time you hit 'em with the real thing, the leader of the pack, the big kahuna, they can't think of a single good reason not to fucking buy it."

Phil is not convinced. "Yeah... okay."

"I've done it before, Phil. It works. You're covering all the bases your competition might have covered. And OMG! – dissing 'em just like that. *It fucking works!*"

Phil looks as if he's been hit by another intense dose of radiotherapy. "Lot of ideas, Leo."

"Problem?" asks Leo.

"God no," says Phil swiftly. "Kev and I can do rejects."

"It's our speciality," asserts Keval proudly.

Phil gets up slowly and uncrumples the much-abused *Advanced DelkrONics* rough. "Here, what do you think of this Leo – minus the crinkles?"

Leo graces the sheet of paper with a cursory glance. "*Advanced Delkronics*. Yeah, okay. Bit old school. It's a concept in search of an execution. Convince me it's an account-winning campaign."

"It'll be a campaign, Leo," says Phil, feeling his body tense up and his temperature rising. "I do know the bloody difference."

"Okay, okay, mate, don't get antsy. Just saying. You finished that radio-whatsit of yours yet?"

"Nearly. Very nearly."

Leo looks at Phil as if his senior copywriter could be sneaking in extra radiotherapy sessions just for the hell of it. He wouldn't put it past the old bugger.

*

When Nancy enters her office, she is irked to discover Mr Grainger already seated there and quite settled in.

"Oh, you're here," she observes, unnecessarily. "Sorry to keep you, Mr Grainger."

"That's okay, Nancy," says the man, cheerily. "Just admiring the pictures."

As the walls are completely bare, Nancy has to smile, despite herself. "It's still Mrs Morrison," she says, "and no, you still can't smoke. So, how's the job hunting?"

"I'm going to try the minicabbing again. My licence is the only thing that's clean. Well, except for my shirt and my teeth." He gives Nancy a quick smile but then just as instantly looks concerned, as if the reality of his situation has begun to intrude. "But if that doesn't work out…"

"Try not to worry about things until they happen," says Nancy, which causes him to stare at her, but she can't tell whether he's impressed by the wisdom or despairing of the lunacy. "Sorry. My husband hates it when I say that."

"How is Phil?"

"Excuse me?"

"Phil, your husband."

"Yes, I know who he is, but…?"

"With his illness. You must be gutted."

Nancy looks back towards the outer office, as if the culprit will immediately offer up the mime of falling on his or her sword.

"Whoa – crossed a line, didn't I?" says Mr Grainger. "Story of my life. *Mea* culprit. No one told me, love – I just overheard. Villains keep their ears open. Hey, you've probably got loads of people to talk to. The ladies here… your mates…"

Nancy cannot believe that they are having this conversation. Yet she is almost shocked to discover, although she would hardly admit it, even to herself, that this isn't totally unwelcome. Go figure, as they say. She is well aware that she doesn't confide in many people – basically, she's a rather private person. A person who hates burdening others with her 'stuff'. More of a listener, really. Always has been. Which possibly isn't helping anyone right now. *But the man's a client, for pity's sake!*

"It's actually… it's actually a very private matter, Mr Grainger."

The man doesn't say anything for a moment but simply looks at her. And saying equally little, she finds herself looking back. She knows what he is seeing. A woman approaching a certain age who seems bound up so tight she could almost explode. He wants to put his arm around her, let her know that he understands. Calm her gently down. Instead, he simply nods.

"Course it is. So, let's talk about me, Mrs Morrison. Maybe it'll take your mind off things, if only for a while." He rests his chin on his hands. And starts to talk.

*

As the days and the early morning hospital sessions grind on, Phil Morrison, predictably, becomes more and more fatigued and the office waste-bin, equally predictably, full to overflowing. Even climbing up onto his radiotherapy table these days takes on the dimensions of an Everest trek, whilst putting on an energised front for Leo and his equally demanding board drains him of so much juice by the end of the day that he sometimes has to take a cab all the costly way home. One memorable occasion, when he did manage to make it onto the tube, an elderly lady gave up her seat for him because he seemed to be on the point of passing out. She appeared to be alone amongst passengers in realising that the man swaying in front of her hadn't simply been out for a very long lunch.

When he does finally arrive home on these evenings, Phil barely has the energy to talk to Todd, let alone swing him round the way he used to. Sometimes he finds that he has fallen asleep over the kitchen table, waking up with a start to discover his wife and daughter quietly clearing up around him.

One evening, two weeks into the treatment, Nancy comes into their bedroom to find Phil still fully clothed and working on his laptop.

"I thought you'd gone to bed ages ago," she says.

He leans towards her almost instinctively and she gently helps him off with his shirt. Nancy tries not to offer too empathic a wince, as she notices once again the redness raw on his chest.

"You've got a nasty boil coming up. On your neck," observes Phil, almost as if he wants to reciprocate. She doesn't say that it can happen when she's stressed, because she sees no need to go there right now. And anyway, there are more important things to discuss.

"Phil…" she begins with almost pointed hesitation, "your dad rang today."

"I do phone him, Nance," he replies over-defensively. "I only spoke to him on… whenever."

"I know – I know."

The uneasy silence causes him to look up and find her gaze moving swiftly away.

"He wants to come and stay, doesn't he? Nance, I don't need that bloody man right now. I really…"

Nancy still won't look at him.

"When's he coming?"

"Saturday."

"What – this Saturday? No, Nancy! *No*."

＊

"*Grandpa's here!*" yells Erica from her bedroom, as she watches a familiar car being parked very carefully right across their driveway.

By the time Grandpa Desmond has managed to extricate himself from his vehicle, Nancy and Todd are at the door to greet him. Nancy can't help thinking how trim and robust the man looks, all tweeded up in his best jacket and tie. Such a contrast to his less-than-thrilled host currently slumping down the stairs.

As Mum and excited son go to help the elderly man with his luggage and flowers and bag of gifts and range of overcoats, Erica gently draws Phil aside.

"Dad. Dad, I did it," she announces, quietly but urgently.

"Did what?" asks a somewhat distracted Phil.

"The invitation. Y'know, for Mum's surprise party. I just got it." She unfolds something from her pocket and proudly shows him. "Here. Quickly. *Quickly!* I used the colour copier down the stationers. If you like it, I can get them all done. *Quick!* What do you think?"

Phil gives the design a cursory glance. His mind is somewhere else. "Colour's a bit washed out. Make sure you get them to bump it up a bit." He glances up again towards the newly parked car, not noticing the look of hurt instantly clouding his daughter's face. "Oh, and Erica, I want you to have a think about the food."

"You *told* me. Three times. I am!"

They watch Desmond hand his suitcase to Todd. It is far too heavy, so Nancy steps in to take it. Noticing this, Desmond takes it back.

"Okay, okay," whispers Phil. "Now, you've got the guest list? We need to order a cake! Yes. Something really special, you know.

Howsabout… that raspberry and cream meringue Mum likes? Yes! I want everything to be just right. Has to be – just right."

"It *will* be! So – did you like the invitation?"

"Yeah, it's fine," mutters Phil, distracted once again.

"Does he *have* to sleep in my room?"

"Yes. Try to be kind to him, Erica. You know what you're like."

"You know what *you're* like," she retorts.

"Got an excuse. He's my dad."

The elderly man approaches, supported in spirit, if not quite physically, by daughter-in-law and grandson. Nancy immediately notices the father's discomfort but also the son, too wrapped up in his own. After a moment's awkwardness, Phil reaches his hand out.

"Hi, Dad."

Desmond responds in kind, as this is clearly the accepted Morrison greeting, but with his other hand he tentatively taps his son's arm. Phil turns away, but not too abruptly, and leads them back into the hallway.

"What is it that one does to get this testicular cancer?" asks Desmond.

"I didn't *do* anything, Dad."

"No, no… I didn't mean… so, how are you feeling?"

Phil and Nancy exchange a look. "I'm fine, Dad. Really. I'm fine." He gazes around, as if pleading for someone else to step in. Todd struggles manfully to lug his grandpa's well-worn suitcase up the stairs.

"Hi, Grandpa," rescues Erica.

"You don't look fine," says Desmond, helpfully. "Hello, Erica, dear. Did you get a second opinion?"

"About the malignant tumour on my right testicle? Yeah. The greengrocer thought it was a wonky potato."

"*Phil!*" warns Nancy quietly, as Desmond hangs up his jacket with inordinate care over one of the children's fleeces.

"Well, at least you've had your lovely family, thank goodness," says Desmond, who prides himself on seeing silver linings.

"You can still fire on one cylinder, you know, Desmond," explains Nancy.

"Too much information, Nance," warns Phil.

Erica toddles off back towards her room with a dramatic sigh, as she does whenever parent sex rears its icky head.

"So, what needs doing, Nancy?" says Desmond, vaguely rolling up his sleeves, without actually creasing his shirt. "I know the kitchen's your territory, dear, but if there's anything else around the house, anything poor old Phil here hasn't the energy for." He cocks his head to one side for Phil. "We'll make sure you're taking it easy, won't we, Nancy? Have your advertising people given you much sick leave?"

"I'm still at work every day, Dad. Got a really big pitch on, actually." He waits in vain for Desmond to ask him about it.

"You'd have thought they'd give you some time off."

"I don't need bloody time off! *I'll have time off when I'm dead!*"

Nancy recognises that Phil is starting to lose it. "Come on Desmond, you've had a long drive. I'll make you a cup of tea."

They go into the kitchen, leaving Phil in the hallway. He looks around, at the door, the stairs, the walls, as if he has no idea where to go and the options are rapidly shrinking. There is a large antique mirror on the wall next to him and he wishes there wasn't.

*

"I can't ask him how long he's staying!" says Nancy that evening.

Phil sits topless on the toilet seat, trying to keep his eyes open, while she spreads a thin layer of cream onto his inflamed chest.

"He's only been here a few hours."

"Seems like months," grumbles Phil. "I am so bloody knackered. Nance, why does he always make me feel like a thirteen-year-old boy?"

"Because you let him?"

"Knew it would be my fault. Well, you're going to have to look after him, sweetheart. I'm leading the pitch on Wednesday."

"Really? Who are you pitching to?"

Phil glares at her, as if she is so out of order. She shrugs, apologetically. "Sorry. Bit tired."

"Try having a major op then getting zapped five times a week."

Nancy starts to say something then realises that she has absolutely nothing to say, or at least nothing she won't immediately regret. So, she simply slaps the lid back on the salve and goes out onto the landing.

Erica, who is on her way upstairs, notices that Nancy is near to tears or violence, so she steers clear and makes for her room. She swings open the door to discover her grandfather removing his dressing gown.

"Sorr-ee!" she almost shrieks, remembering.

"*Shhh!*" urges Nancy.

Erica stomps off with a sigh into her brother's poky room.

"What's going on now?" says Phil from the bathroom but Nancy chooses not to hear.

*

In the morning Desmond just manages to catch Phil as his son is hurrying out of the kitchen, stuffing a couple of small tomatoes in his mouth. He has recently read that this is a good thing to do before radiotherapy. Something to do with lycopene. He makes a mental note to check whether Amazon offers it in capsule form.

"Where are you off to this time in the morning?" asks Desmond. "You look exhausted."

"Really?" says Phil, chewing away. "Can't think why that should be. Just thought I'd fit in a quick round of radiotherapy before work."

"Ah. Yes, of course. I'll give you a lift to the hospital."

"No, it's okay, I can drive myself."

"You don't look like you're up to it."

"Thanks, Dad. Made me feel so much better."

As Phil throws a swift glance at him from the front door, Desmond suddenly crumples. Which is the last thing Phil reckons that he needs right now.

"It isn't right you're going through this – not at your age," sighs the older man. "Wrong way round, isn't it?"

For a moment, they both sense a connection. It appears to jolt them.

"Well, see you tonight then."

When Phil responds his tone is gentler, more conversational. "It's the big agency pitch tomorrow, lots to finish up at work, you know. Probably be a late one."

"Not the best timing, eh? Give me the car keys," says Desmond.

"I told you – I can drive myself, Dad. Thank you."

Desmond grabs the car keys from his son's hand. "Your driving wasn't up to much when you were fit and well."

"That's not true," says Phil, although he fears that it might be, and he really hasn't the energy to argue.

*

Paula appears just as concerned about Phil Morrison when she collects him from the waiting room.

He has been trying to lose himself in today's dry-run and seriously ignore the other radiotherapy patients sitting nearby, some of whom, in their wanness and lack of hair, look far worse than he does. Yet who knows, they might be in the smaller number who mercifully, because of the treatment, survive. Whilst he could be in that minuscule percentage who unfortunately, despite the best of care, sadly don't. He doesn't need this stuff in his head right now, not today, but realises once again that, in his forever racing mind, it is seldom out of it.

As she helps him onto the bed, Paula appears quite stern. "I hope you're not working too hard, Philip."

"I go straight home to bed every day and watch *Emmerdale*."

"Uh huh. So, how's *Mrs* Morrison coping with it all?"

"Nancy? Oh, she just gets on with it, bless her," he says, as he shuffles ever more uncomfortably into the usual position. "Glass half full, you know. Not like me. She's a rock, Paula. A real rock."

The patient might have perceived his rock as slightly less adamantine, had he spotted her emerging from the WH Smith's near her office, ripping open a fresh packet of cigarettes. As she stops to light one, from a newly bought box of matches, a hand comes in and coolly flicks a lighter that stubbornly refuses to work. She looks up to see Mr Grainger flicking away, then fires up as planned with the functioning matches. Her client chucks his dud lighter in a nearby bin.

"Never happens in the movies," says Mr Grainger. Nancy is too busy inhaling to respond. "I thought we didn't smoke."

"Only off duty."

The man smiles knowingly, as he stares at her. "You haven't for years, have you, Nancy?"

"No," she admitted. "Not since the kids came along."

Very gently Mr Grainger takes the cigarette from her hand and stubs it out on the pavement.

"What the hell are you doing?"

"I can't talk about cancer like this. Disrespectful."

"Who wants to talk about cancer?" says Nancy.

The man simply looks at her, saying nothing more, offering only a slight yet open smile and some surprisingly white teeth.

"I'd… best be getting back to work. Not really my break time. Bunking off." She is finding it incredibly hard to keep down the tears that hover like hostages awaiting long-overdue liberation. "I'll see you on Thursday, Mr Grainger. Usual time."

He watches as she goes off. He doesn't see her crying, nor would she wish him to, yet somehow, he knows that she is. And she knows that he knows, which isn't as embarrassing as she might have thought.

*

There are highly finished ads and concept boards stacked against the walls of glass. A mocked-up but nonetheless impressive commercial plays on Leo's massive TV. Cardboard is everywhere, glossy documents litter the table. In this one regard, Leo thinks of himself as old school and possibly even Luddite. He wants items people can pick up and touch, examine and pass around, rather than absolutely everything being on screens and laptops. These guys aren't buying technology, he insists, they've *got* technology. They're buying talent. They're buying ideas. And these are people whose products are geared specifically to those 'who are hands-on, who like to get a grip'.

"So, after Amara does her very serious planning spiel, blah de blah de blah…"

"Thank you, Leo," says Amara, very seriously.

"You know I love you."

"Blah de blah…"

"Camille," he calls back towards the desk, where the young woman is busily typing. "I want that new Spark-Lite film playing in reception as they walk in, the one with the U2 track. Oh, and by the way people, I just heard we're the final agency they're seeing – dunno whether that's good or bad. Saving the best for last, eh? Okay, so Amara sits down, I give a few well-chosen words then it's over to Phil here for the magic."

"Tosser-in-chief," says Phil.

"That's very funny… you're not going to say that? We'll do it all again properly at tonight's rehearsal."

"*Tonight?*" repeats Phil, feeling suddenly sick. "I thought we were rehearsing after lunch."

Leo says nothing for a moment. "The stuff won't all be ready by then."

"Yes, it will, Leo," corrects Phil, "Kev's been beavering away all night on it."

The creative director appears strangely uncomfortable. "Yeah, well, there's some other stuff… it's still being finished."

"What other stuff?" asks Phil.

"Just another idea. Something the new kids came up with."

"What, to throw away?"

"No," says Leo quietly, "to recommend. I asked them to have a go. Sometimes it pays, y'know, to come at it from a fresh angle. You never know what you're going to get."

"So, what did you get?"

"Something a bit more… cutting edge."

Phil feels like he's going back under anaesthetic. The people around him appear to be growing blurry. "Okay. Bit confused here. We're recommending this *as well as* the *Advanced Delkronics* campaign?"

"Look, Phil," says Leo, smiling uncomfortably yet understanding deep down that this is the hard stuff, this is what he gets paid for. "I get that the Delkron guy knows you of old – and that they think they want 'Son of Fish Family' – but you know what, it's my job to *tell* them what they want." He points to the groaning boards. "And – well – that ain't it."

"Firstly," insists Phil, "this stuff is *way* edgier than Fish Family. But second, third and fucking fourth, why didn't you say anything sooner?"

For a moment, Leo appears a bit sheepish. "You had enough on your plate."

Phil tries with Olympic fortitude to remain calm. "Well, okay. I'm a grown-up. As you keep implying. Let's go and see this 'cutting edge' idea, shall we?"

Leo is relieved. The diplomat triumphs, another battle won. "Yeah. Course. It's in the studio. I really want to know what you think, Phil."

Phil gets up from his chair with some difficulty. He knows that the radiotherapy knocks out a lot of the good cells, as well as any of the nastier rogues that might have sneaked in there, but right now he is feeling as if he has damn few of either sort left.

"And then we can decide," he says.

"Phil," says Leo quietly, with a slight smile that he doesn't mean. "An agency ain't a democracy. Not the night before a pitch."

Phil shakes his head, as it finally sinks in. He realises that neither Amara nor Keval are looking at him. "So, I'm going to be presenting a new idea that I haven't even been involved in."

"I *want* you involved," insists Leo. "I'm getting you involved now."

"Bit late in the bloody day! Did you know about this, Amara?"

"Yeah, but I thought you did too." The young planner looks devastated, owning a guilt that Phil knows shouldn't be hers to bear.

"You're still leading the presentation, Phil," says Leo. "You're still the main man."

Phil starts to play with Leo's plane, enjoying its owner's rising panic. You get your jollies where you can these days.

"This is shabby, Leo! And – and underhand."

"It's business, matey. Five million quid's worth. Could you not touch the plane?"

"Business. Uh huh." Phil appears to be weighing his options. He can sense Keval praying that he does nothing stupid. "Well, okay – if we win this business, it's still going to be my account, right? Mine and Kev's. On a day-to-day basis."

"Who else would I give it to? The other team would be working to you. They're kids, Phil. Talented – but kids." He stares directly at Phil. "So, you just present it with max enthusiasm. Yeah? You are a team player, aren't you, Philly?"

'Philly' knows that it isn't very mature but right now he just wants to go home. Where there are people who care. And no surprises.

*

A person's notion of 'home', however, can quite often be at odds with reality. It certainly is around suppertime at the Morrisons.

Todd has the TV blasting, even though his hearing is by far the best in the house, because his mum and sister are having another of their ding-dongs and he doesn't think that his grandpa, whom he can just glimpse coming down the stairs, will be anyone's idea of a peacemaker.

"*I'm just asking for a little bit of help, that's all!*" says Nancy, slamming shut a few cupboard doors that didn't need opening in the first place. "I'm not trying to bring back bloody slavery."

"Yeah, right. I am helping. Actually."

"Yeah, right."

"Hello, you two," says Desmond cheerily, as if their argument has nothing to do with him, which in fairness it hasn't. "Erica, I was beginning to wonder where you were. I've sorted out your room and I've—"

"You've WHAT?" says a horrified Erica, as Todd turns up the TV again.

"You see?" says Nancy, leaping into a total non-sequitur like it was a warm bath. "She was *shopping*, Desmond! I caught her in the High Street."

"Oh, call social services!" says Erica.

"Erica, don't speak to your mother like that," chimes Desmond, "not when she's so worried about your poor dad."

"Thank you, Desmond," says Nancy, "I'm quite capable of dealing with my daughter."

"Yes, of course you are, dear," agrees Desmond swiftly. "My apologies. Oh, nearly forgot, Phil rang just before you came in. Could you please pick him up at, er, 10.30? Yes. From the station. I'll do it if you—"

"*10.30!*" gasps Nancy. "He'll be bloody knackered. Erica, it's Dad's big pitch tomorrow. I want you to keep right out of his way tonight. No noise. No music, no shouting, no phone—"

"How about no Erica? I'll be at Abigail's!"

As Erica storms out, Todd – who had it on the best authority that his sister and Abigail were lifelong enemies – decides to close the living room door.

*

Keval seems as knackered as usual when Phil joins him in the agency lift on the morning of the big day, but at least in his best 'client-jacket' he is looking noticeably nattier. Even his yawns appear more tailored. From the younger man's own perspective, or 'POV' as their scripts so often lay it out, his creative partner simply seems beaten.

Aside from an acknowledging grunt, Phil can barely talk to the young art director. *The last time I felt as anxious as this*, he muses, *is when Nancy went into early labour with Todd. No, I tell a lie, it was just a few weeks ago, in the local hospital.*

He manages to take a slow, audible breath. Keval responds instinctively, taking an equally slow and audible breath, whilst still gazing outwards through the open lift doors. Two *simpatico* souls sharing one as yet to be determined fate. Glory or redundancy – the only two industry options.

As the doors close, the lift ascends with the slow-breathers inside. They say nothing for a couple of floors – each in his own world – until Keval breaks the almost unbearable silence.

"Bad today, was it? Y'know, the radiotherapy."

Phil shrugs for an entire floor. "Actually, it was the best part of the day," he admits eventually. "All downhill from now on."

"Hey, forget about Leo. He's not really going to sack us if we don't win this one."

Phil looks at him then nods. "No, you're right, Kev. He's only going to sack me."

"Thank Christ for that."

Phil stares at him – then smiles. "That jacket should swing it for us."

*

The agency's main presentation room looks like no corporate boardroom a client has ever sat in. Because clients don't want to regard their advertising agency as simply another department or adjunct of themselves. They like to believe it reeks not just of professionalism and commercial competence, but creativity run riot, open-necked abandon, yet still somehow rigidly disciplined and totally focused, in the interests of the brand. Hence the large, private-cinema-sized screen, the discreet state-of-the-art sound system, the cabinets of gleaming and meticulously polished domestic, international and obscure awards. And the better biscuits.

The long walnut table, stretching the length of the room, and the sturdy but comfortable chairs that surround it, smack of immaculate taste and design. Yet care has been taken, as must always be the case, not to suggest that the agency itself is profligate with the money it earns from its impressive roster of hard-working clients. It is a delicate balancing act, one that even extends to the choice of crockery, bottled water and snacks.

Naturally, if the agency does actually represent a client who bottles water, makes furniture or manufactures biscuits, these must rise to the top of the pile (if, however, they make downmarket, self-assembly furniture or custard creams, the same rules might not apply).

Phil, Keval and Amara sit with Leo, in their judiciously allotted places, waiting nervously for the clients to arrive and trying not to fiddle with/peek at the forest of boards arrayed clever-side-to-the-wall behind them.

Seated nearby are the account executives and media planners – the suits – looking through the hard copies of their presentation pages once again, more to jog their memories before addressing their audience than anything else, as it is far too late to change a single word or number or facial expression.

Small talk is being exchanged, most of it puerile, but it does nothing to temper the atmosphere of febrile expectation. It suddenly stops, as they all watch the heavy door from the agency's plush reception area being slowly opened.

Immediately everyone is smiling. The presenters as they dutifully stand up to greet their visitors. The agency's top board directors, from Managing Director downwards, as they usher in the expectant potential clients. These clients themselves, energised to be in one of London's top agencies and eager to discover how the quality products they revere and with which they spend all their working days might be sold to a hopefully burgeoning and responsive audience in these troubling times.

Phil immediately nods to the senior member of the client team, the blunt and overweight silver-haired man he knows from old and with whom he recently reconnected for the briefing. This man, Derek, has brought with him two far younger colleagues, a man and a woman, who are making an excellent job of looking business-like and noncommittal, whilst politely responding to the cordiality on offer and entering the almost mandatory discussion as to how their journey went.

Phil wonders if these visitors know or even care how many careers are on the line here (possibly even theirs, if they make the wrong choice). They are certainly aware that the bonhomie on display is mostly forced and, in reality, this is like a PowerPoint Game of Thrones.

He also muses, for a concerned moment, on whether Derek has already noticed how very different Phil must surely look from their last, quite recent encounter in Nottingham. He hopes that his once and hopefully future client will put it down not to some wasting disease but to simple exhaustion pursuant on burning the midnight oil, in the quest to produce a gangbuster Delkron campaign (or eight).

After all those present have shaken hands, exchanged platitudes, discussed the traffic, weather and local football, and been offered a raft of (non-alcoholic) refreshments, a slightly uneasy silence takes over, thankfully interrupted by an electronic fanfare suddenly blaring through the speakers. Three seconds later, the words *Codling, Capon and Tilbury welcomes Delkron* appear on the screen, along with the two companies' respective logos. Everyone smiles in anticipation, as if the theme from *Lawrence of Arabia* has just begun and something epic is about to follow.

They all dearly hope that it is.

*

By the time Phil scores through the fifth item on the afternoon's full agenda with a free company pencil, he has totted up in his head what he reckons is the combined salaries of everyone around the table. It is pretty colossal, especially if you include the board directors' perks. He has already chomped through more than his fair share of classy chocolate biscuits, because he can sense his energy depleting rapidly after so many radiotherapy sessions. Unusually, he has also drunk so much 'un-decaffeinated' coffee, in order to keep himself awake, that his bladder feels as if it is about to go nuclear.

He comes round from his latest caffeine rush to discover Amara just completing her portion of the afternoon's pitch. The table looks like Hurricane whatever-her-name-is has just hit, with papers and brochures and documents and notepads and iPads and shiny biscuit-wrappers everywhere. And this is *before* the creative work gets hurled around.

Leo is all boyish charm, as he springs up from his chair with enviable if excessive vigour, running his hands as ever through his wayward blond hair.

"Thanks, Amara. Well, okay gentlemen, lady, now you've heard all the boring bits…"

"Didn't think you were actually going to say that," chuckles Amara.

"You should have seen what I originally wrote," joshes Leo back at her.

Phil tries not to squirm, but he can sense all of his colleagues beside him checking out the clients, who don't appear to be hostile or unamused. But neither do they wish to appear won-over or seduced. So, their faces are politely neutral, offering only the odd small, courteous smile. The balancing act between thoroughly demoralising people who are simply doing their best and offering false hope is one both delicate and skilled.

"Right," begins Leo, with a slight laugh in his voice. "Now I could give you a meticulously detailed, bells 'n' whistles, warts 'n' all, kitchen-sinking creative rationale – in all-singing, all-dancing PowerPoint or whatever– that totally justifies everything you're about to see here down to the very last frame. But you know what? The punter doesn't hear all that. We're not standing behind him (or her) rabbiting strategy when they switch on their widescreen telly. So, I truly believe great advertising is advertising that speaks for itself." He points to the pile of gleaming documents on the table. "Anyway, it's all in those hugely expensive, glossy things you'll be taking away with you as going-home presents."

The agency can all sense a slight thawing in the atmosphere. This guy is earning his money.

"So, let's move on to what you've really come for. I'm going to hand you over now to Phil Morrison, one of my most-valued team members – and a DIY buff to his fingertips… if he's still got any."

Phil just stares at the man, who stares meaningfully back. The clients sit up straighter. All eyes are on him, as he rises from his chair with a hesitancy which he hopes the visitors will assume is all part of his anticipation-building 'shtick', while the agency are just praying he doesn't keel over into the remaining posh biscuits.

When he does finally speak, Phil Morrison tries manfully to summon up all the energy that he can, with a begrudging all-too-awareness that the well is only half-full. He has a feeling that even at 'max', he is going to come across as more than a tad lacklustre.

"Er… thanks, Leo. Well, good afternoon. Derek. Delkron." He looks tiredly at the expectant faces – both client and agency. They seem to shift just slightly out of focus, as they shuffle forward expectantly in their seats, so he looks around at the boards still concealing their multifarious riches against the presentation room wall.

"As you can see," he says, pointing towards the display, "you've kept us pretty busy. If you made tree-felling equipment, you'd be laughing!"

"We do," says client Derek. "Ha ha."

"Ah," says Phil, slightly thrown. "Thanks, Derek. So, anyway, you won't be surprised to hear that we're recommending television as our main medium. With poster back-up. Big eye-catching poster back-up. In DIY-speak, we're gonna *nail* it! Uh huh. So, why don't I just take you through our first campaign?"

Phil can sense from his boss's body language that Leo is trying to energise his creative colleague telepathically. Good luck with that.

Throughout all of this preamble, Phil notices that the younger and rather intense male client is making notes and whispering to his female colleague. They nod, occasionally smile, jot things on their pads. Phil wants to ask if he's disturbing them but instead picks up the nearest storyboard, a stylishly drawn version of a potential TV commercial, rendered from Keval's detailed roughs in a dozen colourful frames by an outside design group.

"Okay... so – imagine a man's hand," he begins, setting the scene and hoping that they have at least a scintilla of imagination. "A man's hand powered like a drill, a Delkron drill, a man's powerful hand throbbing as it slowly approaches a solid block of masonry." Phil clicks his fingers and right on cue we hear through the sound system the unmistakable thrum of the most powerful Delkron drill. "The finger goes right through it. Like butter. No problem. Then we gradually dissolve the Delkron 430X Power Drill into this same hand and a voice-over says: 'Delkron. Turn your hand to anything'. And that penultimate frame, in mid-dissolve, between hand and drill, that's your poster right there."

As he gazes at the rapt faces of the clients, clearly quite taken with idea, Phil can almost smell Leo just behind him, staring up at the back of his neck. Remembering the game plan, Phil says, "that's one way of doing it – *but we can do better than that!*" and cursorily throws the storyboard over his head and away.

The clients gawp. WTF? Leo nods. Good boy.

Phil goes through the same procedure, campaign after campaign, board after board, presenting then hurling away. The delivery, however, becomes more jaded and monotone each time, less enthusiastic and committed to the 'script', despite glimpsed hand-gestures from a frustrated Leo encouraging him to 'up the ante', for pity's sake.

"'In the power struggle, there is only one winner, so we tested Delkron against the rest. We tested it on wood, we tested it on masonry, then we tested it on Mr Andy Jackson of Epping' – but we can do better than that!"

Discard!

"'I'm Jason Briggs from *THE BIG DIY DRILL-OFF*, and when I'm transforming properties and lives, I have to make sure I'm transforming them for the better. The best materials, the best people – and the best power tools we can all lay our hands on.'"

Jettison!

"We open on two brawny guys holding rival power drills like they're Colt 45s. Slowly, they make their way towards each other, as if they're about to have a shoot-out. But then, in between them, we find a…"

Abandon!

To his surprise Phil is now finally starting to feel that, despite the tank registering just a flicker above empty, he is sourcing renewed energy from somewhere. Finding his rhythm. He reckons that it must be like that power he has often heard actors avow they can summon. Even if they're feeling like death warmed-up before they step onstage, and maybe one or more limbs is hanging off, Doctor Theatre sees them through until after the final curtain, when they can safely collapse and bleed unapplauded.

"But we can do better than that," he repeats, slowly revealing the beautifully produced storyboard of his beloved 'big' idea. "Now to the campaign I call *Advanced DelkrONics*. See? We open on a Delkron masonry drill, made entirely for our purposes from the toughest, clearest glass – so that we can see every single, beautiful working element. Each and every finely tuned component. Then the camera goes in, and in, and…"

As he presents the idea, a discernible trace of sadness in his voice, he can barely utter that fatal, godforsaken line for one last time.

"*But we can do better than that!*"

By now the clients are practically saying it with him, as he turns with palpable regret to the final board.

Leo leaps up and moves beside him. In for the kill.

"And, indeed, we *can* do better," says the beaming young creative director. "There you've seen five ways to go. Five highly creative ideas. All of them viable, all of them more than respectable. All of them mercilessly rejected. But now, guys…"

Phil steps in again, with impressive enthusiasm. "But now I'm going to show you the *right* way to go, the distinctive way, the unexpected way. The way to put the Delkron name exactly where it deserves to be – at the top of the heap."

The clients look extremely interested. Leo looks extremely pleased. He nods discreetly to the board director on the account, to register that all is going to plan.

Momentously, Phil lifts up the very final storyboard and unfolds it. The artwork is beautifully and quite unusually realised. The drawings are a different style to its predecessors – black and white, with colour highlights. Sequentially they depict a massive waterfall, a herd of elephant, a raging typhoon, clouds scudding across a sky, a volcano in full eruption.

"The theme is," announces Phil, with sonorous respect, "*the power of nature – the nature of power.*"

The clients – with the agency people in consummate mimicry – are staring intently at the work.

"We're going to get right away from the workshop," explains Phil, still with some urgency left in his voice, although he knows that his palms and probably the rest of him are stickily sweating. "Right away from the tool-shed, from the kitchen table, the woodworking, the masonry stone wall. Let the others do that. We're going to grab them with images that reflect the purity and magnitude of natural, raw energy." He points to the storyboard frames. "Like – a waterfall. A herd of elephant. A volcano!"

Something suddenly clicks in his head. Phil Morrison can't quite explain it, but neither can he believe what he is having to do right this second nor the utter garbage that is spewing out of his by now parched and arid mouth.

Were you to ask the man his current feelings, he would simply tell you, with probably as much surprise as that of any onlooker, that he simply cannot be arsed. Not in this life. Not anymore.

Not after all that he has been through, not before all that is still to come.

He shakes his head in bemusement. A gesture that hyper-alert Leo picks up with some perturbation. But perhaps it is just a nervous tic.

"I'm sorry," says a genuinely mystified Phil, "*elephants*? A *volcano*? Well, I suppose it's 'cutting edge'. I mean, it's all in black and white, isn't it? With coloured bits."

A concerned Keval manages to catch Phil's eye and nods towards Leo. The creative director has gone from vaguely disconcerted to quietly incandescent in ten seconds. Meanwhile, the clients are on their own bumpy journey, from genuinely intrigued to just a wee bit confused.

"Yes, very modern – or is it post-modern?" he mumbles, almost to himself. "Dunno. What comes after post-modern? And if you look carefully, I'm sure you'll find a Delkron drill in there somewhere." He points to a tiny object in a corner of the final frame. "Oh, yeah, there's the little fella – see? Just peeking out from in there. Hello."

For the first time, Phil turns and actually looks directly at Leo. He hands him the storyboard. "I think I'm done now, Leo."

"Yes, Phil," agrees the younger man. "I think you probably are."

Phil Morrison quietly picks up his laptop. He walks with it the full length of the room, past the befuddled clients, past the few remaining biscuits and classy documentation, past the stunned members of his board and right out of the presentation.

Just outside the door he passes the two keen young creatives, who stare at him in some bafflement. Phil shrugs apologetically to them, as he walks past, heading for the lift and the exit.

*

"What was all that about?" asks the senior client, not unreasonably, once the door has closed.

"Personal problems," sighs Leo, with touching compassion, shaking his head as the mind inside it races. "Er, family crisis he only just heard about this afternoon. Road accident. Both parents. Terrible. Brave guy. We need more people like Phil... thingy." His spirit immediately flips from pastoral empathy to boyish enthusiasm. "Now, let's give this wicked campaign the presentation it deserves."

By the time Leo has re-presented, with almost exhausting gusto, the one idea that hasn't ended up on the pre-ordained scrapheap, Phil has packed the stuff from his desk into one of those large and rather heavy boxes in which he wishes he had shares and is on his weary way out of the building.

"Early night, Phil?" asks the security man, cheerily.

"Something like that, Arthur."

"You still taking those Jap fish things?"

"Er, yeah."

Arthur looks at Phil. "I'd stop," he says.

*

The kitchen looks showroom-sparkling, yet the family are still happily adding the finishing touches with their trusty and by now well-worn power tools. Even Grandad is up a ladder, fixing a new ceiling fan.

The freshly sanded and varnished door swings open. All eyes turn as Phil comes home, energised and defiant.

"Hi, Dad," says little Todd. "How did it go?"

"I told them where to stuff their new campaign!" chuckles Phil.

"Good for you, love," says Nancy, waving a Delkron jigsaw happily. "I'm sure we can manage on my salary."

"I'll go skiing another year," chirps Erica, "not all the snow will have gone."

Phil hugs her, then kisses Nancy warmly and passionately.

"And best of all, love," he whispers, "it's grown back!"

Nancy's cup runneths over, as Phil smiles, contentedly.

The voice-over intones, "Delkron. Tooled-up for life."

*

As soon as Nancy hears the key turn in the front door, she is there. Only to be confronted by an overloaded Phil, his head barely visible above the iconic box. He looks sheepish and scared. As unwell as she has seen him since he struggled awake from the operation.

And what's with the box?

"Hi, love," she says, with a brightness she doesn't feel. "How did it…?" She catches sight of his face and stops.

Phil dumps his box with a grunt on the stairs and walks past her into the kitchen.

Desmond is unloading the dishwasher as they come in. He is too busy examining a newly cleaned plate to notice his son's arrival.

"Do you find these things really get the dishes as clean as washing by hand?" As he turns, he sees Phil and wishes for a moment that he hadn't. "Oh, hello, Philip." He offers up his most solicitous smile. "How did your big thing go?"

"Appalling, actually. Couldn't have gone worse if I'd sprayed them all with Ebola, now you ask."

"Oh. Oh dear. I'm so sorry."

Erica steams in, gripping her phone as if it contains the nuclear codes. She uses the other hand to swing open the fridge and grab a bunch of grapes.

"Hi, Dad," she says, cheerily.

"Hi."

"Just off to Abigail's. See you."

"'How *are* you, Dad?'" says Phil, in a grumpy mimicking of her voice.

Erica turns to look at him. "Oh. Sorry. I don't have to ask every day, do I?"

"Maybe my pitch day. Maybe that'd be nice."

"You're always pitching for something," says his daughter. "It's what you do. So, did it go okay?"

"No, now you ask. It didn't. Anyway, why are you off to Abigail's? I thought you hated Abigail."

"That was yesterday, Phil," intercedes Nancy, quietly. "It's no big deal."

"*Yes. Yes, it is Nancy*," says Phil, his voice rising. "You need help here. With the house. With my dad."

Desmond, who has prudently decided to busy himself some more with the dishwasher, looks round at this.

"Anyway, Erica ought to be studying, not zipping off."

"I *am* studying," protests Erica. "I *am* helping." To which Phil just sighs.

"Actually, she has been," says Desmond, which only elicits a highly sceptical snort from his son.

"Well, I just can't do anything right, can I?" says Erica, not raising her voice, which curiously makes her sound more justifiably irate towards her father than if she had gone up an octave. "If I help Mum, I should be revising. If I'm revising, I'm leaving her to do it all on her own. I'm told 'Ooh Erica, better stay right out of Dad's way', then guess who's told off by you for not caring and not being around. Hey, I know Dad, why not get that daughter off the Fish Family? Y'know, the one that's prettier and nicer than me. Then you can just write the bloody script for her."

"It's okay, Erica," says Nancy, gently tapping her arm. "You just go off to Abigail's."

"No, hang on, hang on a second, Nancy," says Phil, before Erica can slip out of the kitchen. "So now *I'm* the villain of the piece," he says, laughing bitterly and shaking his head at the sky. "For God's sake, I'm the one with cancer!"

Suddenly Erica is no longer moderating her tone. Suddenly she finds herself screaming at him. "*It's not just your fucking cancer, you know!*"

The silence could break windows.

Everyone appears stunned, no one more so than Erica herself. Desmond starts to load up the dishwasher again, with anything he can find.

"Erica?" says Nancy, praying that the now red-faced teenager won't say more but pretty certain that she will. She knows her daughter when she is on a roll.

"*It's Mum's cancer too!*" continues the young girl, still at a pitch that defies interruption. "Yeah, *and* mine. *And* Todd's. *And* Grandpa's." She can see the confusion growing on her father's face and this appears to anger her even more. "*Huh?* You just don't get it, do you? Maybe 'cos you're not the one who has to see Mum crying all on the quiet, because you're working too bloody much – and she's shit-scared you're going to die."

Nancy tries to interrupt but is given no chance. Phil can't even try – he seems to be in shock.

"But I have to see her. *And* hear her – 'Ooh, yes darling, you just trot off to work now'… 'Good luck with the pitch, love.' She mustn't tell *you* off – oh no, not poor Phil – so I have to get her crap."

"Sweetheart, it's alright. Please," says Nancy, almost unable to look at her husband although she can sense him shaking beside her.

"No. It isn't alright. No! I don't *care* if he's ill. You're knackered. I'm knackered." She points to the living-room, from which they can hear the TV blaring. "I bet the telly's bloody shagged out. I mean, *hello*, that's all Todd does all day."

"Erica, finish now! Phil—"

"No, he has got to listen," insists Erica, kicking the kitchen door closed without turning away. "You can be all grown-up about it, but I don't have to. I'm a child. And I'm sodding hacked off with it all!"

The kitchen door slowly opens. Todd lurks in the doorway looking frightened and eating a biscuit. Nobody seems to notice.

"Do you know *why* I was going to Abigail's just now? Eh? Eh? Do you?" challenges Erica, not waiting for an answer. "*To write your bloody invitations!*"

"Sorry, what invitations?" asks Nancy.

"Nothing. It's nothing," says Phil, swiftly.

"*Yes, it is!*" insists an offended Erica. "*It's her birthday party!*"

Suddenly she starts to cry. It begins with a gasp then swiftly ascends not to a sobbing but to a high-pitched, breathless yelp, a primal heart-rending howl of anguish.

"And I've spoilt it! *I've gone and fucking spoilt it!*"

Now, finally, the words stop. The tears flow. As Phil looks on, stunned and helpless.

Desmond notices Todd, who just watches all this in slightly fearful fascination, his biscuit halfway to his mouth. The elderly man walks over and puts a gentle hand on his grandson's shoulder.

Phil notices none of this. His attention is all on his daughter, as his face begins to crumple, losing whatever was left of his anger and shock and pent-up resentment, replacing it with a sadness so profound he wonders how he is still standing up.

"No... Erica... darling..."

He tries to touch her, helplessly, to make connection but she just moves away, the wound too raw.

"Erica, love, sit down," urges Nancy. "Please. Just sit."

"Don't want to."

"Please, poppet."

"I am *so* sorry, Daddy. I really didn't mean to."

"No. No," says Phil, moving towards her but too scared now to reach out. "It's me, I'm the one who's sorry, lovey. Who should say sorry. So very, very sorry." He looks at Nancy, who is only just holding it together. "I didn't see how worried you were, Nance. How you all were. How you were just – each of you –." He shakes his head. "Why didn't you say?"

"What was I going to say?" says Nancy, perhaps a bit too sharply. "Somebody had to keep the show on the road."

"I just didn't think—"

"You weren't meant to bloody think! "She is shaking her head at the idea. "You were just meant to get well. Oh – and maybe not work so effing hard!"

"I had a job to do. Things didn't stop. I had to work hard!"

"Oh, right," says Nancy, the anger suddenly rising up against her express instruction, "*and hard work never killed anybody!*"

Desmond starts to lead Todd out of the room but Phil walks over and picks up the little boy, ignoring the twinges ripping across his groin as he does so. He senses his mobile buzzing in his pocket but ignores it.

"It's okay, Toddy. We're all a little bit… tired. You know, from all these weeks. But it's alright."

Todd looks across at his sister, who appears less tired than utterly distraught.

"*I can't believe I've spoilt your surprise!*" she wails. "Hey, everyone, this is our crap daughter Erica, who totally ruined our big lovely party."

"No… no," protests Phil, in some desperation, "you didn't ruin anything, darling. Really you didn't. Not a thing. And I reckon Mum's surprised enough as it is."

Erica wipes her eyes on her sleeve. "You're not going to die, are you?" she asks, softly.

Phil can feel Todd in his arms, squirming round to look at him.

"No, love," says Phil, definitively. "I'm not. I'm really not going to die."

When the home phone rings, it comes as something of a relief. Or at least marks a not totally unwelcome change in the evening's febrile atmosphere. They all just look at each other, slightly stunned. Desmond, trying to be useful, scoots to answer it.

"*Dad!*" warns Phil, who knows that everyone who could possibly matter to him is already here in this kitchen, But Desmond is on a mission.

"Good," says Erica, referring back to Phil's confident assertion of immortality. "'Cos I need you to check my English coursework."

Phil smiles at her little joke, so she does too, simultaneously sniffing back up whatever her outburst has caused to unleash.

"English coarse language by the sound of it," says her dad.

"No, this is his father. Who's speaking?" says Desmond, but they don't listen too hard or care too much.

Very gently Phil sets Todd down, as he realises how much he wants to cuddle his daughter right now. "But just don't ask me about maths, okay?" he tells her.

Desmond is suddenly there between them, thrusting the phone towards his son. "Phil – it's 'Leo'?"

"I don't want to talk to him," says Phil, defiantly.

Nancy stares at him.

"I'm afraid he's rather busy," says Desmond, politely. "...No, I'm sorry, I'm sorry Leo, that's not at all possible. But I am quite capable of taking a message in my advanced years, if you'd like to..." Desmond pauses to listen to the clearly excitable young man at the other end. "Mmhmm... mmhmm."

Nancy holds up a bottle of red wine for Phil, who nods as if it's the end of Lent. She starts to pour for them both. Erica throws her a look and her mum brings out another, far smaller glass.

Desmond, still with the phone to his ear, turns to Phil once more. "This Leo chap wants me to tell you that the agency thinks they might have won the account – and that the clients really liked one of your ideas. Advanced Del... something."

"Advanced Delkronics," says Phil. "With the emphasis on the 'ON'." He smiles at Nancy in astonishment. "They went for it. *They bloody went for it!*"

Nancy passes him a large glass of wine.

Desmond is nodding to the phone in a business-like manner. "Yes, alright, I'll tell him." He moves the phone away from his face and turns to Phil. "He says you were right after all, Phil. Bravo. And apparently, if they do get it, he and someone called Kevin will be handling it perfectly well without you." A glumness takes over the elderly man's face. "I believe he's saying you're sacked."

The family look at each other, in shock. Even Todd, who isn't quite sure what exactly is going on but knows for certain that something is.

Nancy and Erica are surprised to see that Phil is smiling. They can also tell from his face that he is as taken aback as they are by his own curious reaction.

"Know something?" he says, "*I'd* sack me*!* I was a bit rubbish. And do you want to know something else? Right now, I just don't bloody care."

Desmond brings the phone back towards him and talks into it. "He says you can take your stupid job and shove it right up your arse!" With that he sets the phone decisively back into its wall-holder.

The family are staring at him. Desmond looks like someone wondering if he might possibly have overstepped his brief.

"Well, no going back on that then," says Phil, quietly.

The others appear in a state of shock.

"Oh – we'll manage," says Nancy, bravely.

Desmond picks up the phone again. "I could call him back," he says, hopefully. His kinfolk just gawp at him, shell-shocked.

Very tentatively, but then more forcefully, Phil Morrison laughs.

He laughs until the still healing scar hurts and his still raw chest burns. He laughs like the idiot in the crappy commercials he has been seeing for days in his head and in his sleep. He laughs because right now there is nothing else he can do, except perhaps kiss and begin the painful yet hopefully healing process of making up. Of finally grasping it instead of losing it. He laughs because he is lopsided and sore and stunned and spent, yet suddenly very much alive, and indeed fortunate to be sipping cheap supermarket wine with the only people in the world who count, in a cosy kitchen that really could do with a bit of DIY but isn't getting it any time soon. He laughs because there *is* a tomorrow. Even if it is on a cold table in a stark, clinical room just a few miles away. Without an office any more to stagger into afterwards. He laughs a tad more more wryly, because he knows that, although his world has been so dramatically shaken up in ways he could never have expected, perhaps for the worse but even possibly for the better (who the hell knows?) life will still go on – and he'll still be a hypochondriac in the morning.

Unless the Japanese invent a pill for it.

LOST SOULS

By way of introduction

It is better to be without a book than to believe it entirely.
(Chinese proverb)

Call me Ambrose.

With apologies to the great Herman Melville. Who, by the way, is a sweetheart – just don't get him started on boats.

Modesty aside, I'm a bit of a scrivener myself, but in my line of work you don't exactly enjoy an excess of free time. To write, to create – or basically to do anything, other than the job in hand. Which, believe me, these days is quite a job. You want to hear the one compensation? It's the people you meet. Alright, they're dead, but like they say, you can't have everything.

Incidentally, did you know you arrive in Heaven in the very last clothes you were wearing? The ultimate outfit. So, little tip – if you're thinking of dying, dress nice.

You're starting to tell yourself this ain't no ordinary story. We ain't talking simple Boy Meets Girl here. Or Hero Kills Bad Guys. By the way, I don't usually say 'ain't'. It's not great English and it's a bit plebeian. I put these critters in just now because, of course, reading this, you can't hear me speak. You can only take a shot at how I sound. So, think of me like you're listening to an average American Joe. Which I am. Sort of. Kinda. Right now. Possibly.

For a while.

(I could be British tomorrow, but Jeez, that accent is tough! You think they still talk like that when nobody's around?)

So, I'm reckoning you probably read more books than I do. Wouldn't be hard. Of course, we get the talking books up where I am – believe me, some of the authors we got here, they won't frigging stop talking them. It's like a scene out of *Fahrenheit 451*. It's also how I know so many first lines. '*It was the best of times, it was the worst of times...*' '*It was a bright cold day in April, and the clocks were striking thirteen...*' Yeah, yeah. But to tell you the truth, I'm more of a movie man myself. Wide-screen extravaganzas, cold-hearted noir, sophisticated romances, screwball comedies. Musicals, I love. Schmaltzier the better. '*Sound of Music*' '*Calamity Jane*.' Don't get me started. When I get the time, of course. Big when.

Hey, you know what clip the BBC in the UK played on their news, the day blissful Fred Astaire died? Only that old Irv Berlin song about him being in *Heaven*.... Makes you realise there is a God.

Not that I ever doubted it! Me? No friggin' way!

Yet, if you had to classify this story – or if you'd prefer me to do this for you, so you know what you're getting into and can decide if you want to put in the hours – I'd say it was sort of a fable. You know, like old Aesop, only earthier. A lot earthier. A tale, if you will, about good and rotten. So much good, quite a bit of rot. And a soupçon of smut. But believe it or not, it happened. It really happened. Look, where I'm coming from – would I lie to you?

Let's make it clear, I'm not talking *rotten* like Hitler rotten, may he fester in the downstairs area, or *good* like, say, Mother Theresa, bless her saintly little heart. Although, to be honest, there's someone you'll meet before long, someone you would not be expecting in a million, who comes pretty close to blessed Mother T.

Yet be warned, there'll be a fair amount of moral turpitude and scuzziness, and even some pretty choice language, maybe more than you're used to. Yes, even you – you know to whom I'm referring. (I asked a couple of random guys here if it's okay to get a bit near the knuckle at times. They said '*sure Ambrose*'. So, props to you, Vladimir and D.H.)

But if you're looking for depth, try *20,000 Leagues Under The Sea.*

It's the kind of story where, despite what I just told you, you might have to suspend your disbelief for a while –if you've come this far, I don't think the suspense is going to kill you. And if you're seeking for morals, like in those other fables, well I'm afraid you'll find a total lack of them but then also a whole damn barrel load. So no shortchange there.

Now, you may think, *Is old Amby going to be this chatty and familiar all the way through the thing?* Like some guy who buttonholes you in a bar, when you only want a quiet drink, and proceeds to tell you his entire life story, until his head falls into your nuts (the ones in a bowl, I mean). Well, don't worry, it will soon start to read more like an ordinary book. You don't get to mix with dead writers without picking up a few tips yourself. And if this isn't exactly literature, just treat it as light relief between those far worthier works you boast to your friends about having ploughed through – *Lost Souls*?– Yeah, believe I read it just after *Ulysses*.'

I'll tell you how you know right off this is a true fable. If I was writing a fiction, I really don't think I'd call my hero Arnie Garth. Would you? It's hardly Rhett Butler. Or Don Quixote. But that's the name his parents gave him, although it wasn't the only thing they called him.

Trust me, I've been spooling back over his life. Literally. Sound and pictures. This is a given, back at my place. It's what you do. Especially in the division where I work. I could do it to you and there's nothing you could do about it. You wouldn't even know, except for maybe a tiny flutter in your stomach, which you'd probably put down to those Jerusalem artichokes or the curry you had for lunch. Scary, huh?

I bet sometimes even you wince when you think of how you used to be, the mischief you got up to. In fact, I often wonder if the difference between good people and bad people is simply that the latter kind don't have their own rewind button. They can't or won't look backwards, so there's nothing to stop them doing the same thing going forwards.

Anyway, if you watched the childhood of Arnie Garth as dutifully as I've been doing, or even just the trailer moments, you could probably guess how he'd end up.

There's that cute little vignette of his mom sitting in their cosy den back in Pittsburgh, breastfeeding her tiny guy and him nearly ripping her left nipple off. But hey, he was a baby, and a mom should be proud she'd passed on good gums and a forceful personality.

Now, scrolling on, here's the time young Arnie and his pals discovered how you can fry things using just a magnifying glass and some really hot sun. Remember that? Things like a blade of grass or some flies stuck on flypaper. Or, in Arnie's case, the family cat staked out belly uppermost on the ground, his little paws tied to tent-pegs. But, as his poor sweet mom said time and again, 'boys will be boys', and in a way, you had to admire the kid's inventiveness. Unless you were a slightly singed feline. Incidentally, Catricia never came back. Last thing I heard she moved to another state and changed her name.

By the time he was thirteen, young Arnie Garth was making and selling his own home movies. All it took was a borrowed camera, a head for heights and one broken brick on the third floor of the local convent. Any vow of silence the poor devout ladies might have taken leapt very soon over that wall.

Yet still the elder Garths reassured each other that their enterprising son would grow out of it, that he'd become older and wiser, as most spirited teenagers do. That he'd put those undoubted God-given skills, both artistic and entrepreneurial, to some good and more socially acceptable use. So, they waited. And waited.

And sure enough, their son grew up and got older.

And sure enough, Mr and Mrs Garth died waiting.

*

We're going into the story now. So, expect a tad more description and a little less conversation. And maybe some fancier and even, dare I say it, derivative writing in certain places. Which, in short, means a bit less me.

So, without further ado about nothing, let's just swiftly fast forward into our narrative. The big picture, as it were. Lights, action, Arnie. As promised, I won't intrude so much, or interfere, except where it's really necessary. But I'll be here, rest assured. And popping in from time to time, so as you don't forget me or who it is that's joining the dots and maybe even calling the shots (my rhymer pal Percy Bysshe would love that one). Sort of a *deus ex machina*, with apologies to the *deus*.

On the way, I'll try to set the scenes for you as best as I can, as I don't expect these are going to be so much like the scenes from your own life. At least, I hope not.

Finally, on what you might call a stylistic note: although all this happened before the Millennium, in a possibly more innocent, less worldwidewebby time, I've made an artistic choice to stick to the present tense. Because tense is exactly what the present was right then. At least for Arnie Garth.

He didn't yet know how tense.

But he sure as hell is going to. In just a few more pages.

As you would probably guess, I'm a sucker for last words. Famous or not. That old Brit Prime Minister Gladstone's 'I feel better now' always kills me. Or the less well-known Zelda Stavisky of Cleveland's 'one more latke – where's the harm?.' (By the way, on a musical note, I'm still waiting for the cremation where they play 'And I Am Telling You, I'm Not Going' from *Dreamgirls*, as the box disappears into the flames. One day.)

But today you should maybe take cognisance of the late Elvis Presley's supposedly final message, uttered to a young lady just minutes before he tragically passed away, 'I'm going to the bathroom to read'.

You could do worse than follow The King.

THREE STEPS TO HEAVEN

Chapter One

Goodness speaks in a whisper, evil shouts. (Tibetan proverb)

"You're so good... you're so big... oh, ooh baby!!"
Words loud and explicit. So loud that if they hadn't just been uttered in a totally soundproof room and the windows and doors hadn't been so scrupulously closed, they would have flown straight out of the big, lavish, multiple-garaged, cerise *hacienda* in the Hollywood Hills, soared over the empty golf cart and bounced like swallows in summer off the obligatory but currently unrippled swimming pool, the one shaped like a large pair of breasts, with round, salmon-pink nipples perfectly tiled into its floor.

As Arnie Garth's nearest neighbours have been heard to say on many occasions, 'taste no object', which coming from them is quite something, considering they have more gold taps than a third-world dictator and a shark tank in the basement.

"That's it, that's it, that is it, lover...!"
Anyone who has just managed to catch these words, in all their exotic, Latino-accented lustfulness, let alone the volcanically mounting urgency of their expression (and, of course, who didn't know Arnie Garth himself too well), would

certainly think that this fortunate man must be one hell of a lover. A description with which the man himself would be forced to agree, although to be honest the jury is still out.

You also won't be surprised to discover that the designer's vision, whoever he or she might be, made so brazenly manifest to outdoor guests and passing aircraft, is continued in spades once you venture within. Taking in the décor – and you'd probably need to keep those shades on for this – you would pretty soon recognise that it is the house that IKEA forgot. All that leopard skin and shiny leather. And this is just the walls. Don't get me started on the furniture. (I know I said I wouldn't pop in that much, but *please!*)

Yet it's the stuff tacked onto these glitzy walls, the prized objects that are so lovingly framed and protected in non-reflective glass, that offer up the final clue. We are probably not talking here the domicile of PhDs in European literature or even, this being the movie capital of the universe, makers of art-house classics. Or that the owner has ever read a book.

First there are the photos. Plenty of photos. Full colour. The works. Blown-up shots of a podgy, balding, medallioned man in his mid-forties, sporting a lavishly cap-toothed grin almost bigger than he is, a suntanned chest in need of a good mow and a pneumatic, scantily dressed companion (a different but clearly interchangeable one in each picture, this being the only noticeable variation, other than maybe the degree of garishness of the man's unbuttoned Hawaiian shirts.) In the expensively manicured and flauntily be-ringed hand not occupied in pressing the flesh, the grinning subject holds aloft some sort of Oscar-like award. At first glance it looks suspiciously like an erect and gilded phallus, but on closer inspection it can be seen to be exactly what it looked like at first glance.

Between each individually-lit photograph is a scaled-down version of a movie poster. One look at the titles of these movies would confirm to you, in an instant or less, the kind of community that would reward its members with shiny, less malleable members to take away and put on their mantelpieces. *An American in Clarice, Last Year in Marian's Bed, Seven Brides for Seven Sisters, A Fistful of Dolores* – I'm certain you get the picture. They're amongst the classics of their genre, big players in the pantheon. You might even have seen a couple or three yourself, but maybe didn't announce it on your Facebook page.

Despite the bordello-style décor, chaises-extra-longues strewn with cushions of all nationalities and a well-equipped if vaguely eclectic bar (Manischewitz? Absinthe?), the room also appears to serve as an office. There is a large, mahogany desk by the sliding windows that is almost bowing under the weight of papers and documents, all battened down against the breeze and the air-conditioning with a few of the original gilded dicks, most of them speckled with cigar-ash like fake snow at Christmas.

At the far end of the room, an ageing engineer with a silver-grey ponytail and a cowboy shirt frayed enough to match his demeanour sits at an elaborate mixing desk, diligently pushing buttons and adjusting levels. On a TV monitor above his head a silent movie plays, but not the kind of which Mack Sennett or Buster Keaton would be particularly proud.

On the screen, in a setting not so dissimilar to this one, only less subtly lit, a visiting pool cleaner, muscles rippling under his tight tee, appears to have taken a shine to the pertly underdressed maid of the house. Rather than setting about the task for which he is presumably being paid, he is enthusiastically demonstrating his equipment to the visibly interested employee, in a furnished cabana by the poolside.

Despite her obvious excitement, the little mischief is not too lost for words to compliment her agile suitor on the length and efficiency of his hose and to enquire exactly how often he likes to clean his pipes. Yet it would be plain to even the least technical of observers that, whilst this young woman is apparent mistress of the well-turned phrase and equally sharp moan of total ecstasy, these latter sounds are in fact emerging via carefully placed speakers from the soundproof booth beneath the screen and behind the glass.

Inside the booth, poised almost on top of the microphone, is a matronly, greying Latino lady, wearing a bored expression, a large but rather shapeless red jumper and a pair of faded blue denims above solid, sandalled feet. Who knows whether this is an accepted trick of her own particular trade, but between moans of unbridled and unusually protracted bliss, she is popping considerable quantities of Ice Breakers sugar-free gum. (Notice the product-placement there – will I get even a free gift pack? Where would they send it?)

"Take me to heaven, baby..."

If she only knew.

Watching all this, from his crocodile leather seat behind the engineer (although sitting is quite clearly something this hyperactive and volatile creature is incapable of doing for more than thirty seconds), is a squatter, rounder and infinitely less patient man. You need only check out the photos on the wall to realise that we are in the presence of the great Arnie Garth himself. In fact, the shirt alone would give it away.

Splayed out across the desk beside him are a group of manila folders, each with a different description stamped in red on their ash-stained covers. *Sales Figures, Budgets, Actors' Agreements.* On another even larger pile are scripts, so many scripts, which, as you would probably expect, are a tad slimmer than those you might picture sitting on the desk of a major Hollywood studio executive. (Action, I hear, takes up a lot less space on the page than dialogue, and these protagonists are nothing if not active.) And scattered all around are colourful fliers for the upcoming annual National Erotic Cinema Awards in Las Vegas. The pornographer's Mecca – you should pardon the expression.

Right now, this celebrated and much-gilded producer is glaring crossly into the aforementioned booth. He appears just as exercised as the young maid currently being dubbed (among other things) on the screen. But nowhere near so pleased about it.

After some seconds the young woman in the cabana, and the considerably older one practically eating the microphone, conveniently reach their explosive and highly professional climaxes at roughly the same time (being a microsecond or two out really doesn't matter so much – the customers aren't buying these epics for the syncing).

Whilst the on-screen starlet attends to the pressing needs of the pool guy, blissfully gasping out her compliments on his sterling extra-curricular work, the kindly and far from spent lady in the sound booth looks beyond the busy engineer to her employer, who is now approaching at some speed. She pops her gum before smiling hopefully at him.

"Was good, no, Señor Garth?" she enquires, in her normal and far huskier voice. Which, if you ask me, is just as attractive and actually far friendlier.

Arnie Garth, whose permanent California tan is turning an angry red, shakes his head and vigorously rubs his temples. He stares at the woman, as if he can't believe how very misguided she is.

"*You call than an orgasm!* Huh? Huh? I've heard hornier death rattles. Do it again and keep doing it until you get it right. And like-you-really-mean-it would help. You've got thirty minutes or I'm calling immigration."

At this point the engineer simultaneously coughs, looks up at Arnie and taps his watch. Arnie stares at him for a second then sighs, as if yet again an unfeeling world has conspired against the perfection-driven artiste.

"No time? Fine. Shit! Okay. We'll go with take forty-three."

The woman, who is almost in tears by now, smiles gratefully and exits the booth.

"Aw, hey, Dorita," says Arnie, throwing her a smile.

The woman stops for a moment, slightly thrown by the unexpected warmth of tone, and looks back at her producer for some sort of solace.

"Make some lunch for us now, eh babe? And don't forget to add plenty of cumin. Ha!"

The woman nods and gives an appreciative little laugh, without quite getting what she picks up from his expression has to be a witticism of sorts, undoubtedly crude, as the majority of the things that emerge from his potty-mouth firmly embrace this component. She makes for the kitchen, humming a Salvadorian folk-song of her youth.

"How do you get away with it, Arnie?" asks the sound engineer, when Dorita has gone. The older man looks simultaneously disgusted, appalled and genuinely fascinated.

"With what?"

"*With what?* Treating people like something you trod in, spouting filth and ugly sexist abuse and not get your head handed to you. Or your cojones."

Arnie throws the man his trademark and vaguely repellent twinkle. "It's a gift, lamebrain. Now get this mix finished or I'll have someone break your fingers. Again."

"You got it, boss."

Dorita's magnificent forty-third orgasm suddenly blasts through the speakers.

Arnie Garth sighs, as he makes for the door. "I'll be on set if you need me."

The harassed producer doesn't notice as he storms out that Dorita herself has returned with a tempting plate of taquitos for her and the engineer. As they munch, they exchange a comradely shake of the head, their mutual gaze focused on the door out of which the bane of their lives, their tormentor-in-chief, the asshole supreme has just barrelled.

They know that he is on his way to give an equally hard time to the poor working stiffs – and this isn't a random description

– currently on set in the guesthouse just twenty feet to the right. But, as ever, the pair are still uncertain as to why the dickhead needs to hop into his golf cart to get there.

*

"Why is everyone standing up!"
Not, you might think, the usual complaint that a harassed producer of movies might voice on set. But this is not a usual producer of movies. At least not those movies that demand big studios, even bigger stars and all the statutory yet often inexplicable cinematographic apparatus. Plus a lot of people standing up.

The movies we are talking about this sweltering LA afternoon involve a cameraman, a sound guy, perhaps a make-up person and, of course, a director. With an efficient but hardly over-stretched wardrobe lady and a keen, young, barely paid boy to lug the lights. All of whom you might expect to discover upright, unless maybe there's a director's chair or two just sitting around. But the stars of this particular genre of movie, the featured artistes, are more often to be encountered in a recumbent posture, on, say, a bed or a sofa (or even, more exotically, though less comfortably, a hammock).

Hence, Arnie Garth's bitter disappointment when he finally steams into the guest house to discover his leading man still in his surgical scrubs, and his regular and extremely healthy-looking leading lady as yet unrelieved of her flimsy, fantasy nurse attire. With a totally pristine hospital bed lying virginally unoccupied between them.

At first no one responds. They all turn towards Arnie, like escaping POWs caught in the searchlights. The handsome and impressively structured (even in scrubs) male lead eventually shrugs sheepishly and looks to his very attractive co-worker for the support he knows that only she can give.

"It's not my fault!" yelps the young woman, unhelpfully, thrusting out her more than ample but currently still decent chest, as if this alone will demonstrate her willingness and indeed enthusiasm to get this show firmly on the road and bedded down.

"It is too," protests the would-be doctor/seducer.

"Is not!"

"Is too!"

Unimpressed by this quick-fire banter, redolent of so much of his early work, the irate producer attempts to ascertain what exactly is or isn't his leading lady's fault, only to be met with a barrage of exclamations and explanations, none of which appears in the least explanatory or even decipherable.

Arnie Garth finds himself massaging his poor temples all over again.

"*Will everyone just shut the fuck up!*" he requests politely (for him) and takes advantage of the respectful silence to dial down his voice from incandescent to the merely homicidal. "Now. What exactly is going on that is in no way Cleo's fault and that is costing me five hundred bucks an hour minimum?"

The leading man, whose name really is Brent Wood, as if his parents aspired to nothing less than porn stardom for their firstborn, points to Cleo and says, "Smell her! Go on, smell her."

Arnie, who seldom does as asked, chooses this time to take the cue and moves closer to Cleo in order to sniff. Then he gently moves her glisteningly incarnadine lips apart and sniffs again. "Little garlic. With a touch of lemon butter. And a hint of Cajun spice..."

"You loved it last night," says Cleo, with a little grin.

"Lower. Sniff lower," orders Brent, unhappy with the way things are going.

As he begins the downward journey, Arnie realises what the younger man is saying and straightens up.

"I get it." He nods. "So?"

"So, I'm allergic to garlic – I'm garlic intolerant," explains Brent, putting his recently acquired medical knowledge to full use. "And I don't want my *schvantz* breaking out in a rash. It is my instrument, after all."

In order to illustrate his point more graphically, the petulant star pulls down his hospital pants. He tries to ignore the fact that the make-up guy is staring across the set at him without blinking.

"So, wear a rubber," suggests Arnie, who knows that every problem has a solution and not quite all of them violent or threatening.

"And what about my other instrument?" protests Brent. Before anyone can pose the obvious question – and we are not talking lyre or harpsichord here – the handsomest guy in the room sticks out his tongue. It is indeed unusually long and flexible. The make-up man is just starting to perspire audibly.

"Okay," says Arnie, rolling up the imaginary sleeves on today's offending Hawaiian shirt. "Here's how we handle this. Like grown ups." He turns to Brent. "Get down to business this *minuto*, garlic guy, or it's back to dinner theatre for you."

"But Arnie," protests the man, rapidly losing his glow and his tan. "I got a wife, a family to support."

Arnie nods, as if in understanding. He holds out a podgy, impeccably manicured hand and grabs the younger man's newly exposed qualifications.

"I am an award-winning producer," he informs his victim, "of high quality, quadruple-X erotica."

If somebody on the small set coughs the word 'porn' under his breath, this producer chooses to ignore it.

"My latest opus, *Everything's Coming up Rosa's,* is nominated in seven categories for this year's National Erotic Cinema Awards, eight if you include foreign language." He squeezes seven times then once more for luck, as if to nail his point. "And I expect to be coming outta that big Vegas room next week with a lotta dicks in my hand. So – I am a big shot. You, you are a little shot blessed with a big shlong. You wanna play here – you do it by my rules."

As she notices that the faces of the two men are drawing closer, mainly because the younger man's knees are starting to buckle and his head to nod forward, Cleo steps between them and deftly wrenches Arnie's crunching hand away. The leading man crumples to the floor.

"*Stop it!* Just stop it, Arnie," she reprimands, as only she can. "I'll run to the store and get some Summer's Eve."

"Does it come in flavors?" enquires the floored lead. "Get Strawberry... I'm a sucker for straw—"

"*No!*" interrupts Arnie, the frustration mounting. "We don't have time for this. Summer's nearly over. All of you – back to work. I don't pay you people to jerk off!"

"Well, actually..."

Arnie turns back with a moan towards his buggy. Which is when he notices a couple of sweet young kids, a boy and a girl, no more than eleven years old, standing in the doorway.

"Who are you?"

"They're mine," explains Brent. "It's 'bring your kids to work day.'"

"*Jesus!* Get 'em outta here. Go – go in the house, kids. Daddy'll come as soon as he... Just *go!*"

As they scoot off, eyes bugging out, and the male lead, still in some pain, collapses onto the bed, Cleo catches up with her departing producer and erstwhile boyfriend.

"Arnie," she protests, "that thing with Brent, that was – well, it was way outta line! You can't just come down here and throw your weight around. *We – we are the talent!*"

A ripple runs round the room:

"Yeah."

"She's right."

"You said it."

Arnie swivels back to face them. Like Charles Laughton giving his best Captain Bligh, the man senses mutiny. But Cleo is no Fletcher Christian and Arnie has fought off tougher insurrections.

"Oh, so you're the 'talent'?"

Cleo nods, still defiant but perhaps not quite so much.

"Actually Cleo, Cleo Cleaves, aka Ada Dubrowski, you're not. You are so not. If anything, you are the talent-less."

The young starlet's fulsome lower lip begins to quiver. She can't believe what she is hearing. And this from the man who discovered her when she came to his office selling Bibles.

"W-what?"

Relishing the effect he is clearly having, her heartless tormentor proceeds with gusto. "What you also are is the jobless. The brain-less. What you *really* are is the fired-less. The fired!"

"*Again*? Arnie, it's me, Cleo. Okay, Ada. Have you forgotten last night? Oil massage, *Casablanca* on Netflix, the shocker…" She sits down, eyes brimming with tears.

The entire room is glaring at Arnie. He shifts focus to address them all. "What am I paying you morons for?"

At this point the director, a small, bespectacled, unassuming guy with bad skin and the accent of a Southern gentleman, feels duty-bound to intervene and speak up for his cast.

"If I may interrupt, Mistuh Garth – Arnie. Miss Cleo here was the only lady in this scene. As you doubtless are aware from the script – an excellent script, by the way, one of your finest – she is the dedicated nurse and Brent the eminent gynaecologist who is very kindly giving her a courtesy examination."

Arnie, never immune to flattery, nods in agreement, as he recalls some of his earlier triumphs. Yet they can't entirely quench his anger this morning. He is still smarting from today's emailed rebuke from the powerful plumbers' union. In the same way that the public has been led unrealistically to believe from cop shows that every crime can be solved within the hour, viewers of Arnie's movies now apparently have the unreasonable expectation that plumbers and other tradesmen, pool cleaners included, will always turn up within minutes or even seconds of a phone call from the lady or female employee of the house.

Instead of answering the man directly, Arnie looks around the room. His eyes fall on the sweet young wardrobe-woman, who is oiling the zip on a pair of workman's overalls in preparation for a future production.

"*You!*" he says, quite shocking her.

She looks up, her lubricating hand just beginning to shake.

"Wanna be a star?"

The young woman nods, too intimidated to refuse.

"Cleo. Guess what – you're rehired. As wardrobe. Take this young lady's oil can and give her your outfit."

To her own annoyance, all that Cleo Cleaves can hear herself saying is, "Thank you, Arnie," which the choleric man doesn't hear anyway, what with all the feverish pacing, the crazy, incessant hammering in his head and the now almost flesh-removing assault by his own hands on his tormented temples. He really should remove all the gold jewellery from his fingers before segueing into heavy stress mode.

"*Listen up, people,*" he announces, clapping his hands. "We are on day seven of a two-day shoot – and I wanna see orgasms! Great big, earth-quaking, San Andreas frigging fault orgasms." He watches his crew as they simply stare at him, scared and transfixed. "You know how to have an orgasm, don't you? You just pucker up your lips and go…" Arnie Garth suddenly grabs his head. "Ohhhhh!"

The cast all look at each other, then – what the hell? – they grab their own heads and imitate the maestro. "Ohhhhh!"

"Gaghhhh!" says Arnie, which is kind of a new one on them, but when in Rome…

"Gaghhhh!" comes the echo.

Now their tutor staggers sideways. So, in unison, the group staggers sideways, which is weird but sort of fun in its own way.

"Hghhhkkk!" continues Arnie, dropping to the floor on his knees.

Quite a climax, think his imitators, far from unimpressed. And not a little envious. They drop down too, with an equally heartfelt and expressive "Hghhhkkk!"

Finally, or at least they hope finally, because they've had enough now with the earth-moving, their boss and mentor gives a long, wavering sigh and sprawls backwards, banging his head on the floor. And so the cast, thinking almost wistfully of *When Harry Met Sally*, do the selfsame dramatically painful sprawl.

"So, was it good for you, Arnie?" murmurs Cleo from her prone position, her face almost scraping the makeshift studio floor. She only begins to be slightly concerned when she sees her producer just lying there, staring upwards, drooling and glassy-eyed.

"*Arnie!*"

Chapter Two

With a sweet tongue and kindness, you can drag an elephant by a hair.
(Persian proverb)

Imagine, if you will, a place as far away as you can get from the hedonistic fleshpots of Hollywood, California, USA. And from the salads.

We are not just talking miles here. We are talking lifestyle, outlook, ambience. We're talking culture, politics, attitudes.

We are talking rain.

So much rain.

Somerset Maugham, who believe me is quite a character, a bit prickly at times, but the man knows from rain, must have been here in England's Lake District when he wrote that eponymous short story of his. Alright, it all took place in Pago Pago or somewhere, which even I've never been to, and I've covered the waterfront. But maybe he came here as a child. I can't believe it rains in double Pago as much as it does here in Rough Fell, The Lake District, Cumbria, UK.

But does Noreen Millburn give a shit?

Every day she is out here, walking her beloved Cumbrian hills. Every day, come rain or – rain. And come mud, sludge, soggy cowpats, flooding ditches and leaking gullies – you name it, she's *shlepped* in it.

Here she is, this sturdy, rough-hewn, Lake District Englishwoman, bad teeth firmly clenched, lagged like a trusty boiler in so many crudely home knit woolly cardigans and scarves that pretty much all you can see of her face, under her faded red and extremely bobbly hat, are a couple of weary yet strangely wild and burning eyes and a drippy nose. Of course, the industrial strength waterproof walking boots, an inheritance from her late mother, aren't home knit, but the heavy-duty socks keeping her gnarled little northern feet toasty inside them most certainly are. She could be any age from fifteen to one hundred and six, but I know for a fact that Noreen Millburn (Miss) is exactly forty-five.

The aforementioned eyes, when they're not obscured by her unfetching but functional headgear, are an unusually pale yet vivid blue, which is the only blue around these parts, except maybe for the odd vein, as the sky is a glowering, moody grey, warning her and the world that there's plenty more wet stuff where this all came from.

Yet Noreen Millburn is not alone as she squelches across the sodden but beloved property bequeathed to her on these moor-covered hills. There is no man with her this afternoon, of course there isn't, nor indeed in her life. She has no need of such distractions or frivolities.

But there is Geoffrey.

"That's it, Geoffrey, you're doing really well, petal. We'll be home very soon."

Geoffrey doesn't understand a thing the woman is saying. And it isn't just the accent, which is weird as they come, unless of course you come from round here, but even then, it has to be pretty weird. Geoffrey is a young, black-faced Herdwick sheep, local to these parts and tough and hardy as they make them. Or as we make them.

A native of these high grounds, Geoffrey can take anything a merciless nature cares to throw at him or drench him with. He can even take his name. Fortunately for Noreen, he can also just about manage the thickly woven rope lead she has slung around his neck, so that he doesn't go wandering off in search of other sheep or other Noreens, although to be honest he'd have to search far and wide for the latter.

The one thing, other than the lead, that might distinguish this sheep from his fellows, is that his front left leg is in a tiny, homemade splint. He is clearly not too uncomfortable with this, so whatever was going on with the poor, damaged limb is fortunately healing. We have, however, no way of knowing the state of his embarrassment or inner mortification, as thankfully there aren't many of his fellow black-faced Herdwicks around and right now he is making a pretty stoic fist of it.

Through the rain that is coming down so thick and fast you'd need only the Maid of the Mist to complete the picture, they can see a small, two-roomed slate stone cottage not too far ahead of them. Totally isolated, just off a poorly maintained dirt road, it stands as it must have stood for generations, four square in its stubborn, stoical greyness, against the slings and arrows and absolute pissing-downs of outrageous Cumbria.

There is a small garden surrounding this extremely modest structure, a plot utterly bereft of flowers or beauty, save perhaps for its shabby window box, but fulsome in the robust, earthy produce that Noreen Millburn cultivates in order to survive and sometimes even to sell. When, that is, she is not giving it away in basketfuls to people more needy than herself, which is another story. Although actually, when you think about it, it's very much this same story but I'll save it for a bit later. I don't want to run ahead of myself as it's getting dark, we're almost home now and we need to get out of this *fershtinkeneh* rain.

Of course, there is no electricity in Noreen's remote little homestead, with its thick stone walls and tiny windows. Nothing so comfortable or self-indulgent. So, when Noreen pushes open the peeling old door – it's never locked – she can only use her other, admittedly heightened, senses to guide her to the kerosene lanterns propped all around the place. Even a person without such sharp senses, even a person with lousy hearing and a seriously stuffed-up nose, even Helen Keller with a cold, would, however, get what's going on here. Such a person would recognise in an instant, from the stench alone, that there is a virtual menagerie inhabiting this tiny dwelling.

Actually, no virtual about it. There's a zoo here and these guys are alive and shitting. In fact, deaf ears and a loss of smell would be a blessing, considering the almighty ruckus and the overpowering reek of dogs, rabbits, at least one goat, a hare, a brace of ferrets and God knows how many cats. Not to mention the rats and the mice. It's still too early for the badgers but the back door is open, and they know the way.

As the warm light gradually unveils the welcoming squalor of the tiny living room, the animals greet their owner in an ear-splitting frenzy of ravenous self-interest. A visitor gazing around (not that there ever are any and not that they could stay more than a couple of seconds without retching or passing out) would notice the ancient and extremely basic furniture. They would spot an ancient wooden rocking chair with a broken rocker and a solitary, fraying cushion. A tiny single bed in a poky room at the rear of the dwelling. A badly framed sampler that reads 'Home, sweet ho' because her mother died weaving it.

Dominating the parlour is a small and battered table, strewn with skeins of rough wool, unidentifiable half-knitted objects that won't look any better when complete, some curious-looking bars of pure white confectionery in bright blue wrappers and relentlessly savaged feeding bowls made from cheap tin. The ash from last night, and a whole lot of other nights, lies greyly in the grate of the fireplace, above which sit fading old photos, in black and white: Noreen as a child, with her equally craggy parents; an assortment of now-deceased sheep and sheepdogs; the cottage at a time it didn't rain, which must have been taken with a pretty fast film.

If you discount the animals – big if – the items you'd probably notice pretty swiftly, because they're scattered all over the place, are the collection boxes. Dozens of them, maybe more than dozens. Scores! Could be a hundred.

Some people still call them tins or cans here but they're all plastic now, with identical slots in the top for coins and, they should be so lucky, paper money. The only difference between all of them being that each one is decked out in the glaring colours and logo of a particular charity or organisation.

One look would tell you that this solitary lady is either a serial mugger of charity workers or that she herself collects for Britain. Just read the boxes and weep. *Help the Aged, Help the Lame, Help the Helpless, Save the Children, Save the Whales, Save the Planet.* Then there are the boxes for all the horrible ailments you most probably know – cancer, of course, MS, Parkinson's, motor neurone, heart failure, leprosy etc., and even more cans for bad stuff you might just have heard of, if you've been studying medicine most of your life, but really wouldn't want your worst enemy or possibly even your mother-in-law to catch – Arizona swamp fever, porphyria, Moebius syndrome, black urine disease, Rasmussen's Encephalitis.

Look further and you'll see the organisations – *Red Cross, Blue Cross, Red Crescent, Greenpeace, Sue Ryder, Cheshire Homes, St Luke's Hospice, Samaritans, Mind, UNICEF, Unesco, UNWRA, CND, JNF, PLO, UTI.* You name it, this lady's got a box for it. The only puzzling thing is that she doesn't have one specifically for osteoporosis of the neck, because that's what she's all lined up for after years of humping all these boxes around. And the only lucky thing for her is that most of them are still pretty empty, even after a long day's rattling, but it doesn't stop a girl from trying.

"I suppose you'll be wanting your dinner now?" says Noreen, idly snapping off a white chunk of something from one of the already opened blue packets and popping it in her mouth.

"What do *you* sodding think?" say all the animals, in their own language.

She hardly has time to fill the bowls before the gang are hitting the table in a feeding frenzy, jaws, paws, tails and claws in ravenous action, not always sticking to their own especially tailored menu. Noreen Millburn would be hard-pressed to explain why she is forcing her 'flock' to eat at the table, but it was something her late parents always insisted on, and what was good enough for her old family is good enough for her new one.

Only Geoffrey, currently impeded, is unable to match the speed of his fellows. Fortunately, Noreen is on hand to slip him a morsel from one of her many voluminous pockets, a practical feature of the sagging, soggy wool, which the limping sheep grabs gratefully and takes to his own little corner.

Staring around with a maternal and only slightly demented grin, our homeowner notices an envelope on the floor. Paw prints aside, it is gleaming white and looks pretty important. Especially with the words *APEX HOLDINGS* printed on the top right and *VERY VERY URGENT* stamped just above the address.

Noreen picks the letter up with a sigh. "Another one for you, Sebastian," she says. And feeds it to her goat.

Chapter Three

You inherit from the dead, not from the sick.
(Congolese proverb)

I'll be frank with you, I'm not too crazy about hospitals.

Wouldn't you think, with what I do, what I've been doing for all these eons and more, I would get used to them? Or maybe you wouldn't, as you don't know yet what exactly I do for a living. Or a dying. Just wait a little longer, you'll find out – unless, of course, you already reckon life's too short.

I wouldn't say this here is a bad hospital. In fact, as hospitals go, it's pretty classy. I mean, it's not like producers of respectable movies are rushed to respectable hospitals and porn brokers get Chicago Abandon-all-Hope. At least not erotica purveyors of Arnie Garth's prominence.

Perhaps it's not quite as brand spanking pristine as the medical set he was just wheeled out of on a gurney, but there are machines like you wouldn't believe all around the hospital bed. You can hardly see poor Arnie for all the stuff that's just beeping and dripping and pulsating all day long, 24/7. He wasn't a big guy to start with, but he looks a whole lot smaller now, with this apparatus hooked-up to all parts north and south. A damn sight paler too.

And even more pathetic.

"*Arnie?… Arnie?!*"

After a few moments – pretty painful moments for poor Cleo Cleaves, who is bending solicitously over him – Arnie Garth blinks his confused and bleary eyes and starts to look around.

"Am I paying for this set?" he asks weakly, which is not so surprising considering Cleo is still in the nurse's uniform she was wearing for Bulge Entertainment's most recently interrupted production, *Fay's Anatomy*. Attire that doesn't look so much like anything the other nurses in this fancy hospital might be wearing, unless there has been an unfortunate laundry incident or a highly unexpected communal growth spurt.

"You're in the hospital, Arnie," explains Cleo. "A real hospital. You had a stroke. And a double heart attack. At exactly the same time. Which is quite rare – the doctors were pretty excited." She finds that she can hardly talk through her tears. "I thought you were going to die!"

With this she clasps the prone man and pulls his balding head towards her, through all the wires and tubes, in a huge emotional hug, looking for a moment as if she has suddenly sprouted a third breast.

In a muffled voice the ailing man, struggling for a pocket of air amidst the quivering flesh, manages to mutter, "Don't worry. If I die, you get to keep your apartment."

Cleo pushes him back angrily, rattling his life-supports. "I don't care about the frigging apartment, Arnie. I was just being nice. Can't you be nice, just this once?"

"Hey!" protests the man, his voice feeble yet insistent. "I didn't get where I am today by being *nice!*"

"You're in intensive care, Arnie."

Arnie has nothing much to say to this, so he is not literally being interrupted when the room doors swing open and another, even more statuesque woman strides purposefully in, classic Louboutin heels clacking on the boarded floor. Yet this particular person would classify as an interruption at the best – or worst – of times. And the fact that she is flanked by two almost identical-looking young men in expensive suits and haircuts, clutching briefcases, doesn't make her arrival any less of an intrusion.

The woman is of an indeterminate age and at first glance would appear to be of Asian origin – Chinese, perhaps, or Korean – although unusually tall. A second glance would correct the first impression, as you might just begin to realise that the perfect smoothness of her skin and distinctive tilt of her eyes is more attributable to surgery than heritage. Indeed, the old joke in her industry is that the cleft in her chin was once her navel. The dazzlingly blonde hair and gargantuan chest would further indicate that nature, rather than being allowed to take its course, has been given all the assistance money can buy. Much of it Arnie's, as it turns out.

"You're not dead," observes the woman, in a throaty, mid-Western drawl.

"Nice to see you too, honey," confirms Arnie. "Who are your friends?"

"Not friends. Too straight for friends. Lawyers."

"*Lawyers*?"

The men nod. One of them is on the cusp of talking but sees his client's terrifying, bruised plum lips begin to open and thinks better of it.

"Divorce lawyers, at first," continues the woman. "But now they're estate attorneys. I called a deathbed vigil to discuss the will. How are you feeling?"

"I'll live, Melisande," says Arnie, defiantly.

"*Shit!*" She turns slowly to her lawyers, which makes them think of a huge liner attempting to change direction. "No deathbed, guys. We're back to the divorce. Go away – but not too far. Could be a false alarm."

The lawyers withdraw gratefully to the relative safety of the hospital corridor. Cleo tries to stand tall in her fake nursing shoes and turns to the visitor.

"Melisande! The guy just had a stroke. And two heart attacks. All at once. You could at least *pretend* to look upset."

"Can't. The Botox won't let me." To the newcomer's credit she gives it a good go, but nothing moves. "See? Now – why don't you hitch up your little nurse's outfit, not that it could take a lot more hitching, and scram. Porn star mistresses have no visitation rights in California."

Cleo shrugs, *Whatever*, and heads sadly for the door. But she knows that she can't leave her producer and lover to this heartless gorgon without one final, gently reassuring word.

"Call me, babe. If you recover."

Throwing the prone and now uncontrollably shaking patient a deeply caring smile – because this is a very sweet and, in her own singular way, rather innocent girl – Cleo carefully manages to manoeuvre past Melisande, without one of those unfortunate bosom collisions so prevalent in their industry. She is hampered in this endeavour, however, by the advent of a real nurse, popping in to see how her patient is doing. On seeing the departing young woman moulded into a tighter and highly abbreviated version of the outfit she herself is wearing, the middle-aged, African American healthcare worker gives a double take of which any silent comedian could be truly proud.

"Pardon me," apologises Cleo, leaving the nurse to deal with the marital discord. She, however, is more concerned with attending to the sick man on the bed and checking his blood pressure and IVs. She chooses to ignore the domestic venom being hurled in both directions, as she can get as much of this as she needs at home.

"I moved outta the house but it's only temporary," explains Melisande, "until I get it back in the settlement."

"Why are you divorcing me?" asks Arnie, which causes even

his nurse to raise her eyebrows. "Thought we had a good thing going. You go your way. I go mine. We file joint returns."

"I've fallen in love with my boyfriend," says Melisande.

"LOVE?" exclaims Arnie, at some volume and with a degree of saliva expulsion that makes both his wife and his nurse recoil. "What is *wrong* with you?" He enlists the poor medical attendant into his diatribe. "Can you believe this, sweetheart? I know you wouldn't think it now, with more structural work to her name than the Statue of Liberty, but in her prime this woman was God's gift to erotica aficionados in fifty states and Canada. She won the National Erotic Cinema Award for Best Three-Way four years running. Now she says she has found true love!"

"A life to be envied," says the nurse, checking his oxygen levels.

"Yeah. Right. I know from love, sister. Love is for wimps."

"Okay – I was hoping we could do this painlessly," persists Melisande. "A simple service. Snappy cremation. Tear-free mascara and a short probate. But I see that's not in the cards. Although…" She turns to the nurse. "What's the hospital's policy on pulling the plug?"

"Fine," says Arnie, gathering strength before the nurse can respond. "You wanna battle? You got it! I will skin you alive. I will leave you poverty-stricken and hopeless, like you were when I picked you up outta the gutter. I'll… melt your silicone!"

His brows begin to knit, as he winces in obvious pain. The nurse appears concerned but Melisande just goads him along.

"Dream on, pornmeister. Good, good. Tell me more!"

"Begging for your next meal, selling that pathetic re-tread of a body to whoever has the small change to pay for it and eyesight bad enough to enjoy it."

"Arnie. Bubeleh," she says, sweetly. "You don't have the balls."

"No? Ask Cleo. I got botchie balls." He nods towards the nurse. "Ask this lady. I got balls you could bowl with. I got balls so big that—"

He suddenly falls back onto the bed, groaning and quivering, his eyes firmly closed. The nurse rushes towards him.

"Is he dead?" asks Melisande, solicitously. "Tell me quick. I can still catch the lawyers."

The nurse checks Arnie's pulse then nods sadly. "He's dead."

Melisande pumps her fists, then notices that the nurse is checking again.

"No, wait. Yes. He still has a pulse. It's a miracle."

"Well, praise the fucking Lord!"

"Ma'am, please watch your mouth. Mr Garth shouldn't be disturbed. He's had a life-threatening event."

"Not life-threatening enough. Call yourself a carer?" Melisande makes for the door. "This ain't over until the short, balding pornographer croaks!"

As the door closes, the relieved nurse makes a final check, then gently raises the sheet and looks downwards. Arnie's eyes pop open.

"What?"

"Just checking for – bedsores."

"Go away."

As the exasperated woman stomps off, Arnie sighs and slowly covers his face with the sheet.

And this is where I come in.

Not that I haven't been here all the time. Perish the thought. I'm kind of what you might call quietly ubiquitous. But this time I get a speaking part.

"Things not looking so rosy on the longevity front, huh brother?" I say, by way of an icebreaker.

Very slowly, Arnie lowers the sheet. What he sees, sitting casually on that chair right next to his hospital bed, is an incredibly handsome and impossibly muscular young man, with dark wavy locks, a gleaming Mediterranean tan and the brazen look of a Greek God. Or, to put it another way, an absolutely premium blend of Bradley Cooper, Tom Cruise and Brad Pitt.

I'm lying, I'm lying!

What our ailing Mr Garth actually notices, somewhat to his surprise, is a pale, rather gaunt fellow, in his late middle-age, and if I'm being brutally honest, maybe a tad on the nondescript side. Yet, even though I say it myself, this is at the very least an extremely clean and reasonably well-turned-out gentleman, in a decent lightweight business suit, with attractively greying hair on some, if not all, of his head and a neat, well-trimmed, salt 'n' pepper moustache.

Needless to say, the patient isn't thrilled to see me. They seldom are.

"*Who the hell are you?* Where d'you come from? How did you get in?"

That sort of thing.

"So many questions. Sheesh. Glad I'm sitting down, Mr Garth. My name is Ambrose."

"And?"

"Just Ambrose. Means 'immortal' but hey, what's in a name? Oh, and I'm here to collect your soul."

So, there you have it. The secret, as they say, is out of the bag. And what a secret! What a bag!

"*Nurse! Security!*"

For a man in his parlous condition, Arnie Garth can scream pretty damn loud. Loud enough to draw that same admittedly intrigued nurse right back in.

"What is it, Mr Garth? Why you yelling?"

"Why you think?" he says, nodding his shiny head and all his drips in my direction. "Who let this guy in? Get rid of him!"

"What guy?"

"Are you blind, lady? *This* guy!"

Now he's pointing straight at me. But, of course, the nurse doesn't see a thing. Except for an empty chair. Hey, it's not her soul I'm after. Yet.

"You're seeing guys?" she says, shaking her head. "This is a

156

new one. I'm fetching the doctor. He will love it."

And she's off again, muttering to herself. Leaving a somewhat bewildered Arnie Garth. And, of course, me.

"Over here," I say, when he looks to the chair again and for one blissful moment doesn't see anything.

Swivelling his head, he finds me right across the private room, on a second, empty bed, playing with an oxygen mask. *Whose Life Is It Anyway?* – now that's my kind of movie. Although a few songs wouldn't have hurt.

"'*Pull back to reveal Ambrose, a commanding man in a smart yet not ostentatious suit. Handsome, with just a hint of masculine cruelty.*'"

Not even a smile. Ah well.

"Nurse couldn't see me, Arnie," I explain, moving back to the chair with a certain fleetness of foot that would even impress my idol Gene Kelly. That man could dance on a cloud.

I'd have thought the selective-seeing bit would be pretty evident by now. It's the other stuff that could require a more detailed explanation.

I must try my best not to sound too bored. That's Rule One – even if you've done this a million times (which, believe me, I have), you should treat each person like they're your only customer.

"To all intents and purposes," I say, "I'm a special effect."

"Cut the crap!" protests Arnie. "I'm a very sick man."

"Oh that, my dear Arnold, is an understatement. You are in a worse shape than honey-bunch John Wayne at the end of *The Alamo*. Can I be honest with you? – and please don't nod, not in your condition. You are inches away from a brain aneurism that will lock you into your body for as long as you live. You'll see, hear, and feel everything. But you won't communicate, not even with a "blink yes or no" code. You'll go slowly insane, and no one will know it. Excepting me, of course."

"I really, really hope you're not a doctor."

"Better than," I tell him. And now I cough a little, which isn't my usual MO, you should understand, but truthfully, I'm just a little embarrassed this time round. "Actually, by rights, Mr Garth, you should be dead already, but there was – well, I'll be honest with you – there was a glitch."

"*A glitch!* I'm still alive because of a glitch?" says Arnie, getting quite chatty now for someone on the brink of virtual extinction. "Well, thank God for glitches, is what I always—"

"Wait – not so much," I say, holding up a hand not as well manicured as my friend's here, but passable. "The glitch is…"

Okay, so now I'm going to have to admit something here, although it pains and troubles me. As I said, I'm feeling just a tad uncomfortable right at this juncture. I won't keep you in the dark too long and I hope you'll forgive my uncharacteristic reticence, but I can feel a huge sigh sinking me into the hospital chair, which is pretty unusual in itself, as I have absolutely no body mass and am basically an apparition.

"See, Mr Garth," I say, a bit sheepishly, "every child that comes into this world, they're given what we call a soul. Bless 'em."

Here's where I pause for dramatic effect, old ham that I am, but also because, I won't lie to you, this is the really tricky bit.

"Well, every child *except one*. Guess who?" And I point to Arnie Garth, with a friendly little wink. Just to lighten the mood.

"*What!*" gasps Arnie, looking not as lightened as I might have hoped. "Why didn't I get a friggin' soul? Who screwed up? I demand a manual recount!"

"Arnie," I explain, with a sympathetic sigh. "I don't give 'em out, fella, I just take 'em back. I'm sure I don't need to tell you about demarcation. I mean, you wouldn't ask your make-up artist to fix a camera that goes on the fritz."

He has to nod at this – the man may be almost irredeemably gross and seriously repellent, but an idiot he is not.

"So, I really don't know why they didn't give you a soul.

Could be a lot of reasons. There was a baby boom, the guys upstairs were overworked, they got distracted some, they plain forgot. It's like they say in the Bible, shit happens. So, imagine my surprise, when you have the fatal stroke and heart attacks, triple whammy, I come down for your soul and – whoops – *hello*?"

"But what's it friggin' matter?" demands Arnie Garth. "Who needs a soul, for God's sake?"

"Ever wonder why you're such an irredeemable bastard?"

The man in the bed looks outraged. "*Me?* Arnie Garth? Come on – people love me!"

I'm sorry, call me unprofessional, but I shake my head so hard at this, I nearly fall off my chair.

"Trust me, pal, you're a shit. A total shit. A shit from shitland. Everyone hates you. Even people who haven't met you hate you already, 'cos it saves time. And you know why you're such a shit? I'll tell you why. You are such a shit because you don't have a soul."

Arnie ponders on this for little more than a beat. A beat in which several thousand people around the world may have died, such is life, but just a beat nonetheless.

"I can live with that," decides Arnie, not offended in the least. "Who needs a soul?"

"Let's see," I ponder. I do a good ponder. "You wanna go somewhere hot and excruciatingly, skin-meltingly painful for all eternity and beyond, when you die?"

"Er, no. Not really."

"Then *you* need one, you schmuck. By the end of the week would be nice."

"*End of the week!*" He pauses for a second, as a thought strikes him, like something he only noticed in the edit. "Hold on, did I hear you say *fatal* stroke?"

"*And* fatal heart attacks. Bubeleh, you don't look this way from a head cold. Actually, you shoulda died today. But hey, fair is fair, this is our mistake. An embarrassing one, I admit. *Nostra culpa.*" I wink at Arnie. People like a wink. "So, I know some people. I pulled a few strings."

"What people? What strings?"

"Such impatience. *Tsk tsk.* To continue – I bent a few rules. At, I might just add, some heavy personal and professional risk. And I got you... wait for it... da daa! An extension."

"Wh-what kind of an extension?" Arnie is staring dumbly at me. Right now he looks so pathetic my heart almost melts. Almost.

"Okay. Here goes," I commence. "If you retrieve your soul by midnight Sunday, we'll overlook the stroke and the heart attacks – which are on hold for now – and possibly even your godawful personality. (Did I mention you're a shit?) So, you get to live out the rest of your natural life. Which actually mightn't be that long, I've seen the inside of your arteries."

"Sunday? *Six days?* Just six friggin' days?"

"Arnie – Heaven can't wait."

The man in the bed looks suddenly chilled. "And... if I don't get it back? This soul thing."

"You'll die and go straight to Hell. Okay, that's you. So, you wanna hear my Humphrey Bogart impression? It's a killer."

"Screw your impressions! Tell me what you people did with my fuckin' soul!"

"Now this I know!"

But I don't tell him straightaway. I give a sort of a pause, like I'm weighing up the best way to break it. This is what you call dramatic tension. Okay, pause over, here we go.

"We gave it to the little girl who was right behind you in the line."

Arnie just stares at me. This I was expecting.

"Say what?" he utters, finally. "*You gave it to a little girl...?*"

"Who was behind you in line. Yup. Little new-born baby female. Popped it in there right alongside her own. Two souls, eh? Quite a first for us."

"Fine," says Arnie, some of the colour, I'm glad to say, coming back into his miserable face. "Okay. Let's look at this rationally, whatever your name is."

"Ambrose." *Is it really so hard to remember?*

"Other guys get a Gabriel. I get a Ambrose. Figures! So, lemme get this straight, Ambrose, I grab my soul back from off of some broad who has two. Mine and her own. You collect it sometime. Hopefully, not too soon. And when I go, I go to heaven, not the other place."

"I am so happy you understand. I really thought this was going to be difficult."

"*Are you out of your fucking mind?*" screams Arnie.

Then he suddenly grabs his head in pain, falls back, dead to the world – until his ratty eyes pop open again just a few interesting seconds later.

"Oh, my God, *I saw the white light!* And there was a sign. *All are welcome...* except maybe for you, Arnie Garth."

"See? I told you. Circle of life. Hakuna Matata. So, you just find this lucky female lady with two souls and—"

"And I rip mine back out of her. With your help. Yeah?"

Here I do one of my celebrated shrugs. "Sort of. In a way. Well, no. Actually."

Now he just stares at me. So, I try to put on my calmest, folksiest, maybe kind of Mr Rogers voice.

"Arnie. You ever been to the Lake District?"

Chapter Four

If you do not travel, you will marry your own sister.
(Mozambican proverb)

We're not quite on location yet – but we are on our way. Get your umbrellas out!

Of course, the hospital in LA was beyond delighted to see the broad Hawaiian back of Arnie Garth departing through their electronic sliding doors into the unrelenting California sunshine. But no more so than their irascible patient was to be doing the exit vertically, on his own two well-shod feet and in an even more vivid shirt than the one in which he first so dramatically and horizontally arrived.

I can't say for certain that the staff were amazed at his remarkable recovery – courtesy of yours truly – but the expression 'the devil looks after his own' was heard on more than one occasion in corridors and cafeterias. Which is hardly a medical supposition but is most certainly a human one (and almost definitely misguided. If I know anything about the downstairs people – and, unfortunately, I know a fair bit – they would have been only too delighted to claim my little turd for eternity and beyond).

I almost wanted to reassure the good but beleaguered hospital folks that this could well be a temporary arrangement and that a more probable scenario would be to see the soulless little homunculus, who gave them such a hard time, well and truly expired by the following weekend, but they would think I was only trying to cheer them up.

So, I kept my own counsel and didn't reveal myself to them, or even indeed to Arnie Garth himself, until we were in one of those iconic London taxis on our way out of Heathrow Airport, after taking an exhausting red-eye from LAX (well, exhausting for him. I sleep like a dead person).

Notice the abrupt change of scene? And it cost me nothing. Bupkis. The magic of the written word. Mind you, it cost Arnie Garth a fortune. Serves the horny little snob right for only travelling first class.

I really wanted to tell this seriously fraught man, whilst he was arranging his mercy-mission at breakneck speed, that the United Kingdom, on which he had never previously set Gucci moccasin, was bigger than he might have assumed in his narrow LA mind. And that Heathrow Airport to the Lake District by black cab would be a major expense. But I had to concur that time was indeed of the essence and that Arnie Garth, one of the nation's wealthiest eroticrats, was not a huge fan of public transport.

The trouble with suddenly manifesting right next to someone who has just had a major heart attack or two is that you could make their heart stop majorly all over again. But it seemed like there was nothing else for it, as I still didn't think that Arnie had quite grasped the challenges of his particular journey. And we are not just talking jetlag.

So here I am, in the back seat of one of London's famous black hansom cabs – a first for me, too – making sure that my 'client', if this is what I may prematurely call him, is up to speed.

"Okay, so I meet this Brit woman – this Madam friggin'

Two-souls," he says, when he has recovered from the inevitable shock and adjusted to my presence. "Then what, Ambien?"

"Then you cut off her head with a mystic sword. And it's Ambrose."

I can see the cab driver in his mirror. A middle-aged Cockney gentleman who clearly thought Christmas and Rosh Hashanah had come all at once when a loud American in the wrong clothes for this time, or indeed any time, hired him from the taxi rank to travel the length of the country, rather than just to make another familiar traffic-laden slog to some plush hotel in the West End. He has no idea who his passenger is talking to – he can see no sign of a phone or an earpiece – and is just beginning to fret that he is going to be several hours on the road with a mad person.

"Say WHAT?" says Arnie Garth.

"I'm kidding, Arnie. That's *Highlander*."

I lower my voice now because this is the serious bit. The part of the plan that I'm not sure this Arnie guy is totally on top of. The big slug of plot I want to reduce down to a manageable size by keeping my cool. "You just have to get her to fall in love with you. Body *and* soul would be good."

This is when he really starts to stare at me. And the cabbie really starts to stare in his mirror at the space where I would be, if he could only see me.

"Get her to fall in love…?" repeats Arnie, looking stunned.

"You got it. By George!"

"Hey, I've always been pretty good getting women in the sack."

"That's nice," says the driver. "I'm a married man myself."

"Fall in *love*, Arnie, not bed," I explain. And, as if this isn't shock enough, quite casually I add the clincher. What this guy I'm (invisibly) with might call the deal-breaker. "Oh – and Arnie, *you have got to fall in love with her, too.*"

Now he is frozen. Now I've caught his full attention.

"I fall in love," says Arnie, robotically.

"Lots of visitors fall in love with England," chirps the cabbie, with a friendly Cockney smile and a sudden yearning for normality. "But they usually wait till we get out of the airport."

"And it has to be true love, my friend. Accept no substitutes. You get me? True love *on both sides*. Or – well, it just won't take."

"True love," repeats Arnie, like it's an expression he never heard before. "What? Like sharing feelings? Sacrificing my needs for hers? Bargaining when she says no to kinky stuff?"

"See? You got two out of three, so I know you can do this."

"Look," he says, raising his voice, "you just keep your part of the deal. Capisce? I don't die."

"Listen, guv," says the cabbie, "I've been driving twenty-five years. Ain't lost a passenger yet."

"*Was I talking to you?*"

"Then who…? My luck – another fruitcake!" The driver turns his attention back to the road. It's going to be a long journey.

Knowing that at least one of us can't be heard, I continue the mission statement and wonder whimsically if I will self-destruct after delivery. "And you both gotta *mean* it, Arnie. No faking it, this time, you hear what I'm saying? You have both to utter those three little words for real and out loud."

"For… real?" whispers Arnie.

"Uh huh. Out loud."

"*I – love – you?*"

The cabbie reaches an arm out behind him and deftly slides closed the glass divider. He is aware that Yanks can be a lot more free with their emotions than the buttoned-up natives of this island, but not on his watch, thank you very much.

"See, once you feel it and say it for real – say it like you *mean* it, Arnie – you're, like the expression goes, 'as one'. Two souls – one housing. You see? Sorta like Siamese soulmates. And you all live happily ever after. Music. Roll credits. Aaahhh."

To my surprise, at this point Arnie Garth actually smiles. His first for a while.

"That's it? So basically, it's what I just said, I gotta score with some babe. Bring it on, Soul Man."

My day just got a lot more difficult.

"No, Arnie," I say gently, as if talking to a three-year old. Not that I get to chat to too many of those, thank the Lord. "You have to make her love you. L-O-V-E, as the late Nat King Cole used to sing. And still does, try and stop him – but that's another story."

Oh, okay, thinks Arnie, his brows making those ridges like deep thinking is something pretty new to him, which I very much suspect it is.

"Well, once she knows that if she doesn't start lovin' me pretty damn quick, she'll be sending me to an early death and straight down to hell, she'd have to be a seriously mean broad not to go the extra mile."

"Oh."

"Whaddaya mean 'oh'?"

"Did I not say this? Mea culpa." I shake my head, somewhat sadly. "Arnie, my friend, you gotta make her love you *without* you revealing what we might both call the 'backstory'. Not that your particular cinematic genre goes gangbusters on backstory. Blow my cover, tell her she got your soul as a twofer with her own in some heavenly bureaucratic balls-up, and you instantly void the offer. Plus, of course, you'll be dead."

"Hey, pal," insists Arnie, with a smile of total (and totally unjustified) smugness, "the only thing getting blown here will be me. You, sir, are looking at the Warren Beatty of hardcore. I can charm any dame I meet."

I have to smile back at him. It's not often one of my guys leaves me to deliver the perfect exit line. Or at least not one they're still alive to hear.

"Arnie, you haven't met Noreen Millburn."

Chapter Five

History is constantly teaching, but it does not find many pupils.
(Austrian proverb)

By the time Arnie Garth's black cab finally – and I can only imagine triumphantly – enters the sleepy little Cumbrian village where this Noreen-two-souls is meant to hang out, I am nowhere to be seen (or to be not-seen) and Arnie's lower back is giving him hell.

So, he is quite relieved when they pull up at the old marketplace in the very heart of Rough Fell. And even more heartened to find, right there on a corner, The Wordsworth Arms, a local pub which advertises rooms to rent.

It is, not unexpectedly, dark and drizzly, so the newcomer has scant opportunity to appreciate the beauty and grandeur of the landscape in which he has surprisingly found himself. He can see only the vaguest outlines of the hills, or maybe even mountains, that surround him. He can, of course, still admire, by the light of the quasi-Victorian streetlamps, the dusty grey stonework of the picturesque village itself, and the rustic Cumbrian charm of this historic market square, with its tiny shops and cafés and replica gibbet. But naturally he does no such thing, because

Arnie Garth, late of LA, doesn't give a shit about scenery. The bucolic makes him nauseous, and he just wants his bed.

When he eventually manages to extricate himself, in some considerable pain, from the steamy rear of the cab, Arnie notices that a few of the locals, who are hovering outside the pub, have chosen to stare fixedly, if slightly blearily, at him. They look as if they could have been here for centuries, in their drab rustic garb, holding dusty pint glasses and being dour and drizzled upon. He wonders for a senseless moment if they actually recognise him – he has been known to do an Alfred Hitchcock in some of his movies (if Hitch ever did a cameo stark naked and treated his surname as a direction). Then he realises that he is still dressed for southern California, in skimpy Hawaiian shirt, linen pants and shades. He starts to shiver.

"Right, guv," says the cabbie, hefting Arnie's Louis Vuitton suitcase from the trunk of his cab and dumping it on the damp and cobbled street. "That'll be five hundred and eighty-seven quid."

"You are fucking kidding me!" says Arnie Garth, which causes the locals to laugh in gentle derision.

"Call it a round six hundred," says the cabbie, as Arnie begins peeling off nearly all the notes from the serious wad in his pocket.

The cab driver grabs the money swiftly and leaps back into his vehicle, glad to see the back of his weird passenger and indeed of the equally mystifying North. But before he leaves, he hurls one final thought into the chill Lakeland air.

"*Anyone going to Heathrow?*"

Always worth a try but sadly, no takers. Yet the Cockney-eyed optimist still switches on his 'for hire' light, as he roars off around the square and back to southern normality.

Arnie lifts his suitcase out of a convenient puddle and trudges towards the pub, nodding to the curious customers, who simply stare in vaguely threatening silence, like assorted townsfolk in a Dracula movie.

The heavy door opens with a creak. Of course it does.

The pub interior, decked out with everything from ancient wooden ploughshares on the ceiling to cracked old pharmaceutical bottles on practically every shelf, is itself like a tired film set. Indeed, some years ago, when he naively thought that his audiences gave a damn about storylines, or at least would appreciate his doing so, Arnie had constructed something not dissimilar that was meant to be set in the Highlands of Scotland. Despite the novelty of pop-up kilts and the tossing of human cabers, *Throb Roy* had not been a success and he had reverted to less atmospheric, LA-style dross.

Determined not to be intimidated by the scrutiny of yet more beery villagers, Arnie drags his now sopping suitcase to the well-stocked and brightly lit bar. Local ales vie with national favourites, whilst above them, lined up like soldiers preparing for battle and imminent vanquishment, is a formidable array of spirits, some of which Arnie has actually heard of and several of which he wouldn't touch unless his mouth was forced open. To his relief the landlord, a huge man with a red face and equally fiery foliage, offers him a warm smile from behind his beard and bar, accompanied by something in an almost impenetrable accent.

"And a good evening to you, sir. What can I get you?"

"Huh?"

The larger man repeats his words, only slower and far louder, which usually works with foreigners. And idiots. Looking at his visitor's attire he senses that he might have struck the double here.

"Bourbon with a twist. And the number of the nearest Sheraton."

"Ah," grins the landlord, from somewhere inside the hair. "You're looking for a place to stay. Well, today's your lucky day, sir."

Arnie seriously doubts it but keeps his own counsel.

"It just so happens we've got a lovely old room available, one of our finest and most historic, with a splendid view of the hills and a spacious bathroom very nearly ensuite. First time in the Lakes, sir?"

"You mean people come back?"

The landlord gives a deep, rumbling laugh. "You've been learning irony on the plane coming over."

He calls to a young woman who, as Arnie now notices with an appreciation both chemical and professional, is bending firmly over a long low table at the far end of the room, in order to collect the empty glasses. "Rosie, kindly escort our new guest to The Windermere Room."

When the young woman slowly slides herself back over the table and turns to stare at Arnie, the visitor's first wish is that she could have been named Noreen. For this is a person with whom Arnie Garth could quite easily imagine falling in love, and of course she with him. Not that he has ever fallen in love with anyone, if he is being honest, except possibly himself. Nor, to his knowledge, has anyone actually uttered those simple, somewhat helpless, all too profoundly exposing words in his vicinity. At least not with any earnestness. Or whilst entirely sober.

This actually doesn't upset him in the least.

He has no need for these crass and humiliating outpourings of affection – well, at least he hadn't until this life-or-death week – and he would in fact have been quite embarrassed, indeed nonplussed, should they ever have been aimed in his direction. When he thinks about it, he does believe that on a couple of occasions Cleo herself might have come pretty close, but he could be mistaking this for something she once said in a movie.

Arnie ponders on this but knows in his heart – if indeed he has one and this hasn't also gone to someone less deserving down the line – that really, he doesn't much care.

In a curious way, Arnie Garth can now almost justify to himself the relentlessly appalling behaviour, in thought, word and deed, that he is well aware causes so many others to think so very badly of him. To detest him, in fact. It was simply an accident of birth. A snafu in the system. Not his fault and nothing he can do about it. Except, of course...

But she's tomorrow's problem.

"This way, sir," says Rosie. "Mind your head," she adds, just a fraction too late to stop him from banging his baldness really hard on a dimly lit and unnecessarily low Tudor beam.

"Owwww!!!!"

He can hear the unmuffled laughter from the locals, as he follows the young woman's appealingly nimble frame up the narrow staircase. He doesn't catch the landlord happily chalking another tick onto a slate behind the bar.

"Ayyyy – ooohhh – owwww!!!" continues Arnie's Elizabethan serenade.

"You really want to watch out for those beams," says Rosie, pertly manoeuvring herself around another hairpin stair-bend.

"Ya think?" grumbles Arnie in the darkness, once again knocking his suitcase into the historic structure's oppressively tight and deceptively curving walls. It's like being on an antique version of Space Mountain.

"Elizabethan folk – they were smaller than we are," explains Rosie. She turns to him with a mischievous grin, as they appear to reach their destination. "Smaller all over, probly."

Before he can fully appreciate this attempt at some form of local hospitality or – dare he think it – flirting, she adds, "So, you in from the Coast?"

"Excuse me?" says Arnie in surprise, letting his suitcase drop so that he can rub his dented and bruising head with both sweaty hands.

Rosie opens the door to the aforementioned Windermere Room, whose dominant attribute could indeed be age. This would seem to apply not simply to the bed and the period furniture, but to the linen, the paintwork, the curtains, the crockery, the television and the dust. In addition to what could well be the original oaken beams and stupidly inadequate windows, the room appears to have retained the original cobwebs and quite possibly odour. There is a large fireplace beside the bed, complete with fully filled brass coal scuttle, neither of which Arnie has the first idea how to use.

Sensing her new guest's unfettered distaste, intercut with a less anticipated sense of mortal terror, whose origins she has no way of guessing, Rosie immediately opens all the windows and starts to plump up the pillows with enviable vigour. Despite all that is going on for him, including his imminent death or worse, Arnie Garth finds that he can't take his eyes off this alluring little domestic, as she busily skitters around the room, straightening and nudging things with solid shoulders, pointy elbows and tiny feet, in an exercise redolent less of Cumbrian welcome than of pure damage limitation.

"You think we've never seen an American before?" she says, in a curiously appealing if not wholly decipherable accent, flicking away what could be biscuit crumbs from a previous guest or century. "You're all over the bloody place round here – like Starbucks. You come up from London, on your way to do Scotland in an afternoon, and you'll fit in some snapping and pottering and a bit of fell-walking for good luck. Some of you even have a go at tracing your ancestors, like they're not all dead and buried. Is that why you're here?"

Arnie, whose current mission is trying not to be an ancestor just yet, shakes his battered head. But Rosie is clearly on a roll.

"We had a film crew in a while back. Took over the whole sodding village and drank everything going. That movie about Wordsworth and Coleridge, did you see it?"

She points to a framed still on the wall, just above a battered kettle and a jug of milk on the turn. It shows a very young and fairly solemn Tom Cruise and an equally stern Denzil Washington wearing frilly shirts and long, curly wigs. Underneath is the logo of the movie, done like two scratchily quilled signatures: *WILL & SAM*.

"That art-house crap?" sneers Arnie. "It only did $10 million domestic. And that was *despite* the Oscar nod for best hair."

Rosie's wide hazel eyes suddenly flame up like those bonfires the Brits light every year to celebrate their Parliament not being blown to smithereens, although some apparently regret it now. She turns to her guest with renewed interest.

"Are you in The Industry?"

Arnie gives a falsely modest shrug. "You just blew my cover. Why do you ask, Rosie?"

"Because I… I'm an actress!"

"Oh, shit. *No shit?*" He dumps his suitcase on the bed, which appears to sink visibly. "So, you appear in the movie?"

The smile instantly vanishes from the young woman's winsomely freckled face. "*No!* I didn't even know they were shooting a poxy movie, did I? I was working in a bar over in Ibiza, wasn't I? Just 'cos I was on holiday, I'd missed every sodding thing, hadn't I? And it is *so* unfair, 'cos I *am* an actress, aren't I? The best one in the whole village! *I was Annie!*"

"Yeah?" says the weary guest, who is losing interest fast.

To Arnie's surprise and instant upturn in interest, the pretty barmaid now gets down on her knees directly in front of him. Before he can fully begin to marvel at the unanticipated but far from unwelcome level of hospitality accorded to people in his industry by young English womanhood – and just as he is wondering if this is in fact a test from heaven – Rosie begins to sing *Maybe* from her musical triumph *Annie*.

"Unbelievable!" proclaims a somewhat thrown Arnie, attempting to maintain enthusiasm. "And so unexpected."

"You like it?" she says, continuing to belt out the famous opening song at an even greater volume.

"'Like' isn't the word, kid. Please stop." He smiles at her in gratitude for the sudden silence. "Hey, maybe I can find a part for you in *Will and Sam – Reloaded!*"

"They're making another *Will and Sam*? But you just said—"

"It did great on DVD. Go figure. Say, did this Wordsmith have a girlfriend?"

"Wordsworth? I don't know... Ooh, ooh, I think he had a sister."

"Even better!" Arnie suddenly looks out of the dusty window, as a cloud crosses the moon. He finds himself shivering and knows that it is not just fatigue. "So, Rosie whatever your name is, star of the future, what can you tell me about a local 'lassie' – Noreen Millburn?"

Rosie gawps at the man for a second. Next comes a frown. Then she begins to laugh. In fact, the laugh continues to build, as if she has just heard the funniest joke going. The sort of mirth that expresses itself out of your nose as well as in your smile.

"Ha! I've got to get back to work. Ha! *Noreen Mill...!*" The laughter soars. She snorts again. "Noreen Millburn!"

Arnie can hear her joyous laughter all the way down the stairs. This would have disturbed him, save for the fact he is fast asleep before she has even avoided the final beam.

Chapter Six

The right answer to a fool is silence. (Afghan proverb)

To Arnie Garth's consternation, as he emerges mid-morning from a long but troubled sleep and another head-banging walk down the stairs, the bar is still pretty crowded with drinkers. They definitely appear to resemble the drinkers of the night before, yet perhaps to the undiscerning eye all Cumbrians, especially the hard-drinking ones, look alike.

The pub's sole transatlantic guest is less surprised by the rain that he can see and hear battering against the hostelry's Tudor windows, obscuring what might otherwise be a rather beautiful view. The very stuff indeed of Ruskinesque watercolours and postcards home. He wonders for a moment if he will ever again be in a mood to appreciate nature's glorious, heaven-bestowed bounty but has to remind himself, if truth be told, that he never really got off on scenery and stuff before this, being far more jazzed up by glitz and neon, tacky suburbia and the buzz of traffic.

Our new guy in town would, however, be the first to admit that today he is dressed to kill. Slick Armani suit, open Versace shirt, shinily expensive Gucci loafers. The Arnie Garth woo-pitching outfit *número uno*. Head-turningly pimp-chic. Looking good, man. No wonder everyone is staring.

Yet, as he ventures into the main bar, with its tarnished horse brasses, old black and white photos of local and long-dead cricket, soccer and darts teams, and seemingly permanent aroma of stale best-bitter, it strikes him that there is something decidedly odd here. At first, Arnie is at a loss to compute what is so disconcerting about a group of staring, semi-moronic drinkers, until he realises that everyone in this fuggy, fusty Tudor room is absolutely silent.

Not just silent. They are all drinking their pints in a weirdly exaggerated, over-animated way, almost as if they are aliens *pretending* to be human boozers in order to blend in, but not quite managing the rudimentary steps. It is only after a few moments that he realises that the drinkers' mouths are actually moving, along with their faces, in that particularly demonstrative manner indicative of lively conversation, yet there is not a single sound emanating from any one of them.

"*What the fuck?*" he mutters. Which, of course, carries in the deepening silence.

Redbeard the Landlord is at it too. He appears to be shouting at him to come over, but without a single accompanying decibel.

When Rosie comes out of the kitchen, carrying three steaming, overcooked English breakfasts on a tray, she immediately understands his bafflement.

"They're background," she explains, somewhat dismissively. "It's what they did in the movie. They're trying to impress you."

Arnie, who thought he was either going insane or being offered a preview of his future trip to hell, sighs in relief. "Yeah? Very good. I am *so* impressed, guys. Leave your names at the bar. Now, Rosie – can you just tell me where I can find Noreen Millburn?"

When everyone in the pub does a massively overemphatic pointing, all in the same direction, towards the open fields beyond, Arnie sighs. Grabbing a lukewarm pork sausage from each of the plates on Rosie's tray, he makes swiftly for the nearest exit.

The sound of silent laughter appears to be ringing in his ears.

*

Some hours later, Arnie knows why this place is called the Lake District.

He reckons he has sunk into one sodden lake or another every second frigging step of the way. This was when he wasn't clambering over stiles – who, in God's name, ever thought stiles were a great idea? – crawling through hedges and trudging through bogs. Of course, he hasn't been getting totally lost on his own. He has had inestimable help from farmers, ramblers, marauding bands of urchins and assorted locals mystifyingly out for a stroll. All of whom, for some inexplicable reason, find the words 'Noreen' and 'Millburn' absolutely hysterical.

By the time he finally sees a wisp of smoke in the distance, which he prays isn't Noreen Millburn self-combusting, Arnie Garth's finest courting outfit is a mud-splattered, shredded mess and he looks like a dripping Rodeo Drive scarecrow.

"This had better be fucking worth it!" he moans into thin damp air. Because somehow, he just knows that I might be listening.

Chapter Seven

It does not matter if your tavern sits in a remote location, so long as the smell of your wine is appealing. (Chinese proverb)

Arnie Garth has just about heard the word 'hovel'.

He had, however, never expected to find himself standing directly outside of one, in the driving British rain. Especially not looking like someone who, after the past few miserable hours, might feel so comfortably at home here.

In some desperation, and to little apparent effect, he attempts to brush off the more dangly and less seeped-in elements of mud and grime from what in happier times, such as this morning, had staked its claim to be his coolest daytime outfit.

He alternates this with shaking his head in a manner which, to the casual observer, might seem disturbingly unhinged, but is today being employed to rid himself of the rough crown of thorns and brambles he senses that he is currently wearing, like Christ on his way to the cross. The resemblance, in his mind, feels like it doesn't end there, as he suspects the day's torture has only just left its first station.

Our dishevelled martyr is about to bang his grubby fist on said hovel's door, when he spies some drenched and wilting flowers in an old window box. Looking around, just in case the Cumbrian flower police might be doing one of its random spot-checks, he swiftly grabs a bunch and arranges them into a makeshift and somewhat pathetic bouquet.

The surplus soil now wiped as best he can from his hands, Arnie Garth smooths down what little there is of his sodden hair, then gives his mouth a bracing spray of Listerine Clean Mint. Finally, he adjusts his crotch and treats himself to another spray down there, because he hasn't notched up his enviable tally of women who do inordinate amounts of sex for a living by having a smelly crotch. For a moment his thoughts turn to Cleo, who must be wondering how and where the hell he is, but the moment passes.

Finally, he gives a solid thump on the door.

And waits.

He has to admit to some nervousness.

After all, he is about to encounter the woman born within seconds of himself who has taken onboard his misplaced soul. And, if Arnie Garth has anything to do with it, the person who will also be the lucky recipient of his ever-loving heart (in the next five days would be good).

When there is no response, he knocks again.

Nothing.

"Don't tell me the stupid bitch is out," he moans into the air, then corrects it to 'stupid broad', just in case.

Finally, when he and his fist have grown weary, Arnie Garth gives the old door a petulant kick. To his surprise, it staggers open on its sagging hinges with a rust-infused creak, and he steps very tentatively inside.

The visitor has just time to register the dim light of candles and oil lamps – and nearly pass out from the horrific stench – when something immense flies across the room and batters into his chest, knocking him backwards onto the room's dusty floor.

"*What the fuccckkk!*" he screams, before receiving a soggy face full of shaggy hair and huge sloppy tongue. For the second time in a matter of days, Arnie Garth believes that he is going to die.

A stern voice from the darkness barks out a command. "*Cheryl! Stop that! Or there is absolutely no story for you tonight!*"

The Old English Sheepdog's lollopy tongue withdraws and its massive face shifts very slightly away, affording Arnie a sight which he would have to admit is not a whole lot better.

"Are you... Noreen Millburn?" he asks, praying for a swift denial and a neighbourly nudge in the right direction.

"I am," says the bobbly-hatted, multi-cardiganed woman.

"Aw, shit," says Arnie Garth.

He reaches up a hand and pulls the huge dog's head back into his field of vision, cutting out Noreen once more.

*

The cup of coffee is vile but at least it is hot and comes with a rudimentary chair. In the flickering light Arnie can see several non-human eyes staring at him with a mixture of menace and curiosity, and one equally disturbing pair of pale blue ones, of unusual lucidity, looking concerned and hardly welcoming.

"I make the coffee myself. From the dandelions outside."

The expectorated liquid lands on the woman's outermost cardigan with a silent splat and finds a home amongst other equally natural, albeit less forcefully delivered, stains. She doesn't even bother to wipe it away.

Arnie Garth stares at his 'host' once again, then ventures a sly but plaintive look heavenwards, as if to say somebody up there really doesn't like me. (NB: We don't, but this is beside the point.) Noreen Millburn has to be the strangest-looking and most bizarre creature he has ever encountered. And this man is from Los Angeles.

He thinks for a moment of the homeless people he sees on the streets back in LA, wearily pushing purloined shopping trolleys filled with their worldly goods, sleeping in parks and under freeways in makeshift tents, panhandling in one of the richest cities in the world. People he passes with barely a glance and without a second thought. They look like guests at the UNICEF Ball compared to this large, woolly woman with the rugged, weatherworn, presumably Lake District face, devoid of make-up or any other mode of concealment, and defiant, prematurely greying hair.

Noreen sits down at the table, so that she can unsettle her visitor more comfortably. Her accent, when she addresses him, comes across as local (circa 1750) and Arnie has to struggle to unravel exactly what she is saying. Even when he does, it makes absolutely no sense, an outcome that fails to surprise him in the slightest.

"I keep telling you people – I am *not* interested," she says, thumping down a large, sandpapery hand on the already rickety table. "And nor is anyone else around here. So please just go away." She points with a knobbly finger towards the door, which is still hanging open and of which Arnie would definitely take rapid advantage were he not on the mission of his amorous life.

"*What people?*" he asks, when the gnarled sounds she is uttering finally identify themselves as what pass for words round here. "I ain't people. I'm Arnie Garth."

Noreen stares at him. "Y-you're not from Apex Holdings… Mr Garth?"

"Who the fu— who the hell are Apex Holdings?" He offers an indulgent laugh. "You got me all wrong, lady. I'm a big Hollywood movie producer…" He pauses for a thoughtful moment. "Of worthy, faith-based, educational films."

The woman looks quite puzzled by this. And not as impressed as she could be. So, Arnie Garth, creative giant, comes up with his masterstroke.

"*And* your long-lost cousin."

He reckons that this is quite inspired. Even though, on looking hard at this Noreen person, whom he seriously doubts has any relatives on two legs, Arnie is already beginning to fear that the whole encounter is an emotional lost cause. A total non-starter in the redemption stakes. A death sentence. If it's true about the Grim Reaper, he could well be staring at her.

"I don't have any cousins," says Noreen Millburn.

"*That's because I'm long lost, you stupid b—*" He stops just in time and ratchets down his anger. Especially as he senses some of the fiercer animals in the room, especially the goats, just preparing to rear. "I mean – I brought flowers!"

He holds up a bunch of pale-green stalks. The more flowery heads are now, thanks to the recent canine assault, strewn all over the floor.

"That's very nice, Mr Garth," says Noreen, never wishing to be impolite. "But I've got flowers, thank you. This is the countryside."

"No kidding." He looks around the dingy, squalid, clearly poverty-ridden old cottage, where strange plastic box things on strings and mounds of knitted woolly objects vie to be the main source of decoration, along with discarded blue wrappers from something unrecognisable. What could pass as admiration, or at least slightly diminished repugnance, colours his face. "Hey, I *love* what you done with this place."

"I haven't done anything with it."

"*Exactly!*" He gestures around the pathetic little parlour. "So many people, they're into… y'know, taste. Cleanliness. Self-respect. But you, Ms Noreen Millburn – you're earthy." He gives her his best, dentally enhanced smile. "I like that in a woman."

For some reason, perhaps nudged by his recent trek and the incessant, gusty rain beating at and through the cottage window, an idea for a movie, involving naked and deeply energetic mudwrestling, slithers like a silty rivulet into his mind.

Somewhere in Slime? Sunday Muddy Sunday? He never ceases to marvel how the fertile creative mind simply refuses to take a break.

Soiling the moment, Noreen thumps his small be-ringed hand with her own heavy fist. As he recoils, she makes a suggestion that takes him completely by surprise.

"Would you like to see something really beautiful, Mr Garth?"

Chapter Eight

A pig used to dirt turns up his nose at rice. (Japanese proverb)

By the time they reach the small lake, barely a pond by local standards, but ravishing in the summer moonlight nonetheless, the rain has miraculously taken a breather. Perhaps it has popped over one of the many adjacent and still stunning mountains, to give the folks on that other side a torrentially hard time.

Arnie Garth, his once fine caramel and cream buffalo leather shoes now encrusted with genuine Cumbrian mud, can at least glimpse the moon now, whose best side dominates the newly cleared sky. If quizzed, not that he is a moon expert, he would be forced to admit that it is indeed larger and possibly even brighter than any moon he has set eyes upon in the past. There are some pretty brilliant stars up there too, in the impressively unpolluted firmament. It is as if someone has poked pinholes in the night then aimed the biggest Klieg light in the world directly at it.

Arnie turns to Noreen, who is staring at the familiar vista with an intensity so rapt she has almost forgotten that her newly arrived and slightly toad-like cousin, long lost and now re-emerged from somewhere or other, is standing right beside her.

"So, where's the beautiful bit?" asks the visitor, just starting to shiver.

Noreen gives a start, which swiftly turns into a throaty chuckle, until she realises that this curious stranger, to whom she hasn't as yet found herself in any way warming but knows in all charity that she must, is completely and utterly serious.

"Just look around you, Mr Garth," she says.

"It's Arnie and I'm lookin'. I been lookin' forever. All I see is scenery and night."

"Well, if Apex Holdings has its way, you won't even see *that!*"

The woman now looks infinitely sad, her wind-hardened face almost caving in with the pain. A block of volcanic Skiddaw slate would be moved to tears.

"No? That is awful!" says an unmoved Arnie Garth, staring into her moistening eyes. "Tell me more, Noreen." He gives her his best smile, tilting his head in the hope that his expensive teeth will glint in the moonlight. "I could listen to you all night."

In movies, even the ones Arnie makes, there are such structural and editing techniques as dissolves or fades, which enable the storyteller to denote the passage of time and hopefully cut out what, for the audience, might be the less involving elements. Such as, for example, the bit between the hunky young plumber parking his van on the posh driveway and the time perhaps a half-hour later, when he leaps upon the delighted and equally posh lady of the house. Which omission might conceivably involve his carrying out the repair of the washing-machine that this subsequently over-grateful lady had actually booked him in to do.

Arnie finds himself wishing that life itself could be as susceptible to an editor's touch. And that he wouldn't still be sitting on a dumb rock beside this apology for a lake, shivering in his cool and now ruined LA clothing, whilst listening to the unintelligible ramblings of a madwoman with whom he has to fall sincerely and genuinely in love within five days, or hellishly die. And, equally impossibly, must induce this sexless swamp-creature to fall madly – or at least sufficiently – in love with him.

"Do you mind if I smoke?" he asks, in a final burst of inspiration, hoping that the heat of a good cigar might ward off almost inevitable hypothermia, if only for a few, warming minutes.

"Of course not, Mr Garth," says Noreen, kindly. "But as a supporter of several lung cancer charities, daily hospice visitor and regular participant in the Pulmonary Pullover Knitathon, I would be remiss if I didn't tell you that you might well die in agonising discomfort as a result."

"Right now, sister, that's the least of my worries," says Arnie Garth, as he lights up one of his precious Romeo y Julietas. "So, tell me about Ajax."

"Apex! I just told you. They want to build it right here – well, just off the road over there." She points into the near distance. "Most of it on my poor late mum's land! In fact, you're sitting just where she's buried."

Arnie begins to squirm. "Must be a first for her. So, what's the problem with a fourteen-screen leisure complex for crissakes? With gyms and shops and bowling alleys and restaurants. You could make a bundle!"

"You would say that. They'd probably be showing your films."

"I wish."

"Nobody seems to understand. I don't *want* money. I'm happy here. This is where I belong. Where I'm wanted. Where I'm needed. This is where I can really do good. All day and every day. *And* night. Including Christmas and Bank Holidays." She pauses for a moment. "On second thoughts…" She rips the cigar out of the bewildered man's mouth and throws it away. "I'm sorry – Arnie. But all life is precious. Even yours."

"Excuse me asking, Noreen – but are you on medication?"

"No."

"You should consider it." Even in the darkness he can feel her staring at him. "Hey, this Latex thing – or whatever – it's your choice. Big deal. Not my problem."

On reflection he decides that he might be better off finding a more seductive point of entry, which, if you think about it, has been his stock-in-trade for years.

"What I mean is, sweetheart – kinfolk – cuz – you should get out more. Schmoozing, networking. Pressing the flesh. Y'know, meeting people."

In the darkness, Arnie can sense his curious companion of the evening flinch. As if somewhere inside all that raw wool and knitted vests, a nerve has been exposed and prodded.

"*I've met – 'people'!*"

Arnie has no idea what to make of this, as it sounded like it was charged with depth and resonance. Our guy doesn't do depth and resonance. So, he is quite relieved when she changes the subject.

"How exactly *are* we related?"

Arnie hadn't fully thought this one through but a name she is seriously unlikely to know springs instantly – and thankfully – to mind.

"Er… exactly through my great-uncle Harry. Harry… Reems."

"Never heard of him."

"No. You wouldn't have. He was kind of… a black sheep."

At this point, with what even Arnie has to concede is impeccable timing, they hear the bleat of a Herdwick coming from right beside them. Arnie had totally forgotten that Geoffrey had joined them for their walk on the wild side.

"Go back to sleep, Geoffrey," coos his foster mum. "So this Mr Reems… ?"

Arnie has no intention of venturing into the lineage and history of the revered Harry Reems, star of *Deep Throat* and *The Devil in Miss Jones*, a man included in the XRCO Hall of Fame (look him up, it'll make your hair curl). But the late, great, ridiculously well-endowed star is going to be a stand-up guy again tonight.

"'Arnie', he'd say, 'if you're ever in' – wherever the hell we are – 'go see Noreen.'" He pauses, remembering those plastic stringy things cluttering up the cottage. "Maybe she can help you… with your leprosy."

Noreen is immediately on the case. In the moonlight Arnie can observe her large eyes, just visible beneath that ridiculous hat, suddenly fill with tears. *How does she do that?* he thinks, wondering, with one eye as ever on niche markets, whether she has other neat tricks.

"You've got *leprosy*, Arnie?"

"It comes and goes," he explains. "Especially… when I'm hungry."

Noreen immediately segues from riven with compassion into wracked with guilt. "Oh, Arnie. I wasn't thinking. I am just so sorry. Can you ever forgive me?"

He can see the bobble on top of her hat quiver with shame.

"I don't get many visitors. Well, not human ones – or Americans. Actually, I don't get any. *Ever.* I've a sort of feeling I know why. I'm not stupid. Oh, just listen to me 'going on'! Would you like something to eat? Yes, of course you would!"

Arnie immediately leaps up from the late Mrs Millburn's makeshift grave, shocking Geoffrey and indeed his equally woolly but slightly more human companion.

"Thought you'd never ask, Señora M! Grab your coat – a little make-up wouldn't hurt – and point me to the nearest Hibachi grill and then we'll—"

He is halted by a massive carrot, as it is deftly withdrawn, like a rabbit from a magician's hat, out of the none-too-pristine top pocket of Noreen's second most uppermost cardigan.

"Here," she offers.

Arnie stares down at it in disgust. "Hey, sister, now Arnie Garth enjoys a good carrot as much as the next man. If the next man is a friggin' vegan nut-job! But I was thinking that maybe we'd go someplace fancy. Y'know, with chairs and stuff. And electricity. Then we could kinda get to know each other."

"I really don't think so," says Noreen. "You see, Mr Garth, I have to be up bright and early in the morning, to clean out the bedpans at the local old peoples' home."

"Boy, you musta done something *really* bad to get that," says the appalled producer. "How many hours did they sentence you to? You have to wear a tunic or—"

"You do talk such rubbish! It's *voluntary*, Arnie. I do it out of love. And then in the afternoon I'm giving blood at two, plasma at three and bone marrow at four. Now come on. Chop chop. I shall give you a lift back to your hotel."

"You drive a car?" says Arnie Garth.

"Not exactly," says Noreen Millburn.

Bouncing up from her rock, as if all the damp and saturated knitting encasing her muscular body weighs nothing, Noreen starts back towards the house at a brisk, no-nonsense pace, leaving Arnie with his carrot. And Geoffrey.

When he stares after her, Noreen Millburn is backlit by that huge, unblemished moon. For a moment, his two-souled Lady of the Lakes appears to emit an unearthly glow. It reminds him, to his horror, of a halo. He suddenly recalls one of his more spiritual movies, *Thong of Bernadette*.

"Jesus Christ!" he says. Turning to follow her, he sees a sleepy sheep looking up at him. Arnie chucks him the unbitten carrot. "Wanna put in a good word for me?" At which old Geoffrey, incontinent at the best of times, simply adds his toxic contribution to the Cumbrian wind.

Chapter Nine

Faint heart never won fair lady. (English proverb)

Arnie has never seen a 1950s BSA motorcycle and sidecar, let alone been transported in one. *Mad Max* springs instantly to mind, but he senses that this journey could be infinitely more deranged.

He doesn't believe that he would be feeling any more uncomfortable if he had simply been parcelled up in cardboard, secured with twine and mailed back to the dismal village in whose environs he has unfortunately found himself.

Our benighted passenger has no illusions that Noreen Millburn, in her World War Two helmet and goggles, can even *hear* his screams over the engine's angry yet oddly asthmatic roar, as the rusty contraption bumps and rattles over what apparently pass as roads in the wilder reaches of England's celebrated Lake District. Arnie sees absolutely nothing to celebrate, as the same black, blue and balding American head that had struck every low-slung Tudor beam just hours before is yet again finding something brain-damagingly unyielding with which to connect.

So, it comes as no surprise to the beery regulars of The Wordsworth Arms to be witnessing their village's (and indeed the entire region's) most eccentric resident enter its local hostelry with a scrunched-up fellow traveller cradled like an oversized infant in her burly arms. But they still keep their distance. (And 'eccentric' is my word, not theirs.)

Arnie is in too much pain to notice the communal recoil on his and Noreen's arrival. But he just catches a muttered, "it's alright, lad – no cans", a remark he misinterprets on first hearing as being mysteriously sexual, until he realises that the crowd is simply expressing its relief that for once in a millennium, Noreen Millburn is not collecting. She is, in fact, doing quite the reverse. The laden woman is clearly delivering.

The universal sigh follows them up the stairs, as they hear Noreen's helmet crash into every beam going, alongside Arnie's yelps as one after another rarely used muscle goes into spasm.

"How's the stiffness?" asks Noreen, as they reach the top of the stairs, where she has been informed that Arnie's room awaits.

"I'm working on it," says Arnie instinctively, employing lines from his old movies to centre and calm him, much in the manner decent people use mantras or affirmations.

She sets him down on the worn carpet outside his room, although his posture remains much the same as when he was in the sidecar. To an observer he would resemble an oversized foetus with a tan.

Noreen gives the heavy but low wooden door a tiny push. It creaks open.

"I musta forgot to lock it." He smiles in what he considers a charming manner. "In my excitement at meeting you after all these years, cousin." A thought suddenly strikes him. "But not such a close relative that we can't…"

"Can't what?" asks a genuinely mystified Noreen, at the doorway.

"Y'know." His mind is racing. "Obviously, the way I am now, the pain I'm in, I'll need your help, Noreen, sweetheart. Undressing. Getting into bed. Ordering breakfast…"

Arnie leads the way, managing to straighten up slightly into what he might consider, were he in a classical frame of mind, a sort of Richard III configuration. Moving round the door, in this summer of his discontent, he can't help but notice, in the dusty, moonlit room, that there is a person already in his bed.

Waving.

He has a pretty good idea who it is. And what she isn't wearing.

Instantly he straightens up and cracks his head on the doorframe. Ignoring the shock and the dizziness, he backs out of the room – right into his deliverer, almost knocking her down the stairs.

"*Mr Garth!*" exclaims Noreen. "What is it?"

"Nothing! It's nothing, my sweet!" He is thinking impressively fast for someone with possibly permanent brain damage. And talking surprisingly quietly. "Y'know, it has been just so great, Noreen," he whispers. "You, me, the stars, the carrot. Funny, I feel like I've known you all my life. Longer, even. And I get like we're truly bonded. You know. *Soulmates in fact.* Please, call me Arnie. Now – go away."

Noreen has no idea whether to feel flattered, valued or dismissed. But she has a lifetime's experience of knowing where she isn't wanted. Which round here is practically everywhere. Except perhaps where she is doing her good work, and even then she senses that the people who value her contribution immensely and are totally overawed by her self-sacrifice (she has even volunteered to catch salmonella in place of someone more vulnerable), still can't help feeling that she is a royal pain in the arse. So, despite being somewhat taken aback, she graciously shrugs and retreats, with her helmeted head bowed low, down the precarious stairs.

"Goodnight, Mr Garth," she mumbles.

As she arrives at the first, semi-lethal turn of the staircase, Noreen Millburn reaches deep into the over-generous pocket of her most intimate home-knitted cardigan and produces a small, white ferret.

"That is a very odd person, Stanley," she informs the bemused rodent.

*

Rosie gives the room's paying guest a massive beam – but not a Tudor one – as he gently closes the door.

"Thank you for winning the war," she smiles, allowing the bed linen to fall where it may.

Arnie smiles at this lovely and incredibly hospitable young woman. He had heard that the Brits could be a bit frosty, but this is a standard of room service for which even Fodor's would award five stars.

"Is this just because I'm a major Hollywood producer, looking to cast his next big movie with local talent?" he asks.

To which she simply grins.

"Hey, it works overseas too!"

Despite the near-concussion, Arnie Garth moves towards Rosie, instinctively unbuttoning his mud-splattered shirt. Remember, this is a guy who found his way here without any moral compass.

Yet a sudden sound from outside in the street makes him pause at the foot of the bed. It is the sputtering of Noreen's ancient motorbike, with its empty sidecar. He immediately drops the button business and offers the expectant young woman an apologetic smile, tinged with more than a hint of genuine, lust-sodden regret.

"Y'know, Annie…"

"Rosie."

"Whatever – y'know, maybe this ain't such a good idea. Tell you the truth, sweetheart, it's a weird old time for me and… I need to concentrate all my energies on… er, well…"

Rosie slinks out of the bed and glides towards him, draped in a very thin and not entirely pristine sheet.

"Don't tell me you're saving yourself for batty Noreen?"

Now she is standing right next to him. Arnie, who has never refused a good thing – or indeed a mediocre thing – is in a mental agony almost the equal of his musculoskeletal one.

"N-n-no way. I-I-I'm married, Rosie! That's it! I'm a married guy!"

She runs a delicate Cumbrian finger down his unshaven face.

"*Oh – and I'm gay!* I'm a gay, married guy! A gay, married, fundamentalist Christian guy" Now he's imploring. "YMCA! ... Chapel of Love... Amazing Grace."

Rosie, who is no stranger to the classics, appears to regard this as catnip and begins to blow in Arnie's ear.

"Rosie!" he begs. "*Please*, baby – you're putting my weak heart at risk. Not to mention my immortal soul."

"You're a big Hollywood producer. You probably don't have a soul."

"I'm frigging working on it!"

Our soulless Hollywood producer watches with something approaching terror as the young woman's luscious lower lip begins to tremble and her soft hazel eyes go frighteningly moist. This whole business, it should be stressed, is not Rosie's customary MO. Far from it. The inferno of her own ambition has actually begun to terrify even her. But opportunities don't grow on trees, not even in the fertile Lakes, and she is just too damn big for Rough Fell.

"So, you don't want me? Is that what you're saying?"

She rustles the sheet.

Arnie immediately bites his knuckles, until the skin begins to crack. But he knows without looking that he is more than a little aroused.

"Er... yeah. Right. You got it. How freaky is that? Oh – and I have a prostate problem. PSA up the kazoo!"

The young, rejected wannabe star is clearly offended. Wrapping the sheet back firmly and semi-modestly around her, she turns away. "Fine. Fine. I have no idea what that is, probably something American, but I'll go then. Oh, Arnie…"

"Yeah?"

She leans into him again and he can smell the intoxicatingly cheap, mass-produced scent in which she appears to have drenched herself. "If you change your mind…?"

"Yeah?"

Rosie, a woman and artiste scorned, deftly picks up the heavy brass coal scuttle from the olde English fireplace and hangs it where his designer-pants are tightest. He winces in pain.

"Light your own fire."

"Good line!" he manages to grunt, before collapsing at the side of the newly vacated bed.

Chapter Ten

We learn the value of things more in their loss than in their enjoyment.
(Latin proverb)

The two elderly gentlemen lean on their walking frames outside the geriatric ward of the hospital, passing the time of day. Sadly, their bodies have long since begun to let them down.

Yet it is their eyes that they believe are particularly betraying them this sunny California morning, when they glimpse the apparition moving towards them at some speed down the long corridor. Statuesque, clad head-to-toe in defiant scarlet, the woman walks purposefully past them on her extraordinarily high heels, a swaying, short-skirted hip just clipping one of the men's metallic corners.

"Hey!" cries the frailer of the two patients in delight. "Weren't you Melisande?"

"Still am, pops!" she replies, without breaking stride.

The old men smile, relieved that whilst the flesh may be dormant, the horny mind never sleeps.

When Melisande arrives in Arnie's room, the bed is neatly made-up and patently untenanted. The same nurse who had the pleasure of meeting her a couple of days earlier is straightening the pillows.

For a moment Melisande pauses, just staring around her. It seems like the right room, but don't they all look the same? It's hardly the Beverley Hills Hotel and even porn goddesses can make mistakes. No, she tells herself, this is definitely the same room in which she last saw the little rat all tubed-up and ready to go.

"Oh, my God!" she cries, sinking to her knees, which isn't the simplest posture to manage, in her figure-clenching dress and all those years of bodily wear and tear.

"Arnie… my husband. He…"

"He's gone," says the nurse, whose name tag reads *Endora*. "Checked out."

"Gone? Checked out?" The megastar grips the woman with both talons. "Oh, Encino. H-he… can't have…"

"Day before yesterday. And it's Endora. Like in *Bewitched*."

"Whatever… my eyes are too full of tears." Melisande suddenly goes into full grieving-widow mode, which curiously involves a certain amount of nifty unbuttoning, as if the venue – so resonant of earlier triumphs – has sparked off a Pavlovian response. "My poor, sweet Arnie! The love of my life! The man to whom I owe everything. Thank God I've got the entire portfolio of his assets to remind me of him." She is already speed-dialling on her cell phone – "Lazlo, he's dead – get the will into probate now!" – when the nurse stops her.

"No, honey. Sorry to break this to you. But he's not dead."

"You said he's gone. Checked out, you said. I friggin' heard you!"

"Of the hospital."

Melisande grabs the woman with both her famously dexterous hands. "You heartless bitch… don't you get any 'bad-news' training? What happened to his clinging-to-life-by-a-thread diagnosis?"

"Musta decided to cling somewhere else."

Melisande begins to shake the poor nurse vigorously. "*So, where the fuck is he?*"

"How would I know?" says the nurse, unravelling herself. "I'm not married to the poor guy. The doctors did tell him it was against their best advice."

Melisande is back on her cell phone. "You hear that? My husband is obviously not mentally competent." She thrusts her phone at the nurse. "Wouldn't you say?"

"He was talking to himself as he left, but he..."

Melisande starts to lighten up. "Are you *listening?*" she barks to the voice at the other end. "Qualified medical witness – 'Endowment' – 'Endoscopy' – something, it's on her badge – will say Arnie Garth's a total nut-job. Draw up the papers, I'll divorce him after we put his sorry ass in a cheap institution with bars on the windows and Bulge Entertainment, with all its back catalogue and pleasure-enhancing merchandise, will be in more mentally stable hands."

The thought of stable hands brings back unbidden but not unpleasant memories, so it is some seconds later when she notices that the nurse is just staring at her.

"*What?*"

"Why not just kill the sorry bastard and put him out of his misery?"

Melisande suddenly stops breathing. She nods thoughtfully. "So, tell me, Eldorado – any tips on that from nursing school?"

Chapter Eleven

Hope is a good breakfast but a bad supper. (Latin proverb)

We're back in the lovely but distinctly chillier Lake District and onto the following morning.

Which, as I'm still utilising the powerfully immediate present tense (as employed by some of my favourite, not so present authors) is actually right this minute. And isn't staying in this actual moment – the very now of things – what all the therapists these days are swearing is the key to a longer, happier life? At least the ones I meet are.

Mind you…

Anyway. Onwards. Avanti!

Arnie Garth, cleansed, shaved and clad in a freshly inappropriate outfit is making his painful way down the stairs to a much-needed English breakfast. Before he can even grab a rustic chair, he hears a commotion in the normally quiet, and by all accounts quaint, village street.

Suddenly, the pub door flies open and locals of all sorts, male and female, old and young, drab and – well, drab – start piling into the pub. They appear in some sort of a panic and within seconds the small, fusty room is full.

"What's up?" asks the bemused guest. "They playin' a Romanian movie in the street?"

The villagers all stare at him, blank faced, as well they might. With a sigh, he strolls over to the pub door and starts to pull it open.

"*What are you doing, man?*" yelps one of the older villagers.

"*Are you mad?*" calls another.

"*Don't go out there!*" warn almost all the rest.

Arnie gives them a look of contemptuous pity – he's seen that movie – and exits onto the newly-vacated sidewalk (or 'pavement', as for some inexplicable reason the Brits need to call it).

Normally the main street of Rough Fell, which is pretty much its only street, would be bustling with people going about their daily business. Arnie can't imagine what such business might be, in this godforsaken place in the middle of nowhere, but he assumes that the locals know and are happy to bustle at it.

This morning, however, the drizzly street is completely empty. He thinks that he does catch one stray person, in the distance, hammering frantically at a closed door, which opens just a fraction, to allow the desperate soul a full-bodied launch inside.

Cars and vans travelling down the road appear suddenly to pick up speed, as if fleeing a major disaster. And a horse can be spotted galloping off, leaving an inordinate amount of fresh manure on the cobbles.

It is the noise that first alerts a bemused Arnie Garth as to the whereabouts and identity of Rough Fell's keenest and most dire threat. He turns to see a strange figure in the distance. A strange, bulky, clanking, chinking figure, lumbering down the High Street like an automaton out of a vintage science-fiction movie, newly landed from a mechanically advanced but merciless planet, come to take over the world without removing a single cardigan. It is pulling a limping and vaguely disgruntled sheep on a rope tied to the waist.

Arnie, who tells himself that he was more than half expecting this, watches as Noreen Millburn makes her jangly and laborious approach.

The woman is almost completely swathed in collection tins and cans and boxes of all colours and causes. They dangle round her neck, hang over her shoulder, droop under her woolly armpits and swing whilst clamped to a thick leather belt. In fact, it appears as if every square inch of her body is given over to good causes. One collecting can, supporting the oft-ignored plight of distressed Cumbrian donkeys, even hangs from the sturdy bobble on her hat. The woman gives a whole new meaning to charity-case.

"*Jesus Christ!*" mutters Arnie Garth. And this is not a religious man. "Good morning, Noreen."

"I'm not talking to you, Mr Garth," says the rattling woman. "Long-lost cousin or not, you're creepy and very odd." Despite her personal antipathy, with a well-practised bob and lunge she shakes a can right in his face. "Spare a little something for some charity or another?"

Arnie is utterly baffled by the entire concept of surrendering money to someone without even the slightest likelihood of profitable return, at least in this life, but naturally puts it down to the sad weirdo having two souls, one of them rightfully his, so maybe it isn't her fault entirely. Although he seriously doubts that he would be into a whole lot of giving or collecting were he himself to retrieve the precious missing item.

"Charity? *What charity?*"

"I know," sighs the despairing collector. "It's so hard to choose, isn't it? The sadness and deprivation in the world. So much suffering. So many poor people. I could weep for—"

"Yeah, yeah. Enough already. I ain't even had breakfast."

"Well, how about…?" She appears lost in thought but then notices the freshly deposited horse manure on the road just ahead of her. "Ooh, look!" she says, in some excitement.

"You gonna wipe its ass?"

Noreen ignores him and rattles off to pick up the recent droppings with her large-mittened hands. She then distributes it all with a brisk flourish into a nearby window box.

"Wonderful for geraniums! Mrs Godber will be thrilled," she smiles, smacking her woolly palms together.

"Good for Mrs Godber," says Arnie, dodging the fallout. "But where does that leave you, Lady Shit-For-Free? Pair of ruined, not very nice gloves. Stinky fingers. Charity is for suckers!"

Arnie Garth can tell by the horrified look on the woman's rosy-cheeked, cosmetic-free face that he might perhaps have said the wrong thing. Again. Especially if he wants Noreen Millburn to warm to him pretty fast – Sunday at the latest – which even he recognises isn't looking hugely probable right now.

He stares into her open mouth, trying to ignore the jagged teeth that he puts down to English dentistry and too many raw vegetables.

"Hey, joking. I'm joking, Noreen! You *know* me, lady. Well, you will. I am such a loveable kidder. Here…"

He reaches into his pocket, produces a nickel and drops it into her tin. She just stares at him in disgust. He finally takes the message on board and laughs.

"What did I tell you? Such a tease! Ask anyone in the porn—Portland, Oregon area."

He reaches into his pocket again, produces a roll of bills and shoves them into a random tin, so that half of them are still proudly sticking out.

"Buy an orphanage or something."

Noreen Millburn's mouth remains open, this time not from horror but in awe.

"Mr Garth… Arnie… that's really generous! No one has ever… if I'm lucky, I get 50p. Usually it's buttons or tiddlywinks – I'm, well, I'm overwhelmed."

"You *are*?" smiles Arnie, in some relief. "Well, that's what

I came here to tell you, kiddo. The reason I'm so friggin' attracted to you is *I'm a philanthropist too!* I– help the lonely and unattractive."

"That's... interesting."

"I give back. Okay, our styles are different – maybe I'm just a tiny bit too brash, too American. You – you're seriously weird and dress like a bag-lady. But deep down, where it counts, in the kishkes, we're kindred spirits, Noreen! With an emphasis on the kin. Hey, enough of the foreplay. You wanna eat dinner tonight?"

"I eat dinner every night," she says, in confusion.

In a cage, hanging outside a pretty little cottage, is a solitary budgie. Casually, Noreen undoes the metal latch and sets the little bird free.

"*I meant with me*, you dumb... I mean, I'd like to take *you* for dinner. Like you was a normal person. Pick you up at seven."

"Oh! Well... alright, Arnie. Thank you. But I'm normally in bed by eight."

"From your lips to God's ears," says a hopeful Arnie Garth, sauntering back towards the Wordsworth Arms for a well-earned breakfast. He doesn't notice Rosie watching him grumpily from an upstairs window, feather duster in her hand, illusions of stardom slowly draining from her heart.

At the little home with the now reeking window box, a door opens. Into the damp morning air wafts a plaintive but all-too-familiar lament.

"*The bugger's done it again!*"

Chapter Twelve

He that feeds upon charity has a cold dinner and no supper.
(Turkish proverb)

A bright red Ferrari 200 is whispering along the narrow country road, through the persistent evening rain. From the state-of-the-art stereo system Tony Bennett sings his crooning heart out, never realising that he is part of some soulless pornographer's increasingly desperate seduction plan.

In the distance, a respectable arrangement of lights gives the hint that here at least could be one building worth stopping for and not just another crumbling farmhouse or hairy-roofed cottage. A flash of oncoming headlights and the angry hoots of some very insistent horns suggest to the arrogant dickhead with the show-offy car that he might be safer sticking to the British side of the road.

When they finally arrive at the exclusive country house hotel, an establishment which a kindly lady at the Rough Fell Post Office has recommended to Arnie as the finest in the Lakes (the landlord at The Wordsworth having insisted that no grub in the area could possibly match his own), the harassed and exhausted driver pulls up with some relief outside the front entrance.

The car is already attracting some admiring looks. And rightly so. It is a vehicle which Arnie has hired at huge expense, with serious hints of future location filming, from a swish dealership in the nearest major centre. Arnie reckons that it makes him look so hot that he could happily even screw himself (an option that has been suggested to him quite often in the past).

Sadly, the same can't be said of his guest for the evening, who appears simply to have altered the layering of her cardigans – so that a former under-cardy is now promoted to top dog. But she has at least added a flower to her bobbly hat, even though it looks more like a fern.

A smart diner in a tuxedo is emerging from the building as they arrive. Arnie hands him the car keys. "This is costing me a bundle to rent," he tells the perplexed man. "So park it close. And no monkeying around with the radio."

Arnie, her attentive escort for the evening, guides Noreen gently towards the hotel doorway, where she stops. Rigid. Frozen. Unable to move. Arnie practically has to drag her into the lobby. He can feel the poor woman shaking, or at least wobbling, under all her layers.

"I have never been anywhere like this before, Arnie," says a wide-eyed and more than somewhat intimidated Noreen Millburn.

"Get outta here!" marvels her host, in well-faked surprise. "Well, Lady Noreen of Rough Fell, eat your heart out! And the evening has only just begun."

Winking suggestively to the intrigued and only slightly repelled receptionist, the not-very-quiet American accompanies his guest for the evening into the sparkling, triple-rosetted, country house hotel restaurant.

"Prepare for the night of your life!"

*

Arnie Garth is quite accustomed to people staring when he enters a classy joint. But he knows that in LA this is because they stare at everyone who comes in, just in case it is someone they know, ought to know or would very much like to know. He rarely fits into any of these categories, as he is in a particular and rather more circumspect niche, albeit a highly lucrative one. Wannabe stars are hardly like to rush up to him in public, or ask to join him at a table in order to demonstrate what they are capable of, as there are laws against such things at mealtimes. Even in LA.

The staring this evening is of a different order.

What on earth is he doing with her? or, *What in God's name is she doing with him?*, is a game played with unremitting joy and blissful meanness all over the globe. It appears to have reached its apogee this drizzly evening. It is not that Arnie is a catch so magnificent that one could expect only a goddess to match his aura. It is simply that the component parts of this intriguing couple would appear to inhabit two totally different worlds. One tackily foreign, the other vaguely subterranean.

Yet Arnie is far less focused on the manner in which other bemused diners are looking at him than he is preoccupied with how intensely his wide-eyed guest is gazing back at them. And not just at *them*. A bedazzled Noreen is taking in everything from the velvety drapes to the gleaming silverware to the glittering chandeliers. And, of course, the sneering yet unctuously subservient waiting staff.

Finally, she turns to Arnie and says, in the same voice she uses for calling her sheep back home and scaring away the foxes from her chickens, "Wouldn't this place make a *fantastic* shelter for the homeless?"

Arnie sighs. He really has no answer to this. Nor, apparently, has the remainder of the restaurant's clientele, who are looking at each other with a mixture of furrowed brows and shaking heads.

"Hey, why don't I order some wine? Red or white? How about three of each?"

"I don't drink, Arnie."

"Of course, you don't," sighs her host, resignedly. "Crystal meth?" Naturally his native wit leaves this particular dazed native simply confused.

A smartly dressed young waiter has been observing them in some disbelief. As if he has drawn the shortest straw, he makes his tentative way to the table and hands each of them a menu. He then sidles swiftly away, fearing they might be infectious, and escapes back into the kitchen, a succession of dramatic sighs left to hover in the air.

"Okay, let's order," says Arnie swiftly, starting to read. He smiles at his guest in what he has been led to believe is his most irresistible manner. And nothing to do with it usually being aimed at young women who aspire to a career in erotic cinema.

Noreen, however, appears to be ducking rather nimbly out of range of this particular megawatt beam, immersed as she is in the tall, leather-bound object she has just been handed.

"I don't understand, Arnie," she says, shaking her head. She is almost in tears. "This menu…"

Arnie checks it out. "It's in French, sweetheart. They do that in fancy places, so everything sounds expensive. Looks like they don't even translate it here, lazy stiffs."

He looks around and snaps his fingers at a waiter with fake insouciance, which causes all the diners around them to pretend even harder not to stare at the couple.

"I'll get penguin-boy."

After a fair amount of judicially ignored snapping, and close to the point at which the unseasonly attired guest is starting to resemble a coked-up Flamenco dancer, another bored waiter strolls languidly over.

" Hi," says Arnie, swiftly shoving a bill into the waiter's top pocket and winking at him. "This is kind of a special occasion. Know what I'm saying?"

The waiter nods, although he can't for a moment deduce what sort of special occasion this could be and would rather not employ his imagination in the exercise. Arnie understands that it probably won't aid the situation to tell him that if Cupid doesn't get his friggin' arrow through all those cardigans by Sunday, this guest from across the pond will have had his Last (criminally overpriced and French) Supper.

"What's good today?" he asks, then smiles at Noreen. "Or should I say, *bon*?"

"No, you shouldn't and it's all good, sir," says the waiter, a bit sniffily, in Arnie's opinion, but hey, this is England. "May I recommend the *brochette d'agneau*?"

"Oh yeah. You most certainly may. I love a good – broshet. And the lady will have the same. But see that you make 'em biggies. None of your *nouvelle* BS. And no skimpin' on the fries."

He winks at Noreen. How can she not love his restaurant presence, his cosmopolitan élan?

The evening is going even better than he expected.

*

"*Ayyyghhhg!!!*"

The mounting shrieks and wails of the bizarre woolly female at table eleven, a person who appears to have decided to savour the Michelin stars whilst resembling the Michelin man, are starting to convert the other diners' already piqued interest into something approaching restaurant trauma.

Unaware of the stares, Noreen is gazing down at her plate of neatly skewered meat as if she has just entered a crime scene. Which perhaps, for her, it is. Arnie, who is all too aware of the unwanted attention, tries frantically to comfort her, before they get both of themselves ejected.

"Noreen! Sweetheart! Cousin. It's not like you *knew* the friggin' sheep! Hey, tell you what – I'll order some carrots. Nice big, raw ones. You're not pals with any oysters, are you?"

The man's comforting is to no avail, his dinner guest is inconsolable. Finally, Noreen Millburn shakes her still-bobbled head.

"I'm not hungry, Arnie. I knew I shouldn't have come." She stares at him in total bewilderment, tears glooping down her face, as she gestures all around the gilded triple-rosette cage. "*This – this isn't me!* Why did you bring me here? You hardly know me!"

Arnie leans across the table and hands Noreen a monogrammed silk handkerchief, hoping that she won't actually discern what happy little body part the monogram designer has cleverly contorted his client's initials to represent. She wipes her eyes and face, then blows her nose with some considerable power. He gestures that she should maybe keep the handkerchief.

When the snorting and subsequent deluge have passed their peak and he can make himself heard without alerting the entire restaurant, who right now appear to be all ears as well as all eyes, Arnie adopts his most sincere and indeed humblest voice (which has been known to work gangbusters in the past).

"Okay, Noreen, sweetheart. It's time I levelled with you. I brought you here because... because..." The man can hardly talk, he is so choked up.

Noreen knows this, because he stutteringly informs her so, before segueing more nimbly into the autobiographical bit.

"Noreen, sugar, people don't know this, don't even suspect it. Of me, Arnie Garth, big shot Hollywood producer of – uplifting, faith-based motion pictures. They think my life must be one long round of adoration and non-alcoholic parties. Truth is, I – I'm alone in the world. Entirely alone. Orphaned. Unmarried. Unloved. Unwanted. Hard to believe, I know."

He allows time for her to interrupt, which she doesn't, so he continues with his final pitch.

"And because – goddammit – you're a very attractive woman, Noreen!"

"No, I'm not."

"You got me. But hey, who needs tits and ass? Those I can…" He has a feeling people are leaning so far over from other tables they're about to topple into the aisles or their entrees, so he dials down to a whisper. "You've got something better than looks, Noreen Millburn. You know what you got?"

"A sheep?"

"No! Forget the friggin' sheep, for crissakes! I'm talkin' about what brings us together. I'm talkin' about our souls."

"*Arseholes?*" says Noreen over-loudly, which would be a conversation stopper anywhere. "What have arseholes got to do with it?"

"*Everything!*"

Arnie is a touch bemused by the reaction, as to his unschooled American ears she is just repeating his sincerities in a silly accent. But he ploughs on.

"What I'm saying is, Noreen sweetiepie, you've got a soul the size of – of the Lake District. In fact…" And at this point he looks around, just in case I, Ambrose, might be listening. "Between you and me, Ms Millburn, you got a soul to spare."

Near the wind, Arnie Garth. Near the wind.

Now that she is persuaded that the man is not, in fact, talking orifice – and despite her own better judgment – Noreen begins genuinely to soften at this.

"Oh… oh… thank you, Arnie. No one has ever said this about me."

"Perhaps it's just 'cos – they couldn't get near enough." He shakes his head, in what he hopes will pass as genuine admiration. "I mean, the way you help people. Not normal decent people… we're talking sad losers here, no-hopers, deadbeats, sickos, dumb stinky livestock." He smiles as a new thought strikes him. "Hey, it... it's like this movie I just been making – about the animal nut. You know, Saint Francis the sissy."

Noreen brightens at this. Her pale blue eyes, which aren't her worst feature, begin to sparkle and gleam.

"*Getaway!* My late mum used to call me Saint Noreen!"

"Get outta here! Well, Saint Noreen – did I tell you I was an orphan? Twice." Tears well in Arnie Garth's cunning little eyes. "Both parents. One to Ebola, the other a stray bullet. I got nobody." His voice begins to crack. "If... if I spend just one more lonely night alone and on my own, by myself, with no one to talk to, no one to care about me, playing solitaire for one and doing other solo stuff, I think I'll surely die." He grabs his napkin and wipes his eyes. "I'm... sorry. I'm so sorry, Noreen. You must think I'm beyond pathetic. Trust me, I don't usually..."

Her strong, cracked hands, which still smell slightly of sheep and goat, despite a goodly rub of her best carbolic (on both her *and* her furry companions), move slowly across the table to make contact with his own. He feels their roughness, as they graze his suntanned skin like sandpaper.

"Oh Arnie. If there's any way I can help...?"

Arnie swiftly removes a hand and grabs a room key from his pocket. "Room forty-three. I'll be up in a minute." He slides it across. "Make yourself at home."

A muffled cheer rises from the surrounding tables, although whether it is from relief or admiration we shall probably never know.

Chapter Thirteen

Character is like pregnancy. It cannot be hidden forever.
(African proverb)

When he enters the small but charming bedroom that he has somewhat optimistically reserved for the occasion, Arnie Garth is happy to discover that Noreen has been sufficiently naive to act upon his invitation, which is always a plus.

He is less delirious that she has managed to find her way onto a TV channel showing an XXX erotic movie. Arnie can only assume that there was a glitch with the previous check-out, as he can hardly believe a fancy hotel like this clicks onto such a channel as a matter of course.

And ask yourself, who else in this story could be responsible?

When he suddenly realises that the movie is in fact one of his own – not exactly a classic but, in its own humble way, a representative example of his oeuvre (with its signature 'positions' instantly identifiable to the connoisseur) – Arnie Garth's surprise turns to alarm. If she catches the opening or closing titles, his name and that of his company are all over it. He may even – he can't quite remember – have a cameo.

Heaven forbid.

"*Arnie – look at this!*" says Noreen, pointing to the screen.

A strappingly handsome archaeologist has completed the unwrapping of a perfectly preserved and well-formed female mummy, one who is apparently more than happy to continue what she was doing two millennia earlier, with some Rameses or another.

"I *know!*" says Arnie, in a shock which, in its own way, is absolutely genuine. "And Noreen, I am just ashamed to be a member of the same species as the vile degenerates who spew out this... garbage! Look at it. Corrupting! Degrading! Never mind the excellent lighting and state-of-the-art camerawork! So different from the highly educational, spiritually uplifting movies I make. Who would even watch *Yummy Mummy*? Or whatever it's called."

"It's not disgusting, Arnie," says Noreen, which causes him to do a double-take of which any comedian would be proud.

"It's not?" he says, suddenly hopeful.

"No. It's sad."

"Of course, it is. You are so right. More than sad. Tragic. *Tsk.* Why, exactly?"

"Do you really need to ask, Arnie?"

He nods. He really does need.

"These young men and women, so beautiful and healthy-looking, they should be learning about feelings. About emotions. And – and yes, about *kindness*. What's more, they ought to be trying to convey these qualities to others. And not just indulge in – in meaningless sex."

"Noreen, you're a mind-reader! We speak the same language, kiddo. And you wanna know something? I feel for you. I do. In a sort of emotionally kind and meaningful way. You wanna use the bathroom first? Maybe spray all those clothes and yourself with something flowery."

The woman stares at him, as if pennies are just beginning to drop and she isn't warming to the sound nor to the thought of picking them up.

"*Arnie!* You said in the restaurant not fifteen minutes ago that you didn't want to be alone. You said you wanted someone to talk to. A conversation."

"I do, sweetheart. I really do." He looks offended. "Hey, I ain't one of those guys that goes straight to sleep afterwards."

Actually, he is, but he supposes he could just about stay awake for a bit, if his life depended on it.

Noreen throws the man a look she wouldn't even give a departing fox who had just ripped the stuffing out of one of her baby lambs. Rising up with some dignity and effort from the bed, she grabs her favourite bobbly hat from the side table, leaving the archaeologist and the mummy to continue making their own pyramid.

Arnie's expression plunges in a scary nanosecond from misguided hopefulness to a desperation that appears inconsolable. Even he, with the sensitivity of a narcissistic stoat, is beginning to realise that he is more than a little out of his depth here and that this particular seduction, unlike those countless others in his predatory past, could be more challenging than he would ever have imagined (dealing, as he is, with someone who most probably doesn't have her entire heart set on a career in erotic cinema).

In an attempt to make his entreaties register above a soundtrack of Ancient Egyptian climaxing, he pleads with the stocky, departing form.

"Noreen! Sweetheart. Wait! *Don't go!*" Arnie summons up all his energies to choke out those three simple words, the ones he has never allowed himself, nor indeed felt even the slightest need, to utter in his entire life. "I – I *love* you!"

The woman stops at the door and turns back to look at him. "*What?*"

"Er… I love you, kid? Genuinely. With meaning. There, I've said it. See, Noreen. Now you gotta stay."

Softening, Noreen comes back until she is standing almost directly in front of this bewildering person, the strange new intruder into her ordered life. Then, unexpectedly, she swings her re-bobbled head away from him and towards the TV. The figures on the screen appear to be performing just for her.

"Alright, Arnie Garth. If you love me, which admittedly is pretty quick work, considering we only just met yesterday, and you didn't even eat my carrot – and, by the way, no one has ever loved me in their entire lives, save perhaps my late mum and dad and possibly Geoffrey – but if you love me, *what colour are my eyes?*"

"Eh?" says Arnie Garth, phased now and stalling for time. What is this, for Pete's sake, *Who Wants to be a Millionaire*? "Well… hey, y'know somethin' – they change in the light. That's what I love about you, Noreen! It's like a filter on a lens. The one I use when I'm – when I'm filming saints – doin' miracles and shit. They're a kind of greenish, bluish, greyish, yellowish… so – I'm a wealthy, successful film producer. How about that?"

He swiftly puts his best arm around her. The one with the gold Rolex and a man's solid platinum bracelet. But this sudden outpouring of affection and jewellery would appear not to diminish her anger. In fact, quite the reverse.

"You don't *love* me, Arnie. You're a creepy little man and—" She motions to the busy TV screen. "For some reason, which I can't for the life of me fathom, you just want to do… *that* with me."

Arnie looks professionally at the screen. "I seriously doubt either of us could do that. The lady's a contortionist. And a devoted mother of three."

"Thank you, Arnie," says Noreen.

"For what, exactly?" he asks, in surprise. "You barely touched your sheep on a stick."

"I have absolutely no idea why you have come all the way to Rough Fell from wherever it is in the world that you live. Or why you are behaving so very strangely. Unless it is for a wager of some sort, which would be unspeakably cruel. But thank you for helping me to see that living on my own, in my little, rundown cottage, with my sheep and my dogs—"

"And your vermin."

"And my... friends, is the *best decision I could have made!*"

Suddenly Arnie smiles. And nods his head. Almost in time with the head-nodding that is now busily going on behind him on the screen.

"I know what you're doing, Noreen Millburn," he laughs. "This is you playing hard to get, right? You tease."

He is surprised by the velocity of the slap, perhaps less so by its thrust. It sends him tumbling over the unlaid bed with a yelp and onto the richly carpeted floor.

"Oh, I am *so* sorry, Mr Garth," gasps a horrified Noreen, staring at his prone and gasping form. She bends over him and slaps him again, just to snap him out of his shock.

He yelps in pain once more.

"Oh! Even more sorry. I don't know what got into me. Although, of course, you did deserve it, you revolting little man." She gives him back his handkerchief, puzzling just for an instant over the design. "But truly, you're more to be pitied than censured. You're still one of God's creatures – I imagine. Now, there's bound to be bruising in the morning. Try some arnica cream. In fact, I've got some in my bag. Here. Spread it liberally."

On this useful little household hint she exits, slamming the door behind her. Arnie rushes to open it once more and yells after her.

"*I'll give you 1000 dollars if you fall in love with me tonight! Pounds! 2000 pounds! 3000 pounds! And a blender!*"

A room service waiter is wheeling a champagne trolley towards them.

"*What about our souls?*" cries Arnie.

"What is it with you and arseholes?" comes the final retort, as she turns the corner towards the lift.

Arnie shakes his head at the waiter, who simply moves on, pretending he didn't hear this.

Alone and disconsolate, he slouches back into the room. Standing on the expensive carpet, he stares glumly at the TV. And that's where he sees me, beside a sarcophagus, under a pile of heaving, trembling limbs. Still dressed in my best suit, but louchely horizontal, I'm staring right out of the screen and giving one of my best and wisest shakes of the head.

Sensing that I probably wasn't there in the original edit, my current favourite unfavourite person smacks the off button on the remote control.

With a long sigh he flops mournfully onto the clean, cost-an-arm-and-a-leg, yet sadly underemployed, kingsize bed.

Chapter Fourteen

Listen to the sound of the river and you will get a trout.
(Irish proverb)

"Owwww! Ow! Shit! Fuck! OY!"

By the time Arnie has once more braved staircase-hell and sourced his table for breakfast, Rosie is right there beside him, holding a steaming pot of coffee. She pours a healthy amount into his awaiting cup and an equal amount onto his lap.

"Breakfast bar's over there. I'll take your order for cooked items when your nuts dry." With this, she walks back towards the kitchen.

Arnie, confused as to where one pain starts and another ends, rises gingerly from the table and pursues her as best he can. He wonders briefly whether insanity actually runs in Rough Fell (or more likely gallops), perhaps as a result of centuries of local inbreeding or simply as a side effect of being British.

"Still mad about the other night?" he hazards.

"The other night?" puzzles Rosie. "Did something happen? Things tend to blur."

She turns away from him and rearranges the individual cereal boxes, so that the already opened ones are at the front.

Arnie offers her his most contrite look, although contrition isn't high on his CV.

"Hey, look kid, you caught me at a bad time, okay?" He shakes his head ruefully. "I... well, truth is, Rosie, I can't afford to get involved right now. It's complicated."

"I'll bet," says the young waitress/barmaid/chambermaid/testicle-scalder, as she buries a browning piece of sliced apple under a just turning tinned-pineapple ring.

"However," says Arnie, in a spasm of inspiration, "I *would* like to hire you in a professional capacity!"

A ring of pineapple with the flat of a dainty but powerful hand behind it hits him square on the cheek.

The guest stares at her, hurt in so many ways. "Why do you people keep *doing* that? I need your help, Rosie! That's all I meant. Your wisdom. Advice. I need it badly. And now would be good."

Naturally, the young woman is sceptical. Wouldn't you be? "And what's in it for me?" she demands, narrowing her fetching but shrewd hazel eyes.

Arnie snaps his fingers. Which, in reality, is the action he employs when he needs time to think, although more usually the thought process relates to the optimum camera angle for something unspeakable.

"Er... well, I decided to get the rights to make *Will & Sam Redux.*"

She stares at him, her face wavering between suspicion and excitement. But he is on a roll.

"The sequel – yeah. Bigger and even more poetic than the one before. And get this – I'm gonna make it a musical! And you, my little undiscovered diva, you get two songs!"

"Yeah, yeah, I wasn't born yesterday. Two songs?"

"It's what I said. I know people – I been making some calls. We've got Lloyd Webber!"

"I don't care! *Two songs!* So, what do you want me to do?"

"Not much. I just need you to answer a very important question, as a prominent young woman of the area *and* a major local talent. How do I get someone like, say, for example, picking a name at random outta thin air, Noreen Millburn, to sorta fall in love with me?"

Rosie stares at him in abject disbelief. "There *is* no one like, say, for example, random Noreen Millburn." She walks towards the kitchen. "I would really stop bashing that little baldy head of yours, if I were you. *Two songs!*"

*

There is something about an olde English village tearoom that distinguishes it from anything else in the world. The moment Arnie Garth enters The Dilly Doily on Rough Fell's historic High Street, he feels that he has been transported either back in time or to an alien planet.

Wondering for a moment if you can physically OD on chintz, he reckons to himself that if the expression 'bull in a china shop' derives from anywhere, it is right here in town. There are more fancy plates on walls, cupboards, pine dressers and tables than he has ever seen all in one place in this life. The unnecessarily lacy tables appear to have been set close together not simply to maximise covers and avoid turning anyone away, but also, as a bonus, to afford the tea-slurpers, china-clinkers and scone-scoffers the opportunity of having their faces squashed by the apologetic backsides of each passing customer, not to mention the more harassed buttocks of the overworked and rather large waitress/proprietor, as she struggles to cut a clotted cream corridor to her destination.

In addition to the overpriced homemade cakes and warm scones (cream and jam extra) and the rich assortment of teas no one really wants, her customers appear to appreciate the luxury of being able to listen in to all the other conversations circulating around them, whilst maintaining the acceptable illusion that they are inhabiting their own little islands, interested in no one bar their immediate table companions. Nowhere do prurient curiosity and Anglo-Saxon aloofness meld so effortlessly as in the cosy rural café.

The only compensation for feeling so out of his depth is that Rosie has finally relented and agreed to impart to him all that he needs to know in the sphere of romancing an Englishwoman. Or Noreen. *Although, God knows why he would want to*, she muses, unless it's a kink even she hasn't heard of.

For his part, Arnie Garth has never witnessed so delicate a mouth accommodating so massive a slice of Black Forest Gateau. The young woman could be a natural, but this isn't why he is here.

"Wmuh lick tuful yu instit dem," she explains.

"Excuse me?"

"Don't you understand English?" she says, wiping her chocolatey lips. "Women like to feel you're interested in them."

Arnie shakes his head and almost laughs. "But I *am* interested in them, Rosie. Will she be a moaner or a screamer? Will she have a G-spot? Will she dress up as a nun…?"

Now it's Rosie's turn at the head shaking, which she does with such vehemence that a flight of errant cherry crumbs splatters him in the face .

"*That you want to hear what they've got to say!* That you really want to know – . You've got to *listen* to them, Arnie."

She starts to pour her tea into a delicate china cup through a metal strainer. It is one of the weirdest things the man has ever seen. He tears himself reluctantly away, in order to process the equal weirdness he has just heard.

"*Listen?*… Really?… Yeah?" He supposes that this Rosie, as a woman, must know whereof she speaks, but it all sounds pretty suspect to him. "Well, okay – hey, I can do that. Sure. I'm a great listener. Gimme something to listen to. C'mon Rosie kid, I'm all ears."

The café proprietor chooses this moment to give his face a tooth-rattling butt-smack on her way to another table with a laden tray. He grabs her apron, jerking her back. "Sweetheart, where's my tall skinny decaff soya macchiato?"

"I told you five times now – this is a sodding *tea room!* Are you bloody deaf or something? Sir."

*

Arnie Garth isn't exactly brimming with confidence as he and his sceptical tutor make their cake-heavy way back to The Wordsworth Arms.

It doesn't aid his mood that Rosie has insisted on practising her dance routines all the way along the busy High Street. Especially as she has managed to interpolate her own cuts and edits into the performance, endowing the whole number with a disconcertingly jerky quality that is starting to hurt Arnie's head in a way that even the malevolent Tudor beams weren't quite able to achieve.

She suddenly stops, right outside the village Post Office. Turning to Arnie, she gives him some of her best and most energetic tap, whilst simultaneously talking in a puffed rhythm that indicates her breathing might need more work. A few locals pause to watch, then realising it's only Rosie, they simply nod, smile and move on.

"Arnie, if you and nutty Noreen have to be together – God knows why, but it's sort of romantic, in a seriously sad and gross way – then you will."

"Y-you think?" he responds, in some surprise.

"I don't just think. I *know!* Get out there and make it happen! You're okay, she's okay. Feel the fear and do it anyway. Men are from Mars, women... aren't." She suddenly begins to sing, "*Tomorrow...*"

Despite her voice being of the type that could cause a walrus to miscarry, Arnie feels strangely elated. "Yeah! I'm gonna do it, Rosie! Gonna do it today. And all I have to do is listen, right? Yeah. Listen."

He goes very quiet and cocks his ear to show Rosie and the world, in a visual way – after all, this a man for whom, in life and work, actions are the loudest speakers – what a real good listener he is. Which is exactly when he hears a familiar sound. A distinctive purr that he knows so well from LA and was hearing again only yesterday in this godforsaken place. A car engine – that of a particular and rather exclusive vehicle, especially in these parts – being started up.

Arnie runs round the corner with a speed that only fear and mounting panic can induce. He discovers a young man in a leather jacket sitting in the newly-rented Ferrari. Not merely sitting in it but, with some visible pleasure, starting it up.

"*Hey! That's my Ferrari!*" protests Arnie.

"Not anymore it isn't," responds the younger man, with a polite but no-nonsense smile. "The company wants it back. Your credit card's been cancelled."

For a moment Arnie can't process the words, although this time it is not simply the bizarre accent impeding their journey to his befuddled brain.

"Say WHAT?"

Whilst the person in the driver's seat is debating whether this is an order or merely an odd exclamation, Arnie compounds the confusion with another arcane muttering.

"*Melisande!*"

"*Melisande!* – indeed," repeats the young man, who has been trained to believe that the customer is always right, even when you are repossessing their car.

"Look, kid. Mister. Sir. Gimme an hour! Yeah? What's an hour? There's this girl. Well, woman. I've got to go see her, now that…" He looks back to his recent relationship coach, who is watching the exchange with interest from the street-corner. Still tapping. "Now that I know the secret, y'know, the key – to really 'communicating' with a person."

"Well, I'll be very happy to explain exactly why we…"

"*Was I talking, shmuck? I need this fucking car back now!*"

"Have a nice day." The driver waves as the Ferrari takes off down the road.

Arnie stands there for a second, just watching it and his future – possibly his entire earthly existence, not to mention afterlife in a temperate climate – disappear pretty swiftly down a foreign hill that is forever England.

He feels a drop of water on his cheek and curses this green and unpleasant land once again for its inexplicable attraction to rain. Until he realises that this time – and possibly for the first time in his life – the unwelcome moisture is coming not from the heavens but from his own bleary eyes.

Arnie turns to Rosie, whose own already wide eyes have opened so much wider that it looks like she just developed a thyroid problem.

"*Arnie?*"

"I gotta… I have to… what the—? Rosie, I'll see ya!"

With this he pelts, in his now pain-inducing Gucci moccasins, swiftly along the same insanely cobbled street down which he has only just watched his last hope roar away. Arnie Garth has no idea where he is going or what he is doing, but at least, he tells himself, he is doing something. He is being proactive. And God will show him the way.

Yeah, right, Arnie. When did you and he last pass the time of day?

"*What about my two numbers?*" yells Rosie, but the strange man has gone.

Chapter Fifteen

There is no such thing as a free lunch. (English proverb)

Just as he is beginning to feel that he has seen every last street of stones and scones, half-timbered Tudor house, overstocked little shop, stinky pub, smelly villager and feral dog in this godforsaken one (crapping) horse town, Arnie Garth's teary eyes spot something that might just save the day. As well as his bacon, sanity and possibly even life, although that's still in the lap of you-know-who.

To his disbelieving eyes, what appears to be a Tudor car sits outside a cottage, in a tiny side-street. The door to the small, rundown dwelling is open and fortunately so are those of this bizarre, half-timbered vehicle. A sturdy, middle-aged lady, looking in her trusty Barbour and tweeds like the centrefold from a back copy of Country Life, is leaning into the rear of what Arnie now divines as being a Morris Traveller, which sounds more like a person than a car.

From some purpose-built and well-stocked shelves, the woman is nimbly sliding out a tray. A tray which looks bafflingly to Arnie like something you might be offered on an airplane. Wondering for a moment whether this could be some sort of cottage industry, where people are employed on a piecemeal basis to pre-flatten and remove the flavour from food before it is loaded onboard, he is better informed when he hears the robust lady call out loudly into the house.

"*Meals on Wheels, Mrs Arbuthnot!*"

As the cottage door has clearly been left open for just this purpose, the cheery deliverer is able to nudge it just a bit wider with a sensible shoe and stroll in bearing today's piping hot, Arbuthnot-friendly lunch.

The moment that the kind woman is out of sight, Arnie walks briskly round to the side of the vehicle. As he had hoped, the keys are still in the ignition. Whilst it is hardly a Ferrari, in fact hardly even a car, it might just serve his purpose.

Nipping in, he slams the door and starts the engine.

Unfortunately, in his enthusiasm to rattle the timbers and drive away, Arnie Garth has omitted to close the back doors. As he puts his foot down, with as much force and determination as possible, he speeds off in one direction whilst several of the meals formerly on wheels take flight in another. At least one member of Rough Fell's more elderly population, staring out of the window in hungry anticipation, wonders at his own sanity and whether this is what the youngsters mean by fast food. As if on a signal, the neighbourhood's cats appear and help to tidy up the littered road.

Arnie, shocked by what he is witnessing through his rearview mirror, and still struggling with the unfamiliar 'stick-shift', slows down for an instant, reaches behind him and just manages to grab a still warm tray before it sets off on its final unexpected journey.

He reckons he might need a full stomach for what lies ahead.

*

Noreen Millburn's cottage may not be too far from a relatively decent road – in fact, the B-something or other borders her outermost field – but the local Meals on Wheels van is just a muddy remnant of its former, much loved and beautifully-preserved self when it chunters down the neglected track and skids to a sludgy halt outside her door.

After a few moments, Arnie Garth struggles painfully out. He wonders almost proudly whether in another life he could have been a rally driver. Surely, they too have been obliged to knock down and crush the occasional lamb on the way to success.

Wiping the food from his chops and a few chops from his car, Arnie Garth ruins another pair of expensive shoes simply by trudging to Noreen's front door.

Before he can knock, a goat appears from the rear of the cottage and nudges the door open for him.

"Thanks," says Arnie, with unusual politeness. "Noreen home?"

The goat nods at the same time as the man is shaking his head and wondering why he is talking to a goat.

It turns out that this particular goat is indeed all talk, as Noreen Millburn is nowhere to be seen. Although, of course, the cottage is so dark and dusty that she could be huddled in a sagging armchair and the casual visitor might not be able to spot her for days, especially with all the spare wool and collecting cans.

After a few moments of scouting around, carefully avoiding the occasional curious rodent, Arnie sees a large, hand-scrawled note on the table. *GONE TO MEETING IN VILLAGE HALL. PLEASE HELP YOURSELF TO FOOD OR MONEY.*

He sighs, half-heartedly rattles a charity can, just in case, then returns at some speed to his recently borrowed dining-car.

Chapter Sixteen

For a greedy man, even his tomb is too small.
(Tajikistani proverb)

Arnie Garth had noticed the Olde Rough Fell Village Hall –
so what's newe? Everything's friggin' olde around here! – when
he had last passed through the small market square. He can't
recall why he had noticed it, perhaps he had spotted more of
those ancient wooden beams across its front and sides and an
instinctive ducking response had kicked in. This time, however,
there is a large banner outside that reads, *Proposed Rough Fell
Leisure Park, Mall and Multiplex – Emergency Meeting* and clear
sounds of activity from within.

Arnie Garth's oeuvre has, of course, never been seen
anywhere near a multiplex in its entire sordid life, although
Arnie himself has passed many a rewarding couple of hours
inside such palaces, watching legitimate mainstream movies
and picking up wonderfully poignant and imaginative cinematic
ideas he can soil, abuse, defile and degrade. Yet hang on – he
vaguely recalls now that Noreen herself was banging on about
something to do with multiplexes and malls, wasn't she, but let's
be honest – who listens? And isn't that the raspy voice of the lady

herself, echoing through the half-open doorway? He can almost smell the cardigans from here.

"*...and in conclusion, lovely, kind and wonderful people of Rough Fell...*"

Yes, that is unmistakably she.

As he walks in, head sensibly bowed, Arnie can feel age and history, like a noxious emission, begin to clog his orifices and cling to his new-worldly pores. Gazing out towards the front of the hall, he notices an impassioned Noreen Millburn, woolly arms flailing but minus charity-cans, addressing the packed house from the podium. He has never seen the bobble on her hat bounce so energetically.

Seated behind Noreen are a group of men in smart business suits and an equally well-turned-out young woman with a laptop. They appear to be listening intently, if you can actually do this when your eyes are rolling faster and faster around your head.

Arnie can only see the backs of the audience from where he is standing, yet even these appear hostile.

Before he can begin to unravel whatever garbage Noreen Millburn of this parish is currently spouting in her curious brogue, he can sense the genuine and fervent passion of its delivery. Arnie wonders if the speaker might ever willingly let rip such unbridled passion for him. Forget the 'ever'. Stroke of midnight Sunday would suit.

"...I know that you're all behind me in saying a great big and extremely polite, 'sorry but no, thank you very much, Apex Holdings, to despoiling our lovely, unique Cumbrian countryside with this horrible multiplex, bowling alley, pizza parlour, fitness centre and designer outlet complex of yours.'"

She turns round to address the most senior of the guys, a portly, greying man, who sports an *APEX HOLDINGS* lapel badge, document case, tie and golfing umbrella.

"No offence to Apex Holdings, by the way, or to you, Mr Edwards. I'm sure you're all very nice."

The Edwards person, who doesn't look particularly nice, makes a smarmy, 'no offence taken, madam, but if you could just quietly go somewhere and die' gesture, but Noreen doesn't see it, as she is back addressing her people and her community, the ones who have known her from childhood and knew her parents and grandparents before that.

"So, I ask you now, dear friends and neighbours of so many years, fellow farmers and landowners, lovers of the countryside, devotees of clean air and natural beauty, to stand up from your chairs and raise your voices. Join me, one and all, in making Apex Holdings hear how you feel. Don't be shy – shout, clap, stamp your feet – let them know we are NOT going to sell off our priceless heritage for shoddy, short-term gain! Come on! All together! Raise the roof!"

Arnie walks round so he can watch this peasants' revolt for himself.

So far, he is the first and only man standing.

"*Now!*" says Noreen. "Well, in your own time." she modifies. "Finish whatever you were doing. No rush… I think we've got the hall till three."

Arnie is now fairly near the front. He spots an empty chair and sits down next to some guy who smells like he might be a local farmer. Or someone for whom personal hygiene isn't yet a credo.

After a few seconds, the hall's newest arrival computes that he is the only person in the room without his arms folded defiantly. Immovably. And in total silence, save for the occasional cough, fart or expectoration.

"Did you hear me, Mrs Davenport?" asks the speaker, just beginning to sound plaintive.

No one will ever know if the aforementioned Mrs D did, in fact, hear this, or at least discern the gist of the argument from Noreen Millburn's slightly desperate arm-waving. After a few more painful seconds, the large, rusty-haired landlord from The

Wordsworth Arms, whom Arnie hadn't hitherto noticed, rises majestically from his seat at the other end of the front row and turns to the assembly.

"And all those in favour of selling off our lovely, priceless heritage for shoddy, short-term gain?"

The room erupts instantaneously into a deafening surge of cheers and frenzied clapping. Hats, sticks and strings of pork sausages are flung in the air. On the raised dais, Mr Edwards and colleagues permit themselves satisfied executive smirks.

Over the commotion, Arnie can make out the odd, shouted comment:

"Sell up, you stupid cow!"

"Sod heritage!"

"Just let them pull your bloody cottage down."

But at this point a sweet old lady, bent over and shaky, using her well-worn stick and the kindliness of a neighbour for support, rises onto her two tiny feet.

Noreen sighs in some relief, as she sees her. "Mrs Davenport?"

"String the obstructive bitch up!" suggests the doughty little Cumbrian.

Noreen sighs with a profound sadness. Her despondency is hardly dispelled by noticing a now sadly familiar figure, in an incongruous linen suit and inappropriate footwear, as he scuttles away at some speed towards the exit.

*

Arnie is back in the Morris Traveller, hitting his phone.

He knows that he is taking a risk, as the 'borrowing' of this insane vehicle has surely been reported by now. And it hardly merges into the crowd. But at least he is parked in a tiny alleyway and most of the village appear to be in the olde hall giving Noreen an olde hard time.

The rank outsider is at a total loss. Having checked his wallet and his pockets, he knows that he has barely enough cash remaining to take a bus ride, let alone hire a car. Not that he has actually seen any buses, even if he wanted one. Stranded. Scuppered. And all because of that venomous, malignant, poisonous wife of his. Qualities which, he has to admit, would quite regularly turn him on, when they weren't being directly targeted at him.

"*Welcome to the American Express Customer Helpline,*" says the recorded voice-message. "*To request your balance press one. To report a lost or stolen card, press two. To query a recent transaction, press three. To increase your credit limit, press four. To complain about your card being frozen by your vengeful partner due to severe mental competency issues, press the teensy little button thing right there in the middle of your handset.*" Arnie dutifully presses five. "*All our lines are busy right now. Please don't wig out. Imagine an idyllic pastoral scene from your childhood.*"

"*Goddammit!*" screams Arnie, only slightly bemused by the tone of this alarmingly specific, targeted new message. He tosses his phone over his shoulder into the back of the van – and guess whose hand reaches out smoothly to catch it, with a Tom Cruise-like deftness that belies his age and lack of physical substance?

"*Ambrose!*"

"You've cut to the chase. I like it. Do I smell food?"

Arnie nods towards the rear of the van, where there are still two lukewarm trays remaining. "You want the beef or the chicken?"

"They would go right through me!" I say, in a moment of light-hearted banter, which I have to say are all too infrequent these days. Most probably because seedy Arnie Garth is facing imminent death and a one-way trip to hell, which can sometimes gnaw away at a sense of humour.

"So, how's it going with Saint Noreen?" I ask, by way of conversation. And, unlike certain people, I am a pretty good listener. "She said those magic words yet, Arnie? You know you've only got three days 'til..."

232

To my surprise, our guy from the City of Angels (no relation) seems unexpectedly bullish. "Hah! I'll have time to spare. You watch, Soul Man. Right now, that poor beleaguered lady needs all the pals she can get. And guess what? She don't have any. Oh, and hey, did *you* know women like it when you listen to them?"

"That's what the Boss says. In fact, she never shuts up about it." I'd continue in this disarmingly droll vein, but Arnie's attention is drawn once more to the mean streets of Rough Fell.

Noreen Millburn is outside the hall now, retreating backwards from the main doorway and just one teeter from toppling dangerously down the rain-splattered stone steps. We can both only sit and watch in fascinated terror, as she edges uneasily away from villagers bent on vengeance. They are moving towards her en masse, anger in their hearts and the prospect of an extremely satisfying thump in their fists. Even Arnie, observing that mob, can see that something needs to be done.

"I can't sell my little cottage and all the land around it that my mum and dad left me!" she protests, above the grumbling and calls for blood. "What about the environment?"

"Bugger the environment," says the ever more red-faced landlord of The Wordsworth Arms. "We want first run movies!"

"We want Dolby Digital 5.1!" says another.

"And deep pan pepperoni!" adds little Mrs Davenport, who is heartily sick of Meals on Wheels.

"You like to help people," cries someone else, "so help us all get bloody rich!"

The other mob members endorse this to the hilt. "*Yeahhhh!*"

Noreen tries to speak but the words simply don't come. She looks like she may very soon burst into tears.

Mr Edwards of Apex Holdings, dapper suit still neatly buttoned over his business-lunch belly, approaches her, wearing an indulgent smile. He addresses the obstructive and currently besieged landowner in a more conciliatory fashion than that of the fired-up locals bent on trampling her to death.

"The people have spoken, Miss Millburn. And I'm rather afraid the people don't much care for your stubborn stance. So, we may have to—"

He is suddenly interrupted by a tidal wave of filthy water, as an old Morris Traveller careers through the massive puddle right in front of him.

"Yuk!" cries Arnie, shouting empathically out of the open window to the man in the previously pristine pinstripe. "You may wanna change your pants there, pal." He throws open the passenger door, praying that it won't fall off altogether. "Noreen, get in, will ya!"

"I will," agrees Noreen gratefully, shuffling with maximum clumsiness into the vacant seat and slamming the door. She looks around the vehicle, although it doesn't really require much introduction. "Why do you have Mrs Wainwright's Meals on Wheels van, Mr Garth?"

Arnie says nothing. He just stares at her. Out of the corner of his eye he glimpses an economy-size wicker man being swiftly erected on the nearby village green. Just in case.

After a moment, having received no explanation, Noreen shrugs and moves on.

"Oh, Arnie, I-I just want to go home."

Arnie says nothing once again. He simply nods. And cocks his head.

"No," she decides on impulse, "*I want to get right out of Rough Fell altogether!*"

Arnie repeats the nothing. And simply smiles.

"And I don't *bloody* care where – oh, excuse my French! *Arnie*?" asks Noreen Millburn, beginning to stare at her driver with puzzlement. "Are you okay?"

He nods again and continues to drive on what he still considers the stupid side of the road.

"Aren't you talking to me?" she enquires in some concern. "Is it because of what happened in the hotel bedroom? When that terrible film was playing. Did I hit you too hard?"

He just shakes his head.

A voice from behind him butts in, if indeed a person can butt in on a headshake. "You can overdo the listening shtick, you know," I tell the idiot. "*Talk to her!*"

Arnie nods again, this time in understanding, and turns to his bemused passenger. "So, Noreen, you got any hobbies?"

"*Jesus!*" I say, then offer a silent apology skywards. (You can't be too careful these days.) "For pity's sake, Garth, tell the poor lady something she wants to hear! '*You got any hobbies!*' Tell her you'll take her away from all this. Somewhere nice! Somewhere romantic!"

"Yeah, right," scoffs Arnie, turning to talk to the back seat. "I'm outta cash, my credit cards have all been nixed, the bank thinks I'm a person *non gratis* and I'm driving a hot delivery van! Literally!"

"You're talking to food trays, Arnie," observes Noreen Millburn.

I have to think for a moment.

Yes, me. I. Your narrator. Ambrose.

Hey, even Collectors of Immortal Souls, Upper Level, Grade 27 – 06 – D, we gotta pause for rumination once in a blue moon.

"*I got it,*" I cry, in some elation. Okay, okay, I know it's not like Izzy Newton and the falling Golden Delicious thing or old Alby Einstein with his famous theory, but in its own way it has moment. "Go to Manchester Airport right now. The information desk. There'll be a passport for Noreen and two tickets to a super-romantic destination, with swanky hotel reservations in your name."

I can do this sort of thing. When absolutely essential for the plot. Don't ask.

"Business Class?" says Arnie, to which a stare is the only word I can think of. "Whatever. You're an angel."

"Workin' on it!" I josh and disappear from his view before he can ask any more leading, or just plain irritating, questions.

Noreen is gawping at the empty rear of the car and then at Arnie, hoping without huge hope for some sort of an explanation. "Er... Arnie?"

"Eh. Oh, I... have conversations with my poor, dead, departed mother."

Noreen beams at this – her first of the day. "*I do too!* My mum, I mean, not yours. The very same thing, Arnie – every night without fail!"

"What are you – *nuts?*"

They say little more until they approach the airport. Or maybe Noreen still talks but Arnie has simply stopped listening.

Chapter Seventeen

Watch out for the unexpected mushroom. (Sicilian proverb)

Mrs Angela Wainwright's Meals on Wheels van, rarely seen in these environs or, indeed, anywhere outside Rough Fell, is rapidly approaching Terminal 2 of Manchester Airport. Arnie finds himself really concentrating, reckoning that if the people round here are only too ready to make big mistakes with their cars and their roads, they're bound to have cooked up something equally screwy with their car parks.

He can already sense the woolly head of the passenger beside him whirring around like something out of a horror movie. Which, of course, reminds him of his first and now classic award-winner *The Sexorcist*. Happy days that now seem so very long ago. He wonders if he will ever produce another erotic masterpiece and go to bed just one more glorious time with a new and golden dick in his hands. It doesn't bear thinking about. And, of course, he has far more pressing concerns.

"Arnie," yelps Noreen, "*this is an airport!*"

"Hey, you been around, kid."

"No," admits Noreen. "I've never even been out of Rough Fell. I've never even seen Manchester!"

"Well, today's your lucky day. You're not going to. C'mon."

He parks the car in the first bay he finds. Let Mrs Whatever-her-name-is get a ticket.

"But Arnie..."

"Noreen, get out of the friggin' car!" He sees her face and softens. "Hey, you said you wanted out."

He starts to walk towards the terminal, pretty sure that Noreen will follow. Which she does.

"*But I can't just leave the country!*"

"Sure, you can! I'll break this to you gently, kid, but back in Wuthering Heights, everyone hates your guts."

Everything about Noreen Millburn suddenly sinks. Her spirit, her eyes, her cardigans. Even the ragged bobble on top of today's particularly unfortunate choice of headgear appears to wilt in sadness.

"I know that, Arnie," she sighs. "I do realise that everyone hates me. I think I've always known it."

Arnie suddenly pauses in his single-minded airport dash. Despite himself, he turns back to listen.

"But ever since I was a little girl, I've had this... well, this overwhelming compulsion to help people. Even if they don't want to be helped. I have absolutely no idea where it comes from but sometimes it's almost like – well, like a curse. A real curse. You can understand this, can't you?"

Arnie just nods his head. "No."

Noreen concedes this, with a sigh of genuine hopelessness. "Where are you taking me, Arnie Garth?"

"Er... well, Noreen Millstream, it's kind of like, well, like a surprise."

When her look becomes sceptical, he throws open his arms in supplication. "Hey, have I ever let you down?"

"Well, there was last night in the hotel..."

"It was a rhetorical question! *Jee-sus!*"

Several fraught minutes later, Arnie Garth of Los Angeles finds himself standing rigidly at the airport information desk, not quite believing what he is seeing. Noreen hovers some distance away, doing much the same thing, but for hugely different reasons.

But whilst her head is still turning around every which way in abject wonder and amazement, Arnie's has begun to shake in sheer terror. With a healthy amount of fury mixed in. All of it aimed at the envelope he has just picked up, the universe in general and, whilst I don't like to boast, more than possibly at me in particular.

Although most people in the airport – indeed, in the Stockport and Greater Manchester area – can probably hear poor Arnie as his recently dumbfounded mouth begins to break through its dumbness and foundness, Noreen Millburn, late of the middle-of-nowhere, is still too busy attempting to take in the overwhelmingly alien bustle and noise.

Beneath the cardigans and the vests, she can feel her whole body trembling. It can't be excitement, at least not so far as she is aware, because she rarely becomes excited or indeed has anything to be excited about. But it is most definitely shock. Suddenly her whole vista has changed. Converted, as if by sorcery, to a dizzying panorama of lights, escalators, people and suitcases on the move, fast food outlets, public toilets, mewling infants, uniformed officials, men holding up surnames.

Yet it is what is absent that is equally disturbing. Not a hill, lake, field, cottage or sheep in sight.

Sheep! Noreen suddenly gasps in panic. "Oh, my Lord – Geoffrey!"

"*Las fucking Vegas? No! There has gotta be a mistake!*"

Now she hears him and moves towards the desk, from which he has instructed her to maintain a respectable distance.

"Is everything alright, Arnie?" she asks.

Arnie gives her one of the smarmiest and least genuine beams in a long history of profound insincerity. "The gods are smiling, Noreen!"

He hands her the passport that came with the ticket envelope. Inside the latter he had also discovered a paltry amount of United States cash.

"I've never had a passport," says Noreen, flicking through it. "How did you...?"

"I know people," says Arnie, with a clumsy wink. He digs back into the envelope just in case there's another goodie or, with luck, a cyanide capsule buried between the low value dollar bills. Instead of which, he finds a slip of paper. It is a receipt for the Lakeland Home for Limping Sheep. He hands it to Noreen.

"I think of everything," he says.

No, Arnie. You don't. But I do. Because in times of crisis, well you have to.

Yet I have to be honest with you, dear readers, this is truly a very fraught and highly critical stage in our celestial game of souls. As you know, this whole sorry situation, this heavenly cock-up, this shit's-happening ragout, it's all virgin territory for me.

As guys say where I come from, we're winging it here.

Chapter Eighteen

Clumsy birds have need of early flight. (Chinese proverb)

Arnie Garth is remembering the first plane ride he ever took.

It was an internal from Pittsburgh to Los Angeles and he still recalls the excitement. He would have to admit that the fact he was a juvenile and on the run probably added to the adrenaline rush, but nonetheless, that first heady sensation as the massive steel pterodactyl left the ground needed no embellishment.

He is pretty sure, however, that he never uttered sounds comparable to those produced by his fellow-passenger just a half hour earlier, sounds sufficiently disturbing to cause the remaining 243 passengers to wonder if air was seeping in at some speed from somewhere that it really shouldn't. Only his muted but swift suggestion that the keening Noreen perhaps had a spare carrot in her bag to chomp on prevented an uncomfortable blip from developing into a major incident.

If he had to define the exact nature of the sound, Arnie Garth would be forced to say that, whilst it might be composed of a hardly unanticipated dollop of helpless terror and alarm, there was undoubtedly a dash of pure exhilaration in the mix. A "wheeee!!!" alongside the "whoaaaa!!!" He wonders if this might bode well for the future but has to admit that the link between a declaration of undying love and, say, a nun going on her first trip to Six Flags Magic Mountain, has yet to be proven.

The Virgin Airlines flight to Las Vegas has completed its ascent, despite the momentary panic. And, perhaps because of the heady events of the past few days, Arnie Garth has suddenly fallen asleep.

Come on, who can blame him? The guy has had two major heart attacks *and* a stroke, discovered that through a celestial clerical error he's without a soul in the world and will most probably go to hell on Sunday, had his funds cut off by a malevolent porn star wife, was forced to drag himself through nine kinds of mud to check out his potential 'soulmate', finally met her with all that this entailed and, perhaps most taxingly, had to decipher the rural Cumbrian accent. And don't get me started on his laundry. Wouldn't you relish a bit of shut eye?

It is when he suddenly wakes up that Arnie Garth's panic starts. Noreen is nowhere to be seen. He wonders for a moment whether the urge to go home and be with her stinky animals has been too hard to resist. Of course, she could just be in the bathroom, but somehow, he can't or would rather not picture her there. So, where?

It is her voice he catches first. Sheep-herdingly loud and quite unmistakeable. He looks along the aisle. Up ahead the crew are serving meals. And so is Noreen.

"Here you go, my dear," she informs a bemused passenger, as she hands him his tray. "And if you do fancy any fruit with that, I believe I've got a banana in one of my pockets."

"Ma'am," says a stewardess politely, but firmly, "could you please just put the gentleman's haddock down and return to your seat?"

"Alright, my lovely. But I'm just down there, next to that odd-looking little balding man with the crumpled suit and the unhealthy tan. Call me if you need me. You're on your feet all day, you deserve a rest."

They both look towards the man answering the description. He is beckoning wildly.

"Did you have a good sleep, Arnie?" says Noreen, plonking herself back down with a plane-rattling thud. "You must be so tired. What with all the travelling. And the funny business."

"What funny business?"

"*You* know. The posh country hotel? And you pretending that you didn't know where we were flying off to today, you dafty. I'm still totally mystified, but after that horrible Apex meeting, well, I'm just glad to be away for a while." She suddenly appears quite sad. "Mind, if you want to know the truth, I'm already missing everyone."

"Everyone?"

"Well, not human, of course." She turns to him, with interest. "I never asked you, Arnie – do you have anyone waiting for you at home who isn't human?"

"Yeah," sighs Arnie, regretfully, "but I'm workin' on it."

When the food arrives and Noreen establishes that no animal has been harmed or killed in its making, she turns to Arnie and asks him about their destination, a question he knew would be coming.

"What's this Las Vegas like, Arnie? Well, from what you've heard."

"Er…"

"I think maybe I've seen the name in our local travel agent's window. But I don't have a TV or a wireless and I never ever look at a newspaper, so I'm afraid I may be a wee bit unworldly."

"It's one of your best qualities, Noreen," pounces Arnie, "your not being from this world. Or planet. It's… well, it's what I've come to love about you."

"*Really?*"

"Would I lie?" he lies. Yet, to his surprise, he is not exactly

243

finding the dearth of worldliness in this singular woman, to whom he is mystically and mystifyingly linked, the absolute worst thing in the world. In fact, right now, as the intimidating prospect of Las Vegas, city of eternal sin, looms large, it might almost be considered the best.

"Las Vegas?" He sighs. "Well, just look at it on the map, sweetheart. It's in the middle of the desert, for fu— for Pete's sake. Very hot and very dull. Too hot, to be honest – so best just to stay in the hotel. All the time. 24/7. And, oh, how they hate the English because of... the whole independence thing. So, if I were you, I'd not talk to a soul. Not even the staff. And if anyone mentions my name or says they know me or my... inspirational, faith-based work, they're lying."

"Are you *sure* we're related, Arnie?" asks Noreen Millburn, grappling with a tiny packet of vacuum-sealed cheddar.

Arnie closes his eyes and tries to imagine what might happen next.

Good luck with that, Mr Garth.

THE ROAD TO HELL

Chapter Nineteen

Choose your inn before dark, get back on the road before dawn.
(Chinese proverb)

Imagine you've never been to Vegas.

Could be you haven't, but unless you've been stuck in a cave or a submarine or a rundown cottage in the drizzly north-west of England all your days, you probably have some idea of how it looks. And sounds. Even how it smells.

Now imagine you're Noreen Millburn, first time in an airport, first time in a plane, first time in a US cab (or, indeed, any sort of cab). Come on, work with me.

Suddenly, just a few heady hours after you woke up at home in your animal-refuge-cum-hovel, you're driving past the shiny black pyramid of the Luxor, the white soaring towers of the Excalibur, moving with all the other traffic past the MGM Grand and the Bellagio, with its magnificent fountains, and Paris with its mini-Eiffel, that almost makes you believe you're really there, if you're an idiot, even though you're nowhere near. Caesar's Palace in all its decadent splendour, the Mirage with its erupting volcano. The Flamingo. The Venetian. The Jerusalem with its Wailing Wall. (I made that one up, but trust me, there's a lot of people in Vegas wailing.)

All around town billboards encourage you to shop, gamble, eat and enjoy stellar performances by people you never heard of in your life.

"It doesn't look that dull, Arnie," says Noreen, perceptively, resisting all attempts by Arnie to block her views out of the cab window.

Arnie is forced to agree. "You are right, Noreen!" he says in surprise. "They musta built it up a bit. And here was I, planning a restful few days just communing with the spirits and being closer to God's own earth." He offers up a sigh of deep regret. "I prefer how it used to be. Mile after mile of sand and tumbleweed, clear blue skies, mother nature in the raw. Just a man and his maker in perfect harmony in the sweltering desert. You know, like Moses and Jesus and – and Priscilla."

"I don't know Saint Priscilla. But look over there, you can still see the mountains. They're so beautiful."

"Maybe we can see them from our hotel room."

"Room?"

"*Rooms*! I meant rooms. That kinda adjoin. If…"

Arnie Garth looks around for help. For me, even. And then at his watch. There are no clocks in Vegas, supposedly so that gamblers don't know the time and we can all stay awake 24/7. But Arnie Garth knows, even without checking, that his own clock is ticking and that his ticker is talking.

He gazes across at our lady of the cardigans, whose eyes are almost popping out of her head. In that failing heart of his, Arnie is by this time pretty certain that someone like her, someone so relentlessly, helplessly, painfully good and unworldly, nice even, could never in a million decades fall for someone possibly not quite so nice, such as for example him. They never have and they never will. Especially not here, in this not so nice city.

And, try as he might, dear God has he tried, he is most surely not falling for this intensely decent, not unlikeable but curiously pitiful creature, which apparently is a major part of the whole deal. Not even when she turns to him, her pale but luminous blue eyes suffused with innocent wonder and her bobbly head so full and reeling that she is unable to speak, only to shake her head and sigh.

He notices that they are leaving the more lavish part of town to enter what even he might call the scuzzy section. And Arnie Garth knows from scuzzy. Strip joints, fast food outlets, sex shops. He wonders for a moment what Noreen will make of this descent and why the hell I, good old reliable Ambrose, am being such a cheapskate. Unless, of course, I'm on a budget.

The cab suddenly veers down an alley and parks beside a dingy entrance.

"Here we are," says the cab driver, as if he is equally miffed to be directed way off his normal classy track. "The Dime After Dime Motel. Livin' the dream."

"Enough already," says Arnie.

"Is this where we are staying, Arnie?" asks Noreen, her interest clearly piqued but not yet, at least so far as he can ascertain, utterly soured by disappointment. But it's early days.

"Reckon so, sweetheart." He taps her woolly-mittened hand. Probably the only such extremity in Nevada, which is itself a state of extremes. "It's where Mother Teresa would stay whenever she was in town. And Gandhi. I thought that would mean something to you."

"Oh yes. The minister at our church has talked about Mother Teresa. But I never knew she came here."

"It's where she did her best work."

*

The first thing Arnie Garth notices when he enters the grim motel lobby – well, the first thing after the fug and the flickering light and the stench of bitter disappointment – is a large and vivid poster on the notice board. It reads, *LAS VEGAS WELCOMES THE NATIONAL EROTIC CINEMA AWARDS*. A bright red banner stripped across it, covering some of the more explicit artwork, screams, *TONITE!*

The first thing Arnie Garth does, after he pushes Noreen Millburn out of the way and towards the small reception desk, is to rip said poster off the wall, muttering something about a violent antipathy to lazy spelling.

"Thank you, Ambrose," he mutters into the dusty air. Wondering, perhaps not for the first time, whether I truly am on his side (you don't have to tell me about unreliable narrators – my place is full of them. Sometimes they don't even turn up). Yet to whom else is he going to turn? He hasn't a soul in the world!

Arnie swiftly realises that even Noreen may be drawing comparisons between The Dime After Dime and that exquisite country house hotel to which Arnie had fruitlessly treated her just a couple of nights earlier. Or perhaps she has already spotted the glaring differences. It is, to be frank, the distance between a red carpet and something you just trod in. But if his guest has indeed entertained such thoughts, she is certainly not airing them or passing judgment and still simply appears overawed. Yet Arnie finds himself cursing Melisande for depriving him of his usual suite at The Tropicana.

The guy at reception graciously takes time out from the twin demands of picking his teeth and wiping his hands on a string vest to greet the new arrivals. Whilst most hotel receptionists, especially in Las Vegas, are trained to take every registering guest, however striking, bizarre or unsettling, in their professional stride, Arnie can feel the man's eyes swivelling between himself and Noreen as if these two are part of a human story he would for once, even with all his experience, be at a total loss to unravel. And, of course, he would be absolutely correct in this assumption.

"So, how many hours d'you want?" he asks, eyeing their lack of luggage.

Arnie looks at a curious Noreen. "It's an American thing." He taps the desk. "We're staying until Sunday."

"What happens Sunday, Arnie?" asks Noreen.

You don't wanna know, he thinks, but says, softly, "Everything shuts down. For church."

"Double room?" asks the man, working really hard not to picture anything.

"Sure," tries Arnie.

"No, thank you, sir," says Noreen. "We're cousins."

"I've seen worse," says the man, who undoubtedly has.

Chapter Twenty

When poverty comes in the door, love flies out the window.
(German proverb)

Arnie would have been delighted to learn that the only room available this evening in the Dime After Dime was the Penthouse Suite, were it not for the fact that the bed he has nobly chosen as his own is a lumpy, threadbare sofa in the outer chamber, with stains he really doesn't want to think about (he recalls an erotica colleague of his once observing that whenever you discover stains such as these, they always resemble a map of Ireland, which Arnie somehow felt showed a Celtic heritage, a love of geography or a life best unexamined).

Noreen's accommodation is hardly a giant leap upwards, but the woman appears utterly thrilled. Arnie can only assume that this is because she really needed to get out of Dodge for a while, as even with his monstrous ego he can't quite believe that the main draw could be sharing a crummy suite with her American cousin, however long or lost.

Well, at least this time the TV isn't on.

And this is still the city of dreams and hope, so he reckons he had better make the most of it. With a flourish, he trots over to the window and pulls back the moth-eaten drapes.

"Here you go, Noreen – *Vegas!*"

She stares at the brick wall for a few moments. It appears to reach up almost to the sky, without even a window or a lurid sign to break the monotony. He feels his heart sink like the cranky elevator they just got off.

"Do you know, Arnie?" says Noreen, as she examines the offending structure, without even a hint of disappointment. "I never really considered the workmanship that goes into constructing a wall like this. See how firm and even every single one of those bricks is. So many men must have worked so hard together, as a team, making sure that whoever was eventually going to live inside was safe and warm and secure. I do hope nobody hurt themselves in the process. I collect for the brickies' benevolent fund back home, you know – the Hod of God it's called – although, of course, in Rough Fell the buildings are all so small. Thank you for giving me something to truly think about."

"Are you for real?" asks Arnie, and not for the first time.

But the bouncing bobble has already moved on and Noreen has discovered something else new and equally wonderful. A tiny freezer. She opens it and turns to her host, a face of undiluted radiance bathed in the refrigerated glow.

"Arnie – *look!* Isn't that thoughtful?"

Before he can talk her through the economics of hotel hospitality – and politely warn her off – she is already examining a miniature Jack Daniels.

"They've even got drinks for dwarves!"

"That's America for you. Built on kindness." He smiles at her, with only a hint of desperation and a swift reminder not to talk her through his legendary *Snow White Trash* movie. "Now they're strictly non-alcoholic, Noreen. Nevada's a dry state. So, you just drink as many as you like."

"Oh, I shall," promises Noreen, "thank you." She catches herself in an only slightly cracked mirror and appears visibly shocked. "But look at me, Arnie. You didn't even give me time to pack. I need to go out and get myself some clothes and things. Do they have a Help The Aged shop here?"

"A *what*?" Arnie sighs once again at the sheer hopelessness of life, until a thought occurs, which he half dismisses the moment he utters it, if not before. "You remember to bring your credit cards?"

"I don't have credit cards, Arnie. As my dear mum always said, 'Neither a borrower nor a lender be.'"

"Of course she did. Well, my credit cards are kaput, thanks to Meli – thanks to melifluously donating to animal charities and the blessed evangelists and stuff. And I've only got…" He looks in his wallet and sighs. "Eight dollars. So, if you want new clothes in this burg, it looks like there's only one thing to do."

Noreen nods in complete understanding. From her voluminous handbag she deftly extricates a large bundle of wool skewered with needles. "I'll be as quick as I can."

Arnie's eyes go skyward. Looking for me, perhaps. "Lord, give me strength."

No, straight to board level.

Grabbing Noreen – and her hefty handbag – he drags her out of the room.

Chapter Twenty-One

Better an ounce of luck than a pound of gold.
(Yiddish proverb)

Arnie Garth has a pretty good idea that no one he knows (or, more critically, who knows him), especially no one here in Vegas for the prestigious NECA awards ceremony this evening, will be gambling their lives away in the tiny For Luck's Sake Casino, just a few short yards down the dingy alleyway from their motel. Or, indeed, would be seen dead anywhere near this part of town (although this is a notion that right now he doesn't care to examine too earnestly).

He is, of course, all too aware that in even the most rarefied and sumptuous of establishments in this unique city, the level of glamour rarely approaches those heights that the great unversed are led, from movies and beach-reads, to expect with all their yearning hearts. Casino Royales, they are not – with handsome, tuxedoed men making lickerish eye contact over roulette wheels with glamorous women dripping in diamonds, Valentina and unbridled lust. Yet Arnie still realises that in this less than royal casino, his country's legendary oasis of neon and kitsch has struck a new, depressing low.

At first glance, a visitor might believe that they have stumbled into the annual convention of morbidly obese geriatrics, Middle America chapter. The fat is almost moving on its own, as ageing players attempt to fit their massive legs under gambling tables or squidge onto tiny, groaning stools, like human blueberry muffins.

Noreen can't help but notice the bulging body of an elderly man being wheeled out of the room on an extra-large gurney, his pale and rigid hand still gripped vice-like onto the now severed handle of a slot machine. His wife, remaining seated at her own machine, watches him in sadness, until the sound of dropping coins lures her back.

"It's how he'd have wanted to go," she tells the oddly dressed and gawping Englishwoman.

Noreen isn't even listening. Not that she can hear much above the cacophony of bells, balls and bullshit. She simply stares around her, as the South American natives must have stared when they first saw the Spanish galleons emerging out of the mist. This is so outside anything we have ever seen or could reasonably have imagined, therefore it cannot, in fact, be real.

"I don't understand, Arnie. Are these people *gambling*?"

"I'm afraid they must be, Noreen. I am so sorry, I had no idea," he apologises. "I thought it was a clothes shop. But now that we're here..."

"My poor mum always told me gambling was wrong."

"It kills me I'll never meet her," mutters Arnie, at the same time squatting down a few inches.

"In fact, one of my charities is... what are you *doing* down there, Arnie?" she asks, glancing floorwards to his balding head.

"Eh? Er... your handbag – well, shopping bag – was coming open. There are some bad people here." He smiles up at her and talks softly, then realises that this is impossible, as the noise around them is almost deafening. So, he shouts upwards in the direction of her ear. "Hey, gambling *is* wrong, Noreen. If you lose. But we don't have that luxury." He pulls out a reasonably impressive wad of British five-pound notes from whatever is lurking in the stringy, home-knitted cave. "Awwww shit! What's this? Don't you have any real money?"

"Arnie, please don't touch that money! It's for the new hydrotherapy wing at the Ullswater Hospital for Serious Childhood Diseases."

"Now, you just made that up," he tells her, as he flashes the wad to a passing cashier. "Hey, toots, what can I get for this?"

Moments later, Arnie and Noreen are sitting beside the frayed and fading cloth of a crowded blackjack table. As ever, it is occupied by frayed and faded people, obsessively guarding their piles of chips like bloated squirrels.

Noreen clasps her bag tightly into her woolly cardigan, mindful of Arnie's warnings. As all of her cash, however, is currently sitting in little plastic discs on the table, she now has precious little remaining on her person to be stolen, except perhaps for her virtue and that is looking pretty safe right now.

The dealer, a swarthy, cadaverous man who seems as if he is on a starvation diet just to make his customers feel bad, deals them their first card.

"Thank you very much, sir," says Noreen with a smile, causing the dealer to glare at her, sensing some sort of dangerously foreign sarcasm beneath the almost impenetrable accent.

She starts to examine the card with an embarrassed smile, as if she has just been handed a billet-doux and is attempting to decipher its intent.

"The object of the game, Noreen, is to get as near to twenty-one as you can," explains Arnie, "but not more than twenty-one. I know it sounds complicated, but—"

Noreen is suddenly beside herself with giddily grateful excitement. "It's *Pontoon!*" she shrieks. The perspiration already on her brow, perhaps from wearing an excess of cardigans in the desert, begins to glide down her face, intermingling with very tiny tears of joy. "Oh, Arnie. I used to play it with my mum for peanuts."

"Nothing changes, does it?" says Arnie.

Noreen stares at the dealer, with an intensity that Arnie has never seen before, taking even the gaunt employee and his corpulent patrons by surprise.

"*Twist!*"

The dealer looks confused.

"*Hit me*, Noreen," explains Arnie, pushing the chips out onto the table.

"You really are a pervert, aren't you?" she mutters, before asking the dealer to twist again.

"Like I did last summer," mutters an elderly gentleman sitting nearby, smiling leerily at Noreen, which she ignores as he is being odd.

Robotically, the dealer delivers a third card. He and Arnie can see instantly that she has reached the magical number and pretty soon Noreen is up to speed.

"*Pontoon!*" she screams, which means absolutely nothing to anybody around the table, who all wonder why she is into bridges.

Having screamed sufficiently, Noreen Millburn now begins to jump up and down, clapping her lake-ravaged hands in delight. Arnie simply stares at her, not quite believing his eyes. He has seen elements of this fervour before, when Noreen has been droning on about all the noble things she would like to do in this world, most of them involving colostomy bags or prosthetics, but he never expected to witness it at a worn-out blackjack table in the ass-end of Las Vegas. Whilst it may not be bringing her any closer to loving him, or saving his miserable life, he finds himself strangely warmed by this. And surprisingly heartened.

Shepherding the precious pile of winning chips closer towards them, he grins at her.

"See, Noreen? Gambling is a wonderful thing. Think of all the good you can do with this."

Her pale blue eyes begin to sparkle. "You're right, Arnie!"

For some reason, Noreen begins to look around the drab casino. Her glance falls on a glassy-eyed, raddled-looking woman in her forties, hovering some distance away. She is wearing a glitzy, very low-cut top, an extremely short, tight skirt and black fishnet tights that end in bright green high heels curling dangerously into each other, as she manoeuvres between the tables and the human lard.

The woman smiles hopefully but unsuccessfully at various men in turn, as she approaches Arnie's table. Noreen immediately grabs all her chips and thrusts them into the stunned woman's vermilion-nailed hands.

"Here you are, dear. You buy yourself some good warm clothes. I have heard that even deserts can get cold at nights."

Before this lady of the desert-night can fully grasp the kind sentiment and, more importantly, its physical manifestation, Arnie briskly grabs the charity chips back from her and scurries off with Noreen to the nearest cashier.

Once he has the winnings safely stuffed deep in her bag, he hustles a bemused but considerably richer Noreen out of the casino and into the darkening alley. Cries of 'Indian giver' and 'asshole' ring in his ears.

"I forgot to tell you, sweetheart," he explains to his charge, "helping the downtrodden is frowned upon in Vegas. It's the American way. Go figure."

Noreen simply nods, prepared to be surprised by nothing in this strangest of all possible worlds.

"Now let's go and get you all dolled up. As befits a companion of Arnie Garth." He pauses for a moment. "And there are... perfectly adequate places right around here."

He suddenly finds himself, with a shiver, recalling the poor fat guy on the gurney and wonders what he, Arnie Garth, will be gripping onto when it's his turn to die. Which looks like it could well be in just a couple of days. He really hopes it's something softer than the handle of a flashing Las Vegas slot machine.

Chapter Twenty-Two

Do not dress in clothes made of leaves when going to put out a fire. (Chinese Proverb)

Despite his best endeavours and entreaties – indeed, begging might not be too harsh a word – Arnie Garth has found himself encroaching on the one place he least wants to be at this daunting time, this particular week. This wretched evening. The celebrated Las Vegas Strip, as night (and NECA) approach.

Looking all around him, he steps tentatively out of the fashion shop into which Noreen had only minutes ago dragged his sorry ass. In fact, she had yanked him with all her strength and a capacious bag brimming with those black-and-white dollar things the lovely casino people had just handed to her.

On his way here from that same casino, Arnie has wisely managed to find himself a large but cheap hat, practically a Stetson (if Stetsons come striped in red and gold) that affords him some sort of camouflage, coming down as it does over his balding head and right to the bridge of his nose.

"It's almost as if you don't want people to see you, Arnie," Noreen had said, peering under the massive garment into his shifty little eyes.

"Actually, you're right, Noreen," admitted the lavishly behatted man, a tad ruefully. "See, in my business, you get crazy autograph hunters and wannabe movie stars hounding you all the time. 24/7 and more. 'Sign this for my citizenship teacher, Mr Garth.' 'Can I play Archbishop of Canterbury in your new film, Mr Garth?'"

"You must show me one of your movies one day."

"Noreen, I would be honoured," Arnie Garth had said. *I should live so long*, Arnie Garth had thought.

Fortunately, at this point, Noreen had spotted the clothes shop that had her name on it. Well, not literally 'Noreen Millburn' – who in their right mind would call a fashion outlet Noreen Millburn? I doubt even Noreen Millburn would do that – but it was called It's So You, and right then Noreen was as 'so you' as you can get.

So now Arnie and her – or 'you' – are strolling out of the shop. He with his cheap 'I've stayed and played in Vegas' Stetson pulled down low, she with all her old, shapeless cardigans scrunched into a large plastic bag and a brand new, sparkly, diamanté-studded, shapeless cardigan buttoned up around her sturdy Cumbrian frame.

"You really think it suits me, Arnie?" asks Noreen coyly, as they hit the Strip.

"*Suits you?*" says Arnie, vaguely, as his head jerks around like a coked-up meerkat, seeking people and even posters to avoid. "Honey, you were born to wear that… thing."

He suddenly notices one of his DVDs on prominent display in a window – 'Arnie Garth presents *Breakfast on Tiffany's*', and swiftly steers her away.

"Well, thank you, Arnie Garth," continues an oblivious Noreen, patently intoxicated by the new sensations of the day and possibly the first compliment of her life. Even Arnie, with his much-practised lack of perception, can detect that the usual, wind-battered ruddiness in her cosmetically unenhanced

Cumbrian cheeks has been supplanted by a new and different glow, one that appears to generate from within rather than being purely elemental.

"And now," she announces, with a hugely satisfied smile, "I have got a surprise for *you!*"

"You bought the matching panties?"

"*You!*" she says matily, punching his shoulder so hard that his hat slips to a jauntier angle and he develops a bruise that could last beyond death. "No, silly man," explains an excited Noreen, "I asked the lovely kind American lady in the shop for the best restaurant round here. I know you like your food – that's why you're such a podge."

"I'm not such—"

"You're a little porker, Arnie. Anyway, *guess what?* Tonight, I am going to take *you* to dinner! With my – what do you call them? – winnings. Just as friends, mind. No funny stuff."

Arnie stares at her in total panic. "*No way!*" he cries, adding swiftly, "I mean, no way to dinner, Noreen. As for the funny stuff…"

"Now Arnie, I am not taking 'no way' for an answer. It's the very *least* I can do after you rescued me from that awfully cruel lot back home and dragged me halfway across the world, for reasons I still can't quite fathom."

"I just have this irresistible urge to help people in need." He smiles, because you have to grab the moments as they fall. "Hey, I surely don't have to tell you what that's like, cuz… Saint Noreen."

"No indeed, Arnie. I just never thought that anyone else felt the same way as I do."

"Very few people do. Hardly anyone. So, you and me, meeting up like this, is what you call a magical coincidence. Yeah? And you know what Einstein said about coincidence."

"I don't even know about Einstein."

"Who does? Well, anyway, he said that coincidence is

'God's way of staying anonymous'. Isn't that beautiful, Noreen? That God himself is the guy putting us together. Reminds me of one of my movies. In fact, *all* of them. Did you know Faith Baste was one of my leading ladies?"

"Really? Then you must tell me all about her. At that restaurant."

"Aww, Noreen," says Arnie, "can't we just eat in our nice, cosy room? And stare at our lovely… wall. Y'know, just you and me. Together. The two of us. I… don't feel like being around people right now. Especially the sorta people in this town."

Noreen looks shocked. "*Eat in the room!* And let this lovely new cardie go to waste? No wonder you never married, Mr Stick-in-the-Mud. I want to eat out." She digs her hand deep into her bag and pulls out a tiny, white ferret. "And so does Stanley."

*

"*Ambrose!*"

Arnie Garth's worst nightmare seems about to come true. He can almost feel his treacherous heart caving in and whatever it is that causes strokes sneaking straight back to give him another one. This time for keeps.

"*Ambrose!*" he cries again but isn't certain whether he is actually crying it out loud.

"*Ambrose indeed!*" endorses Noreen, thinking that it must be a word Americans use to express awe and delight, which – to no one's surprise more than her own – is a little like what she is feeling right now. (And who knows, perhaps one day the word Ambrose might mean just that! Stranger things have happened. A few of them could be about to happen this very evening.)

The couple, who are of course nowhere near a couple, are standing outside one of Las Vegas's most magnificent and luxurious hotels, the shimmering lights bathing the marble columns and their persons in a warm neon glow.

All along their slow and wondrous journey here they've passed billboards and illuminated signs announcing that tonight is NECA night. That magical occasion when glittering and somewhat indecent prizes are presented to the lucky and talented winners of the National Erotic Cinema Awards. The goody bags – or, as they are termed here, the Woody Bags – handed out to the invited guests are themselves worthy of prizes. That Arnie Garth, founder and CEO of Bulge Entertainment, should be here in town amongst the illustrious throng – the *titeratti*, as the press have dubbed them – is a given. That this is the last place Arnie Garth would wish to be seen right now, with so wildly innocent a companion, a human being light years from indecent, is a given ten times over.

"*This* is where she recommended we go eat?" says Arnie, staring at the faultlessly awesome hotel with dissembled incredulity.

"I think so. Yes. This is the place. What's wrong with it, Arnie?"

"What's wrong with it? What's… er… *wrong* with it? I'll tell you what's wrong with it, Noreen… sweetheart."

He can see that she is waiting, as she admires the knee-trembling splendour, the classic design, as she watches smart cars arrive and even smarter men in their multi-coloured tuxedos alight and escort staggeringly well-proportioned young ladies in their elegant fake-furs and very little else. Not your everyday Vegas clientele, as I've pointed out. But this is a special night. And this place Noreen happens to have chosen – or to which she has kindly been signposted – just happens to be the venue for those aforementioned, highly prestigious and much trumpeted dirty movie awards.

Who knew?

"It's a *dive*, Noreen!" announces Arnie Garth, his voice a tad too high. "A hell-hole! That cardigan – *that cardigan* –deserves somewhere far better. I know this little Italian place. You'll love it. I really got into those guys' food when… I was in Rome… shooting the musical biopic of Pope John Paul. The seventh." He grabs a solid, diamanté arm and yanks her away from the unbearable shoddiness of it all.

A confused Noreen finds herself being almost dragged halfway back along the Strip. Well, no *almost* about it. If Arnie Garth has even the remotest chance of 'seducing' this strange and saintly creature into loving him unconditionally, he really needs to steer them both as far away from the notorious NECA as possible. Even though it is usually one of the pinnacles of his sleazy but stellar career and none more so than tonight, when he and his cast are up for several of the major awards. Some of them almost prosecutable.

This dragging, however, is not quite as simple as he might have thought. For a start, Arnie is smaller than Noreen and nowhere near as strong. The effort is also compounded to a huge degree by Noreen being rooted to the spot in her serious work boots – or, in fact, to several spots – in utter and repeated mesmerisation at what this miraculous place has to offer.

"Oh, Arnie, the lights are so beautiful! Can this really be a place of sin?"

"Only the seven deadly ones. Plus, a couple or three more. Boy, I'm so hungry. You know what they say in Nevada – hasta la pasta!"

"I never heard that."

Before they can reach the only safe refuge of true squalor, a voice stops them. "Pssst! Hey!"

They turn to find a slightly seedy-looking man in a fraying brown suit and two-tone shoes stepping out of the bushes lining Caesar's Palace. He is shaking his head in a distinctly nervous fashion, like he is having some sort of argument with himself, and looks practically on the verge of tears. As if he has an empathy detector built in, the man immediately focuses his full attention on the lady in the twinkling *schmatter*.

"Can you help me please, ma'am? I-I've been – well, I've been such a fool! See, I've gambled away everything I've got. *Everything!* Including my kid's college money and my sweet wife's liver transplant fund. The only thing I have left is… is this watch my dear late mother gave me." He pulls up his sleeve. It is indeed a fine-looking piece of jewellery. Noreen's stare lands on it for a brief, admiring moment but is soon firmly back on the man again. "It's a Cartier, see?" he points out. "Cartier. From France. And I-I'd be *so* grateful if you'd give me just fifty bucks for it, so I-I could afford my bus fare home to face the music." At this he blinks back the tears of sorrow and guilt, staring earnestly into Noreen's already moist eyes.

"Oh, you poor man! Of course!" She fishes in her bag, bringing out a tiny ferret, which throws the man a little, but then some bills. "Here's – let me see – it says one hundred dollars on it, will that—"

Before the man in the brown suit can snatch it, Arnie is right there, grabbing his skinny arm with a firm, unyielding hand. Noreen gasps in shock.

"*Arnie!*"

With his other hand, Arnie pulls up the stunned man's sleeve. There are at least half a dozen identical timepieces running up his arm. Noreen is open-mouthed and gawping.

"And just for future reference, shmuck? 'Cartier' *doesn't* begin with a 'K'."

"Fuck you!" responds the man. "With a 'c' *and* a 'k'!" With this snappy exit line, he runs off down the street.

"Shame on you!" calls Arnie. "Does your mom know what you do for a living?"

"Or your poor sweet wife and kid," adds Noreen, then realises how she might have got that bit wrong. Arnie looks at her and notices that she appears quite upset. "Arnie… he was so… I truly thought he…"

Arnie puts an arm round her, squeezing the diamanté and

feeling a shoulder like toughened granite. "I know, baby," he comforts her. "But hey, not all Americans are scuzzballs."

"I know you aren't a scuzzball, Arnie. Whatever they are."

When Arnie nods to her this time, staring into that disconcertingly innocent, make-up-free face and those oh so trusting pale-blue eyes, he senses a curious and completely unfamiliar sensation starting to wash over him. He wonders for a moment if it is fear or IBS or even imminent heart failure, then realises – with a total shock of the new to his system – that it might very well be guilt.

He shakes his head briskly, as if ridding himself of a wasp.

"C'mon, kiddo, let's eat.

Chapter Twenty-Three

Cold tea and cold rice are bearable, cold looks and cold words are not. (Japanese Proverb)

Arnie is chowing down on a huge plate of steaming hot fettuccine, when he senses Noreen staring up at him from her overabundant salad.

"What?" he says, meeting her kindly gaze. "I got some on my nose?"

"No. Well, yes." Noreen smiles. "And your chin. And your... but, it's just nice to see you enjoying yourself."

Arnie looks around the busy Italian restaurant in case anyone might be listening. The massive room is designed like a trattoria built to feed half of Naples and packed with lively and universally enormous, homegrown tourists, most of whom could be mistaken for participants in the final stages of a national pasta eating contest. But fortunately, they don't resemble anyone he knows in his chosen field (except maybe that oversexed corpulent couple in *Beauty and Obese*).

He shakes his head and sighs. "Saint Noreen. Listen, kid," he says, philosophically, "life is shit, and then you croak. You gotta get your jollies where you can."

"Well… I suppose I am, aren't I? Getting my 'jollies'. You do talk funny, Mr Garth." She smiles to herself. "Do you know, I feel quite jolly just being with you. Isn't that curious?" She demolishes a huge chunk of mango then squirms at the unexpected taste. "Oh, I thought that was a stewed turnip. How odd. Not horrible though. What was I saying – yes, me, batty old Noreen Millburn, who has never been out of the Lake District in her life. Or eaten one of these size-of-a-house salads. Or met a maker of so many educational, religious films."

He shrugs, modestly.

"Of course, I was really upset with that watch-shmuck earlier, but now… well, strange as it may seem, I'm almost a little bit glad I'm here."

Arnie thinks for a moment. And finds himself so taken aback by his own thinking that the quivering mound of fettucine on his fork is paused en route to his open mouth.

"You know something," he says quietly, "so am I, Noreen. Almost a little bit glad *you're* here. Sweetheart."

Noreen suddenly looks concerned. The gentle smile fades from her face. "Hang on. How do I know you're not just trying to get me into bed again? Like you did back in—"

"*No. No, Noreen!*" interrupts Arnie. He is being quite insistent. "Really. I-I don't want to sleep with you. In fact, I'm not sexually attracted to you in any whichway whatsoever. To be honest, I wouldn't go for you poached."

"Oh, Arnie," she smiles, gratefully. "You're just saying that."

"I'm not. Really, you… you gotta believe me, Noreen. In fact, you're the first lady I ever took out to dinner since puberty and didn't want to jump her bones. Save perhaps my mom."

"That is so sweet, Arnie," says Noreen, genuinely touched. "But technically – I'm taking *you* to dinner."

Arnie laughs out loud, causing others around to stare. Curiously, unlike on certain previous occasions, the diners here have been far too preoccupied with their groaning plates to pick up on the disparity between two of their more unusual fellow diners. And they're not really over-bothered now.

"Yeah! How about that? A dame treating *me* to my food. Another first."

To his surprise, she suddenly taps his tanned and compact hand with her own larger, far paler one.

"Oh, Arnie. You must be such a lonely man."

Arnie doesn't say anything for quite a while. Noreen wonders if he even heard and whether it is worth saying again.

"You must be—"

"Yeah, I heard," says Arnie finally. And then he nods, as if this is something that has only just dawned on him. Which, in truth, it probably only just has. At least for real, not as a lecherous ploy. He leans across the table, trying to avoid her salad with his elbows. "Y'know, Noreen," he says, with an almost resigned sigh, his eyes just starting to brim. "I really do think I am. What you said."

Their eyes meet, hers pale blue and suffused with so much empathy, his squitty-brown and slightly moist. Even Arnie Garth would be hard-pressed to deny that this is what one could call a moment. The sort of thing you might even see in films. Not the type he makes, of course, when the script is more likely to say that their thighs meet, but something he has definitely seen on a screen somewhere.

He hardly dares to entertain the thought, but could this really be the time – the life-saving, death-defying instant – when things might just be starting to change? He leans even closer towards her. And closer...

"*Arnie!*" comes a cry from the doorway.

The moist-eyed man thus addressed freezes for an instant, mid-moment, eyes immediately drying. Very slowly, he turns around.

Noreen watches as the face of Arnie Garth, previously bathed in an unusually calm and almost peaceful glow, suddenly develops an expression she has seen only once before on a man, when as a young girl she had opened the door to her parents' bedroom and found her rugged, hard-drinking, sheepherding father in bed with a Georgette Heyer novel.

Her companion's shock and horror, and – dare she label it – *shame,* is unmistakeable. Yet Noreen Millburn has absolutely no idea why.

The approaching crowd – and there must be at least a dozen of them – appear at first glance to be extremely sociable and indeed highly elated to catch her hitherto attentive dinner companion unawares at his table. Alright, the ladies aren't wearing a huge amount of clothing, but it is the desert for heavens' sake. And no one in the restaurant is exactly dressed to the nines. Or even to the fives.

The group certainly does look excessively healthy, especially up top, of which in the ladies' case you can see rather a lot. Actually, the men's case too, as their silky shirts are mostly unbuttoned, revealing far less spare fat than their fellow dinners. Far less chest hair too, interestingly. And more jewellery.

Noreen doesn't personally warm to heavy make-up and bright mascara and long false eyelashes and piercings and tattoos and bustiers and that sort of stuff, but she likes to think that she is not one of those people who disapprove of what others do. This would hardly be charitable or in the spirit of live and let live – and, indeed, help live – to which she has always generously subscribed. And if the gentlemen want to wear a lot of gold and nipple adornments with their formal wear, then good for them. She is sure that they have worked hard for it. And they certainly appear to have the bodies.

What she does find a little more difficult to compute, or at least align comfortably in her mind, is how these clearly very jolly and extremely glamorous people might fit into her current benefactor's world of educational and faith-based filmmaking. She can hardly envisage any of these lovely ladies taking on the role of Saint Joan of Arc or that sweet little Mother Teresa, or indeed imagine any of the men here, despite their pigmentation, giving their Bishop Desmond Tutus, but she has heard somewhere that actors can be extremely versatile.

As she is pondering this and taking in the scene with some considerable, yet far from judgmental, interest, the newcomers are all over Arnie, slapping and kissing, hugging and fondling, all the while muttering excited comments which she clearly finds some difficulty in fully deciphering.

Arnie thanks every God for small mercies.

"Hey, guy, we didn't see you at the awards," says one of the back-slapping men.

"Naw, well, you know," Arnie explains, comprehensively, checking in all the time with Noreen, who is thankfully still struggling. "Hey, well, it's been so great catchin' up with you…"

"Haven't seen you since the wrap party for *Malcolm Triple-X*," says one of the young women, throwing her arms and everything else around him, until all Noreen can see is a shiny globe of sweaty nakedness glistening under the lights, which could belong to any of them. She hopes Arnie isn't going to suffocate, as she really doesn't relish giving him mouth-to-mouth. Anyway, she has only ever done it on sheep, so it might not be the same.

A tall Latino man, who Noreen has to admit is rather good-looking, is inspecting her with unmasked curiosity.

"This your date?" he asks Arnie. Before Arnie can even half shrug, the guy continues *sotto voce* into Arnie's ear. "She's gotta do something very special."

Noreen does, in fact, hear this and is rather flattered that the attractive man can tell just by glancing at her that she is one for performing unsung good works back home.

Before Arnie can respond, not that he possibly could, another of the actresses bends down and French kisses him, her long and versatile tongue venturing so far inside his mouth and with such bulging freneticism, that it looks like she is transferring food for him to store in his cheeks through the winter.

Noreen feels that she has to pose the question, because surely even in America a gentleman would introduce a dinner guest to his friends, as this gushing, exuberant throng would clearly appear to be.

"Who are these people, Arnie?"

"I never seen them before in my life," says Arnie, to which everyone laughs, even Noreen. Such a witty guy.

A strapping young man in a white sleeveless tuxedo and explicit arm tattoos smiles at Noreen. "He gonna put you into one of his movies?" he asks, with what looks like a genuine interest.

"I-I can't act," stammers Noreen.

"Neither can I, hon," laughs a very pretty young woman. "*But I just won three Woodys!*"

On this she commences to draw out from a large bag a clutch of the distinctive golden awards we first met in Arnie's office, which has to seem like an age ago but really wasn't. With remarkable speed and a burst of tepid fettuccine, Arnie is up and shielding the offending items from Noreen's curious gaze. He manages to push the well-won Woodys swiftly back into the surprised young lady's bag.

Yet, even in this time of life-threatening crisis, Arnie Garth can't help himself from wondering if these glittering prizes had in fact been awarded to productions from his own prestigious stable. Professional pride is a hard baby to tame.

Fortunately – or not – Arnie doesn't have long to wait.

"Your *Shakespeare Trilogy* won the Woody Supreme!" announces another pneumatic young star.

By now, the entire restaurant appears to be staring in the direction of this exotic group. Some of the female diners, however, are taking time out from their own gawping in order to check on exactly where their husbands' and young sons' bulging eyes are focused.

"You don't say," says Arnie, really wishing that they hadn't.

"*Shakespeare*, Arnie!" says Noreen. "That is so wonderful. Do you know, at school I was very partial to Shakespeare. 'Tomorrow and tomorrow and tomorrow…'"

The gang all nod graciously, working really hard to decipher the words through the seriously screwy accent. One of the players finally gets there.

"You would enjoy these classics, ma'am," he says. "*King's Leer!*"

"Isn't that *King*…?"

"*A Midsummer Night's Wet Dream*," recalls another, blissfully. Arnie tries to cough over the offending one-syllable word but possibly not loud enough.

"A Mid-*what*?"

"And not forgetting *Coriol's Anus!*" announces another tuxedoed guy, with tears in his eyes.

"Coriolanus, yeah," corrects Arnie, pedantically, with a fearful, games-up smile.

"*Arnie*…?" says Noreen, as she takes an even closer, rather more critical look at the assembled, admiring bevy.

"Ye-es, sweetheart?" he responds, fearfully.

"What kind of films *do* you make?"

"What kind…? Well, they're kind of… y'know, as I said, educational. For people who find life hard. No, scrap the hard. Difficult. Lonely. Lonely guys. Y'know, like me! They're sorta public service movies! Yeah."

"You shoulda been at the awards!" coos one of the pretty public servants. "There was like this major retrospective of Arnie's oeuvre. You remember *The Best Rears of our Wives*? It was so classy."

Very slowly, Noreen Millburn rises from the table, wrapping her new American cardigan tightly around her sturdy but shaking Cumbrian frame, as if for protection.

"You lied to me, Mr Garth," she says, in quiet but angry sadness. "You are no longer my friend. *Or* my cousin!"

Attempting, with some considerable difficulty, to hold back the tears, the desolate woman squeezes a frantic path through the glitzy gang around the table. With a muttered 'excuse me', Noreen stumbles brokenly off towards the exit and the great unknown.

"*Noreen! Wait!*" cries Arnie. "*You're killing me here!*"

He scrambles through the confused yet strangely fascinated group and rushes out after his fleeing lifeline in utter desperation.

The colleagues from his industry appear quite perturbed. They look at each other in genuine concern. Finally, one of the actresses voices what they are all secretly thinking.

"Homely is the next big thing. You heard it here first."

Chapter Twenty-Four

If you are ready to believe, you are easy to deceive.
(Darkovan proverb)

Arnie Garth doesn't notice the gleaming white stretch limousine that has just pulled up outside Caesar's Palace Hotel.

Why should he? The city is full of stretch limos. A visiting alien would get scared off because they'd assume earthlings round here all had massive legs.

The benighted man is far too busy chasing after his very soul, any sight of which – let alone hope – he appears to have lost in the bustling, jostling, excitable, night-time crowd.

The passenger alighting from this particular white limo does, however, see Arnie.

It is the voice that stops her first. A voice screaming into the air yet almost lost in the hubbub around it. But when you have lived with a voice for so many irritating years, you tend to be able to pick it out from the crowd, like a mother in a busy maternity ward lactating at the sound of her newborn's cries (although this particular person has never lactated for anyone, on or off camera).

"*Noreen!*" yelps the voice, in clear and plaintive desperation.

"Come back! I need you so bad – my life will be Hell without you. And that ain't hyperbole. *Noreen*! I'll give you anything! More sheep... bigger cans – for charity that is, not, y'know... a gigantic farm in the ass-end of nowhere. *Anything!*"

Let's be honest, Las Vegas was truly a bit of a no-brainer.

It is the very first place Mrs Melisande Garth might have expected her devious rat of a still-breathing husband to make for, especially on awards night. He has never been known to miss an opportunity to be recognised and lauded by his peers.

When, however, her investigators had first informed her that Arnie Garth had bolted directly from his LA hospital bed to somewhere in a bleak godforsaken north-western corner of England – *England for Crissakes!* – she had been totally mystified. Yet, at the same time, she had found herself feeling curiously ecstatic and, on this occasion, no faking was involved.

Ecstatic because the evidence presented to her, at great personal expense, was clearly a major indicator of mental derangement. She wouldn't have been surprised to discover that 'flight to Cumbria' is actually on the accepted dementia checklist for doctors and psychiatrists, along with being unable to recall the current year or the name of the sitting President.

Stopping her errant husband's credit cards had been a serious weapon in her arsenal, but by no means the only one. She had intended simply to use it as a tool to restrict his spending before his clearly imminent death – and hopefully even to hasten it. Yet this serendipitous sighting of the swine-in-question, as he cries out the name of another woman in the very thoroughfare on which Melisande is alighting, in words that suggest this is not merely another of his mid-life, Trump-like flings with a none-too-choosy porn starlet, is a potential game-changer. It is an accepted fact in the adult entertainment industry that no porn starlet is ever called Noreen or owns a sheep farm. That is one perversion too far.

A new and desperate sense of urgency has just been brought to the proceedings. Mrs Garth is now obliged to regroup and ponder swiftly on what deeply Machiavellian change of strategy this fortunate glimpsing might entail. The ageing icon tells herself that what has just been revealed to her was no accident. It must have been a sign from God. (And perhaps, in this, she is not wholly mistaken.)

"*Oh, my shit! It's Melisande!*"

The Botoxed face, formerly like thunder, immediately converts to one of total disdain, as she confronts the sorry huddle of fans who have recognised her. They are uniformly male, balding, chubby, wearing heavy metal T-shirts and clutching DVD covers and magazines.

Instinctively, she starts to unbutton. They all get their cameras out.

Sometimes she really does wish that she was still plain Doris Armstretter from Bowling Green, Ky.

*

The Penthouse Suite at the Dime After Dime is empty when Arnie steams back in.

He can't imagine where else Noreen might have gone. To the best of his knowledge, there aren't any sheep in Las Vegas.

The night reception guy isn't particularly helpful.

"I'm looking for a big homely British chick," says Arnie, in some considerable panic. "Wearing a diamanté cardigan."

Without even looking up from the register, the clerk reaches down under his desk and pulls up a thick, spiral-bound volume. He slides it over to Arnie. "Pages forty-nine to sixty-two."

Arnie glares at him and rushes back out into the cruel and sultry night.

*

Meantime Melisande Garth, newly disembarked at her infinitely smarter and more tastefully excessive hotel, clicks briskly down the plush corridor to her room. She is accompanied by an assistant organiser of the side events that always garland the major erotica awards ceremonies. This younger and clearly very efficient Asian woman is scrolling a spreadsheet on her laptop, whilst lugging Melisande's bulging suitcase.

"And at midnight, Ms Melisande, you are performing... girl on girl. On girl. At the Crazy Horse."

"Screw the Crazy Horse!"

"That's on Tuesday."

The great star suddenly stops mid-corridor and turns to face the young woman.

"Honey, I am having a crisis here, okay? Capisce? I'm crising. My mentally challenged lummox of a husband is about to give *my* inheritance away to what I'm guessing is some dentally retarded, Limey moneygrabber he picked up on his batshit crazy little jaunt across the pond. So, the only way I'd honor any of those stupid commitments of yours with any enthusiasm is if he kindly keeled over and died without having the chance to change his frigging will..." She trails off, struck by a sudden and absolutely brilliant notion. She can't understand why she hasn't thought of it already. But it's never too late.

Except, of course, for cheating bastard husbands.

Melisande Garth, known only to her legion of fans by her first name, whistles jauntily to herself, as she waves her key card at room 805, whipping her cell phone from the bag in one swift, practised move and grabbing her case with the other. All she hears before she slams the door on the helpless young woman is, "But what about the Crazy...."

This is probably the moment when the young woman decides that this entertainment internship isn't exactly what she had been led to believe, but Melisande is far too busy to care.

"Hi. Irving?" she whispers throatily into the phone, aiming

her still impressive body towards the minibar. "It's Melisande! Mel – yeah, Doris... I'm good... they're healing. Say, you remember that little 'difference of opinion' you had with Stormy Petrel's agent? Her late agent, yeah. Who was that guy you...?... Why would anyone be bugging my phone? Irv, I may be dirty but I'm clean.... yeah?... Big Louie? Sounds about right. You got his number?"

Melisande Garth can feel herself smiling. Something she had never believed that, emotionally or structurally, she might ever be able to do again.

Chapter Twenty-Five

It is easy to tempt a frog to the river. (Serbian proverb)

Many Americans believe that once you've seen the wondrous Venetian Hotel in Las Vegas, with its meticulous recreation of the grandeur and beauty of the City of Water, there is absolutely no need to sort out your passport and shlep to the other side of the planet to see its historic and slowly crumbling inspiration.

After all, this far more accessible version has no disgorging cruise ships, no unsavoury smells, no confusing currency, less garlic and far fewer Italians. What's more, aside from all the 'locals' speaking relatively intelligible English, it has people-mover sidewalks, a branch of Madame Tussaud's and giant Buddha statues. Suck on that, Venezia.

The Venetian does, of course, also have a casino. In fact, more than one. Why wouldn't it – this is surely its raison d'etre (or should I say, ragion d'essere)?

The clientele of this sumptuous Italianate gambling den, on such a balmy summer evening, whilst perhaps not so greatly surpassing the innate sophistication and glamour of their For Luck's Sake counterparts, are distinctly better-off and looking considerably more pleased with themselves, in these stunning and impressively lavish surroundings.

To be fair, some of the visitors have gussied and spruced up for the occasion, taking their lead perhaps from Hollywood movies, rather than any enforceable, ultra-strict dress code.

One person, however, doesn't appear to have received the bulletin and is still looking more like a refugee from *Ryan's Daughter* or *How Green Was My Valley*, albeit with a touch of diamanté thrown in.

She is also losing control of her newly acquired booty big time. That poor kids' hospital back in Ullswater, UK, looks like it might just have to go begging elsewhere for its new hydrotherapy wing.

"Twenty-nine red," announces the unsmiling croupier, matter-of-factly. As if lives and futures and children's educations don't depend on it.

Noreen Millburn sighs, watching the lion's share of her chips being scooped away from her. She really has no idea why she has fled here of all places nor why she has suddenly developed a seemingly uncontrollable urge to plunge headlong into her first deadly or at least quite precarious sin.

The moment she fled that awful restaurant – well, it was really rather a lovely restaurant and she had been so enjoying her obscenely large salad – she had absolutely no idea where her clumpy Lakeland walking boots would lead her. It was almost as if she had been helplessly propelled along that apparently world-famous, bustling, neon-drenched strip by pure, adrenaline-saturated shock.

Shock at the wicked betrayal by a man she had been very slightly just beginning not wholly to dislike. Even greater shock at herself for being so naive as to believe that a manifestly disreputable little slug like this Mr Garth would have devoted his life and energies to making educational films about the saintly and the good, while quite patently he was a sleazy but clearly prime-moving purveyor of the most soulless and saddest exploitative content known to man. And possibly woman, she wasn't that clued-up on porn audience demographics.

Even when she had plunged into the vast hotel lobby – stunned almost to immobility by its exquisite domed ceiling, with all that gilt and those hand-painted frescoes – she had no idea that her feet would lead her almost inexorably down the unimaginatively named Restaurant Row towards the Venetian Casino. And, once there, you could have knocked her down with a feather, as her old mum used to say, to find herself sitting with all these exotic people, some with bottoms the sizes of which she had never encountered before, at least not on anything that wasn't reared for its milk. She has no idea what has gotten into her and, perhaps more disconcertingly, even less idea how to get it out.

"Can I bring you anything, ma'am?"

The waitress is smiling down at her and seems very kind. Noreen checks her dad's old wristwatch, which she wears constantly. It is still on Cumbrian time, so she is really quite clueless.

"Horlicks, please," she tells the girl. Always a safe bet. "Four sugars."

"I'm afraid I don't know that one."

"*Really?*" says a surprised Noreen, who thought the whole world would be endeared to her favourite milky bedtime drink. "Ovaltine?" she hazards, but is met with a polite shake of the head and a delicate retreat.

Noreen simply sighs and surveys the meagre remnants of her once healthy stash. She is so wrapped up in her thoughts and her sadness that she doesn't immediately register the inordinately smooth, deep and rather delicious voice almost in her left ear.

"*Bet on black thirteen.*"

The last thing Noreen Millburn needs right now is advice from a stranger or, indeed, a conversation with anyone. So, she chooses not to look at the adjacent person proffering it. Even if the speaker really does have a voice that goes down to his boots and is having rather the same effect on her anatomy. But she was brought up not to be impolite. Intensely annoying, perhaps, but never rude.

"I'm sorry, sir," she says, without taking her eye off the currently immobile roulette-wheel. "I'm really in no mood for…"

Yet as she tries to utter these words of dismissal, she feels a curious power so much stronger than even her own fierce determination, a primal force compelling her to crane her still-bobbled head around and upwards towards the sound.

And now she sees him.

A tall, unbelievably handsome, tastefully dressed gentleman, with skin of a rich blackness she can only compare to that of her beloved Herdwick sheep, when they are newly born. But, of course, this gentleman is most probably much the same age as her and, not being a Herdwick, unlikely to lighten with time, save perhaps for some distinguished grey in later life.

The man is wearing the most immaculately tailored suit of cream linen, without, so far as she can ascertain, a single crease or wrinkle. It is as if it has been laminated over what she can only imagine is an equally exquisite body, with that rich and, to her sheltered Cumbrian eyes, relatively unfamiliar human skin colour going all the way down. He makes everyone else in this incredible room, even the smartest, look as if they have crawled in from their own particular slum in their workaday rags.

Noreen observes, as an unexpected flush surges through her quivering frame like a crashing wave (a phenomenon of which, she is certain, he must be all too aware), that this man is smiling at her. Not just with his mouth and all those splendidly regular and dazzling teeth, but also with his cavernously deep brown eyes. Everything about him appears to sparkle, as if someone gave him a spritz of premium fairy dust just before he came in.

"My name's Lyle," he says, in that same profoundly musical voice.

But, of course, she thinks, *what other voice would he use?*

"I didn't mean to interrupt."

"N-no. No, you did-n't," stutters Noreen, thinking that she has never heard the name Lyle before, except on a Golden Syrup tin. "H-h-h-h-hello. I'm Noreen. Noreen Millburn. Miss."

"Well, Noreen Millburn, Miss – go on. Please. Place your bet."

With this he glides his impeccably (but in no way prissily) manicured hand over hers and uses it to push all of her remaining chips firmly onto black thirteen. She shudders, pleasurably, at the unexpected warmth of his touch. *What in heaven's name is going on here?,* she thinks to herself.

The wheel is spun. Noreen's head moves up and down and around, the bobble on her hat bouncing wildly, as if to some native rhythm from a country she's never heard of, as it follows the movement of the tiny but mesmerising white ball. Round and round it goes, making that distinctive sound that really is like no other, except perhaps for the curious death rattle I once heard on an old Guatemalan fisherman, when I arrived just a moment too early.

Whoa! I'm back again and hark at me interfering in the narrative, at what I truly believe has to be one of the most – if not *the* most – crucial points in this entire sorry saga. Unforgivable of me, I know. And quite unprofessional. The real scribes upstairs would be plotzing. But okay, now that I'm here, I have to tell you that unlike certain other occurrences hitherto, this particular development isn't exactly what I had in mind. No sirree. Not by a long shot. Not my MO, as they say. And where it's going to take us, God only knows.

Possibly.

You can almost see the ears on gamblers all around the table twitching in unison to the ominous sound of that mischievous demon ball as it smacks the sides more and more portentously. While the huge and beautiful wheel slows inexorably down. Slower and slower. Until finally the unpredictable little guy settles firmly into the cosy number twelve slot. Noreen stares at it, looking really upset. *Bugger!* she thinks, then swiftly berates herself for her unspoken language.

But suddenly, to her consternation, the tiny ball leaps straight up again from its resting place. Right into the air.

As everyone gawps it simply hovers up there for maybe a second, then slowly moves right across the entire wheel and drops smartly back down again directly into number thirteen.

"*Thirteen black!*" announces the croupier, looking slightly more engaged than anyone has seen him hitherto.

Noreen is considerably more engaged. She is, in fact, beside herself with engagement (whilst everyone else around the table is turning to everyone else who isn't them and saying, "*did you see that?*" or, "*did you fucking* see *that!*")

"Yes! *Yes!*" she screams. Without thinking, Noreen turns to a beaming Lyle and gives him a huge hug. She instantly realises what she has done and not just because Lyle is ceasing to breathe. "Oh. Excuse me. Sir. I got carried away. But – thank you. Thank you *so* much!"

Lyle is appealingly modest. "Noreen, it was surely my pleasure." He smiles to himself for a moment and those sensational eyes close, as if he is deep in thought. "Noreen… *Noreen* – such a wondrous name. It conjures up so many magical images."

She nods. "Does it?"

"Uh huh. Let's see now… hmmm… it is, how shall I put it, *redolent*. Yes, redolent – of rolling green fields… of friendly, rough-haired sheep… mmhmm… and of mountains. *Yes!* Big, beautiful, imposing mountains. Whoa! Hey – a lake! In fact, a whole district of lakes!"

Noreen's mouth opens wide enough to suck in a roulette wheel. "That is amazing! *I live in the Lake District!* And I keep sheep. And... my absolute favourite is my black faced sheep! That's Geoffrey."

"No!" cries Lyle, clapping his long, slim fingers together. "I would so love to hear more about Geoffrey. And, of course, any other sheep or livestock you may have in your social circle, should you feel so inclined." His voice lowers. "Noreen, Ms Millburn, might I be so bold as to whisk you away?"

Noreen doesn't answer. She can't answer, she has no words. Never having been whisked, she simply stares into this extraordinary man's utterly beautiful face, unblinking, unthinking. His eyes appear to be reading her very soul. Or possibly souls. Were this person Lyle to tell her that she was a helicopter right now, the bobble on her hat would immediately whirl around and around and she would soar happily up to the ceiling.

But he doesn't. He simply – and very gently – takes her hand.

Chapter Twenty-Six

*The seagull thinks it is an act of kindness to give the
fish a lift in the air. (Irish proverb)*

Had Lyle of the sharp suit and nice hands whisked Noreen
Millburn (Ms), from Rough Fell, Cumbria, England, up to the
moon or another even more distant planet, it would not have
been more disorienting and unbelievable than what he shows
her on this endless, please-never-let-it-end evening.

They begin at the Treasure Island, with its stunning blue-
water lagoon and mesmeric Cirque de Soleil production. Yet
this has hardly commenced, when she finds herself watching the
huge volcano erupt at The Mirage.

Paris, Ancient Rome, the Wild West, Hollywood. It is as if she
is being taken on a trip around the world, escorted by a singular
being whom she met only minutes ago but is already starting to
feel that she has known forever.

Noreen realises that she has hardly uttered a single word –
unless you count 'ooh', 'aah' and a melange of sharp intakes of
breath as being part of accepted vocabulary – until they reach
the famed Bellagio resort, with its stupendous ballet of dancing
fountains.

"So beautiful," she says, finally, which is just about all that she can manage right now, although she is feeling and thinking so much more, as the lights play on her entranced English face and the delicate spray lands like a caress on her pale, unembellished skin. "Thank you so much, Mr Lyle."

"It is my pleasure, Miss Noreen, and no more than you deserve." He smiles kindly. "I had thought that as you are so fond of lakes, you would enjoy being on the shores of Italy's Lake Como."

"Are we in Italy, Lyle?" ask Noreen, who after all this wouldn't be a bit surprised.

"You are so charming, dear Noreen," he laughs, his extraordinary teeth sparkling even more brightly in the night-time air. He appears to have a larger complement of them than anyone she has ever met. "No, I haven't transported you across the seas to Italia. But some clever gentleman has – at a cost of nearly two billion dollars."

"Goodness," she says, "that's more than..." She stops at this point as she has no idea what this figure is more than, because she has never heard such a figure in her life.

"It is indeed." Lyle smiles again, but this time with his long linen arm around her. Noreen can feel the extraordinary warmth almost singeing her brand new cardigan but feels no desire to escape.

"May I take you shopping?" he asks, gently.

"*They've got a Tesco too!*" she yelps excitedly, fishing in her bag for her purse.

*

Noreen Millburn's initial disappointment that her favourite supermarket is not to be found anywhere within the glass-enclosed luxury of the Via Bellagio dissolves into confusion when she discovers that she has not heard of a single shop that is.

Tiffany, Dior, Chanel, Gucci, Prada. They don't even sound like real names. Where's the Boots and the WHSmith? Where's the Oxfam and Barnardo's? Yet the merchandise within these small but brightly lit emporiums does indeed look extraordinary, whilst resembling in no conceivable way anything a person might usefully wear or use.

She can hear Lyle sweetly offering to buy her anything and everything under the sun, but despite being almost totally under the spell of this kindly yet alluring vision, who for some unfathomable reason wants to be really nice to her, possibly because of her name and provenance, she is determined not to let him go through too much of his hard-earned money this evening.

Although the man has graciously offered a brief explanation, she is still not quite certain as to exactly how he has become as wealthy as he clearly is, but this is possibly because 'dabbling' is not a profession they have in the Lakes. It's probably an American thing, like ranching or barbecuing.

After some persuasion and a fair deal more walking (no problem at all in her very practical hiking boots), Noreen does agree to accompany her new friend into a very clean and clinical beauty shop, which he appears to know, where the young ladies are happy to work late and are, as he explains, always excited to meet a challenge.

"I shall leave you in their capable hands," he tells Noreen, as he guides her towards a welcoming group of white-clad and clearly enthusiastic professionals.

Noreen, soon to be quite alone once more in this alarming new world, finds herself wanting to beg the virtual stranger (yet possibly also her first ever bestie) not to go. But, somehow, she knows in her heart that whatever the beautiful person does must clearly be for the best and that her tall dark saviour in the fine linen suit will definitely be back very soon to do some more whisking.

Chapter Twenty-Seven

You don't go searching for bones in a lion's den.
(Somali proverb)

You're probably wondering, with all this going on, what about Arnie?

If you're not, I sure as hell am.

I know the situation. I know the rules. The man has only a couple of days to retrieve his misplaced soul and save his own rotten life. And, of course, as the old song goes, to fall in love and be loved in return, etc etc. So okay, I'll admit, I have my concerns.

Unsurprisingly, Arnie Garth is pretty worried too. If Noreen isn't exactly his meal ticket (especially after the meal Melisande just made of his finances), she is most certainly his lifejacket. And he is starting to feel that he is totally drowning without her.

One would think that it shouldn't be so onerous a task to find a dumpy English shepherdess without a hint of make-up, wearing a woolly red bobble-hat, a new but still appalling cardigan and ancient mud-stained hiking boots in Vegas. She wouldn't exactly blend in with the crowd (unless, of course, there's an English shepherdess convention in town. Stranger things…).

The only person, however, even vaguely resembling Noreen Millburn of Rough Fell, at least in the glittery cardigan department, turned out to be an octogenarian from Nebraska, who had believed all her birthdays just arrived at once, when Arnie grabbed her and excitedly spun her round.

In his cascading desperation, Arnie even storms into a pretty little 24-hour wedding chapel, where a young Korean couple dressed identically as WALL-E are being married by Elvis Presley (if the King was ever an anorexic Polynesian in her sixties). The cries of 'mazeltov' are appreciated but Noreen Millburn is nowhere to be seen.

His hopes are raised momentarily as he steams out of the ceremony, when he feels fingers of considerable power grip him around the arm.

"Noreen?" he says, spinning round in some relief. He discovers a large man in his forties beaming down at him.

"*Noreen?*" says the confused man. "Hey, Arnie, don't you remember me?"

Arnie shakes his head, so the man makes a thrusting gesture with his hips, rolls his eyes back into his head and puckers his lips. "Ooooooooooooooooohhhh!" he goes.

"*Midas Welby Spring!*" cries Arnie, greeting the legendary porn star. "Didn't recognise you with your clothes on. How you doing?"

"Great! Just waitin' on the missus. We're renewin' our vows tonight. Twenty years!"

"Well, isn't that just fine, in this day and age."

"Thanks, pal!" says the man. "Hey, make sure you send all my lovin' to Melisande. I used to have such a ball humpin' your wife."

"She'll appreciate that."

Arnie really doesn't need to be reminded about Melisande right now. And what other breeds of malice she might currently have aforethought of. *Well, at least she doesn't know where I am,* he tells himself in some relief. And thankfully she hasn't a clue about Noreen.

Otherwise, heaven only knows what she might do.

*

From her window on the fourteenth floor of Caesar's Palace, Melisande Garth is staring down on the plebeians milling around below.

If they only knew I was here, she thinks, all too aware that she has given special and regular pleasure to so many of them in the privacy of their own homes. She sometimes wonders exactly how many of these people, when actually being with a real woman rather than a thermoplastic equivalent or their own ever-loving selves, actually whisper her name under their hot rancid breath. And how large a percentage pronounce it wrong.

The knock on her door is sharp and insistent.

"About time!"

She strides smartly across the luxurious room, her high Louboutin heels only just supporting those famously long, enviably flexible legs and statuesque, tribute-to-science body. Throwing open the door, she looks straight ahead down an endless and seemingly empty corridor. And offers it a puzzled frown.

Suddenly she feels something tugging at the hem of her Balmain micro skirt.

Looking down, she sees a male person no more than four feet high, dressed almost entirely in the most supple leather, with a head completely shaven, save for a greying pigtail in a solid silver band.

"*Who in the name of God are you?*" asks Melisande.

"I'm Big Louie," says the man, striding confidently into the room.

Chapter Twenty-Eight

In the face of love and death, courage is useless.
(Spanish proverb)

The convivial Tequila Bar at Bally's Hotel is the twenty-eighth bar in Las Vegas that Arnie Garth has visited in the past few hours, in an increasingly fruitless search for his errant soulmate.

He has precious little idea why he should be looking for Noreen Millburn in hotel bars at all. There has been no prior evidence of predilection for alcohol, and it is hardly likely that Vegas hostelries have suddenly opened a franchise for dandelion tea (although he wouldn't actually put it past them). He can only think that a tiny hint was dropped when he passed one of those cleverly changing advertising sites on the strip and thought that he might just have caught a glimpse of my good self beaming out at him with a rather delicious cocktail in my hand. He might have done, he might not – who knows in this city built on sand and illusion?

By the time he pushes his way through the rabble to the busy Bally barman (excuse the alliteration – blame Bally's for boasting a busy bar), all he really knows for certain is that he desperately deserves a drink. But he supposes that he has to persist in making the same hapless enquiry.

"Bourbon, rocks. Biggie. Hey, don't s'pose you've seen a weird-looking English broad with lousy fashion sense and built like a truck?"

The woman sitting next to him at the bar slowly turns towards Arnie. He knows that it will be just one of those irritating persons with all her PC, ultra-liberal, feminist bullshit, although he is surprised to sense that, for once, even he is offended by the words that just flew out of his ignorant, chauvinist, filter-free mouth. Go figure.

Well, whatever, he's not going to give this particular sweetheart the pleasure of taking righteous umbrage right into his face. So, he turns the other way.

"That is *very* rude!" comes the inevitable reply. Yet not in the expected accent.

This time it is Arnie's turn to revolve slowly towards his neighbour. What he sees inspires in him a sudden and pretty urgent need to sit. He pushes the little guy on his other side off his barstool onto the floor and manages to plonk himself down before his legs completely give way.

"N-Noreen?"

The woman says nothing. Probably because she feels that a full Vegas makeover, big hairstyling, brand new, clingy designer frock and strappy Jimmy Choos speak with infinitely more eloquence than words. Especially when that fresh frock reveals attributes hitherto buried beneath several different and possibly even historic layers of Cumbrian wool.

"Where'd you get those – I mean that? I mean, all of it?"

"Well, Arnie," begins Noreen, unable to stop a smile from pulling those newly *'Autumn-Plum-ed'* and actually rather lush lips apart. Even what's behind them looks better, but surely she can't have had dentistry since they last met? Or added more teeth. "You'll never believe this—"

Arnie doesn't get the opportunity to put his credulity to the test, as he is halted by what even he would consider to be the most attractive male voice he has ever heard in his life.

"*Noreen!*" says Lyle, ignoring the podgy, balding guy in the tacky shirt seated beside her. "Your winnings, my English rose." Handing his newly transformed companion a huge roll of twenty-dollar bills, he announces, "Time to paint the town a deep, deep red. My favourite color!"

"*Who the hell are you?*" asks Arnie, unsurprisingly.

Lyle doesn't lose a single millimetre of smile. In fact, it broadens, as his rich chestnut eyes sparkle even more noticeably.

"And you must be Arnie. I've heard so much about you, you rascal. How could you have let this incredible creature escape?"

For a moment, Arnie can say nothing. Although he has to admit, if only to himself, that Noreen does indeed look like a different woman. Not your routinely, all-American gorgeous, yet somehow… how come he never noticed, he for whom the superficial goes really really deep?

He realises that he has to stand his ground.

"Huh?" he says.

Arnie would admit to some difficulty in looking away from this clearly beautiful man. He even wonders for a moment if the guy would ever consider a starring role in one of his— *No! Focus!*

"Noreen!" he chides. "I am shocked!"

"*Shocked?*" she responds, raising her voice. "Arnie Garth, you make sex films!"

"Only to pay my way through medical school!"

"Let's go, Lyle," says Noreen, throwing Arnie a last sorrowful, withering look. She snatches up her trusty handbag and a bulging carrier containing her discarded walking boots and cardigans old and new. Pausing only to hand the barman, whose family pictures are on a shelf behind him, some serious money for his partially deaf daughter's further education, she slips a lacy arm through that of the taller, infinitely more handsome man and they glide gracefully out of the bar.

Lyle turns at the door, to offer Arnie a comradely farewell wave.

"*Noreen!*" cries Arnie, watching his spiritual meal ticket – well, his Last Supper ticket – stroll obliviously away. "Don't leave lonely, orphaned, friendless me here on my own. Flying solo. Kindly Saint Noreen! *What about the curse?*"

"Hey, fella," admonishes the barman, "this is a family town!"

Arnie sighs. The jig would appear to be very much up. Before any serious jigging has even been attempted. How can he, Arnie Garth from lowly downtown Pittsburgh, compete with – *that?* Urbane, sophisticated, tall. And drop dead gorgeous, you should pardon the expression.

As he nurses his bourbon and signals the now hostile bartender for another, Arnie mulls on where he might have gone wrong in his life. Looking at the whole situation, clinically and totally dispassionately, he reckons that the objective answer is 'every-fucking-where'.

He downs his bourbon in one.

Every man has a defining moment in his life. This is the moment Arnie Garth decides that he can't just sit here on his own in the swish Tequila Bar at Bally's, staring hopelessly and morosely into an empty glass, his one hope of avoiding extinction newly vanished on fetchingly high heels into the neon mist. He didn't get anywhere in this life staring into an empty glass. Not Arnie Garth. No sirree.

He signals the barman for a refill.

Chapter Twenty-Nine

After a landslide, one more can be expected.
(Faroese proverb)

Arnie is actually pretty good at holding his drink.

He has held enough for a lot of people by the time he finds himself in the Crazy Girls showroom at the Planet Hollywood resort, watching a line of topless chorus girls kicking their leggy way to the front of the stage. Old habits die hard, and in one sense he finds it quite comforting to gaze at attractive young women wearing precious little clothing, in what now look pretty certain to be his final hours here on his own personal, far less glamorous planet. Okay, the whole show is relatively tasteful and restrained, but beggars can't be choosers.

So, he is pretty surprised when his bleary eyes are finally able to focus on what's actually going on up there.

"*Holy shit!*" he says, managing to offend an oversized, middle-aged couple sitting squashily beside him, who don't want that kind of talk when they are watching decent, respectable adult entertainment.

Yet I can't totally blame the guy for his language. Not this time. Because what – or more accurately, *who* – he has just seen up there, on that glitzy stage, *c'est moi!* I'm in my nice business suit – of course I am, it's a working day – but I have pulled my best Brooks Brothers shirt right up to my neck and am doing identical choreography to the lovely young ladies to my left and right. Naturally, they can't see me, and neither can anyone else. Excepting, of course, you know who. Which is a bit of a shame because, even though I say it myself, I am quite the mover.

But I have a job to do.

So, as soon as Arnie realises that his piggy little eyes aren't exactly deceiving him, I direct him with a nod to sidle over to the side of the stage. Which is easier said than done, as Middle America doesn't exactly come with much legroom.

"*What the?*" is what he predictably starts mouthing, even before he reaches me.

"I know I'm going against the critical consensus," I tell him, "but I quite enjoyed *Showgirls*." Industry talk – helps to break the ice. "How goes it, Arnie?"

Arnie is not so far gone he can't figure that folks might find it strange him talking pretty animatedly to an empty space at the side of the stage, but he is certainly way past the stage of giving a damn.

"As bad as it gets, Ambrose," he replies, although to be honest this is not entirely new information. I may not be one hundred percent omnipresent but I've been around. "Noreen knows I'm a big erotica producer – *and* by the way a major award winner yet again – so now she's been and had a gangbuster makeover and gone off with some show-offy black dude. So, it's goodnight and good luck."

"Hey, well win her back."

"It ain't that easy, mister! This guy, he's handsome… charismatic… *magnetic*. I personally think he's kind of stunning, in a completely non-homosexual way."

Now I'll level with you, because if there's one thing I've learned from the Dead Poets Society – and I *do* mean dead

– it's that a writer has to respect his or her readers. Another thing I know is you probably do have to be a little bit afraid of Virginia Woolf, but that's another story. See, since I discovered the rather large fly recently dropping unannounced into the ointment (Fly? A *scorpion*!), I haven't been entirely sure how to play this. Because I know that now, with these new and completely unforeseen circumstances – hey, total omniscience is also above my paygrade – I have to impart a clear and present sense of urgency into my man. Not that the whole thing isn't pretty damn urgent anyway. But, well, you know me and my sense of drama.

"*Oh, God!*" I gasp, dramatically. "*What was his name?* Quick, Arnie – what was his name?"

"How the hell would— Miles or Niles or…"

"Say it isn't Lyle?"

"That's it! Lyle!"

"*Jesus Christ!*" I say into his face. And I mean it. But I also admit that letting my entire body be enveloped in a crackling blue light is a bit Spielberg, bless him.

"*Jesus Christ?*" repeats Arnie, thinking anything's possible.

"It's an expression!"

I grab the trembling man by both shoulders, which of course he doesn't feel, because I'm totally weightless and also on a very strict diet, but it does help to make the point (and, ethereal or not, I can still smell his boozy breath, which trust me could wake the dead).

"Well, congratulations Arnie. Know who you just met? The name Satan ring any bells? Beelzebub? Diablo? Lucifer? Old Nick? Jack Nicholson in that movie with the pretty witches?"

"He definitely said his name was Lyle."

"That's just another aka! To the world, he's Lyle. To us, he's *formally known as Prince of Darkness!*"

Arnie just stares at me. "Shit!" he says, in horror. "Now I've got *him* on my case too?"

By this time my guy is completely freaked out. If he had hair, it would be turning white. *Wouldn't yours?* To discover that the girl of your dreams has gone straight over to the Devil! Okay, Noreen probably isn't the stuff that Arnie's dreams are usually made of, but she has certainly been on his waking and sleeping mind since at least Tuesday.

And if Lyle isn't quite the devil yet – I'm not the world expert on Satanic pecking orders, so sue me – he is certainly one of the devil's disciples. Which reminds me of a play by George Bernard Shaw, but don't get me started on late Irish playwrights. Not if you want to know what happens with Arnie and Noreen and Lyle by Sunday. Which I'm pretty damn interested in myself, by the way. Especially as to how this Lyle guy knew about the whole soul-misplacement *mishigas* forty-five years ago. You think there's a mole in heaven? Call for George Smiley!

Anyway, I'm so busy mulling over all these new complications, I almost don't notice that someone else is on the opposite side of the stage from yours truly, her thickly mascaraed eyes glued on an agitated husband talking feverishly into thin air.

And she has a far smaller gentleman watching right along with her.

Lucky I can lipread.

"*That him?*" exclaims Big Louie, who can't quite believe what he is looking at and would rather look at what's taking off on the stage just above him.

"Yeah. That's my Arnie. Talking to himself again. They tell me he did that at the hospital. How did you track him down?"

"I got my sources."

One of the dancers winks at him from the stage. He gives her a flip of his ponytail.

"And pretty much everyone in this burg owes Big Louie a favor."

Despite herself, Melisande is clearly impressed.

"Any idea what the hell he's doing here?" asks Big Louie.

"*Who knows?*" screeches Melisande, but quietly. "He's finally flipped. Guy's a danger to himself and others. That's why I want him... you know."

The diminutive man nods sagely. "It's the humane thing to do."

Chapter Thirty

A firm resolve pierces even a rock. (Japanese proverb)

Noreen Millburn is firmly back at The Bellagio, this time in the magnificent lobby, gazing in awe at the ceiling where artificial light plays on the massive Chihuly glass sculpture, the famous *Flori Di Como,* revealing such rich, vibrant colours that they put her own adored Lakeland blooms to shame. She wonders how on earth they manage to clean it and hopes that it isn't dangerous for the poor people employed to do so. The tiniest piece of glass in your eye and…

Yet she finds her attention swinging inexorably back to another work of art, one that is currently standing at the reception desk. The awestruck Englishwoman can't quite believe that an almost godlike man such as Lyle would be the least bit interested in someone so very much lesser such as she. She hadn't until this evening – or morning, or whatever blessed time of the day or night it is – believed that any man would give her a second look (she's seen the first look they give and it's usually one of disdain or repulsion). Well, maybe Arnie would look twice, especially now that there is more of her on show, but he hardly counts, considering what he clearly likes to gaze upon in extreme close-up for a living.

She still can't help, however, feeling the tiniest of pangs when she recalls the poor man's genuine and quite abject loneliness – and the fact of his bringing her all this way in the first place, indeed rescuing her, however bizarre his choice of destination. But she knows all too well that this is simply her obsession for helping dumb animals and it is high time she began to help herself.

Wrenching her eyes away from Lyle for just one tricky moment, Noreen notices that people are glancing at her, but not with that usual look of 'what's the bloody cat dragged in now?' that she has been accustomed to receiving for as long as she can remember. Even at school she was regarded as the podgy weirdo with the nits, despite the fact she offered to do everybody's homework for free and would let anyone stroke her ferret. Now she genuinely believes that the glances are more benign, possibly even admiring. Or at least envious. Especially when they follow her, as she moves a bit wonkily on her new high heels towards the striking man by the desk.

The female receptionist is staring up at Lyle with perfectly understandable lust, compounded by a profound professional regret.

"I am so sorry, Mr... Lyle. I'm afraid we don't have the kind of suite you're looking for that is currently unoccupied."

Lyle fixes his darkly unblinking gaze on the receptionist, staring right into her eyes. "Would you mind checking again, please?"

Noreen doesn't notice that his own wonderfully expressive eyes are suddenly suffused with a reddish glow. Nor that for a brief second those of the receptionist are catching the powerful beam full blast.

The young woman's expression goes instantly blank. "Of course," she says, robotically and turns to her computer. "Ah yes! I am so sorry. I spoke in error. The Presidential Suite is absolutely free." She hands her new guest a key card. "It's on the top floor. Enjoy!"

Noreen looks at Lyle with a radiance she normally reserves for sunset over one of her favourite lakes or the birth of a new lamb. *The Presidential Suite!* She is not quite certain why she is allowing herself to be transported upwards to the very heights of luxury by someone who is an almost total stranger, but this whole situation for some reason feels completely and rather happily out of her control.

She is no more certain as to who the President actually is these days, or what he is President of, but she hopes that he has left his suite tidy.

*

As if tracking the scent of a particularly elusive quarry, it is Arnie's turn to be at The Venetian now.

Not that he wants to be here.

Where he really wants to be is back in his sleazy hotel room, staring at that wall, as his day has already lasted way too long, and it is only by some miracle that he is still awake and functioning. But since the prospect looms large of a far longer, not to say eternal, rest in a place even hotter than Vegas, he has kindly agreed to indulge me.

I haven't been on a gondola since those days of Casanova. Don't get me started.

"You ever see *Death in Venice*?" I ask, as a conversational opener. "Oh. Excuse me. My bad. How about *Don't Look Now*?"

"How about shutting the fuck up?" says Arnie, which elicits a funny look from the gondolier, who of course speaks English and, so far as he knows, has only one passenger in his boat. "What the hell does Satan want with Noreen Millburn?"

I have to sigh at this. As does the gondolier, to be honest.

"*Noreen has two souls, dummy!*" I explain, politely. "She's a twofer! Claim one, get one free! Think of the PR bonanza in delivering that good sweet lady over to the dark side! Plus, she's the finest, kindest, charitablest person on the planet. And a virgin to boot. You know how tempting that is to a player like His Satanic Majesty? Catnip! You saw *The Exorcist.*"

"Noreen… gives Lucifer a hard-on?"

Now the gondolier knows he has a crazy on board.

"The boss is gonna do the lambada on my head for this," I tell Arnie, who just stares at me. "The Lord moves in mysterious ways. You have *got* to win her back, Arnie."

"*Me?* From Lyle? Oh, yeah. Sure! Arnie Garth versus Lord of the Flies. What's the support fight? Godzilla versus Kermit the Frog?"

The gondolier isn't even listening now. In the old days you could spot the nut-jobs straight off. These days they might just be talking on the phone. But he didn't see any earbuds on this guy.

"So that's it?" I exclaim. "You're just going to abandon the poor lady? Hey, you got her into this."

"*Me?* I got her—"

"Tomayto – tomato! Okay. I helped. With the best of intentions! But Arnie, if not you to the rescue – who else?"

"That – it's not my problem. I'm done for, anyway."

"He's going to *seduce* her, Arnie!" I tell him, in some frustration. "He's got moves you'd kill for. And hey, once she's given her body to the Devil, you think her soul – correction, her *souls* – will be far behind?"

Now Arnie turns to me. And I have to admit that for once even I am moved. Mind you, considering that most of the clientele I deal with are seconds short of rigor mortis, this has to be a bit more involving.

"Listen, Ambrose," he sighs, shaking his little balding head (I think he lost that stupid hat of his at the seventeenth bar). "It's over. Capisce? Noreen's never gonna fall in love with me. *Never ever!* Maybe there was a teensy bit of a chance once. Perhaps over that Italian supper, who knows? But now – with what she's found out about me, and the new demon on the block, say hello to hopeless."

"Maybe so," I am sadly obliged to agree. "But Arnie Garth, do you really wanna consign that poor, sweet lady to the fires of eternal damnation? Perpetual pain and torment. The Carpenters playing on an eternal loop. You think she deserves that? *Do you?*"

Arnie starts to writhe around on the plush nautical upholstery. The man seems totally torn.

" I – look, it's none of my business. *I can't help Noreen!* I can't even help myself, for crissakes! I'm nothing! I'm nobody. Comparatively speaking. Anyway, I… I don't know where he's taken her."

"The Bellagio."

"*You had to tell me!*"

"And it won't be the maid's room. Have a nice night."

There. I've said all I can say. So, with a farewell nod of my head, I step nimbly out of the elegant boat onto the water. And walk unsplashily away right down the centre of the mini Grand Canal. An oldie but a goodie.

"Siegfried and Roy, eat your heart out," I say to deaf ears.

Arnie remains alone in the gondola, conflicting emotions and impulses playing over his tormented face, like he's doing a screen test for Dr Jekyll and Mr Hyde. Until finally, he makes a decision.

"*Oh, for God's sake!*" he cries, into the tastefully painted and masterfully lit fake Venetian skies. Thrusting both hands into the water, he starts paddling towards the jetty. It isn't a tactic you see many passengers going for, but it does speed up the whole process and, on disembarkation, the gondolier has to admit he is quite glad to see the back of him.

Chapter Thirty-One

It is easy to tempt a frog to the river. (Serbian proverb)

The suite is like nothing Noreen Millburn has ever seen.

Considering that until very recently she had seen nothing much outside of a ramshackle old hovel in northern England, a few hills of the rugged kind and a cobbled Lakeland village, this is perhaps not saying a great deal. But even the full tally of what has she has witnessed in Las Vegas itself over these past few surreal hours seriously pales against her surroundings right this minute.

It is not that a single suite of rooms, however presidential, can be even more lavish than a string of dancing fountains, breathtaking floorshows, vast Italianate lobbies or palatial casinos – logic would clearly dictate otherwise. What has nailed Noreen to the spot, with her eyes and mouth doing almost cartoon-like things, is that practically everything in the expansive set of rooms is something that she has encountered before – a sofa, a table, a bed, a bathroom... okay, that weird thing she can glimpse in the bathroom that is something between a toilet and a tub confuses her – yet of a grandeur, design and elegance that makes her suspect they are of a totally different species. And that she has been silently transported to an alien planet, perhaps one inhabited solely by giants blessed with impeccable taste.

Noreen has to sit down. She does so with some force, plonking herself onto a comfy-looking leather chair that immediately reclines and almost sends her flying over the top.

"*Whee!*" she cries, like a child on a rollercoaster.

Lyle smiles with pleasure. "Horizontal works for you. Excuse me a moment, Noreen."

Her charming host steps into the bedroom and, in what can't have been more than two seconds max, returns wearing the same adorable smile but a completely different outfit.

Noreen has never before seen a man in a red, velvet dressing gown and Turkish slippers, holding a long cigarette holder. This is not the outfit her father slipped into when he came home from a long day on the fells with his livestock – taking his cap off did it for him – and no other man has ever changed his attire in her presence.

"Ahhhh, that's better," says Lyle. "What was it dear Dorothy Parker was once meant to have said, something about getting 'out of that wet coat and into a dry martini'?"

Noreen is about to say that she doesn't know Miss or Mrs Parker but is rendered quite speechless by the fact that Lyle's cigarette appears to be happily lighting itself on just a commanding gaze from its owner.

When she has recovered from what must have surely been a trick of the light, or indeed her lightheadedness after so long awake (not that she could sleep with all this going on – and anyway, she is accustomed to often staying up all night for her needy badgers), Noreen finds a large remote control. As she has never felt the need for a television or indeed for anything electronic, she has not come across such an object, so she can be forgiven for pressing a button or two. Suddenly the drapes open with a soft purring sound, to reveal a private terrace and compact, blue-tiled swimming pool, the whole set-up lit with multicoloured fairy lights.

"Oh, my God!" says Noreen, throwing caution to the wind. She stands up and almost twirls. "This is incredible, Lyle. It's like the best sort of dream. Even without the livestock."

In less than a second, Lyle is across the vast room and beside her. His hand, now alightling on her exposed shoulder, sends a rush of heat around her body that she hasn't experienced since she rescued a poor squirrel that had fallen down the open chimney and into her crackling winter fireplace (Jeremy still comes to visit).

"If it is a dream," says Lyle, mellifluously, "I just pray that I never wake up, is all. I don't think I've ever met a woman quite as beautiful as you, Noreen."

"Oh you!" she says, smacking him hard on his shoulder, a blow which sends even Lyle reeling. "I'm not beaut— *look at me!* No one could call me beautiful, and no one ever has. Sheep-face is about as near—"

Lyle immediately interrupts, shaking his exquisitely sculpted head. "Because no one's ever seen right into your souls – *soul!*"

He beckons for the enraptured woman to sit on the leather chair, which is still resolutely on the recline, and settles himself right next to her. The hem of his dressing gown has slid away to reveal the first ebony leg Noreen has ever seen. She can't seem to steer her admiring eyes away from it. She almost feels that she would like to get out the Pledge and polish it, like the finest antique furniture, which is in itself unusual, as she has never been an assiduous duster in the past.

Without moving a finger, Lyle reclines the chair a little further and glides a fraction closer to her. More than a fraction, if we are measuring, although it feels as if he has hardly moved. Their faces are now inches apart.

"Most women, Noreen," he whispers, yet still with that profound resonance, "most women in this town – they're no more than glossy billboards for some Silicon Valley surgeons. The kind of ladies your sleazy friend Arnie is so drawn to. But you – you just let mother nature take its inexorable course."

"I try my best," she says, not entirely certain what he's talking about.

Lyle reaches out with slim, strong fingers and cups her newly plucked chin.

"W-what are you doing?" she asks, never having had her chin or anything else cupped, so far as she can recall.

Lyle shakes his head and withdraws his hand, slightly. "I apologise, Noreen, for my appearing too forward. I'm just being swept along on a torrent of emotions that I'm utterly powerless to stem. They're rattling my spirit and my very frame, in a way that has never happened to me before. Tell me to stop – and I'll go somewhere cold and desolate and never bother you again."

Noreen says nothing but she is clearly giving the option some thought. Although not a great deal. This isn't like some of her really big decisions, such as should she donate one of her kidneys for transplant (in fact, she had at one time offered up both kidneys but was rejected just in case being bonkers was cellular).

Lyle's face moves closer to hers. Noreen instinctively closes her eyes. So she doesn't notice, as her paramour licks his perfect lips, that his tongue is just a tiny bit forked.

Suddenly they hear a violent, cracking sound and turn in shock. Someone is hammering at or possibly even kicking in the door to their luxury suite.

Arnie, now clearly in the most excruciating pain, barrels one-footedly into the room. He looks both determined and terrified. But mostly terrified.

"Shit! That is one heavy door. Noreen – *stop!* You're about to shtup Satan!"

Noreen just glares at the intruder, miffed that a mood she was rather enjoying has been so impolitely crapped upon.

"*Arnie!*" she berates. "Have you been drinking? On an empty stomach?"

Before he can respond, not that he feels that this is the dominant question requiring an answer, Lyle is beside him, a warm yet somehow irredeemably evil smile on his face.

"Hello, Arnie," he says in that wonderful voice Arnie is just beginning to loathe, "you look like you're about to self-combust. Or would you like some help?"

Arnie, who knows that the Devil gets all the best lines, decides there is no point in competing. So, his response is terse and to the point. "C'mon, Noreen! We're getting out of here!"

He moves to grab her wrist, but Noreen smacks him away, adding a pain in his arm to the one in his foot and an even larger one where his soul should be.

"We are not going *anywhere!*" insists Noreen. "I'm a big girl, Arnie. I can take care of myself… or Lyle can."

"But he's the devil!"

"No, Arnie. He's in real estate. He told me in the lift coming up here."

"Same difference. C'mon!"

Arnie, who is himself all fired-up by now, makes a sudden lunge for Noreen, causing her massive old handbag, which was still wrapped around a newly exposed arm, to go flying onto the floor. Its contents – knitting, spare bobbly hat, peppermints, et al., – spill out.

Then the fallen bag begins to move.

The threesome watch in some fascination as the well-worn relic, which Lyle had been unable to persuade her to replace, shuffles of its own accord across the plush, grade-A carpet.

Eventually, Stanley the ferret pops his little head out and scurries away.

Taking advantage of the furry distraction, Arnie commences to drag Noreen, who is now scouring the room in some desperation for her favourite rodent (whilst plaintively calling out his name). They shuffle towards the battered door. Arnie grabs the door-handle then immediately pulls back his hand as it begins to sizzle.

"*Owwww! Ooohh!* Hot!"

He glares through the steam at a smiling Lyle, as Noreen slips away from her ineffectual, would-be rescuer and returns to the safe harbour of the other male's warm, welcoming arms. This slimmer and infinitely better-looking gentleman adopts a conciliatory tone whilst throwing Arnie a look of comradely disdain.

"Arnie, sport. Accept it like a mensch. You lost."

"Oh," says Arnie, weakly, following it up with a muttered, "go to Hell!"

"But it's my day off," laughs the taller man.

As Arnie turns to leave, knowing now that his own end-of days have just played the numbers game and lost, there is a knock at what is left of the door.

"Ahhhh," says Lyle, with a little, self-congratulatory nod. "Room service. *Entrez!*"

A room service waiter wheels in a large trolley shrouded almost to the floor in a pristine white linen tablecloth and groaning with food of the finest quality. There are more oysters on display than Arnie has ever seen, and he has been a big oyster guy in the past, especially since learning they could be an aphrodisiac. He wonders if this is still the intention today, although he has to admit Noreen isn't looking like she needs much crustacean encouragement.

Lyle tips the waiter in a manner that behoves the suit and the man exits rather contentedly. Arnie, meanwhile, revs up for one final implore. Although he can't help grabbing a couple of oysters for the journey.

"Noreen… please," he says, as he chews. "I can't compete with this guy. Hey, who could? Warren Beatty, circa 1972, maybe. I don't even know why I'm here, except… I need you.

Really. See, for reasons I won't bore you with, if you don't come with me right this minute, I'm a goner."

Noreen looks seriously puzzled. Despite what is, by her own reckoning, a rather over-dramatic entreaty, she finds herself feeling vaguely impressed. The man for once looks almost sincere, as if the entire brash façade that was Arnie Garth is crumbling. She is not exactly certain what to say, but before she can even utter a word, she and her duelling menfolk hear a gruff, disembodied voice.

"*You're a goner anyway, pal!*"

It appears to be coming from within the large room service trolley.

Noreen simply assumes that a talking trolley is yet another marvel this extraordinary place has to offer. However, as they stare at it in wonder, a very small, leather-clad arm appears from beneath the fine white tablecloth. The arm is all the more interesting because the expensively gloved hand attached to it clutches a compact but lethal Ruger SR40c handgun plus tailored silencer.

Big Louie climbs out from inside the trolley and freezes the room. Even Lyle looks a tad cold.

Noreen is the first to break the silence. "It's okay!" she says, excitedly. "I *know* what he wants."

She scoots over to the suite's well-stocked minibar and starts scooping out the miniatures. Shot-sized malt whiskeys, assorted baby bourbons, mini-Tequilas and gin-lets fill her arms. Smiling benevolently, she thrusts them all towards the diminutive newcomer.

"I hope you enjoy them," she says, "please don't thank me."

Ignoring the generous if bizarre invitation to Lilliputian bacchanalia by this equally strange person, Big Louie walks straight over to a totally bemused Arnie. Pointing the barrel of the gun in his direction, he shakes his head rather sadly.

"Hate to do this, pal. I love your work."

"Thanks, the *Little Big Men* movie got a blockbuster small audience – but this is a mistake!" says Arnie.

"Tell that to your old lady."

"Old lady?" says Noreen.

"My *mother* wants to kill me?" cries Arnie, with fake incredulity.

"You're an orphan," reminds Noreen, who by now has become rather angry. Not just at Arnie's bursting in on her lovely and rather promising evening but at this new and quite belligerent intruder, pretending he's a very small cowboy or something. She does get, however, that Las Vegas is a city of artifice, so perhaps she is not investing this compact gentleman with the gravitas he might be accustomed to expect.

"I meant step-mom," corrects Arnie, swiftly. "My *stepmother* wants to kill me?"

"No more talk," says the latest visitor, "and sorry, guys, no witnesses. Wrong place, wrong time. Shit happens. Say your prayers. We respect all denominations."

"Fire away," says Arnie, resignedly. He is more than a little exhausted by now and has quite run out of ideas. "I was going this route in a coupla days anyway. But hey, guy to guy, give the dame a free pass."

The smaller man regretfully shrugs his refusal and levels the weapon upwards at Arnie's head. As he starts to squeeze the trigger, something small and furry flies through the air towards him at great speed and clamps its powerful little jaws on Big Louie's favourite ear.

"*Arrghhhh!*" screams the bitten man, as you would if Stanley the flying ferret had started eating your face. Unsurprisingly, the gun goes off, sending a bullet that whistles past Arnie's trembling head and passes right through Lyle. Mildly annoyed, the wearer of the Coward-ish dressing gown examines the neat hole in the fabric, front and rear.

Arnie seizes the moment and leaps towards his would-be

assassin, knocking him backwards into the trolley and sending oysters, champagne and other amatory aids flying. Then Big Louie's favourite pornographer grabs Noreen firmly by the arm. "*Now* do you wanna leave?"

"Yes, please, Arnie!" says Noreen, grabbing up all her bags and thinking to herself that this really is getting to be a bit of a habit.

They run out of the room. Away from the struggling assassin. Away from the devilish Lothario in the punctured dressing gown. Away from that low round thing in the bathroom she would have loved to soak her aching feet in.

Lyle stares after them. To his chagrin, he has to admit to having been taken a tad off guard by these quite unexpected and unwelcome impediments to mutually assured seduction.

From the corridor he hears a long, high-pitched whistle which, were he of this earth, might have split his eardrums. This is followed by a frantic scurrying as Stanley, Lakeland warrior-ferret, dashes across the room and out of the door, brandishing a small but dangerous German firearm in his tight little mouth.

In the corridor a pair of young newly-weds, she in a relatively sane white wedding-dress, he in a smart rented tux, are gaily returning to their room. They watch the speedy, gun-toting creature as it flashes past them.

"Wow," says the young man, impressed. "Talk about security."

Chapter Thirty-Two

There is no escape from heaven's web. (Japanese proverb)

"So, tell me if I've got this wrong please, Arnie. We were mixed up in a… mob smack?"

Arnie and Noreen are on their way to the airport. For his money, he can't get out of Vegas quick enough. Although in truth it can only be Noreen's money, leftovers from her recent good fortune, that will effect this essential change of scene.

"Hit," corrects Arnie, who would prefer to snatch a few moments of precious shut-eye, as the endless day/night is beginning to catch up with him. Even though these next few hours will very likely be the last he actually enjoys on this earth (and I'm using 'enjoy' in its loosest sense).

"Hit," repeats Noreen. "Because… Lyle was forcing you to make those horrible sexy films, when all you really wanted to do was produce religious documentaries?"

"Exactly right. They were crucifying me, Noreen. And I had refused to do it anymore. Even on pain of death. So, Lyle set that little guy onto me. And used you as bait. Sorry Noreen, but he's a bad omen, that guy. If you know that movie. And I just saved a little thing called your life. So, you gotta love me, right?"

Noreen is not saying anything.

"*Right, Noreen?!*" he repeats, the level of desperation in his voice rising dramatically, alongside the intensity of his gaze.

Nothing more is said until they reach the airport, and a disconsolate Arnie goes to buy the air tickets with Noreen's devil-gotten gains, leaving his reluctant lover by a bookstore.

He returns after about fifteen minutes to find that Noreen has vanished. After some frantic and pissed-off searching, he spots activity at one of the airport's many slot machines. What surprises Arnie even more than the act itself is the fervid, almost compulsive manner in which Noreen is feeding in those precious coins.

"Noreen?"

She doesn't hear him.

"*Noreen!* The flight leaves in fifteen minutes. Will ya come on, for crissakes?"

"Just one more spin, Arnie!"

Arnie shakes his head. Yet, as he watches the strange Englishwoman going almost manic with her strong right hand, he is surprised to find his exasperation tempered by an emotion he has so rarely experienced, that he might be hard pressed, even if pushed, to give it a name. But for the moment, let's call it affection.

This feeling grows even stronger when the dour woman in airport security asks Noreen to put anything metal in the tray provided and Noreen upends the giant bucket of newly-gotten quarters she has been carrying in her voluminous bag.

*

Big Louie is far less elated, as he takes a shower in his hotel room.

He has googled all that he can glean about ferret bites and rabies and is just hoping for the best, as he squeezes and soaps and rubs. The furry little bastard did seem pretty clean and well-groomed when it was hanging onto his ear, although the whiteness of its fur could have been falsely reassuring.

The frustrated hitman is so immersed in his de-ferreting, he fails to notice through the steam that the bathroom door has opened and a shadowy figure is moving towards him.

He finishes his shower, grabs a towel and emerges from the stall to find himself two feet away from Melisande. Before he can ask her how the hell she got in, his eager client is bombarding him with questions.

"Well? Is it done? Am I a widow already? I brought my mourning outfit…" She produces a tiny black thong from her handbag. "Why've you got a new love bite? I don't pay my contractors to get bitten."

"You coulda told me about the vicious little rodent."

"Hey – he was still my husband!"

The disgruntled killer points to his face. "A coked-up ferret. Nearly took my goddam ear off." After waiting some seconds for sympathy he is clearly never likely to receive, even if Stanley had bitten his entire head off, he gives his report. "They got away."

Melisande is incandescent, which fortunately the Botox will let her do. "*Got away!* You moron! *Got away!* The little turd could change his will at any time and leave the whole bundle to that weird Limey bitch. And then go and die on me. They could be anywhere by now."

Big Louie shakes his un-ponytailed head, spreading shower water onto her low-cut, ultra-short red dress. He has often thought that there must be an unofficial dress-code for off-duty porn stars and reckons that you can usually recognise them the same way you can spot off-duty cops.

"Cool it, sister. I got a guy at the airport. They're on their way to LA. I'll catch up with him there. Now, would you mind giving me a little privacy while I get dressed?"

Melisande just scoffs. "Hey, pal, nothing I ain't seen before."

Big Louie shrugs and drops the towel. The woman simply nods. At least now she knows how he got his name.

Chapter Thirty-Three

If you do not travel, you will marry your own sister.
(Mozambican proverb)

Noreen and Arnie are fast asleep on each other's shoulders in their second cab of the morning. When they finally arrive at the address Arnie had yelled at him, the driver wakes them up by screeching onto the kerb and smacking his horn.

Noreen, who has changed back on the plane into her old Lakeland attire (which, frankly, she finds far more comfortable, albeit a bit sweaty) is quite confused. She has absolutely no idea where she is. Arnie knows exactly where he is but is just as confused, because he still has barely an idea in his head as to how and whether he is ever going to survive this unholy celestial shitstorm.

"So, this isn't your house, Arnie?" says Noreen, trying to puzzle it out, as they approach the apartment block.

"No. It ain't anyone's house. They're what you call apartments. But my old bachelor pad is being made over. I'm having the prayer room reconsecrated." He can feel the scepticism like a chill Cumbrian breeze. "Little faith-based producer joke. Got a ton of them."

"So, whose is this – apartment?"

"This place? Well… it belongs to… to my sister. Yeah. I called sis from the airport. You'll love her," he says, pressing the button. "She's a nurse."

"*Hello?*" barks the sisterly voice out of the entry phone.

"It's me. Everything tidy?"

"Yeah, sure."

"Mother-visiting tidy?"

"Oh. Oh *crap!*"

Arnie decides that he and Noreen should ignore the elevator and walk slowly up the stairs. Very slowly. Especially, he enthuses, as she loves hills so much. Whilst he explains to his companion that he also needs the exercise, Arnie Garth is quite aware that the current occupant of the apartment to which they're ascending is frantically doing what has become known in the industry as 'pressing the ESC button' – ESC being Erotica Spring Clean.

Posters that once boasted *Schindler's Lust*, *The 400 Blow-Jobs* and *Glad He Ate Her* will now, with a quick swivel on the picture hook, hopefully feature Cleopatra Cleaves in *The Life of Marie Curie*, *The Amelia Earhart Story* and *Mother of God!*

When she finally opens the door to Arnie and Noreen, the aforementioned star is unsurprisingly flushed and panting. She skilfully manages to turn these features into delirious enthusiasm for whoever has just shown up at her door.

"*Arnie!*" she screams, a touch over-effusively. "Welcome back! We were so worried." She hugs him affectionately and slips a sisterly tongue down his throat. At the same time, she swiftly sizes up the curiously woolly person he has brought with him, but unusually finds herself completely stumped.

"Er Cleo, this is Noreen. Noreen Millwheel. From England, somewhere. Noreen – say hi to Cleo. Short for Cleopatra. Noreen needs the bathroom."

"No, I—"

Arnie shoves her towards a room down the hall. "There you go, baby. Fully ensuite."

"Well, maybe I will just spend a penny," says Noreen, with a shrug. "Then you must tell me – Cleopatra – if there's anything I can do. Ironing, cleaning, blood transfusion…"

Noreen has barely closed the bathroom door when Cleo grabs Arnie by the wilting Hawaiian collar.

"You've got some nerve, Arnie Garth! You fire my ass, have a double coronary *and* a stroke, skip town, I don't know if you're alive or dead, then suddenly you turn up on my doorstep—"

Arnie is about to interrupt.

"Alright, technically *your* doorstep – expecting what? Travellers aid! And who's that person – my replacement?"

"She's… well, she's… see, she…"

Arnie pauses and takes her hand, which feels so incredibly soft and smooth compared to that of his recent, hard-weathered companion. Yet there was something so – how could he put it? – so real and, well, honest, about the earthy Millburn extremity. No! He can't go there. This is too important. Here goes.

"Okay, Cleo, that weird woman in the bathroom, see, she's the dame who's got my soul – had it since we were born, same day, same minute, same moment, heavenly balls-up, don't ask – and I need to make her fall in love with me ASAP to get it back, so we are 'as one', as the saying goes, and I can give Hell a miss and just grab me a few more precious years down here. Only, she can't genuinely tell me she loves me *or* – which is just as unlikely – me tell her the same thing, if I'm already a dead guy, which could happen, because I think Melisande has hired a very scary hit-man of restricted growth but excellent fashion sense and God knows who else, maybe even Satan himself, to kill me and stop her from falling for me and getting mentioned in my will. Which is why I can't go home right now. You see?"

Cleo stares at him for a moment. "You're pathetic," she says and stomps back into the kitchen.

Arnie slumps down in Cleo's easiest chair. He can hear the faucet running, so Noreen will be back again very soon and this whole dizzying, mad charade will continue and undoubtedly conclude. But unlike his movies, more with a whimper than a bang.

What he can't see from his chair, of course, is Noreen scrabbling around in the fascinatingly well-equipped bathroom for some carbolic soap. But when he catches her sudden yelp, followed by the sounds of objects cascading and clattering into the washbasin, he realises that the amenity's current occupant must have discovered the cupboard where Cleo keeps her dildos, vibrators, love beads and, very graciously, Viagra. Sometimes Arnie Garth feels that if there is a God, he must be tuning in to the Arnie channel right now just to give himself a good laugh.

As soon as the bathroom noises tail off, Arnie hears Cleo in the kitchen banging cupboard doors and generally slamming around. He leaps up to mollify her.

"Cleo? Cleo, sweetie, please! You've got to help me!"

She begins to make herself a health drink with too many vegetables and unwarranted vigour, as Arnie looks back in concern towards the bathroom.

"*Please!* It – it's too screwy to explain but I got nowhere else to go. I need you to help me look after Noreen and-and she mustn't know *anything* about what you do for a living or what I do for that matter. Oh – or the little fact that I'm *married*. Okay? She... wouldn't approve."

The clattering only gets worse.

"Oh, well I'm so sorry your new girlfriend wouldn't approve of me. Like I should be ashamed of having sex on camera with multiple partners and simulating incredible orgasms, just so that sad lonely guys all over the USA and elsewhere can ..." She pauses here, because she doesn't immediately feel that she has made the killer argument. From down the hall, we hear the bathroom door open.

"Please! *Please!* Cleo!" whispers Arnie, even more frantically. "Trust me. Hey, who turned your life around when you turned up at my little office, barely more than a kid, selling whatdyamacallits?"

"Bibles."

Noreen arrives in the doorway of the kitchen and halts, as if she can sense some vestigial weirdness between the pair of them. Arnie looks nervously from one woman to the other and back again, twice, on tenterhooks.

"Hey, Noreen." Cleo smiles. "You look like you could use a nice cool radish and lettuce and carrot and eggplant smoothie."

Arnie shoots Cleo a look of supreme gratitude but then simply can't help himself. "Lettuce? Radishes? Shit, Cleo – don't tell me you've turned into a friggin' *vegan!* Not that there's anything wrong with that!"

"I'm on a diet!" protests Cleo. "I've got to lose two inches off my ass. According to my prod–"

"*Nutritionist!*" explains Arnie swiftly. "Okay. Okay. So, tell you what, I'll go get food. *Real* food. My treat. You guys sit tight. Noreen – whatever you want – name it."

"Oohh, anything I want." She closes her eyes.

"Anything. You name it."

"Well, Arnie, my most favourite thing in the whole world, which I'm missing so much more than anything right now – except maybe my sheep, of course – is Kendal Mint Cake."

"Uh huh. Whatever else you want – name it."

Noreen's face sags into a look of utter disappointment.

"Okay. Fine," sighs Arnie. "There's a British shop in Santa Monica sells crappy English food. It's only an hour. Each way."

He turns to go, waiting for a 'don't be silly, pizza will do'. Instead, he feels a strong hand on his arm.

"Arnie... thank you." Noreen kisses him on the cheek. "You've turned out to be a real friend."

Noreen Millburn is surprised to watch Arnie's face fall.

"*Friend*?" he moans. "What is with this friend shit? I don't wanna be your friggin' friend! Who has time for friends?"

He storms out of the apartment, seething with frustration. The angry bang from the door segues into an embarrassed silence.

Cleo smiles a bit uneasily at her new guest, feeling that it is all on her now to be a good hostess and lighten the mood.

"So, Noreen. Do they do hot-tub three-ways in England?"

Chapter Thirty-Four

Give thanks for a little and you will find a lot.
(Nigerian proverb)

To Arnie Garth's delight, The Olde Englyshe Shoppe in Santa Monica has one remaining bar of Kendal Mint Cake, which in fact comprises the entire stock and which the relieved proprietor is only too pleased to offload.

Arnie is far less delighted when he samples a tiny corner of the famed Cumbrian confection. As he spits it out over a passing tourist, he starts to realise how seriously depressed he is and how even the taste of this incredibly sweet English delicacy can seem so bitter on his tongue.

Such is his deepening gloom.

He begins to wander up the celebrated Third Street Promenade, all bright lights and sparkling shop fronts, and feels even more miserable. Passing the seemingly endless parade of smart stores, cinemas and restaurants, all he can see are people enjoying themselves, couples young and old kissing and cuddling, apparently without a care in the world. Even the homeless appear more content than he is.

As he reaches Venice Beach, wisely resisting the temptation to nibble off more minty corners, he notices amongst the even more happy and generally better constructed couples, of all ethnicities and orientations, two dogs contentedly copulating behind a car. Finding himself supremely envious at this point marks a new low in his fall from what he has until now considered a reasonably fulfilling life.

Yet he begins to wonder, just at the time that this same life is going to be snatched cruelly and unjustly away, through absolutely no fault of his own, whether in truth happiness or even basic contentment have eluded him at every stage on his journey. And if a life solely devoted to petty crime, serial adultery, loveless sex and heavy pornography was truly that enriching.

It is more than Arnie Garth can bear.

The sun is sinking spectacularly, mockingly, back into the sea, when Arnie for some reason retraces his steps to Santa Monica and its celebrated beach. Yet instead of looking for a cab, he finds himself standing on the bridge over the busy Pacific Coast Highway.

Leaning over and looking down onto the swiftly moving traffic.

Deep in thought.

*

Noreen is just starting to become worried.

It is quite late, and she has never had this trouble in the past sourcing her regular supply of Kendal Mint Cake. Perhaps, she thinks, it isn't quite the minty staple of an American diet she might have supposed.

She senses Arnie's very pleasant and rather pretty sister staring at her in some concern.

"He's been gone for hours!" worries Noreen, looking over towards the window. "Oh, Cleopatra, do you think he's had an accident?"

"Arnie? He doesn't have accidents, hon, he causes them."

Cleo softens her tone as a new and very different thought strikes her. "Hey, you're missing him, aren't you?"

"*Missing him? Me? No!*" She looks thoughtful, playing nervously with the worn wooden toggle on her uppermost cardigan. "Well, maybe… a bit. Daft, eh?"

Cleo smiles. "Daft. Arnie does sort of grow on you. Like… like thrush."

Noreen suddenly leaps up and dashes over to where she had dumped her bulging bag.

"Ooh, I know!" she enthuses. "Let's *knit* something for him."

As if on cue, Stanley's head pops up out of her bag, holding a bundle of wool in his sharp little teeth.

"*Jesus!*" says Cleo Cleaves, not unimpressed.

*

Arnie is still on that bridge.

This time he is gripping the edge. He looks down over the highway and practices hefting himself up and over, like a golfer before he finally tees off.

Behind him an elderly, white-haired gentleman in faded jogging-gear and an old straw hat is approaching very slowly. When he sees Arnie he stops, although to an observer it might be tricky to distinguish this from his jogging.

"Hey," says the kind old guy softly, not wishing to unduly frighten the man on the bridge. "You doin' what I think you're doin'?"

Arnie doesn't even turn round. "It's not like I got options, pops. My life sucks. I'm going straight to Hell – why wait?"

The elderly man moves round, so that he can see Arnie and look him straight in the morose, hangdog eye.

"*Are you kidding, pal?*" He grins. "The world's a wonderful place. And hey, just think what it would be like if you'd never been a part of it."

Arnie pauses in his hefting, closes his eyes and thinks about what this stooped but wise old fellow has just said to him.

He hears a parade in progress. In his mind he pictures a vast cohort of gleaming, red-uniformed, baton-twirling people. On closer inspection, he can see that the parade is being led by some familiar figures – people he knows well or has encountered sometime throughout his life. There's his wife Melisande, in a stunningly provocative and joyous outfit. And here are a beaming Dorita and Ron, from his domestic sound booth, accompanied by his erstwhile stars, Brent and Cleo. Close behind are Big Louie and Lyle, happily arm in arm with myself, Noreen, Rosie in her *Annie* costume, the hairy Landlord from The Wordsworth Arms and a petite, smiling, grey-haired lady, wearing a sweatshirt that says *MOM* on the front.

Behind them, joining hands with a glittering array of America's foremost, grade-X erotic talent of all sexes are panhandlers, the homeless, the halt and the lame. What unites them all in this massive gathering is the look of total ecstasy on their faces and the fact that they have all come together to mark the occasion of Arnie Garth's non-existence by singing 'Oh Happy Day' in resoundingly euphoric unison.

Arnie opens his eyes and turns to the gently smiling old gentleman. "Thanks for nothing, wrinkledick," he says.

*

While Arnie is hovering between a not so wonderful life and a pretty messy demise, a flight from Las Vegas is about to begin its descent.

The door to the toilet at the rear of the plane opens and Melisande emerges, looking slightly flushed. A few moments later, Big Louie follows her out.

Melisande notices an elderly lady in a nearby aisle seat staring up at her in some shock.

"Oh, *what*?" says the legendary star, curtly. "Like you've never made it in an airplane john with a well-hung, homicidal dwarf!"

The elderly lady simply shrugs contritely.

Chapter Thirty-Five

Honesty is like an icicle – once it melts, that is the end of it.
(American proverb)

Noreen has run out of wool, which she supposes was inevitable in the circumstances. So Cleo is selflessly helping to increase the supply, by allowing the rabid knitter to unravel an old woollen dress of hers, which wasn't exactly flowing to begin with.

The owner of the dress is kindly wearing it, in order to avoid unnecessary tangles. She is consistently walking across the room to check the window, which at least helps to keep the strands taut.

"Knit even faster, hon!" she suddenly urges. "His cab just pulled up."

When Arnie returns a few minutes later, using his own key, Noreen leaps up and runs over to him in order to bestow one of her fondest and most asphyxiating hugs. Aside from stunning the man and reducing his supply of oxygen, she also succeeds in leaving Cleo wearing little more than a woolly pelmet.

"Hey, ease up, lady," says Arnie, extricating himself and regaining his breath. "It's only friggin' mint cake."

"Screw the mint cake, Arnie," says Noreen, showing an

impressively swift uptake of the local vernacular. "I was so worried. I thought you were dead!"

"Watch this space," says Arnie, before his mind can fully process how someone without any vested interest whatsoever might be the slightest bit exercised over whether he lives or dies.

"So… Noreen," he says, more gently, "how've you been? Cleo treating you okay?"

"Champion, Arnie. And I am making you a nice, warm cardie of your very own."

"Where I'm going that's just what I'll need," he moans. Yet, once again, he finds himself wrong-footed. "Hey, back up! You're… you're making something for me? *Why*, Noreen? My cash has all been stopped by my… my creditors. I can't even pay you for the friggin' wool."

"Oh Arnie, it's a gift. I made it for you because… well… because…"

She finds that she can't truly put her reasons into words. Nor can she fathom why she has reasons in the first place. Yet when this very curious man, who has rescued her from the mob (two very different mobs, actually, Cumbrian and Nevadan), dragging her halfway across the world in the process, and with whom she has had enough adventures to last a lifetime, puts his hand into his pocket and delivers up a by now pretty crushed slab of warm Kendal Mint Cake, with only the tiniest corner bitten off, she knows that she just has to hug him all over again.

It is when she is delivering this mother of all embraces and Arnie is smiling hopefully (even as he gasps for air), that Noreen notices the photograph.

It is one of several on Cleo's wall, beside her lovely, faith-based movie posters. Noreen walks towards it, still clutching Arnie to her solid frame.

As she takes in the picture, she drops her human package onto the ground with a thud.

"Hey! Don't stop now, babe," says Arnie, who has been quite pleased with how this is going.

Instead of resuming the hug, Noreen Millburn gives Arnie Garth a massive slap across the face that sends him crashing against the wall. Right next to the photo that Noreen has spotted.

It is a picture of Arnie and Melisande's wedding. The bride wears a sweet little white leather micro skirt with fetching white half-cup peek-a-boo bra and lacy veil. Cleo – like the other bridesmaids – is dressed as a naughty schoolgirl. The ripped best man wears only a fig leaf – and this not very adeptly.

Arnie has no idea what just happened, but he can tell from Cleo's gawping face that something sure did.

"*You pig!*" says Noreen. "How could you?"

"Hey," says Arnie, misunderstanding, "from my angle it looked like you were doing most of the work!"

"Er... Arnie?" says Cleo, nodding towards the photograph. Arnie very slowly turns and far more swiftly understands.

"You're *married*!" accuses Noreen. "To *that!*"

"Only legally!" explains Arnie. "Listen, Noreen sweetheart, there's no love there. It was purely business."

"And I know what *sort* of business, don't I? Or Arnie, I was just beginning to think..." She stops and he wonders if he is noticing a moistness in her actually rather striking pale blue eyes. "How can I trust you ever again? I'm sorry – I want to go home!"

"But it was only one lie, cousin," lies Arnie. "One teeny, tiny, minuscule lie! I'd never lie to you about anything else! Noreen, please... you can't go! Not now, not for one tiny, fuckin' minuscule, shitty little lie!"

"Arnie Garth!" chides a doubly-shocked Noreen. "How can you use language like that in front of your lovely sister?"

"Whoa, girlfriend," says Cleo. "*Sister*? He told you I...? Hey, I ain't his sister, Noreen! I'm his mistress!"

"Two lies," says Arnie. "Two teeny, fuckin' miniscule—"

But Noreen has already stormed out of the room. The ever-loyal and much travelled Stanley follows, pausing only to bite Arnie hard on his ankle on the way.

Arnie and Cleo exchange looks as the front door slams once again.

Chapter Thirty-Six

Words are like bullets. If they escape, you can't
catch them again. (African proverb)

Noreen Millburn has never hailed a cab before, in either the Old World or the New, but she knows how to raise an arm. For safety's sake, this very first time, she decides to wave at least two arms, plus an outstretched, walking-booted leg for luck.

"Where is the fire, senora?" says the cab driver, pulling into the kerb.

For a moment Noreen wonders if her ignorance of all things worldly has caused her to flag down the wrong type of vehicle, but soon realises that this is just the man being American, or whatever he is, and leaps straight in.

"Okay. Where we goin'?" asks the cabbie, starting the meter.

"The airport, please!" says Noreen, with some urgency. But it is barely a second before she changes her mind. "No, wait. I-I need someone to talk to."

"I not a therapist."

"Oh, no. Sorry, sir. I didn't mean you." She thinks on this for a little while. "Now this may seem a rather odd request…"

The cab driver, who is originally from Salvador, rolls his eyes and prepares for a cemetery run. Here we go.

On the other side of the street, a man is watching through the open window of a large black Mercedes. And smiling broadly. Anyone passing might assume he was alone, until a woman's unexpressive face bobs up from the depths and follows his gaze.

"Looks like someone ain't too happy," observes Big Louie, still grinning.

"Not just her," says Melisande, pointing to the doorway of the apartment block. Arnie is rushing out into the street, with Cleo close behind.

"*Noreen!*" he screams, in some desperation. "Come back here, you stupid, pig-headed, judgmental broad!"

Cleo is already unlocking her car. "Cut the sweet talk, Arnie – and get in!"

"Only my rat of a husband would use one slut to catch another," opines Melisande, as they watch Cleo's car speed off after the cab. "How many bullets you got in that gun?"

"Plenty for everyone, baby – including the ferret," laughs Big Louie, who really is in a very good mood today.

He revs the big Mercedes and joins the convoy.

*

The cab driver, who isn't totally heartless, hates it when a passenger cries. Especially a female, although he does find male blubbers pretty embarrassing.

"You okay, lady?" he asks, softly. Well, softly for him.

"Yes, thank you, sir," says Noreen, who is clearly far from alright.

She senses that the extraordinary events of the past few days, compounded by the shocking tsunami of lies, just as she was quite unexpectedly beginning to warm a fraction to that disreputable but actually rather sad little man, have gone to her very soul. (If she only knew!)

Noreen burrows feverishly in her handbag. Nudging Stanley aside, she fishes something out. "Would you like some Kendal Mint Cake, sir? You'll find this hard to believe, but I've suddenly gone right off it."

The cabbie takes the barely-nibbled bar. "Okay. Gracias, senora. I try anything once."

*

As Cleo's small car rapidly approaches the cab, Arnie doesn't really need to concentrate on where Noreen is going. The only place that she knows in LA is the airport. But with every mile they travel, the signature on his death warrant is drawing closer and closer to completion.

Cleo is just confused.

As a mistress, she realises all too well that she doesn't have exclusive rights to the desolate-looking guy beside her. A man who pays for her apartment, provides her with regular work and for whom she would reluctantly admit, despite his manifest failings, to having a certain cockeyed affection. Yet, as a warm and generous person, with a feeling for humanity and a genuine interest in what makes them tick, she would quite like to know what the holy fuck is going on.

"What is it *with* this woman, Arnie?" She turns to glance at his face. And now she laughs, without any trace of bitterness. "Oh no! Ha! Oh my! She's got to you, ain't she?"

"*What?* Nah! Noreen? Got to me. Look at her! You nuts? Nah."

Now Cleo takes her eyes completely off the road in order to challenge her passenger and stare him out. Never a wise move on the freeway but perhaps even less prudent on this particular chase.

"*Hey, this ain't the way to LAX!*" yells Arnie.

With a jolt Cleo switches her gaze back to the car ahead and watches it veer smoothly off in a totally new and unexpected direction. She only just manages to screech her way onto the road less travelled and keep on its tail.

"I've always wanted to 'follow that cab,'" she says, excitedly.

*

Behind Cleo and Arnie, the Louie-mobile makes much the same manoeuvre, with more horse-power but an equivalent degree of surprise.

"Where the hell are they going?" wonders Melisande, out loud. "You think it's to a lawyer?"

"Don't you worry, baby," reassures the hit-man. "Like it says on my website, we always aim to please."

Chapter Thirty-Seven

A man who touches the bottom of a soup plate with a ball of foofoo is no longer searching for soup. (African proverb)

The sign reads: *NOAH'S PARK – WHERE THE BIBLE COMES TO WILD-LIFE!*

"This could be the mostest closest thing to what you looking for," says the cabbie, a bit uncertainly, as he pulls up near the busy entrance. "You wan' me to keep the meter runnin', while you check it out?"

"No, thank you, sir," says Noreen, clambering out. "I think this would appear to be just the ticket." She notices with some gratification that the man is treating himself to a huge chunk of Kendal Mint Cake, while he is parked. "Thank you very much, sir. How much do I owe you?"

The cabbie doesn't answer. He suddenly slams open the door and dashes out of the cab, still holding the Mint Cake wrapper. "*Fuggedaboudit!*" he cries, looking suddenly untanned. "I gotta find me a bucket!"

Noreen shrugs and looks through the railings into the huge theme park. She can hear children and families joyfully laughing and screaming and vomiting, as biblical music of the

Elmer Bernstein variety blares out through all the loudspeakers. Heavenly choirs, harps, a lot of brass. You know the sort of thing (well, you think you do. Know the one place you won't find 'heavenly' choirs? Got it in one!).

Beyond the fast rides and the even faster food outlets, Noreen Millburn believes that she can spot several large enclosures, which might just contain whatever it is she is looking for.

Stopping at the pay desk to buy her all-inclusive entrance ticket, she notices a tall, white-bearded man on the other side of the railings. He is wearing biblical robes, with a headdress and leather sandals, and carries a wooden staff. The man appears to be directing people towards the attractions of their choice.

When it is her turn, Noreen gently but urgently enquires of the man if there might, by the remotest chance, be a very specific resource for the solace she so desperately craves in these tumultuous times.

The tall man strokes his distinguished beard and nods sagely, as he listens and attempts to decipher the accent. One that he would have to admit he has never heard before and hopefully will never have cause to lay ears on again.

"Take thee a left by ye tribe of skunks," he says sagely, pointing his knobbly staff down one of the many busy walkways. "A friggin' wideth left."

Fuelled with anticipation and an almost unbridled excitement, Noreen Millburn weaves her way at some speed through the happy families towards her destination. She has just turned a corner and disappeared from view, when Arnie and Cleo reach the first of what they both assume is a troupe of helpful Noahs.

"You seen a curious but in her own, go-figure way not wholly unappealing Englishwoman?"

"You seeneth an optician?"

Arnie can tell that this is not a man in love with his job nor, most probably, the fortunate beneficiary of a one-to-one relationship with his God. But he does smite the air with an outstretched hand in the direction of the skunkery, so Arnie nods his thanks and drags a fascinated Cleo away.

At various points en route children are discovering all sorts of small animals to pet and torment and larger ones at which to gaze in wide-eyed wonder. As well as parents and grandparents, there are minders and leaders of groups of little ones, all hoping that they will return to their transport after a fulfilling day with near as dammit the contingent they started out with.

A sonorous voice on the Tannoy announces, "List to me, all ye Noah's Park visitors. Do not forget the Ararat Dinery hath a special today on Ham Sandwiches, Shem Donuts and Japheth Pizzas. Just try not to flood in all at once, folks!"

Directed towards a totally different sector of the park, because by the time of this third enquiry the jaded 'entry Noah' was verily growing bored, an armed and lethal hit-man has his heart set on human game. He feels a curious tapping on his belly and turns to see a little girl stroking him like a pet. Big Louie decides not to kill her but, as with so many things, telling her that he intends to do so has much the same effect.

The man has never rubbed out a mark in a family amusement park before, especially not in a venue of a quasi-biblical nature, but there's always a first time and it will be something to talk about at the annual conference.

*

"*Think, Arnie!*" urges Cleo, still not entirely certain why she feels quite so involved. It must be that, as a genuinely sensitive and almost spiritual being, despite her somewhat frowned-upon day job, she has imbibed Arnie's panic and urgency by some form of osmosis. "Where would she go?"

"She's Miss Looney Tunes," says a mystified but not unaffectionate Arnie. "How the hell would I know?"

Cleo can sense eyes on her and not just those of the meerkats in the nearby enclosure. She turns to see a pleasantly nondescript man in his late thirties, standing with his chubby wife and two bouncy young children. The father is smiling at Cleo, in some excitement.

"Say, excuse me for interrupting," he says, "but haven't we met somewhere?"

Cleo is just about to respond, in a kindly and hopefully tactful manner, when the man suddenly shakes his head like he has just been attacked by a swarm of tsetse flies and drags his intrigued children away.

"No… no, you're no one… I never saw you in anything. Er, met you anywhere. C'mon kids."

"Happens all the time," she tells Arnie. "It's like when you see your gynaecologist squeezing melons in the 7/11."

Arnie has stopped listening. He grabs Cleo by the arm. "I got a hunch. Come on!"

Whilst Cleo, who loves animals of all kinds, would really like to take her time and enjoy all that this only slightly tacky theme park has to offer, she can sense that Arnie has a particular destination in mind. He is frantically reading all the signs out loud.

"*Beasts of the field*… no. *Locusts*… no. *Asses*… who wants to see an animal's ass…?"

They finally spy Noreen crouching in what has been billed as *The Manger*. This all feels a bit New Testament to Arnie, but he would have to admit that he's no expert. He does have to congratulate himself, however, on a correct assumption that he'd find his quarry having a powwow with a sheep. A sheep who curiously appears to be listening to every damn word she says.

Those visitors, young and old, hovering around the curiously over-cocooned and majorly bobbled woman appear slightly disconcerted but wouldn't deny that they are also quite intrigued. As indeed are the other sheep.

Noreen, of course, is totally oblivious to the growing circle of people nearby, which now includes a riveted Arnie and Cleo.

"Now I do know that you're not one of my lovely, raggy-haired Cumbrian Herdwicks," she confides, "but I think you'll probably understand. If you can follow my accent, that is. Which apparently not everybody here can.

"You see, I've got these queer feelings like I've never ever felt before – right here, swirling around in my gut. I don't *think* it's wind, because it's not making me let off, the way it usually does back home when I've splashed out and had one turnip too many – I'm sure you know the feeling… anyway, that's all well and good, but whatever this new churning is that's getting me all in a sweat and a muddle, *I want to get rid of it!* Because if it is what I think – what I *fear* it might be – well, it's all wrong, isn't it? *Why?* You ask me why? Okay, I'll tell you why. Because he's a lying, married, dirty-minded, bad-mannered, foul-mouthed, married, woman-exploiting, ill-tempered, selfish, married sex-fiend. With a very nice mistress."

Arnie edges closer towards her, through the fascinated crowd. He can sense that the bulk of their interest is not so much on the weirdo chewing the fat with a sheep but on the surprisingly attentive sheep chewing his cud with a sort-of-human.

"So, what should I do?" she continues. "Go back to him – or go home? Everything I love is at home – but for some reason, alright I *know* the reason, the people at home don't seem to love me. Especially now that flipping Apex Holdings is stirring up the whole village against me. But to remain even a moment longer in the presence of an irresponsible good-for-nothing like *that!* What do you…?"

She pauses, because to her surprise she hears a familiar voice beside her. Even less credibly, she is pretty certain that it is addressing another of Noah's sheep.

"You got a minute?" says Arnie, which fortunately for him

the sheep has, as they generally tend not to have an undue amount on their agenda, other than munching grass, a task this one still appears well able to do. "You see, there's this screwy English broad. Hey, between you and me, she ain't gonna win no beauty contest... but, you know, not so hideous, in a crazy, foreign way. Nice hooters – six cardigans down. Great eyes. Sweet sorta smile. Kindly soul. Decent person. And, for reasons I won't bore you with, 'cos truly they don't make me look so good, I been trying every which way to get into her panties. Which, incidentally, are probably made from the same stuff you got on your back.

"Aw, come on, don't give me that look, you're a sheep of the world. But – well, it didn't happen. Instead she – I hate to say this, but she kinda got into my... into my head. Okay, more than my head. You hear what I'm saying?"

Noreen has stopped her own chatter and is clearly listening to the adjacent man-to-ovine conversation.

"And, I gotta tell you," continues Arnie, "that may not be nearly enough. How I'm just starting to feel, I mean. Not when the big day of reckoning comes. Which, by the way, is pretty damn soon – don't ask me how I know."

Noreen turns back to her woolly listener and talks just a bit louder. "If he could only *turn* himself into a straightforward, honest, morally upright, generous, respectful, thoroughly decent human being..."

"Hey, lady," says Arnie, "you're talking to a sheep!"

As their audience drifts away, the two would-be Dr Dolittles look at each other a bit helplessly. Even, what you and I might call, sheepishly.

"*Arnie!*"

Arnie Garth registers Cleo's sudden yelp and knows immediately that this is not the excited cry of an animal lover.

Turning away from the manger, he recognises – well, how could he not? – the hitman from the Bellagio, with the same small but lethal weapon partially but not fully concealed in his hand. Noreen sees him too and gives him a little wave of recognition, although recalling their past encounter, she is pretty sure that he isn't here for the animals.

Despite it being barely more than a high-pitched whisper, Arnie registers every sinister word.

"Time's up, pornmeister. Why don't we go somewhere quiet? We don't want to upset the kiddies. You too, lady."

"No, it's okay," says Cleo. "I'm good."

"If memory serves, you're great. But that isn't the issue here."

"Hey, fella," says Arnie, "whatever your name is…"

"Big Louie."

"*Yeah*? Well, I'm guessing that has to be 'cos you're— never mind. Can we keep the ladies out of it?"

"Absolutely," endorses Cleo. She tries to take advantage of this conversational interlude by making a sudden play for the gun. Until she feels something hard digging sharply into her lower ribs and a pair of only slightly softer items pushing into her upper back.

"I take it you're not just pleased to see me, Melisande," says Cleo, as the other three move on.

Chapter Thirty-Eight

Better ruined ten times than dead once.
(Judaeo/German proverb)

The ark itself, clearly the main attraction of the park, is a suitably massive structure, engineered in several different types of local wood. (In fact, most everything except 'gopher wood', which is what old Noah originally built it from. But you try asking him what the heck *that* was!)

To add to the 'authenticity', the replica vessel hosts a respectable assortment of real live animals (but not the xylophagous ones – wood-eaters to you!) and also features finely-crafted animatronic models of the many creatures, some now extinct, that he might well have taken with him on his Mediterranean cruise.

As a further treat, the attraction offers a walk-through of the sort of living quarters the big guy and his family would have used. And possibly even the rooms to which they'd flee when they couldn't any longer stand the stench.

What really singles this ark out from the other biblically-themed attractions, however, is that it sits in a large expanse of water and every hour, on the hour, it rocks like crazy in a makeshift storm. Fake lightning, thunderclaps, sounds of God's ancient creatures getting biblically over-excited, the works. People have been known to get seasick just from the motion, so it is probably best to enjoy the experience before lunch or wearing those wristbands from your local pharmacy. What keeps the real animals sane in there is a secret known only to the park's veterinarians.

Right now, a board beside the entrance booth boasts, in Hebraic-style lettering: *Passeth not! Next Flood – 3.00*. An attendant, sitting in the entrance booth in his predictably ancient gear, halts our threesome. He points imperiously to the board.

"Sorry folks, we don't saileth until three. Eth."

Big Louie reaches up and knocks him cold with his gun butt. He then turns to a shocked Arnie and Noreen.

"Hey, it's just work. Some of my best friends are Jewish."

When the curious threesome climb the wooden ramp into the currently empty attraction, some more reluctantly than others, they find the imposing structure big, dark and – although none would profess to be regular ark-goers – pretty authentic. Unsurprisingly, the animals behind the reinforced glass – raccoons, aardvarks, squirrels, are all in twos.

"Ain't this great?" says Big Louie, waving his weapon around enthusiastically. "My kids would love it."

"Oh, are they also…?"

"Don't go there, Noreen," warns Arnie, before turning to address their potential executioner man to man. "Hey, fella, let the lady go, why don't ya? She's got nothing to do with this. And ooh, I just remembered – and I kid you not – it's my birthday today. Howsabout that? So, it's this lady's too. Happy birthday, Noreen."

"Thank you, Arnie, but it's not my birthday," corrects a slightly puzzled Noreen. "Not until December."

"Huh?" says Arnie.

Big Louie just shrugs thoughtfully, but he can hear Melisande's voice in his ear, even though she is clearly still on shore, attending to other business. *Don't listen to the lousy schmoozer. You're being paid to do a job. Friggin' do it!*

The hitman nods, berating himself for almost forgetting that the customer, however vindictive and possibly demented, is always right. Very slowly, because he refuses to be rushed, he raises his weapon.

"I'll make it swift and painless," he promises.

Suddenly a brilliant flash of lightning seems to set the ark ablaze. This is accompanied almost immediately by deafening claps of thunder that reverberate from every loudspeaker in the craft, cleverly concealed in massive and well-spaced rams' horns, because the original prototype probably didn't have a state-of-the-art sound system.

Despite not being three o'clock, the ark slowly begins to pitch and roll. Instinctively the vessel's three human inhabitants glance out of a small side window. They notice that the stunned entrance booth attendant has fallen onto his starting lever. And is very slowly and unconsciously pushing it towards maximum tempest.

The animals – even those that have been skilfully crafted in LA workshops – begin to yelp and howl as the awe-inspiring light show, soundscape and highly-calibrated motion control all mount in simulated, God-like wrath towards their peaks. The two chimpanzees in the cage beside them are particularly exercised. (The use of real beasts for these purposes had been widely condemned by California's animal lovers, who came head-to-head with fundamentalist Christian organisations, with the latter declaring that it was both instructive and authentic and if God hadn't wanted Noah's animals to weather the storms at sea, he would have commanded Noah to build a plane.)

"*Shit!*" says Big Louie, addressing his prospective victims. "Okay, now normally, I let my marks – that's what we call them, for those of you who've never been in a hit before – normally, I let you do the 'last words' shtick. It's corny but folks say they like it. But time's getting on and I ain't a good sailor. So – ladies first."

Pointing the gun directly at Noreen, who is literally out of her depth, Big Louie roots himself squarely on the rocking terrain and starts to squeeze the trigger.

Without even thinking – perhaps because if he were to think, he'd think twice – Arnie dives sideways, throwing his smallish body right in front of Noreen's slightly larger and much woollier one. Directly in the path of any intended bullet.

"*Run!*" screams her saviour, over the apocalyptic din.

Big Louie's finger is pressing down further and harder.

"Arnie! *No!*" cries a horrified Noreen, as the hitman fires.

They all three hear the sound as the bullet leaves the gun.

Yet to their surprise they can also *see* this same lethal bullet – actually *watch* it – heading dead straight but unusually slowly, compared to what they assume is a bullet's normal velocity, towards Arnie's (eternally) exposed chest. Straight and apparently unstoppable, as bullets tend to be. Even the curiously slow ones. Until, at a particularly crucial moment, just millimetres from the intended target, this very same bullet is caught quite deftly in a rather elegant, outstretched hand. A dark and familiar hand, especially to Noreen.

Lyle's hand.

"Number one with a bullet," he says. "Ain't that the truth?" The smile is as sparkling as ever and the linen suit just as uncreased.

"*How the hell did you do that?*" asks a seriously impressed Big Louie, who is well accustomed to guys catching a bullet but rarely quite like this. "And who the fuck *are* you?"

"You don't want to know," says Arnie, wondering with some dread, despite his obvious relief, how the smooth-talking devil with the to-die-for voice is hoping to exact his gratitude.

"He's a friend of mine," comes a voice from they know not whither, if we're going to stay in a biblical vein.

They all spin around wildly until their eyes end up in the monkey cage. Sitting between two monkeys – doing the old 'see no, hear no, speak no evil' trick – is none other than your old friend Ambrose. Or me, as I like to call myself.

Arnie looks baffled. Well, to be honest, everyone looks baffled, but our Mr Garth looks baffled from way back.

"A friend? *A friend!*" he says, looking from me to Lyle and back to yours truly again. It doesn't help that Lyle is smiling. Well, hell, we're both smiling. Arnie still isn't, but you can't have everything. "Hey, what gives, you guys?" he demands to know. And seriously, who can blame him? "I got a day to live, maybe less, I got no soul, 'cos of you dipshits, this lady's got two, I'm going straight to Hell on my birthday – *and you're... smiling!*"

Noreen and the little chap are just stood stock still and staring. They might as well have been put together in the same workshop that made these fake animals. God knows what they must be thinking (well, of course, being omniscient...).

Time to leave my cage.

So, I bid goodbye to my fellow primates, who are still rolling around a bit but are clearly used to it, or maybe drugged down to the keester with anti-nausea pills, and take a little stroll through the plate glass. Neatly done, even though I say so myself.

And now I come right up to Lyle.

I try to keep a straight face, by not looking at his ultra-gorgeous one, but I'm sorry, sue me, I just can't do it. Within seconds Lyle and I are leaning on each other for support, cracking up like a couple of drunken school kids.

"*No soul!*" I snort.

"*Straight to Hell!*" cries Lyle, the tears rolling down his immaculately sculpted cheeks.

Of course, by this time Big Louie has had enough. After all, we're interrupting his business. It's a workday and time is money. I understand this.

"You two freaks," he growls, which actually is still quite alarming, despite the higher pitch. "*Freeze!*" He points his gun at both of us, which isn't too tricky, as we remain quite huddled.

"No, friend, you freeze," I reply, quick as a flash. And let's just say icicles instantly hang from his cute little nose and the guy isn't going anywhere in a hurry. I don't do this sort of thing often – hey, I'm basically just a civil servant – but it's good to have a trick or three up your sleeve. This time, Lyle and I give each other a special high five. "I got that from *Batman Returns*," I tell him.

"Excuse me," says Noreen Millburn, putting her hand up, which isn't really necessary, but appreciated all the same. "Would somebody please mind explaining? This is my first time in North America."

Arnie turns to Lyle with an important question. "You're not... Satan?"

"Afraid not, Arnie," giggles Lyle. "I do a good Satan though."

"And a terrific Liza Minnelli!" I add, because I believe in credit where it's due. "Okay. Denouement time. The 'lost soul' scenario – y'know, bad day in the sorting office, baby boom, uh oh, where's his soul? Oopsy! It's... well, I kid you not, it's bullshit."

"Excuse me?" gasps Arnie. "It's *what?!*"

"Bullshit, Arnie," explains Noreen. " It's what bulls—"

"I *know* what it is, Noreen." The poor man looks so bewildered. "Ambrose, I thought you people forgot to give me a soul."

"*As if!*" I tell him, with a rather appealing smile. "You've had one all the time, kiddo! Not a biggie, granted. But the little dude's in there somewhere, you silly sleazeball."

"Yeah?" Arnie points towards Noreen, who has no idea what's going on. And remember, we're still in the midst of a perfect storm here. Thunder, lightning, tossing. The works. "Well, what about goody two-souls? Saint Noreen."

352

I let Lyle take up the slack, now that he's managed to dial down the hysterical laughter. "Oh, nutty Noreen here," he says in that to-die-for voice. "Nutty but *beautiful* Noreen, she has got a great big one. Widescreen, Dolby, the full monty, the big kahuna. But trust me, Arnie, it's still just a single soul."

Noreen's face is a picture. Well, even more of a picture. "Excuse me, Lyle," she says, again with the raised hand (what is this – third grade?). "But who exactly are you?"

"Well… I suppose you could call me – *the Ark Angel!*" Now he's laughing so much, he's got stuff coming out his nose, which only he can make look cool. "I am so sorry, Noreen – I truly apologise – but this guy, this Ambrose, he always makes me crack up. It's what makes the job bearable. I mean, it's not like there's a salary." He gives her the softest, kindest, most unsatanic smile. "Okay. Truth time. I'm just a simple clerk, Noreen. In the depot. Like Amby here. Logging souls in, logging souls out. In and out. In and out. They don't call it eternity for nothing."

"We got bored," I add. "Hey, we're only flesh and blood."

"No, we're not," says Lyle. Such a pedant.

Time for backstory. The real one. No more unreliable narrator stuff, which I have to tell you again, in case you feel just a tad duped, is an acknowledged literary device. I got it from Agatha Christie herself. A real lady. You can imagine how thrilled *she* is to be with dead people 24/7.

"So, one day," I explain, "when we were particularly bored—"

"Bored to death," contributes Lyle.

"Was I expositing?" I chide him. "So, one day – one tedious day – we decided to see if we could hook up the two least likely people in the whole entire universe. The vilest, scuzziest, sleaziest, most unedifying man…"

"That's you, Arnie," adds Noreen, helpfully.

"And the sweetest, kindest, dearest woman," says Lyle.

"Ain't that the truth," says Arnie, looking over at Noreen

with a look I've hitherto never seen on his face, but always been hoping against hope I just might.

"We simply wanted to see, with all the obstacles and challenges and setbacks we could throw in your way, if you could ever fall in love," I conclude.

"So... have you?" asks Lyle, hopefully. Such a softie.

Noreen and Arnie just gaze at each other. In silence. In wonder.

"Jesus Christ, who do you have to screw to get a hit on this fucking ship?"

They all turn to see Melisande. She is soaking wet and pointing a little gun. She fires without waiting for an answer, as it was a rhetorical question.

Chapter Thirty-Nine

Justice begins at home. (Portuguese proverb)

All that Arnie can see, when he finally opens his eyes, is a bright, unearthly white.

The walls are white, the sheets are white. Even Noreen is white. And as for Lyle and myself, we are back in our working clothes. Which are – you've guessed it – a rather soothing yet distinguished ivory colour. Okay, white.

Noreen is smiling down on him, staring concernedly at the bandage around his head.

"So, this is Heaven," says Arnie, blinking in the almost dazzling light. "Hello, everyone."

"Don't be a twit, Arnie," says Noreen. "Melisande missed you by a mile."

"The boat was swaying so much, the bullet just hit the *EXIT* sign. Well, the *EXODUS* sign," explains Lyle, in that delicious voice. "Which unfortunately fell on your follically-challenged head."

"But you're still alive, pardner!" I gave him my best John Wayne.

"What about Cleo?"

"We found her in the trunk of Big Louie's car," says Lyle.

Arnie gasps in horror.

"Alive and unharmed. But I've a feeling she doesn't want to see you for a while."

"The police say Melisande's going to go down for a good long time," says Noreen.

"It's what made her a star," says Arnie, which Noreen doesn't understand but it makes we guys chuckle. We may be angels, but we're no angels.

Arnie Garth looks around the hospital room, but I like to believe he's talking to Noreen. "So – where do we go from here?"

I look at Lyle and he looks back at me and we both decide to just fade away.

"Well," says Noreen, "I don't know about you, Arnie, but I think it's high time that I went back home."

EIGHTEEN MONTHS LATER – GIVE OR TAKE

Chapter Forty

In the long run, even a dog will compromise with the cat.
(Hungarian proverb)

As evening laps over the solitary little cottage, like a breeze rippling on her favourite lake, Noreen sits beside the crackling fire with her precious white ferret on her lap, knitting a garment that is clearly only suitable for an animal or a small, four-legged child.

The dramas of Las Vegas and Los Angeles appear like the flames in her hearth, flickering yet still dangerously potent. Occasionally, she wonders how events can in certain ways seem so distant whilst remaining quite firmly etched in her mind.

She hears the familiar sound of sheep being herded and so she sits and waits. Eventually the door opens, and a man enters in a heavy, windproof coat and thick boots, coated and clagged with fragments of wool and fine Cumbrian mud.

"Did you put Ambrose, Lyle and Cleo where they belong?" asks Noreen.

"Yeah," says the man, "they're with the other guys in the pen."

"The little lambs," says Noreen, fondly.

"You're looking good, sweetheart," says the smiling sheepherder.

"Well, it's a big night, isn't it, love? Hadn't you better get changed? It's very late."

"Hey, don't you fret. You saw that James Bond movie when he's got this great tux under his diving gear, sharp as a knife?"

Noreen looks blank.

"No, course you didn't." He rips off his coat and waterproof trousers to reveal a dazzling white dinner jacket. "Da da! I ever tell you about my *Oooo Oooo Seven* series: *Doctor, Yes!, Thunderballs, For Your Thighs Only?*"

It only takes a glare from Noreen.

"Sorry. Old habits…"

A door at the back of the tiny parlour opens and a sudden rush of dazzling golden light floods in. The peace of the cosy room is shattered by a blast of noise, mechanical and human. Pulsating Muzak invades the cottage.

Standing in the doorway, in a glittering, low-cut evening gown is Rosie, late of The Wordsworth Arms.

"C'mon, you two!" she chides, but with a cheeky smile. "Especially you, Noreen Millburn – don't you know what time it is?" She throws out her bare freckled arms and begins to sing 'Maybe This Time' from *Cabaret*, until Arnie signals 'enough'.

As if on a signal, Noreen Millburn shucks off her oldest and lumpiest cardigan, to flaunt her own dazzling, figure-embracing evening wear.

Arnie can't help shaking his head in admiration. How had he been so blind to this woman? Okay, maybe the cardigans, the bobbly hat, the grime under a plethora of charity cans didn't help. And the fact that her true beauty still derives mainly from the very best place – within. Or, if you're going to go there, the undeniable truth that deep down he was extremely shallow.

Holding out his arm, he escorts his adored Limey wife to the door.

*

The gleaming casino, newly built onto the rear of Noreen's ancient cottage, is far smaller than those she once experienced in another brief but eventful life, on a distant, bizarre continent, yet in its own way it is absolutely perfect.

There are the usual gambling tables, roulette wheels, slot machines, cocktail waitresses, plus a few stalls representing the Rough Fell equivalents of Tiffany's and Gucci. And, of course, a well-stocked bar with local brews, because this is England, and nothing happens without beer.

Standing beside the tables and machines, itching for the go-ahead to play and lose their shirts, are the villagers who were once so hostile. Dressed in their finest drab, they turn as one to see Rough Fell's most unusual yet now most welcome power-couple.

"Hello, everyone," greets Noreen. "Welcome to *Geoffrey's Palace*. Now, come on and just make yourselves comfortable. And remember, all proceeds go to charity." She catches Arnie's eye. "Well, almost all. Let's not get too Mother Teresa about it."

Arnie moves even closer to her and steals a cuddle, as he whispers in her ear. "Have I told you lately that I love you?"

Noreen turns to him and, in that bizarre Lakeland accent he has just begun to decipher and even almost to enjoy, she says so sweetly, "Cut the crapola, Arnie. We've got a business to run."

He smiles and looks right across the crowded and, by now, raucous room. In a corner, Lyle and I are making the elderly sheep called Geoffrey, in whose honour this very Cumbrian casino is named, magically disappear. Of course, to anyone watching, it's just a sheep on its own that keeps vanishing and turning up again, which is quite an attraction in itself.

You probably didn't expect, did you, when you began this chronicle, this fable of good and rotten, that it would end with a spasmodically disappearing, gammy-legged Herdwick. But isn't that the magic of literature?

To paraphrase the last line of that classic *Anne of Green*

Gables – 'God's in his heaven, all's right with the world', whispers rakish heavenly matchmaker Ambrose, to a highly confused Cumbrian sheep. As his two no longer lost souls look on.

A PERFECT
MURDER STORY

The Script Clinic – *where scripts can only get better*
46 Chiswick High Road, London W4 2LU
www.thescriptclinic.co.uk

Mr D. Crispin   June 14ᵗʰ 2023
PO Box 1463
Oxford OX1 2LG

Dear Mr Crispin,

Re: 'The Perfect Murder'

Thank you for sending us the above-named script, which we really enjoyed reading.

   We have taken into account that this is the first movie you have written, so we've tried to be as helpful and constructive as we can. (We appreciate that you have chosen to use traditional mail, but should you prefer, you can also email us at any time.)

   You will find our detailed report attached, but writers often find it useful to receive a brief summary of our thoughts.

1. The story is quite simple, possibly too simple, and whilst the characters are interesting, they are perhaps a bit too one-dimensional.

2. We can quite understand why your main character might wish to murder his wife, given her appallingly cruel and callous behaviour towards him (endorsed, as you say, and even compounded, by her devoted but equally awful mother). Yet to make him a man utterly without flaws, and her a woman with absolutely no redeeming features, doesn't quite allow, in our eyes, for sufficient light and

shade, and perhaps strains credibility too much to make for a satisfyingly well-rounded story.

3. Your choice of a murder weapon – the exotic and apparently undetectable poison – might well work in terms of making the murder perfect, but we do not believe that he could simply buy the item over the internet, in the manner you suggest (otherwise everybody would be doing it!). And do remember that the husband is nearly always the first person to be investigated – as he usually has the dominant motive!

4. We suggest that you work on developing the characters and find a means for the killing that is totally plausible, yet one that we, the audience (and hopefully the police), have never seen before.

We hope that this isn't too discouraging and look forward to reading the next draft.

Yours sincerely,
The Consultants at The Script Clinic

TSC

The Script Clinic – *where scripts can only get better*
46 Chiswick High Road, London W4 2LU
www.thescriptclinic.co.uk

Mr D. Crispin
PO Box 1463
Oxford OX1 2LG

August 20th 2023

Dear Mr Crispin,

Re: 'The Perfect Murder'

Thank you for submitting the above-named script once again, and for marking your revisions so clearly in blue. Please find our detailed report attached.

Writers often find it useful to receive a brief summary of our thoughts.

1. We are afraid that we still have the same note vis-à-vis your lead characters. The benighted husband does again appear to be a paragon of virtue, whilst his soon-to-be-despatched spouse and her mum are like the creatures that Hell forgot. Today's audiences, in our experience, demand a tad more nuance.

2. Whilst it is readily accepted that people can, on occasion, be 'scared' to death, we think in reality that you might find this a somewhat more difficult task than your script allows, especially given that the wife, inconveniently, has no prior heart condition. You could, of course, provide her with one – she is your own creation, to do with as you will. But pretending to hang oneself in the bathroom (page 35) is not only quite a difficult and possibly dangerous effect to

pull off without serious injury, it might also, if the marital relationship is as disastrous as you describe, be in truth a source of some relief to the lady on her return from a major shopping trip (rather than the guaranteed road to oblivion that you envisage).

3. Once again, our recommendations are a) concentrate on character and b) find that elusive, foolproof murder method, if this is indeed what you wish to be the core of your story. (This is far more difficult than it might appear, and there is nothing to say that audiences really *want* someone to get away with it. They actually love the elements of detection and deduction – the winnowing away of suspects. Think of Hercule Poirot.)

We hope that you have found these thoughts helpful and look forward to reading the next draft.

Yours sincerely,
The Consultants at The Script Clinic

TSC

The Script Clinic – *where scripts can only get better*
46 Chiswick High Road, London W4 2LU
www.thescriptclinic.co.uk

Mr D. Crispin   September 23rd 2023
PO Box 1463
Oxford OX1 2LG

Dear Mr Crispin,

Re: 'The Perfect Murder'

Thank you for submitting the above-named script once more, and for marking your latest revisions in puce. It makes for an easy contrast to your earlier blue.

We have attached our detailed report, but writers often find it useful to receive a brief summary of our thoughts.

1. We appreciate that you have so readily taken on board our notes about character but do feel you may still need to advance this a little further. Making the wife both a marriage and bereavement counsellor could, in some way, diminish her almost total vileness, whilst adding a welcome touch of irony that the audience might enjoy. And giving the monstrously-put-upon yet almost saint-like husband a secret life as a sniffer of bicycle seats does indeed take his character in a new and uniquely gross direction. ('Snurd' is a word none of us had actually come across, so thank you for this.) But we do think that these pursuits, whilst colourful, feel slightly 'bolted on', as opposed to what might be considered more usefully organic.

369

2. Perhaps some sort of back story, provided it is not too laboured, would provide further insight into how your warring husband and wife have arrived at this parlous state. This might furnish the initial readers of your script – and hopefully your eventual audience – with sufficient clues as to what could possibly have brought them together in the first place. Audiences are people – as are, occasionally, script-readers at film studios – so they are intensely interested in human nature and why people behave as they do.

3. Yet again, the exact mechanics of murder appear to be the pivotal problem. We cannot emphasise too strongly that if it is your desire, as your scripts suggest, that this crime be totally undetectable, and your newly widowed hero is to sail (or in his case cycle) blissfully unshackled into the sunset, it shouldn't be a crime that any of we armchair/cinema-seat detectives could ourselves solve quite happily before the lights go up.

4. It is for the above reason that we think a hit-and-run when the wife walks home from her Pilates class might be quite tricky to pull off. This is not to say that we are totally dismissing the car as murder weapon, but streets do have houses with windows and nosy neighbours, and bodies hit at a speed necessary to guarantee fatality usually tend to leave their impression on the chassis that connects with them. (And the only cameras we should be thinking about are those at your director's command!)

5. At Script Clinic we pride ourselves on seeking out solutions as well as problems. So, we have been scouring your script for, as it were, clues to assist you in your quest. You mention in passing (on page 21) that the wife is an insomniac. She uses a CD recorded by her hypnotherapist to assist her in gliding swiftly off to sleep. A certain haunting piece of music on this CD would appear always to do the trick. Currently, this has no plot significance and is simply a neat piece of

observation, allowing Norman to lie in bed and fantasise undisturbed on life without Doreen. (Indeed, you have a long dream sequence to this effect, which is possibly the most imaginative, albeit superfluous, feature of your script.) We wonder if something currently no more than a fleeting tangent to your plot might in fact be of more practical use? This is purely a suggestion and could be totally unworkable, but we offer it in the spirit of constructive cooperation. (And think about the soundtrack possibilities!)

We hope that this is of some encouragement and look forward to reading the next draft.

Yours sincerely,
The Consultants at The Script Clinic.

TSC

The Script Clinic – *where scripts can only get better*
46 Chiswick High Road, London W4 2LU
www.thescriptclinic.co.uk

Mr D. Crispin   November 22nd 2023
PO Box 1463
Oxford OX1 2LG

Dear Mr Crispin,

Re: 'The Perfect Murder'

Thank you for submitting the above-named script once again. We must commend you on your indomitable spirit. It is this type of determination that turns scripts into movies!

And we are grateful, as always, for your marking your revisions in yet another colour. The script is taking on the aspect of a rainbow, which is no bad thing these days.

We have attached our detailed report, but writers often find it useful to receive a brief summary of our thoughts.

1. You appear to have taken our note on backstory quite literally. However, we are not entirely certain that revealing the beleaguered husband, in flashbacks, to have come from a home bathed almost to the point of drowning in kindness and civility, whilst the wife appears to have been brought up by the Borgias, actively advances your story. We are not saying that backgrounds don't serve to establish character, it is rather that you have still to find a way to make these characters totally credible.

2. If we can give one note that might help – you seem to be totally in love with Norman whilst despising Doreen with a

vengeance. Sometimes observing your protagonists through a less jaundiced and more dispassionate lens can subtly allow the audience to make their own judgments. They will learn to hate Doreen for themselves, as we all do here at TSC, which will be far more gratifying.

3. Concerning the murder itself, we are intrigued by how enthusiastically you have taken on board our suggestion as regards the sleep CD. If indeed the playing of that particular piece of music induces an almost instant slumber in Doreen, then contriving to slip it into a CD that the husband himself has made for her is very interesting. (Assuming, in the present state of their relationship, that a 'mix-tape' would still be something he would make and that she would readily accept.)

4. However, most people don't carry portable CD players around with them anymore, as they tend to have their music on their phones. And the likelihood of Doreen listening to that particular 'sleep track' at the exact moment she is strolling in front of a speeding juggernaut is unfortunately relatively small. In a perfect murder you can't really afford to be hit 'n' miss. (Excuse the pun!) If you are intending to submit a further draft – and we suspect, unless you have run out of colours, that you most probably are – then it is this area on which it could pay to concentrate.

5. Might we suggest that you devise a situation in which Doreen would gratefully accept such a CD from Norman, and a foolproof manner in which the playing of that particular somniferous track could lead to her sudden death? In an earlier draft you suggested tampering with her car. Might Doreen be driving this same car, but instead of monkeying with the mechanics, Norman has simply popped a CD into the player, and the 'killer track' plays at the moment it will do the most damage?

As ever, we trust that you have found this feedback constructive. We look forward to reading the next draft, should you decide to consult us once more.

Yours sincerely,
The Consultants at The Script Clinic

The Script Clinic – *where scripts can only get better*
46 Chiswick High Road, London W4 2LU
www.thescriptclinic.co.uk

Mr D. Crispin   December 21st 2023
PO Box 1463
Oxford OX1 2LG

Dear Mr Crispin,

Re: 'The Perfect Murder'

I have to say that, here at The Script Clinic, we have all been thoroughly looking forward to reading yet another draft of 'The Perfect Murder'.

It is not often we find a script by a brand new writer that, whilst perhaps lacking as yet in several basic elements of craft, is written with such white-hot fervour. It is rare indeed to read a 'passion project' in this particular genre.

We are, of course, grateful yet again for your marking your revisions in another colour. Perhaps if this doesn't happen as a movie, you might consider submitting the script itself to the Turner Prize judges. (Just our little joke!)

We have attached our detailed report, but as you doubtless know by now, writers often find it useful to receive a brief summary of our thoughts.

1. We are interested to note new and helpful additions since the last draft. Whilst the husband's taking out a massive life insurance policy on his wife will inevitably focus even more suspicion on him, it does, of course, furnish him (and us) with a useful extra motive for murder, alongside the fact that Doreen is irredeemably horrid.

2. The above will, as indeed you have anticipated, add even more fuel to the flame of homicidal perfection. There must be no conceivable way that the crime could be attributed to the husband. We shall return to this, as we have had some thoughts.

3. Your suggestion that Norman and Doreen are on holiday somewhere with narrow mountain roads and treacherous bends is an excellent one. Playing an instant-sleep CD whilst driving on such a road would increase enormously the chances of a nasty – and dare we hope, fatal – accident. Especially on a wet or icy winter's night.

4. However, your idea that Norman can simply leap out of the passenger seat at the appropriate moment is fraught with dangers. Especially for Norman.

5. So here is our suggestion: he isn't in the car at all. Not only is he not in the car, he isn't even in the vicinity. He could indeed be miles away. A remote murder – and a murder somewhere remote – would add a new wrinkle to a well-worn genre. Does this notion appeal to you?

6. Should you honour us with another draft, perhaps we shall find this conceit developed. What is, of course, especially appealing, is that were the murder to be successful and the vehicle, along with poor Doreen, to end up a total write-off (or, indeed, even if Doreen is the *only* thing 'totalled' or 'written-off'), no one – not even the keenest of investigators – will be the least bit bothered about a CD that was playing at the time. Why would they?

We look forward once again to your next draft, should you feel we might still be of assistance.

We wish you and your family a very merry – and hopefully not too murderous (!) – Christmas.

Yours sincerely,
The Consultants at The Script Clinic

TSC

The Script Clinic – *where scripts can only get better*
46 Chiswick High Road, London W4 2LU
www.thescriptclinic.co.uk

Mr D. Crispin   January 10th 2024
PO Box 1463
Oxford OX1 2LG

Dear Mr Crispin,

Re: 'The Perfect Murder'

Happy New Year, Mr Crispin. You've done it again!

Once more you have set our combined creative juices here at The Script Clinic sizzling – or whatever juices do!

Firstly, can we say once more that your use of different tints for each set of corrections adds both colour and convenience to our world.

You firmly requested in your covering letter that we 'forget the character stuff' for the time being. Clearly and, in our opinion, quite wisely, you would prefer to prioritise plot. So here goes:

1. Your latest draft tells us that Norman, who is a highly successful, self-made businessman, has given his wife, as a surprise Valentine treat, a week in a remote Snowdonian cottage, an area she has loved since childhood. This is apparently a gesture of rapprochement on his part (although we, of course, suspect quite the reverse).

2. As the cottage is high up on a mountain road and there is no internet access, we concur that it is perfectly plausible that Norman should decide to venture down into the local

town on the fateful day to pick up and send important messages.

3. Furthermore, he thoughtfully wouldn't wish to leave Doreen in such lofty isolation without a car. Rather than using the push-bike you say he has brought with him, which would make his journey on the steep hill both long and treacherous, especially his return in the dark, might we suggest that he uses a local cab company?

4. He can book his cab from the working landline in the cottage the same afternoon on which he expresses a need to make such a journey. This way there would be independent evidence that he was nowhere near the scene of the crime. (And the one cab company in town, should they even be questioned after the event, would confirm that no further cabs to return back up the hill were booked at any point by Norman).

5. Your plan for getting Doreen to make that hopefully fatal downhill drive is fraught with dangers – but not, as yet, of the right sort! In your script (page 72), Norman calls her to say that he has had a nasty accident on his bike and is seriously ill in the local hospital. If Doreen's feelings for Norman are as you describe, we would suggest that this – or indeed any other misfortune to befall him – might not immediately cause her to drop everything and dash recklessly towards him in blind but loving panic. (Although she may indeed play a lively CD when she eventually gets going!)

6. You have described Doreen's devotion to her unspeakable mother in some detail – perhaps too much detail – in every draft. What if Norman calls Doreen from the town, quite late on that winter evening, and tells her that he has just received a distressing call from her mother's neighbour? (Someone who has only their mobile numbers to hand, but 'apparently' couldn't seem to get through on Doreen's.)

- Norman could explain in his call that this concerned person has just told him some awful news: Doreen's poor mum has suffered a really terrible fall, slipping on her path and smashing her head on the steps of her house. She was rushed away by an ambulance just minutes ago.
- Norman tells Doreen not to make any calls – the ambulance won't even have arrived at the hospital yet. She must simply get to town just as quickly as she can and pick him up by the town hall.
- As you know, we are very drawn to the sleep-track being on a mix-CD that Norman has made. But whilst 'favourite songs of Doreen' might work in less distressing circumstances, perhaps 'favourite and meaningful tracks of Doreen's poor mum' will better serve Norman's purpose on this occasion. (Songs from the shows etc, with some easy listening thrown in.) Norman could tell Doreen on this final phone call that, by the purest chance, he had made such a CD as a gift for his mother-in-law, and that it was already in the car's CD player, awaiting Doreen's final approval. Norman feels certain that it might truly bring some comfort and calm to Doreen while she drives to meet him.

We humbly suggest that this combination of panic, excess speed, daughterly affection, winter darkness, an emotional musical selection – with, of course, the interpolated instant-sleep track – could be sufficient to send driver and car into a fatal tailspin on this notoriously treacherous road. End of Doreen, end of car (and CD), end of story. And, of course, who would suspect that it was anything other than a dreadful accident? His poor wife was just driving down to the little town to meet her devoted husband for a romantic Valentine's Day supper (perhaps Norman should book a restaurant table for two that evening in the town, just to dot the final 'i' and provide a reason for his earlier phone call to the cottage, should anyone bother to check).

Of course, these are only suggestions. We look forward to reading how you choose to develop them.

We hope 2024 will be your year, Mr Crispin.

Yours sincerely,
The Consultants at The Script Clinic

From the Abingdon Weekly News, February 17ᵗʰ 2024

ABINGDON WOMAN DIES IN FATAL SNOWDONIA PLUNGE.

Mrs Davina Cracknell of Eastbury Villas, Abingdon, died on Valentine's night when her BMW plunged off a mountain road in a remote region of Snowdonia.

Mrs Cracknell, who was driving to meet her husband, Abingdon businessman Neville Cracknell, for an intimate Valentine's dinner in the nearby town, is assumed to have died instantly.

A local farmer, Mr Robert McKee, who witnessed the incident from the window of his cottage, noticed a car driving at enormous speed then suddenly going out of control. "It started just weaving all over the road," he said, "like the poor driver had suddenly lost the plot and suffered a stroke or something. Next thing I saw was a massive ball of flame."

The deceased, who was a JP and Relate counsellor, leaves a grieving husband and a mother.

TSC

The Script Clinic – *where scripts can only get better*
46 Chiswick High Road, London W4 2LU
www.thescriptclinic.co.uk

Mr D. Crispin   August 14th 2024
PO Box 1463
Oxford OX1 2LG

Dear Mr Crispin,

Re: 'The Perfect Murder'

As it has been some months since we last heard from you, we are just writing to say that we trust you have been satisfied with our service to date.

We are currently offering a reduced rate on script consultation for our valued clients. If you would like to send us your latest draft of 'The Perfect Murder', or any other script, we would be more than happy to read it.

If, on the other hand, you have found a *productive* home for 'The Perfect Murder', do please tell us. We are always delighted when something on which we have hopefully assisted comes to happy fruition.

Yours sincerely,
The Consultants at The Script Clinic

Acknowledgements

Thank you to my wonderful agent Christina Pickworth for seeing the potential of Einstein.

My gratitude to David Ian Neville and Petra Fried for helping me to realise I Can't Be Ill, I'm a Hypochondriac. And to the radiographers at Mount Vernon Hospital, Northwood, for making me well enough to tell my story. (Or at least the semi-fictionalised story I decided to tell.)

Appreciation to Paul Alexander and Alan Moskowitz for assisting me in the quest to find my Lost Souls.

And finally to everyone at The Book Guild for giving my guys of all lengths a home.

Paul A. Mendelson graduated from Cambridge with a first in law which did him no use at at all, as he became an award-winning advertising copywriter then a BAFTA-nominated screenwriter.

He created several long-running BBC comedy series, including *May to December* and *My Hero* and has worked in London and LA.

Paul has written nine novels, including two for children (9+). He scripts all his books and four have been optioned for movies. His novel *Must Have GSOH* was the only UK Finalist in the 2023 Screencraft Cinematic Book Contest.